A Life Full of Quarks

C. W. Johnson

Baryon Dreams Press

Contents

All histories are imaginary; this one especially.

For you

Part I: A Nuclear Family

"We need books that affect us like a disaster, that grieve us deeply, like the death of someone we loved more than ourselves, like being banished into forests far from everyone, like a suicide." —Franz Kafka

I, Paleontologist

When I was young, I wanted to be a paleontologist, to unearth things both terrifying and long dead. I suppose this memoir is not very different.

For me, dinosaurs were the gateway drug into science. It came through serendipity: not through spilling chemicals into my breakfast cereal, or through finding a patch of mold in the shape of a Stegosaurus, but through my mother falling asleep without putting me to bed.

My father thought TV turned your brains into oatmeal. My mother, on the other hand, would simply say, "Switch it off if you hear your father come in, Johnny." She had a free-range philosophy of parenting. Meals, she believed, should be spontaneous acts of invention, unfettered by planning. Sporadic housecleaning occurred whenever she couldn't find the book she wanted. Growing up in a long-lost era, my older sister and I played without supervision in the awkward toupee of trees on the hill behind our house, and if we ever came to her crying, her only question would be, "Do you require hospitalization?"

Unfortunately for me, she was stricter about bedtimes for six-year-olds, though this could be postponed when she was enjoying her TV shows. I thought it unfair that she got to dictate what we watched: boring husband-and-wife detectives and deadpan psychologists. One evening, while she snored on the couch, I tiptoed to the TV, and hoping to find some cartoons (I didn't realize they weren't on in the evenings back then), I turned the dial until I stumbled upon a late-night movie that grabbed my attention with long, sharp teeth. It was about dinosaurs—*dinosaurs eating people.*

It was crude stop-motion animation, yet to me at that age, it looked utterly real: long necks swaying above the treetops; massive feet making the earth shudder and ripple like my aunt's green Jell-O salad; row after row of monstrous dentition. My heart squeezed each time a dinosaur gobbled up another victim.

When I finally felt about to burst from fright, I shut off the TV and stood very still, trying to listen over the pounding of my pulse. The summer was feral and warm, and windows had been left open to cool the house. From the sofa came my mother's brassy snores. Then through the open windows, just as in the movie, I heard a slow, steady, ominous thudding.

Dinosaurs—*outside my house.* I almost peed myself.

There was no point in waking my mother. I knew now from experience that an Allosaurus could be standing right behind her, and she'd just tell me I had an overactive imagination. So, I ran out to my father's home laboratory. It was really just our garage, but he had filled it with equipment, and whenever he came home from the university where he taught science, he retreated there. When he did, my mother would sigh, sip her glass, and say, "Well, it gives him something to do."

The lab was a magical and scary place, smelling of oil and ozone and burnt metal. When I went in, my father greeted me, "Hello, John." His welding goggles made him look like a giant bug. He had not actually turned into one, a misunderstanding I wouldn't make a second time. Besides, he had gotten rid of all the cans of Raid. "Not sleepy?" he asked.

"Di... Dinosaur!" I managed to stammer.

"You know, I loved dinosaurs when I was your age," he said with a dry smile. "Magnificent creatures. We humans killed off the mammalian megafauna, of course, but I wonder how would we have fared against a stalking Ceratosaurus, or if we could have brought down a Barosaurus."

"No," I said, barely above a whisper; I didn't want the dinosaur to hear me. I could imagine its hot breath on my neck, reeking of blood. "Outside!"

The goggles were cold and unsympathetic. "John, dinosaurs died out a long time ago. Except for birds. Did you know birds are descended from dinosaurs? Like for dinner just last night, you ate—"

"No, I heard it!" I insisted. I felt panic flood my guts.

After taking off his goggles and adjusting his black-framed glasses, he led me out to the front yard. "To make a claim, we must provide evidence, no matter how fearful the search." He was always saying things like that.

Of course, we found nothing. "Not even a footprint," my father said. "A relief—and yet a bit of a disappointment, isn't it?"

I nodded, my heart still pounding fast, expecting that at any moment, a set of massive teeth would burst out of hiding in the bushes and rip us to red shreds.

Inside, he poked at my mother. "Anne. Anne...? It's ten o'clock. Do you know where your children are?"

She just groaned and turned over on the sofa.

In the morning, beside my breakfast cereal was a book. Its edges were worn, its cover scratched, but inside, there were brightly colored pictures of dinosaurs lumbering through steam-bath swamps and posing in front of puffing volcanoes, as if the dinosaur realtor had said, "Who doesn't want an active volcano in the neighborhood? It adds so much character!"

After I finished my cornflakes, I sat on the front steps and leafed through the pages. It was the summer between kindergarten and first grade for me, although I was already reading several grades ahead. Our dog, Bessie, came and laid her head on my lap as I pored over the pictures and sounded out the names letter by letter.

I heard footsteps behind me—my father. "Do you like the book, John? Let's take a walk," he said, not waiting for an answer.

We went out the front gate, past a lawn more weeds than grass. My father crouched on the concrete sidewalk. "You're too young to have thought about time much," he began. "But let's imagine the width of this crack in the sidewalk as measuring your life so far." He placed the tip of his index finger on the concrete ahead of it. "This is my life so far. And this, the length of my thumb, is how old our country is."

He straightened up and took a short step. "This takes us back two thousand years, to the time of the Roman Empire, to the time of Jesus."

"Like Gramma talks about," I offered.

"Like your grandmother talks about, a lot, yes." He cleared his throat, then took two full strides. "And this is about ten thousand years ago—the beginning of agriculture."

Walking on to the next house, he said, "Now we've gone back about a hundred thousand years, when modern humans began to leave Africa." Then he strode off down the street and turned the corner, with me and Bessie following.

At the next street, my father held my hand as we crossed. "Here is a million years back, when hominids were coming out of the trees and venturing onto the African savanna."

We kept walking. The houses gave way to storefronts, and we passed by shops and restaurants and the local veterinarian's office. "Are we getting ice cream?" I asked, full of hope.

"Hmm? No, John. Now we're about ten million years back, the middle of the Miocene. No humans at all, just early primates. We're barely a sixth of the way to the Cretaceous; we have to go six times as far to find the last of the dinosaurs. Do you see, John? Dinosaurs have been dead a long, long time."

"Jane says…" I began. Three years older than me, my only sibling was a reliable source of misinformation.

"John, listen. You don't have to be afraid of dinosaurs. They are so far away from our lifetimes that it's hard to even imagine. Remember that museum we visited at the beginning of the summer?"

I nodded.

"Remember the skeletons? Those were dinosaur bones. That's all that's left of them: bones that we dig up from the earth."

In the morning, I began to dig. In the summer, I spent most of my time outdoors, trailed by Bessie. This was a time when suburbs still had gentle oases of green; relentless development had not yet choked out all but unnatural life. Our house sat on half an acre of land, backed up against an inconstant stream and a gentle slope that led to bristly patches of trees yearning to be a forest. Scattered through our backyard were rickety sheds housing the remains of my father's failed experiments. Overhead and between the trees, he had strung up sheets of plastic and foil, part of a cosmic ray detector that ran into the house. When the sun was high and hot, Bessie and I sheltered in their shade.

I picked a likely spot, a low point not far from the dry carcass of the stream, and began to clumsily shovel the loamy ground. Bessie sniffed at the soil I overturned, then lay down and fell asleep.

All I found were roots, rocks, and some old tin cans. So, after lunch (peanut butter toast and lemonade, huffily made by my sister, Jane, at my mother's direction from the sofa), I dug some more.

That night at dinner, I had my dinosaur book open. Grinning, my father patted me on the back. "You enjoying it?" he asked.

"Uh-huh."

My sister glanced at a page. "They're from Noah's flood. That's what Gramma says."

My dad frowned. "Your grandmother doesn't know—"

"What she knows, Alan, is how to push your buttons," my mother said from the kitchen.

"Who? Your mother, or Jane?"

My mother didn't answer.

That night, the fear rattling my bones had dissipated. I heard no dinosaurs stomping outside the house. I imagined *they* were now terrified, frightened that I might dig up their bones and stick them in a museum. (My imagination was fertile, but imprecise, casting dinosaurs both as fossils and as living, breathing monsters.) In my bed, I felt safe and triumphant.

After breakfast, I dragged the spade to the far corner of the backyard. I was surprised to see, squatting in the hole I had dug, a little blonde girl about my age. She scooped up dirt with both hands and patted it into a little mound. Already she'd made several rows of mounds, so she had been at work for some time.

"What're you doing?" I asked curiously.

She glanced up and wiped her snub nose, leaving behind a smear of mud. "Making stuff." She had green eyes and was wearing a dark blue dress with white stars on it. Bessie cautiously sniffed the girl, then lay down at her feet and looked over at me; she approved of the girl.

To me, the stipple of mounds looked like the armor plates on the back of an Ankylosaurus I'd seen in my book, but I wasn't sure. "What are you making?"

The girl straightened and surveyed her handiwork. "Friends," she said. Then she amended, "Followers."

"Where do you live?" I asked.

She eyed me with suspicion. "I'm not lost."

"Oh," I said uncertainly. "Um... This is my backyard. I was digging here."

She looked at the ground and frowned. "What're you digging for?"

"Dinosaurs. Dinosaur bones."

She wiped her nose again, depositing more dirt. "Like a paleontologist?" She said the word fluently, as if it she had been saying it all her life. Immediately, I had a crush on her.

"Do you want to help?" I asked.

She shrugged. "I'll watch." She stepped out of the hole, and with hands on hips, looked on as I resumed digging. I dug hard, wanting to impress my new friend.

The sun was high in the sky, I was sweating, and my hands hurt when my shovel hit something, the concussion traveling through my arms all the way to my head. With the shovel's metal edge, I scraped away a bit more and saw a flash of white.

The girl squatted down and put a finger to the white surface. "What is it?"

"Bone," I said, with all the confidence I could muster. "A big one." Together we brushed away the dirt, revealing a curved surface, huge, bigger than me.

"Oh," said the girl. "Neat."

My heart leapt. Then I heard my mother call out, "John, lunch!" I grabbed the girl's hand, and together we ran to the house, with Bessie loping after.

As I stomped into the house, my mother began, "Johnny, are you—" She stopped when she saw the dirt on my hands and shoes and all down the front of my shirt, and the little girl next to me with mud on her nose. My father would have frowned, but my mother threw her head back and laughed. Today she was in one of her good moods. "You might want to wash up first." She eyed the girl. "And who's your friend here?"

"I'm not lost," the girl repeated with a defiant gaze.

My mother smiled. "I'm relieved to hear it," she said as she placed a plate before the girl.

I squirmed all the way through lunch, only taking a couple of bites of my sandwich before saying, "Can we be excused, please?" as I slid out of my seat.

"Your friend's not finished," my mother admonished, and it was true: the girl was still eating her sandwich.

"Just a minute," the girl said with her mouth full. I stood there, torn between impatience and wanting to be extra-special nice and considerate. Not looking at me, she took a couple more deliberate bites, then swallowed and put down the uneaten crust.

"That was tasty," she said to my mother. "Thank you."

"What wonderful manners you have! Maybe you can give Johnny a few pointers."

The girl glanced over at me. "Okay."

Back at the dig, my excitement became tempered by dismay as I realized just how big my find was. Even as I dreamed of a femur bigger than me, I realized there was no way I could get it out of the ground myself. But I was reluctant to go to my father for help. Since he was a scientist, everyone would think *he* discovered it.

My solution was this: I would break off a big chunk of bone, give it to my father to analyze without telling him where I'd found it (the fact that he might wander into the backyard and see the gaping hole didn't occur to me), and only after he had confirmed it to be an ancient dinosaur bone and called in experts and journalists would I show them the site of my discovery.

I hit the bone so hard the clanging hurt our dog Bessie's ears, and she slunk away. Nothing happened. "It won't break," I said in frustration.

The little girl stared intently at the bone, as if trying to imagine a world eons ago. "Drop a rock on it," she said at last.

My admiration for her ballooned. I dragged a ladder out to the back and found the biggest stone in the backyard I could lift, a small boulder the size of my own head. Slowly, I lugged the stone to the top of the ladder, then unceremoniously dropped it on the bone. It made a satisfying *crack*!

After two more drops, I could see crevices on the surface. I felt bad, damaging my find like this, but I didn't see any other way to preserve my claim to discovery. I lugged the stone to the top of the ladder once more.

"Be careful," the girl warned.

This time, when the stone hit, it made a gaping hole and plunged on through. I jumped off the ladder halfway down and stared into the blackness. An awful smell—the stench of a million years—came wafting up. And then it was followed by a thick, viscous brown fluid. Yelping, I stepped back. The brown seepage bubbled out, starting to fill the hole I had dug.

"Uh-oh," said the girl. Her brow furrowed.

My heart squeezing with fear over what I had unleashed, I abandoned my new friend and raced back to the house. I went into the bathroom to scrub my face and hands before changing my clothes.

That's when I noticed the toilet backing up.

I was almost as thrilled to see the backhoe that excavated the broken sewer line as I would be to see any dinosaur. It too had a loud diesel roar that rattled the windows, and there was something powerful and prehistoric in the way its single arm scraped the earth.

My mother wouldn't let me get close enough to watch, more as punishment than protection. She carried a tray of refreshments to the workmen, while from inside, I stewed, brimming with a green brew of jealousy and remorse. From that distance, I couldn't hear any voices, but through the back window, I saw her gesture back to me, and both she and the foreman laughed uproariously.

The girl, held blameless, had been allowed to stay outside. She stood close enough that she had to cover her ears on account of the noise, but when she glanced back at the house, I saw her gleeful grin. Then her head whipped around in the other direction as a woman arrived in the backyard. With her head down, the girl walked over to her mother—I assumed that's who she was—and buried her face against the woman's leg. The girl's mother shook hands with my mother, who gestured at the circus of construction in the backyard, and they too laughed together. As daughter and mother walked away, the little girl turned and waved to me, leaving me both hopelessly in love and with a sharp pang of loss.

When my mother walked back to the porch, she scraped the mud off the bottoms of her shoes. "Your father, naturally, claims to have a faculty meeting today. Since when do they have faculty meetings in the middle of summer?"

I was standing on my toes and squinting, intently watching the backhoe growl and buck as it bit into the dirt.

"Your father also failed to tell you that dinosaur bones aren't conveniently found in backyards. You have to trek far out into the desert, where it's hot and dry, and your camel dies, leaving you stranded. Or you have to hang off the edge of a cliff, a thousand feet up, trying to hammer a bone out of rock. I don't like heights, Johnny, do you?"

I looked up at her. "I don't think I want to be a paleontologist," I said, enunciating the word as carefully as the girl had.

"Good boy," she said, tousling my hair.

"But what kind of scientist is dad?"

She sighed.

After dinner, my father wiped his glasses on his shirt and said, "John, come out to the lab with me. You, too, Jane."

A squat, heavy box sat on his workbench. Out of it ran thick cables, and it had a small hole about ten centimeters across.

"I can only open up the window for a few seconds at a time. Jane, with your healthy skepticism, perhaps you should look first." He threw a switch, and the box hummed, the hole beginning to glow.

"What is this?" I asked.

He smiled. "This, my children, is a window back—if my calculations are correct—to the Jurassic."

"A time machine?" Jane asked, clear incredulity in her voice.

"A time window—the largest I can make. The power required grows as the fifth power of the area." The humming grew into a brutish growl, overlaid with sounds like metal tearing. Squinting through the window, I glimpsed a sunlit riot of green, and on a distant horizon, a herd of many-horned beasts. Into the window, my father thrust a pair of large tongs and pulled out a flower, its petals a bright bloody red shot through with yellow veins. It had an awful smell—not sweet, but like rotting hamburger meat—and a huge, ugly yellow stamen almost snapped in half by the tongs. "Ah, we've reached the Cretaceous, not the Jurassic," he said. "Flowering plants." Swinging it over to Jane, he said, "Here you go, little Weena," and dropped the flower into her open hands.

She stared at it for a moment, her mouth a twisted map of shock and dismay. Then she threw it on the concrete floor of the garage and ground it under the heel of her sneakers. "It's a trick," she said. "A lie. Like Santa Claus and the Tooth Fairy." She kicked the pulpy mass under a tool cabinet.

"But Santa Claus and the Tooth Fairy are made up," our father said. "I've always been honest about them. That flower—that was proof. You won't find any plant like that today. Now I have to get another one." He pushed his glasses up to his forehead and peered at some dials. "The capacitors have to recharge—half an hour."

We trooped inside the house. My father directed us children to wash dishes. When I took too long to dry the plates, Jane splashed soapy water onto me, and I cried. My father sent Jane stomping up to her room, and shooing me aside, took command of the sink.

Unwatched, I snuck back to the garage. The air around the time window's massive capacitors, each the size of a gallon-sized milk carton, was taut, shimmering. I threw the switch. Again the machine began to hum, low at first, then increasing in volume and pitch, just short of a squeal. The time window, which had been empty and dark, glowed like the innermost blue of a candle flame. I leaned close to the window, blinking against the sudden brightness, and for a moment I again caught a glimpse of a green landscape. I grabbed the tongs.

Suddenly, a shadow blocked the window. A huge eye, yellow and saurian, peered out at me.

With a panicked yelp, I shoved the tongs through the window, provoking an anguished roar. I dropped the tongs, letting them bang against the edges of the window. Blue sparks danced. The tongs clattered to the floor, bent by the shorn edge of a hole in time and space.

Without warning, the tip of a huge black claw poked through the time window. My heart squeezed, and I jumped back, peeing my pants. The claw filled the time window and pressed against the edges, causing more sparks and a foul, burning scent. The interior of the machine began to glow a demonic red, and a cry of pain came through the window. Then the machine burst into flames. The humming abruptly broke off, and all the lights blinked out. The claw tip, now a lump of sizzling charcoal, fell to the floor.

The garage door burst open, and by the jack-o'-lantern light of the flames, my father raced to the fire extinguisher our mother had made him install in the lab. A few quick puffs of white smothered the fire, plunging us into complete darkness. I heard a crunch as my father stepped on the carbonized remnant of the claw.

Then all was silent, until my mother's voice came from within the house: "Alan? Alan! What the hell have you done now?"

A week later, when I was no longer grounded, I asked my mother if I could invite over the girl I'd discovered in the backyard. I assumed my mother, who knew everything, could contact the girl's family.

My mother said gently, "I'm sorry, Johnny, they moved away. That's why your little friend was hiding out in our backyard. She didn't want to go."

In the garage, which stank of burnt electrolytic paste, all I found was coarse black powder where my father had stepped on the fried dinosaur claw. On hands and knees, I hunted for the flower Jane had pulverized and kicked under the tool cabinet, but spotted nothing, save for a single yellow speck that could have been Mesozoic pollen. When I breathed out, the speck of maybe-pollen whirled away, and I couldn't find it again, any more than I could find that little blonde girl who wasn't lost.

Sometimes at night, I dreamed about her and her wide green eyes. Other times, I dreamed about the dinosaurs, crowding in the dark around my bed. They muttered threats for digging up their bones, for poking their eyes, for shearing off their beautiful sharp claws. "We'll get you," those terrible lizards promised. "We'll have our revenge. We've had millions of years to dream up all sorts of ways to make your life miserable and lonely."

A couple of years later, my mother sent me to a therapist, briefly, whom I told about the dinosaurs. He nodded and said those dinosaurs were a way for my mind to address the traumas of childhood. But I noticed that behind his thick glasses, his eyes looked vaguely yellow and saurian, and his ill-fitting clothes could have easily concealed a twitching tail. I decided *he* was a dinosaur, too, and I refused to see him again.

Now that you've asked about my life story, I am digging away at my memories, to recreate, like a diorama in a museum, a history. My history. To answer you, I've become a paleontologist once more.

The Assassin Neutrino

It was the smallest of things, or so my father said. But it took away the biggest thing in my world.

In my memory, my childhood summers run together, because the plots were all the same. I went barefoot for weeks, collected bugs and odd rocks, lived out centuries in imaginary worlds, and lay under the backyard trees, eating plums and orange soda floats. I seldom played with friends, because I was an odd child who didn't have many. Following me around loyally was the only friend I needed: our old mutt, Bessie.

If I fell and skinned my knee, my father lectured me on balance and caution—this coming from a man who kept a chunk of pitchblende on his desk, a man who tested electrical connections with a wet finger. If I went to my mother, she'd lean out of her chaise lounge and pour out a bit of her drink onto it, saying, "There, that should sterilize it." But if I went to our dog, Bessie, she licked my face. And when I was lonely or sullen or crying, her wet red tongue washed me all over with love.

Early in the summer between—I think—first and second grade, Bessie lost her appetite. When I poured out her kibble, she turned her nose away. I ate a few to show her it was good, but she just looked at me, unconvinced. So, at dinner, as my father talked about his latest experiments and my sister begged to go to her friend Lucy's house, I dropped a piece of gristly meat on the floor. Normally, fallen food was immediately snatched up. But Bessie, panting on the linoleum, merely sniffed it, then left it in its splash of oily gravy.

A day later, I tried to push some kibble into her mouth, but she clamped her jaw tight. And at night, Bessie had trouble sleeping. She shifted restlessly, unable to get comfortable, and she wheezed, the air rumbling in and out of her like a freight train.

Fear and guilt drove me to my father at his lab bench in the garage.

"Do you want something, John?" he asked without turning from his experiment.

I shook my head, then burst into tears.

"Did you hurt yourself? Did your mother say something to you?"

"Bessie... Bessie won't eat," I got out between sobs. "Something's wrong!"

My father whistled for Bessie. She trotted in wearily, and she took it stoically as he poked at her gut. "Hmm..." He lifted her onto a table and wheeled over some massive equipment. I patted Bessie on her head as she looked at me, her eyes black as night.

"John, stand away. I'm taking some x-rays. It could hurt you."

"Then won't it hurt Bessie?"

"Hmm... If Bessie is really sick, the danger from illness outweighs the danger from x-rays. Do you understand?"

I didn't, but nonetheless, I backed away. There was a humming sound and a series of sharp thumps, with the acrid tang of ozone.

That afternoon, my father found me and Bessie out under a gingko tree, hiding from the summer heat. He had an intense look on his face—one that normally meant he was happy. I thought this meant good news. "Is Bessie going to be okay?"

"Can you show me exactly where she sleeps?"

We all went into my room. I lay down on my bed, and Bessie curled into a comma on the floor next to me.

"Hmm..." my father said, looking down at the floor and then up at the ceiling. With his fingers, he seemed to draw lines in the air.

"Come with me," he finally said.

We climbed into the attic. Crouched beneath the eaves of the roof, he pushed aside one of the heavy boxes that contained my grandfather's crumbling butterfly collection and pointed out long, flat sheets of plastic he had wrapped in aluminum foil. Through a mesh-covered vent, we could see into the backyard, where he had strung up similar sheets between trees.

"You don't know this, but right now, there are cosmic rays from outer space raining down upon us. These detect them."

My father built things. To my mother's despair, he never fixed anything useful, like the lawnmower or the toilet or the stove, but he had built his own x-ray machine, his own radio telescope, his own gene sequencer.

"Cosmic rays are high-energy protons traveling across the galaxy. Most of the time, they pass harmlessly through us. But sometimes when the cosmic rays strike an atom, they create a neutrino. Do you know what a neutrino is? A neutrino is a kind of subatomic particle. It's quite important, and yet it's like a ghost, difficult to detect, able to travel through thousands of miles of rock or metal and not be stopped. A neutrino could pass all the way from the far side of the Earth and come up at our feet."

We clambered out of the attic. "I checked through my records, and about a year ago, there was an event," he said. "There was no incoming track from the attic, so it must have been a neutrino, but there was an upward spall of charged particles. And the nexus, best as I can figure, was right where Bessie sleeps beside your bed."

Back in the garage, he picked up a black x-ray film and handed it to me. In one corner my father had scratched, *DOG, mixed breed, 11 yrs, 20 kg*. Beneath it, he had added, *Local B = 0.47 G*. I still have that x-ray film, and now, armed with my own degree in physics, I know he meant the Earth's personal magnetic field.

In the x-ray, Bessie's bones were a chalky white, and her soft, comforting flesh had been reduced to a pale, floury shadow. Running through her body, in spiral curves like the arms of a galaxy, were puffy clumps.

He ran a finger over the film. "See? Amazing. The tumors draw an ionization path. Even a year later, it's quite clear. I had wondered if building my own cosmic ray detector was a bit daft—you should have heard your mother on the subject—but this ... this has paid off. It's known that naturally occurring ionizing radiation can trigger a carcinoma, but for the first time, I can put the pieces together. I can even identify the original particle that did it, a neutrino piercing from the other side of the Earth."

I tugged at his sleeve. "But will she be okay?"

"Who? ... Oh, the dog. I'm sorry, I'm afraid not."

My father talked excitedly about it over dinner. Whenever he sat down with us for dinner—and whenever it occurred to my mother to make dinner—it was to lecture us about his latest project. My mother swirled her glass, the ice tumbling endlessly, while Jane and I stuck our tongues out at each other when neither parent was looking.

"It seems a little thing, but really, it's huge," my father said, his fork poised over his mashed potatoes. "I'm thinking of sending this to *Science*. Or maybe *Nature*."

"Don't make faces at your brother," my mother said wearily.

"He started it."

"I did not!"

"Cosmic ray research has been obsessed with the highest energies, the mysteries of the 'knee' and the 'ankle,' whereas this might nudge a return to lower energies, to..."

"To the buttocks?" my mother suggested. Jane and I giggled.

My father loaded his fork with potatoes and waved it at my mother. "People worry about radiation from x-rays and electric fields from power lines—"

"And now you'll make them worry about cosmic rays, is that it? I can see the letters to the editor pouring in, demanding an end to cosmic radiation."

"You can't turn it off—"

"I know that. Jesus, Alan." She shivered. "But you do have a way of making me feel ... well, vulnerable." She put a hand on her stomach.

My father leaned forward. "The best thing would be to not smoke or drink."

"You know I've cut back. I wish you'd stop haranguing me. It's only when the kids get on my nerves."

Jane looked back and forth at our parents. "What are you talking about?"

My mother and father shared a glance. "Well," my father said slowly, "I suppose—"

"I'm having a baby," my mother broke in. "A new brother for you two."

"Or sister. Frankly, those tests don't always—"

"Test schmest. It's a boy."

I looked down at my plate. Tracks of gravy led from a sad, indifferent clump of gray-green peas to a tensely coiled lump of fat. "Couldn't we just fix Bessie instead?"

The day was so hot that the blue of the sky seemed bleached white. I found Bessie panting beneath a bush. She looked across the lawn, burning brown in the summer sun, as if she were looking elsewhere—as if she were looking into eternity.

I got out my red wagon with the wobbly rear wheel. Bessie didn't have the strength to hop up into the wagon, but she had gotten so thin under her long fur that I had no trouble lifting her. My mother was asleep in her chaise lounge beneath her umbrella, her glass empty and drying in the heat.

Nowadays, children are forbidden to reconnoiter even a single suburban block. Back then, Bessie and I would tramp halfway across town without hesitation. The vet's office was a mile away, wedged between a dry cleaner and a pizza joint. After the scratchy heat of the summer day, the lobby of the vet's office felt cool. "My dog's real sick," I said.

The vet was a large, tall man with a barrel-like belly. In a small room painted bone white, he examined Bessie. "I'll need to take an x-ray."

I pulled out the x-ray my father had taken. The vet held it up to the light and squinted. "Where did you get this?" he asked.

"My father has a machine he built in the garage."

Handing me back the x-ray, the vet left the room. After a while, I began to fear that he had forgotten us, but just as I was getting up, the vet came in, followed by my red-faced father.

"John, we're going home."

"Your dog, Professor Chant," the vet put in. "She's riddled with tumors—"

"I know. I doubt there's anything you can do." My father turned to leave.

"She's in a great deal of pain." The vet blocked the door, and he was even taller and wider than my father.

"I have one more x-ray to take. I can extrapolate back and confirm—"

"And your son is in pain, sir, from watching her suffer."

My father's shoulders slumped, and he turned and knelt by me. "Bessie's suffered enough, John. It's time to let to her go."

"I'll give you a minute," the vet said, backing out and closing the door.

"Can't you do anything?" I asked my father. "I promise I'll do all my chores and never complain."

"I'm sorry, John. We have to say goodbye."

"But you can fix anything."

"Not this, John. Not this."

We buried Bessie in the backyard. I cried the whole time my father dug the shallow grave, while my mother put her arms around me and kissed the top of my head. Even Jane, who had said "Yuck!" whenever Bessie licked her and who complained about dog hair around the house, laid flowers on the freshly turned earth and burst into tears.

Later, my father came into my room as I was playing on the floor. "John, do you have Bessie's x-ray?" He walked around, lifting up books and toys. "I need it to write my paper."

"I forgot it at the vet's," I lied.

He must have heard the sullen tone in my voice, for he said, "We all miss Bessie."

I looked up at him. "Can you fix your time window? Even a little bit?" I didn't need it to go all the way back to the Mesozoic, only a few weeks into the past. I wanted so badly to see Bessie again.

He looked uncomfortable. "I'm afraid not." It was only years later, when I realized the risk that he had taken in constructing the time window, that I understood his refusal.

He started to leave, then paused at my door. "John, you know we love you. Your mother and I, we love you so much. Our love for you is as big as a galaxy. You know what a galaxy is, don't you?"

I nodded. He had shown me a galaxy that past winter, just after Christmas. We had looked through a telescope to see it, and even though he told me it was a vast collection of stars, I could cover it with a thumb held at arm's length. It was both enormous and tiny, like a neutrino, like his love for me.

The next month, I found a big glass terrarium in my room. It was a pastiche of a desert, with sand and a single basaltic rock and a plastic cactus, but it also contained, splayed out like an indolent beachgoer, a thick, fat-bellied lizard, its pebbly black skin striped with pale yellow. I thought it was a rubber lizard until it flicked out a long, thin black tongue.

I jumped back, into my father, who was now standing behind me. "Do you like him?"

I pressed my face against the glass. "It's a lizard."

"It's a Mexican beaded lizard, a cousin of the Gila monster. You'll have to be careful because they have venomous fangs." He leaned down next to me and took off his glasses to squint into the terrarium, though I knew he couldn't see more than a few inches without corrective lenses. "What do you think?"

A few times since Bessie died, I'd had nightmares about dinosaurs. They smelled bad and came out of the toilet, and my sister laughed as they ate me. Nonetheless, it occurred to me that having one monster around to scare off the others might not be a bad thing.

My mother was less impressed. "Oh, Christ on toast, Alan, this is your worst idea ever! And there's some competition for that spot."

"I thought it would give him some company. Besides..." He hesitated.

"You've got some scheme, haven't you?"

"Well, to be honest, John's beaded lizard—"

"Paul," I cut in. "His name is Paul." During the past year, I had briefly been friends with a boy named Paul, before his mother forbade him from playing with me.

"Well, Paul has a brother," my father said. "I was approached to take on an unusual contract—apparently I have developed a reputation for unusual experiments—"

"'Apparently'?" my mother said, her eyebrows raised. "There's doubt about this?"

"A colleague of mine has developed a new anti-tumor agent," he continued, ignoring her comment. "But they had trouble with the animal experiment review board. Some activist smuggled out pictures of mice with large tumors, causing an uproar. So, I suggested the Gila monster as a subject. No one will protest experimentation on a Gila monster. But we couldn't get any, so we got Mexican beaded lizards." He coughed. "John's is the control. The other is out in the lab."

"Will they be able to visit each other?" I asked. "Maybe the one in your lab is lonely."

"I don't think lizards get lonely," my father said. "Not much for affection."

"And so, you concluded it would make a good pet for your son," my mother said.

We went out to the garage lab, where he wheeled a terrarium containing the other beaded lizard, another lump of black and yellow in a small puddle of sand, over to a machine I recognized.

"You're going to take an x-ray?"

"Yes, to establish a baseline. That way, when tumors develop—"

"You mean like with Bessie?"

Even my father could hear the crack of pain in my voice. "Yes. And you were very sad after she got sick and died. We don't want that to happen, to dogs or to people."

He explained that a tumor is tissue that grows uncontrollably. Healthy cells have instructions to be skin cells, muscle cells, kidney cells, and so on. But tumors forget their identities, and grow without direction. "Doctors have tried killing tumors with medicine," he said, "but the drugs take a toll on healthy tissues as well. This drug is different. It restores normal instructions to the tumor, forces it to remember what kind of tissue it's supposed to be. We're going to try it on this lizard."

He showed me another vial, filled with a thick pale yellow fluid, and attached a hypodermic needle. "This is transmissible sarcoma. I got it off a dead coyote I found months ago. Thought I might have use for it someday." Putting on heavy gloves, he reached into the terrarium and pressed the lizard's head down against the sand. With the other, he jabbed the hypodermic needle into the lizard's thick, thrashing tail.

The lizard hissed and thrashed horribly, scattering sand. Startled, I stepped back, bumping against my father's workbench, sending tools clattering to the concrete floor. A gluey feeling settled in my stomach as I witnessed the lizard's distress and panic.

"It's okay, John," my father said. He let go of the lizard. "You know, it probably needs a name, too. You gave your lizard a name ... um, Patrick..."

"Paul," I said. "But he's going to die, isn't he?"

"Well, I'm hoping the medicine will stop that." He paused. "So, how about a name?"

I stared down at the lizard. "Fatty McStupid," I said in barely a whisper.

My father snorted. "That's not a very nice name. Our good thoughts matter."

Fine words from a man who had just injected a lizard with cancer.

"Ernie," I blurted. "Paul's brother's name is Ernie."

My father leaned over the terrarium. "Hello, Ernie." He put away the hypodermic needle, then started to pick up the tools I had scattered.

"Aren't you going to give Ernie the, uh ... the medicine?" I asked.

Perhaps my voice was a bit plaintive, because my father stopped and looked at me.

"I want to wait a few weeks, until Ernie starts to develop tumors. But I have the medicine right here, all ready for him." He took a heavy metal box and unlatched it. Inside were several vials, filled with a viscous fluid the color of pink bubble gum.

As he closed the box, my father said, "John, can I trust you?" I nodded. "How about I give you the chore of feeding Ernie? I have to go out of town tomorrow. You'll feed Paul anyway, of course. That way, you can be my junior assistant. How's that?"

Saturday, Gramma came to pick up Jane. They spent every Saturday at the local food closet, packing up and handing out groceries to needy families. As always, Gramma said to me, "You can come with us. The Lord loves a cheerful helper."

"I, uh, was going to read," I said lamely.

Gramma frowned. "Instead of stultifying your brain with made-up stories," she said, "it'd do you good to see more of the real world."

I looked down. I hated to think what she would have said had she known I was straight-out lying about reading.

From the couch, my mother called out, "Don't worry, Johnny, the real world is overrated."

My father had left that morning, rising in the coffee-colored predawn to fly to Washington, DC. Soon after, Jane and Gramma left, and my mother was snoring on the sofa.

I went to the bookshelves and pulled down a volume of the encyclopedia to read up on Mexican beaded lizards and Gila monsters. I was beginning to warm up to the idea of my own personal monster. If only I could trap all my terrors in a glass terrarium.

My father had forgotten to tell me what to feed Paul and Ernie. According to the encyclopedia, Gila monsters ate mice, smaller lizards, and bird eggs. So, I went into the kitchen and broke a couple of eggs into a frying pan. Between my mother's irregular cooking and Jane's frequent refusal to cook for me, I had already picked up some basic culinary skills.

I hated runny eggs, but my father loved them. The encyclopedia was not specific on how Gila monsters preferred their eggs, so I split the difference. Upstairs, I carefully slid one fried egg into the terrarium with Paul, then took the other into the garage for Ernie. After washing the pan, I found Paul desultorily chewing his egg.

"I miss Bessie," I told him. "I don't love you."

Unfazed, Paul kept chewing the egg, a bit of yolk running down his jaw.

I lay down on my bed and opened up one of my books. When I looked up, Paul's egg was all gone. When I checked in the garage, however, Ernie hadn't touched his egg. Maybe he wanted something more enticing; I didn't like fried eggs all that much myself.

After leafing through several cookbooks, I found a recipe for a Southwest omelet. *That should make him feel at home*, I thought. We didn't have all the ingredients, so I had to substitute black pepper for green pepper and mayonnaise for the sour cream, but at last, I had a nice, pseudo-Southwest omelet. Good enough for a lizard, at least.

I plopped it into the terrarium. Ernie turned his head away. My heart raced with panic. This was exactly the way Bessie had refused food when she had fallen sick. "I'm sorry I said I didn't love Paul," I told Ernie. "I didn't mean it. I love him. I love you, too." But Ernie continued his hunger strike.

I didn't want my father to come home to find Ernie dead. And my body still rang with grief for Bessie. Another death, even of a lizard... I teared up just thinking about it.

I opened the box of vials filled with pink fluid. Medicine, my father had said. A syringe as thick as a thumb lay on the workbench. After donning heavy protective gloves and standing on a step stool, I reached into the terrarium, held Ernie down, and plunged the needle in.

When I came back, I was relieved to see that both the omelet and the fried egg were gone. After school, I fried an egg for Paul and made another omelet for Ernie. Paul chewed at his egg, but Ernie pounced on the omelet as if it might run away.

Soon I was making Ernie two omelets a day. If I didn't, he scrabbled horribly against the glass of his terrarium. *"I'm starving!"* he seemed to say.

When I told my mother we'd run out of eggs, she waved a hand. "There's money in my purse. You can go to the corner store by yourself, can't you?"

I hoped my father would be pleased at how responsible I'd been. True, Ernie had doubled in size and looked like a little fat man stuffed into a beaded lizard suit. He had even developed a double chin, a look which did not suit a venomous lizard.

Cooking two omelets a day was a strain. Fortunately, as Ernie got bigger, he became less fussy about what he ate. I fed him soggy cereal, stale zucchini bread, moldy cheese, and frozen blocks of leftovers I found in the back of the freezer. Despite his hearty appetite, when I went to bed and closed my eyes, I saw a cloud of tumors wheeling in the dark. Was he getting better? Was the medicine working?

I decided to x-ray Ernie. He had gotten so heavy he was hard to wrestle out of the terrarium tank. I had put on heavy gloves, which was wise, because he naughtily tried to bite me.

"Stay," I told him. But he skittered off the table, fell to the floor with a hideous *plop!* and dashed under a workbench. He wouldn't come when I called his name, so I went inside to cook a tempting omelet. But when I returned to the garage, skillet in hand, he wasn't under the workbench—and the door to the backyard was open.

My father was upset Ernie had disappeared. He asked me over and over if I knew what happened. I told my father I had fed Ernie Saturday morning, which was true, and that I hadn't seen him since, which was also more or less true.

"This experiment is important, John. Very important to me." He sighed and walked out of the room.

My sister stood in the doorway. "You're going to go to hell for lying."

"And you'll go to double hell if you tattle," I warned.

Jane frowned. "There's no such thing as double hell."

Nevertheless, I felt awful. For months, I searched for Ernie. In the backyard, some of my father's cosmic ray detectors had been gnawed on, but Ernie had moved on. I rode my bike up and down the streets and tramped through the woods behind our house. No sign of him. I imagined him lonely—as lonely as I was without Bessie. I hoped that wherever he was, he had found a home, safe from tumors and needles and whatever else might cast cold fear into the heart of a monster.

Tales from the Genetic Code

When I was in second grade, Jane and I briefly had a live-in nanny. This is how it happened.

Second grade started disastrously for me, much worse than the start of *your* second-grade year. My father gave me a chemistry set to celebrate the start of a new school year. In his enthusiasm, he accidentally started a small chemical fire that brought a fire truck to our house and landed us in the emergency room for smoke inhalation.

Missing the first day of class did not endear me to my first second-grade teacher, Mr. Yerkes, whose prime ambition was for his class to remain second-grade district champions in crippleball, a local sport that made dodgeball look kind and gentle. I had no talent for sports (and my father's explanation that humans' ability to throw accurately distinguishes us from other primates did not make me feel better), and bringing a venomous lizard for show-and-tell did not raise my status in the eyes of either Mr. Yerkes or the crippleball captain/class bully, Steve Snoever.

I then did what I thought any reasonable person would do: I tried to make an invisibility potion using my chemistry set, plus other ingredients from my father's lab. I failed to make myself unseen by Mr. Yerkes and Steve Snoever, but I did accidentally make my classroom—a permanent temporary trailer module—weirdly hard to see, like a smudge in the air. This brought both the fire department *and* the bomb squad, and after I stammered out an explanation involving "chemicals," the decontamination unit declared the trailer module condemned—and my mother was condemned to a visit from my school's assistant vice principal.

Exhausted and exasperated after the visit, my mother stretched out on the sofa with her feet up and eyes closed, vibrating with anger. "I don't have the energy right now," she said, feigning bored indifference with a slow drawl—not that she fooled any of us. "But I can't ignore this. So, pretend I am angry. Visualize me yelling and throwing things and, I don't know, making threats." One hand she waved at us, and the other she curled protectively over the bump of her stomach.

"God... Don't ask me what kind of threats. I don't have the energy to dream up a threat. Just imagine terrible threats—the kind that give you nightmares."

My father cleared his throat. "You know, Anne, perhaps you—"

She rattled the ice in her glass at him. "You're not in any position to lecture me, Alan," she snapped, and he winced, as if she had snapped him with a wet towel. "I got enough of a lecture from that man from Johnny's school. A sweaty little man with halitosis. I swear to God, I can still smell it, like pickled fish shit. The smell must have gotten into the furniture. The assistant vice principal—I think that's who he was—he talked at me for most of an hour. I guess when you're an assistant vice principal, you get practice in making a short story long. And the short story is that Johnny can't go back to that school."

My father sat hunched over on the ottoman. I suppose he could have been more uncomfortable if he had been sitting on an ottoman of nails instead of worn red velvet, but it was unlikely.

I didn't dare open my mouth any more than to say, "I'm sorry." The atmosphere was so taut, I feared I might throw up.

"Oh, Johnny... I want to be angry at you, but my motherly instincts demand that I defend you. Those instincts are very annoying and very hard to ignore." She opened her eyes. "The good news—or at least, the less bad news—is that I found a school that will take you. But it's a half-hour drive away. In my condition, I'm not going to drive every day. I'm just not."

My father slumped a fraction farther. "But I can't drive him. I'm double-teaching this semester, both morning and afternoon."

"It's a wonder we have a son left." She rubbed the bridge of her nose. "I can't handle two kids on my own, not now."

That was how Shahra came to live with us.

"You're fat," I blurted out when introduced to her.

"John, that's rude," my father snapped.

My face grew hot. I hadn't meant to be rude. But my father always said a good scientist reported his observations, coolly and impersonally.

Shahra laughed, her black hair bobbing. "Why, John, I *am* fat! Maybe I'm as jolly as fat old Santa Claus."

"Santa Claus is a lie," my sister said. "A lie from the devil."

Shahra's right eyebrow rose. "Well, maybe not so jolly as that."

Our father told her, "Your task is to keep track of these two."

"Radio collars?" Shahra asked.

My father turned to my mother. "I can see why you thought of her."

"Want to see my room?" I asked Shahra.

"I suppose I might as well figure out all your hiding places," she said with a shrug.

First stop on the tour was the terrarium, home to my Mexican beaded lizard. "This is Paul. We used to have a dog, Bessie, but she died. I got Paul to keep me company. He had a brother, Ernie, but Ernie, um... Ernie escaped." I decided not to go into details.

Shahra leaned forward until her nose nearly touched the glass. "The beaded lizard's venom won't kill you, but it would hurt like fire. You'd survive, but remember the pain, and stay away from beaded lizards."

"My father's going to like you," I said.

At my new school, I met my new teacher. "You're John Chant? I'm Mr. Tolentino." Mr. Tolentino was also plump, like a sack of grain that had settled and bulged out at the bottom. He had thick glasses like my father, and a gentle face. Altogether, he looked like a grown-up nerd. He looked like my future.

After the bell rang and the class drifted in, Mr. Tolentino introduced me to the other kids. He handed out papers, then knelt by my desk. "It's a math test," he said, "but since you just arrived, it won't count."

"I don't mind," I said. "I like tests."

The test was easy. I wrote down the answers, and when I looked up, Mr. Tolentino was still correcting some papers, and the other kids still had their heads bowed over their desks.

Bored, I used the margins of the test to make up a story based upon my answers. The first answer was 12, so I wrote, *There were once twelve knights.* The second answer was 121, so I wrote, *... who had to fight one hundred and twenty-one monsters.* The third answer was 8: *to rescue eight princesses.*

Here I paused. In my few weeks at my former school, the only warm moment had been after show-and-tell, when a girl in my class, Becky, told me she liked my venomous lizard, Paul. Blonde with pigtails, Becky reminded me of my first crush, the girl who hadn't been lost, the girl who had witnessed me breaking the sewer line. For that deep reason, Becky became my second crush.

In my second second-grade class, I amended my math test to read, *eight princesses all named Becky. 43. After killing forty-three of the monsters... 3. ... three of the knights had been killed.* I drew their bodies with broken monster teeth sticking out of them, adding, *and the nine remaining knights said, "If one and only one more of us is killed, then each one of us will get a Princess Becky."*

"But if five of us are killed," said another knight, "then each of the remaining four of us will get two Princess Beckies."

"That's assuming the Princess Beckies even want to be with us," said another knight. "They all might already have boyfriends." The next answer was 81, so I wrote, *"They might each have eighty-one boyfriends."*

The next morning, Mr. Tolentino handed back the tests, and as he gave me mine, he said quietly, "Can I see you at recess, John?"

My heart froze. Did he think I had cheated? Was he angry about the story and the pictures? My test didn't have a single mark on it.

All through that first hour, I felt like I was going to throw up. When the recess bell rang and the other kids ran outside, I sat at my desk with my hands folded, ready for the firing squad.

Mr. Tolentino smiled at me. "John, I'd like for you to take another test, if you don't mind missing recess and part of the next period."

I started to break out in a cold sweat. "Those were my answers on the test, honest!"

Mr. Tolentino raised a palm. "Of course, John. You did very well, and the school would like to evaluate you more. I already called your mother," he said, which put another spot of cold fear into my heart, "and she gave her permission."

(I later found out she had said, "Oh, go ahead. His father does all kinds of tests on him. Experiments, actually.")

He walked me down the hall to another room and opened the door. "Charlotte," he said, "this is John. John, this is Mrs. Mullins."

"Thank you, Henry," she said to Mr. Tolentino. Mrs. Mullins was pretty and petite and had long brown hair, burnished to a bronze sheen, and wore bright red lipstick. If the point of the lipstick was to impress seven-year-old boys, she succeeded. Women on television wore lipstick—even street-hardened policewomen as they took down drug dealers and thieves with a flourish of the handcuffs—but my mother hardly ever did. One time my mother did put on lipstick, and I stared as if I didn't recognize her. "Are you going to be on TV?" I asked. My mother had laughed and said, "No, we're just going to a fancy-pants restaurant." And it was true: my father, standing right beside her, *was* wearing his fanciest pants, though his mouth turned down at her remark. Later, they had left the restaurant halfway through dinner when the babysitter called them in hysterics, because my beaded lizard, Paul, had escaped, and I asked her to help me find him.

That's why, when introduced to Mrs. Mullins, I blurted out, "Are you going to a fancy-pants restaurant?"

Mrs. Mullins said gently, "Maybe later. Right now, I'm going to be giving you a test, okay?"

The test was a lot of questions, some with words and analogies, others with numbers, and for some I had to draw a picture.

When it was over, she smiled. "Well, John, I have to add up your score, but I think I'm going to be having you in my gifted program for an hour each day. Do you have any questions?"

I raised my hand, as I had been taught. "Was that an IQ test?"

"Of a sort."

"My father says IQ tests aren't very good. All they measure is how good you do on IQ tests."

"Well, your father has a point." I noticed a smudge of lipstick on her teeth. "But we don't have a better tool to identify gifted kids."

I raised my hand again. "Are you going to have a baby?" She looked startled for a moment, and I added, "My mother is."

She glanced down at her belly. "You're a perceptive little boy, aren't you?"

Aristotle thought the universe was layered like a wedding cake, if there were wedding cakes in ancient Greece. The bottom layer was earth, all mud and mess. Then came water, cool and sweet, and air, which gives us breath. Above that was the fire that lit our minds—some of us, at least—and uppermost, the starry firmament, ethereal and perfect, an admonishment to our muddy, human imperfections.

Our house was layered, too, though in the opposite order. The ground floor was neat and tidy, if my mother remembered to tell us kids to clean up. On the second floor were the bedrooms, where entropy had a sure foothold. My mother never bugged me about making my bed or cleaning my room. The second-floor hallway was cluttered with toys no one had played with for years. My father didn't like the disorder, but since he himself hoarded tools and parts out in the garage, he walked around the mess as if it had been sprayed with an invisibility solution. The attic crowning the house like an outsized wig was chaos incarnate, full of unorganized boxes and gangs of mice. Sometimes I let Paul run loose in the attic. Corralled a few days later, he was full-bellied and as happy as a venomous lizard could be.

After driving me home from school, Shahra disappeared into her room, which had previously been my mother's library, on the second floor. Soon, a smell like vinegar and nail polish remover wafted out of it.

"What are you doing?" Jane asked, having pushed open the door without a knock.

Shahra sat on the floor, surrounded by dozens of flasks of clear liquid, and in front of her was a large, flat machine, covered with lines that looked like smeared makeup. A centrifuge spun like a roulette wheel making up for years of lost bets, and next to it, a flask was shaking to a rumba beat. It reminded me of our garage.

"A little sideline I picked up," Shahra said. "After your mom shut down her lab, I went to work for Professor Romatschke."

"You knew our mother?" Jane asked. "From before?"

"You mean, like B.F.? 'Before Family'? Yeah. I was a student tech in her actinide lab. She was the queen of *f*-valence chemistry."

"My mother was a scientist?" I asked. "Like my father?"

Jane rolled her eyes. "You're so *ignorant*. Of course she was!"

"Not quite like him, I don't think," Shahra said. "But yes, your mom was a scientist, and a drill sergeant in the lab. She gave me hell, but I sure learned a lot. Then she took maternity leave when she was pregnant with you, Jane, and I switched to biochem."

I said to Jane, "You ruined her career."

Jane folded her arms. "I don't care. Science is stupid. It pretends God doesn't exist."

A little firecracker of laughter exploded out of Shahra. "I see. Well, little miss Jane, God exists, and so does the devil, but their names are evolution and entropy. Entropy, that's physics, your father's realm. But evolution shapes us and our future." Shahra leaned in close. Her breath smelled of spearmint. "Your mom or dad ever leave a note for you?" Jane and I nodded. "Your body is made up of trillions of tiny cells—"

"My father showed us that, in his microscope," I said.

She cleared her throat. "Inside each of those cells are tens of thousands of these little notes. They're called—"

"DNA," I supplied. "Do you think we're babies?"

Shahra smiled and explained that the notes were called genes, written with DNA. Genes told our bodies how to grow and work, and how to get better when sick. "They even influence what you do and how you feel."

I asked, "Can we read these notes?"

Shahra stood up and stretched like an oversized house cat. "I was hoping you'd ask."

These notes, our genes, the instructions for our lives had been heavily edited over millions and millions of years, Shahra went on. But many of the crossed-out words and sentences were still there, jumbled in with our working genes.

"These crossed-out genes, they're introns. Some people call them 'junk DNA.' But they aren't junk. They make up more than ninety percent of your DNA. Professor Romatschke realized they tell us about our past and our future."

"Like a time machine," I said. "My father built a time machine. Well, a time window—"

"That was a fake," Jane interrupted. "And this is a fake, too."

Shahra raised an eyebrow. "Genetics is fake? But you have your mother's brown eyes. You inherited her genes for that. You also inherited her caustic tongue."

"What did *I* inherit?" I asked.

Shahra took a Q-tip out of a box and waved it like a magic wand. "Open your mouth. You haven't been kissing anyone lately, have you? Wouldn't want a contaminated sample." My face reddened with embarrassment as she swabbed the inside of my cheek. Shahra then swirled the Q-tip in a test tube of clear liquid. "Professor Romatschke found she could uncover your past and your future by reading your introns. For this, she was expelled from the ivory tower."

Jane screwed up her face. "Fortune telling? That's the work—"

"—of the devil. I could've predicted you'd say that without DNA." Shahra glanced at the test tube, then at me. "Give me a day, and I'll tell you your history and your fate."

The next day, Jane and I squeezed into Shahra's room. Shahra sat shoeless on the floor. We kids stood, because all the horizontal surfaces, the desk, the windowsill, the chair, were covered with flasks and beakers and bottles of reagents. Even the floor was littered with sheets of paper, surrounding a large, flat device.

"Yesterday, I grew more of your cells and pulled out the DNA. Your DNA then got chopped up, and I added markers. Imagine taking a book and cutting out all the pages, and then looking for specific words or phrases on each page. Then this thing, it's called an electrophoresis—"

"Lectofor...see..." I echoed.

"Ee-lect-troh-for-ee-siss," Shahra corrected. "The markers have different weights and mobility, so I have them run a bit of a race to see what your instructions are." She had me sit on the floor beside her, with the electrophoresis sheet between us.

"How can you read this?" I asked. "It's just smears and shadows."

"Good analogy, John," Shahra said. "That's life. Your life is written here in the book of Watson and Crick, and poor Rosalind Franklin, but smeared and hidden by shadow and hard to read." She tapped the paper. "Let's see... You like a girl at school..."

Jane began singing softly, "John loves Be-cky, John loves Be-eh-cky..."

"Shut up!"

"... but that's just more biochemical scripts running through your brain, genes whispering to you. You'll take after your father," she continued, "become a physicist like him. You have his gifts, his curiosity, his inventiveness. Your faults will be different. You will see beauties and monsters, and sometimes they'll be one and the same. You'll look at things in a way no one else has. You..." And then her voice hung up.

"What?" I asked.

Shahra pursed her lips, hesitating, the way I did when I had trouble saying a long, multisyllabic word.

"Is it about Becky? Will he marry Be-eck-ky?" Jane crooned, singing the name with a chiaroscuro of taunting.

But Shahra shook her head. "Love will elude you for a long time, and loneliness will be your companion."

My body felt all weird and squishy when she said this. Later in life, when I remembered this, I also remembered the dig in my backyard, the girl who wasn't lost, the saurian eye glaring at me through the time window, the smell of a burning claw—and my dream of dinosaurs standing around my bed, cursing me across the eons. Only it wasn't a dream; it was written in my DNA.

I liked Mrs. Mullins. She was always kind and spoke gently, as if I were a glass unicorn. When she came to pick me up from Mr. Tolentino's class, she said, "I've been thinking about a project to engage you with. Henry here says you like dinosaurs?"

I had mixed feelings about dinosaurs. "What, you mean like a diorama, like Suzi makes?" Suzi Chen meticulously recreated murder scenes from Sherlock Holmes novels. In fact, when Mrs. Mullins wasn't watching, she would prick her finger with a needle and used her own blood create a puddle beneath the victim. "That looks so realistic!" Mrs. Mullins would then exclaim.

"Why, yes," Mr. Tolentino rumbled. "I guess you could call it a *dino*-rama."

Mrs. Mullins laughed so hard that she bumped shoulders with Mr. Tolentino.

That evening, Shahra showed us an electrophoresis sheet she had prepared from a sample of Jane's DNA. Jane had been reluctant, but in the end, her curiosity—dictated, I suppose, by her DNA—got the better of her.

I sat across on the floor across from Shahra, bouncy with excitement, but Jane refused to sit down. She stood in the doorway with her arms crossed, straight and brittle like a dried stick. "I know you're making this up to make fun of me," she said. "And God."

Shahra took out a magnifying glass and went up and down the columns of bands. "You know, this God phase of yours isn't going to last. You will become a spectacular, messy sinner like the rest of us. You, uh, won't be a virgin your whole life. You'll have a mess of kids." She leaned over to me and said in a loud stage whisper, "Living in a mobile home in a trailer park," and I giggled.

Jane's face twisted up. "Eww." Then she looked over at me. "Let's see if *she* will do it."

By "she," Jane meant our mother.

"Oh ... my ... God," my mother said after Jane rambled on incoherently. "Shahrazad Sattari, what are you up to? This isn't Esme's 'genomancy,' is it?"

"Well, yeah. But just for entertainment."

"That's what Esme said—at first. Then she started to believe her own ravings. She wrote to the CIA and the Pentagon and the White House and CBS news and God knows who else. In the end, she claimed Jean Dixon was trying to poison her."

Shahra twisted her foot on our grimy carpet, the way you might rub out a cigarette. Jane nudged me, and I held out a Q-tip swab to our mother. "Open wide."

Shahra showed me how to spread the cells on a petri dish. A day later, we harvested them, then lysed them with a reagent to get the DNA out of the nuclei. "Like unwrapping a present on your birthday," Shahra said. She demonstrated the reagents used to break apart the DNA, and how to add markers, short nucleotide sequences attached to polymers that would recognize and grab onto certain DNA sequences. This was spread as a thin film across Western gel paper and carefully inserted into the electrophoresis machine to draw out the bands.

"How do you know what it means?" I asked Shahra.

She showed me a small notebook crammed with sketches and notes: the configuration of bands, notations on nucleotide sequences, and interpretations. Some were straightforward: "susceptible to milk allergies" or "prone to alcoholism" or "tendency to introversion." Others were more cryptic: "many miles for a short journey," "after the mountain comes the valley," and other phrases that I later wondered whether they had been cribbed directly from the *I Ching*.

We went to my mother and presented the results. "You have a will like iron, but beware, for iron rusts," Shahra began.

"What is this, a DNA fortune cookie?"

"It gets better," Shahra assured her. "You once ran an empire—your lab—and you will become the mother of an even greater empire."

My mother laughed. "I'm glad to hear my children will survive childhood. The question is, will I survive theirs?"

I could see in Shahra's eyes how she still worshipped my mother. "Yes and no."

"Well, that sounds ominous. Also, confusing. What about Alan? He can't miss out on the fun. Alan. Alan! Get in here. Johnny, take a sample from your father."

My father sputtered and fussed and refused until my mother called him a no-fun, wet-as-a-pee-soaked-blanket, cold-rain-on-the-worst-parade-ever fuddy-duddy.

A day later, he was sitting on the couch, looking uncomfortable. My mother laughed. "Wish I had popcorn!"

"Let's get this over with," he muttered.

Shahra unfolded the electrophoresis chart on our living room carpet with a great deal of showmanship. "Let's see. Perfect hearing. You wear corrective lenses. And yet you don't see or hear what is right before you."

She scanned the columns. "Oh, this is old," she said. "Very old. Your great-to-the-forty-thousandth grandfather was a *Homo habilis*, one of the ancestors of humanity."

My father smiled, a crinkly, wrinkly smile like the edge of an oyster shell, and just as sharp and as salty. "Okay, I'll play along. And this ancestor, this monkey-man, was he smarter than his fellow hominids?"

Shahra shook her head. "No. He was scrawny and wheezed a lot, and the alpha males threw rocks at him. But when the alphas ventured out for food, this fellow stayed behind and screwed the females." She glanced over at me and winked.

"I don't think that's an appropriate comment..."

"Lighten up, Alan," my mother snapped. She took an ice cube out of her glass and threw it at him. "The boy didn't understand a word she said."

My father pursed his lips. "John understands far more than we think."

For a while in Mrs. Mullins's gifted class, I tried making stop-motion Super 8 movies with Tommy Dorigo. But I wanted to act out a battle between dinosaurs (part of me thought a tribute might appease them), while Tommy wanted to dramatize Lee's victory at the second battle of Bull Run. I suggested a compromise: replace the Union troops with plastic dinosaurs. When we both started crying, Mrs. Mullins separated us.

"Here's another suggestion for you, John. I know your father is a scientist—"

"My mother, too."

"—and since there's a science fair in a few months, I was thinking that would be a good activity for you. But no chemistry."

"How about, um, biology?" I asked.

The next day, when I came in from morning recess, Mrs. Mullins was wiping something off of Mr. Tolentino's face. "Can I take sample from both of you?" I asked. "For my science project."

Mr. Tolentino and Mrs. Mullins exchanged a smile. "Sure, John," Mr. Tolentino said. "Anything for science."

I swabbed samples from inside their cheeks, then followed Mrs. Mullins to her classroom. From each kid, I took samples, except for Tommy, who shrank in fear when I brandished a Q-tip at him.

I spent a happy afternoon isolating the DNA and running electrophoresis gels, admittedly with Shahra carefully guiding and correcting me. My father kept stopping by the door to Shahra's room to watch. "Well, at least I guess it's good lab skills," he said several times.

"Problem, Mr. Chant?" Shahra asked. She knew using "mister" rather than "professor" or "doctor" irritated him.

My father frowned. "Well, it's cargo cult science. It's got all the forms and fetishes of science: the test tubes, the reagents, the charts and notes. But it's like building an airplane out of bamboo and palm leaves and expecting it to fly, to bring back trade goods. There's no real content."

"There's more content here than you'll let yourself see."

"Hmm," my father said noncommittally.

When Shahra dropped me off at school on a crisp fall day, the trees shedding their rust-colored leaves, my arms were full of electrophoresis sheets and notes.

Mr. Tolentino said, "So, what did you find out?"

I made a show of looking at his electrophoresis sheet and consulting my notes. "Let's see... When you were young, you wanted to join the Army, but couldn't."

"That's right. I—"

"A problem with your heart. It's inconstant, it—"

"That's amazing, John!" Mr. Tolentino's eyes grew wide behind his glasses. "I have a heart murmur. This is... Wow."

At recess, I didn't even wait for Mrs. Mullins, but at the bell, ran straight to her classroom. I had all the electrophoresis sheets spread out by the time the other kids drifted in.

"I'm pleased you found something that has you so fired you up," Mrs. Mullins said. "The science fair is still weeks away."

I did the readings for the other kids. Suzi would head a huge corporation. Mikey would invent something to change people's lives. Gina would become an unsung poet, but would be happiest of all.

Mrs. Mullins said, "And what about me?"

"I didn't analyze it yet." I had produced the electrophoresis gel, but had saved reading it for last, like a big chocolate cloud dessert, in order to savor it. "I could do it right now." Even then, I liked to show off.

Spreading the gel blot on a desk and leafing through Shahra's notebook, I began to read. "You've had disappointments in life, but managed to overcome them. Your family didn't always approve of your choices." Mrs. Mullins nodded her head a fraction. "When you were young, you wanted to ... to join the Ar—"

I stopped, my stomach scrunched in anxiety. Something was wrong. I had tried so hard to not mix up anything. Quickly I scanned down the lines, pushing down my taut sense of panic. Something looked familiar. I had always had a good memory; I used to entertain my mother by reciting the *TV Guide* for her. "What's on tonight, Johnny?" she'd ask, and having read it on Sunday, I could reel off the schedule from 7:00 to 10:00 p.m., including the capsule summaries, on Thursday night.

I pulled out Mr. Tolentino's gel and laid it out next to Mrs. Mullin's, their names written in blocky letters on top. About half of the lines matched up.

A little bead of sweat trickled down from my armpits. "Uh..."

Mrs. Mullins had gone pale. She reached for the electrophoresis sheets. "I'm sorry, John, I think the baby must have ruined my sample. You'll have to throw away—"

"You've been kissing Mr. Tolentino," I said without thinking.

The other kids laughed.

Mrs. Mullins could have bluffed her way out of it. If she had laughed it off, the inevitable playground talk and lunchroom gossip would have dissipated. But the color in her face drained away as she clapped a hand to her mouth—and the whole class saw it. I was telling the truth.

I couldn't stop myself from asking the other question beating in my mind like a moth against a light. "Is the baby Mr. Tolentino's, too?"

Less than a week later, *Mr.* Mullins promptly initiated divorce proceedings against his wife, and also threatened to sue Mr. Tolentino and the school.

One evening, we got a long phone call after dinner. My mother listened, trying to interrupt a couple of times. "I don't see how that's his fault," she said several times. She looked over at me, but rolled her eyes. "I see," she said.

"Well, Johnny," she told me after hanging up, "looks like you're going back to your old school."

She turned to Shahra, who said, with hardly any bitterness, "Let me guess: you don't need me anymore."

My mother smiled. "You always were the quick one."

The Turing Testaments

One morning, my bedroom door banged open so hard that I thought, *He's finally done it. He's blown us all up.* I wished my father had let me sleep a few minutes more. But it was Jane in the doorway, her arms spread wide, a bird ready to fly. "It's time!" she sang out.

"For what?" I asked, but she was already gone. In my dinosaur-and-spaceship pajamas, I thundered after her and down the stairs.

Our mother clutched her rounded belly, a cannonball ready to be fired at the world, as our father steered her out the front door. "Your damn experiment can wait, Alan," she said testily.

"It *is* waiting," he said. "We're going."

"I don't think we'll make the hospital in time." But she had a smile on her face, and when she turned and said to Jane and me, "Don't burn the house down," her tone was merry. "Or turn it invisible."

"They won't get into any mischief," Gramma said.

"Oh, Ma, it was just an expression," my mother said, then added to my father, "No, the back seat. I don't think I can sit upright."

Jane and I waved as they drove down the street. It had been an indifferent winter, and the little snow we had gotten shortly after the new year had already turned to muddy slush under bright blue skies. "You get ready for school now," Gramma said.

Classes had only just resumed after the Christmas break. I was back at my first school, but in Miss Garcia's class. I saw Mr. Yerkes in the schoolyard, but he always acted as if I were invisible. Unfortunately, I was definitely not invisible to Steve Snoever, who threw red rubber balls at me whenever he got the chance. Because, despite unseasonably mild temperatures, we were all bundled up in heavy winter coats, I barely felt the blows. That day, he bounced one off my head and shouted "Ha!" in triumph. But then I overheard Becky say, "That's not very nice," which more than made up for the sting of the ball. She was still in Mr. Yerkes's class, and we hadn't spoken once since my return. But her defense of me gave my heart a lift, as if it were tied to a balloon, and in my mind, it was almost as if we were engaged—though I didn't really know what that meant.

The rest of school passed in a blur. I remember running home and being disappointed that the driveway was still empty. I remember the beans and franks we ate for dinner. I remember peppering Gramma with questions, each of which she met with "When you're older." I was excited and baffled, a state Jane heightened by filling my head with stories contradictory and impossible.

There must have been a phone call, but I never heard it. Instead, the sound of a car door slamming woke me. My window was full of darkness and stars. I leapt out of bed and pounded on my sister's door. "They're home!"

Gramma met us on the stairs. "Back to bed, both of you."

"But..." Jane began to protest.

"I don't want a sound out of either of you. Your mother needs the two of you to go to sleep without making a sound."

Lying in my bed, I heard the front door open, the low rumble of my father's voice, and Gramma's answer. Then I heard something horrible. At first, I thought they were killing a cat—*someone* was killing a cat—until I realized it was my mother crying.

When I cracked open my door, Gramma loomed into view. "I catch you out of bed again, and I'll give you a whipping that'll pass down into legend."

"But what happened?"

Her tone softened. "In the morning, Johnny. In the morning."

My mother's sobbing kept me awake all night. I lay in bed, too terrified to move, even when a yellow sunrise filled the window.

At last, Gramma summoned me downstairs. Jane, her hair disheveled, was already pouring herself a bowl of cornflakes. She looked up at me, startled, and a cold hand gripped my guts. I had never seen her look so frightened, and it made me frightened, too.

Another squall of wailing came through the ceiling. To say our mother cried makes her sound like a little girl who skinned her knee and dribbled a few tears. But our mother's grief was a wild storm, waves of anguish sweeping through the house with such ferocity that the walls swayed with her sobs. I didn't know how she kept it up.

I thought maybe something bad had happened to my father, except he drifted down the stairs, his face gray, his glasses smudged. At the kitchen table, he embraced first Jane, then me. He looked so much like a ghost that I stiffened, thinking his arms might go right through me. He opened his mouth to say something, then burst into sobs. I had never seen him sob like that, and my stomach curdled in terror to witness it.

At the dining room table, Jane had her hands folded in front of her. She said to me with all seriousness and with translucent mucus dripping from her nose,

"John, you need to pray." When I looked quizzically at her, she said, "Pray to Jesus to save the baby."

When she said that, it felt like the floor had vanished from beneath me, and I was falling without end.

Gramma had just stepped out of the kitchen as Jane was saying this. She went over and kissed the top of Jane's head. "I'm sorry, dear," Gramma said. "Jesus took the baby away." Seeing Jane's open mouth, she added, "Sometimes bad things have to happen. We have to trust that Jesus is doing this for your family's good."

Jane looked lost and perplexed. Then her face completely changed. I could see something happen inside of her, like hidden clockwork. Her eyes turned to cold pebbles, and she said, "Well, Jesus sure is a goddamned asshole," and as Gramma looked on in astonished horror, Jane ran upstairs and slammed shut her door.

There and then, Jane set aside her faith.

For three nights and three days, our mother refused to eat, refused to sleep, did nothing but cry and cry and cry. I wasn't sure how to feel myself—sad, confused, and alone, I suppose. After another night where we were kept awake by our mother's keening, Jane slipped into my room. We never had been easy allies, but we found ourselves with no one else to turn to.

"Do you think she would have cried like this for one of us?" she asked.

On the third day, in the late afternoon, the sobbing suddenly stopped. My heart froze mid-beat. Had my mother also choked, turned blue-gray, and died? I ran to my parents' bedroom, but stopped before touching the doorknob. I still heard crying, but a different voice, a different pitch—a burbly gurgling.

Slowly, I pushed open the door. My father stood fiddling with his glasses beside the bed where my mother lay, her hair disheveled, her face and eyes red and puffed, but with a beatific smile on her face. In her arms, she had something swaddled in a blanket—something mewling. It was a cassette tape player, making the sounds of a baby crying. The cries sounded familiar. My father was trying to reflect my mother's calm smile, but his face twitched as if gophers were tunneling beneath the skin.

It was his voice on the tape. His.

My mother carried the cassette player around all day long, cradling it in her arms. She tugged at her blouse, started to bare her breast—she had damp spots where the milk leaked out—but my father intercepted her. "He, uh, he needs a special diet. Because of everything he went through. I'll take care of that."

"Oh, Alan," my mother said. "You have no idea what to do with a baby. You dropped Johnny on his head, remember?"

When my mother slept, my father surreptitiously changed the batteries. I caught him out in the garage, making cooing noises into the microphone. When he saw me, he froze, then shrugged and continued by adding a little gurgle. He mashed down the stop button. "Your mother has burdens you can never understand," he said as he wrapped the cassette player in a blanket. "She was so happy to be having another baby. She..."

He stopped, lost in thought, the way he did when contemplating an equation, and I thought he forgot I was there. After a while, he said, "Who can explain these things? This..." He waved the cassette recorder. "This will help her get through the next few days."

Six months later, however, my mother was trying to teach the cassette tape player to sit up. "Both Jane and John were sitting up by this time. But Robbie isn't even rolling over." I think it was Jane who suggested the name Robbie.

My father glanced at us, aware of how closely we were following the conversation. "Should I call Dr. Rizzo for an appointment?" she continued. Rizzo was our sporadic pediatrician. I hadn't seen him for two years.

"Er, no. Robbie is a special case, and I have a colleague, or rather, a colleague of a colleague who's a ... well, a specialist in this special kind of special case."

Out in his garage workshop, sitting on a stool, I watched him rig up spring-loaded limbs that would turn the cassette tape player over and make it wobble upright. My mother was delighted. Her laughter rang out bright and clear like a brass bell. She even hugged and kissed my father, right in front of Jane and me.

Her surge of happiness cheered up my father for a while, creating a positive feedback loop. He spent hours in his workshop upgrading "Robbie." Robbie babbled nonsense syllables and responded when my mother cooed at him. Robbie's little servo arms reached out and grabbed at things that my mother had to take away, saying with a lilt, "Oh no, not *that* for you." And my father hummed happily as he watched my mother on the floor attending to Robbie, then went back to the lab to help Robbie "grow up."

"Robbie was a little late in learning to walk," my mother said later. In truth, my father had sweat blood—or maybe cerebrospinal fluid—to make Robbie's internal gyroscope work. While everyone was relieved that her moods no longer soaked the house like a typhoon, her chirping over Robbie began to grate on us, and my father was not pleased by my mother's expectation.

Out in the garage, my father had stacks of blueprints and schematics and piles of joints, motors, gears, and pulleys. Books and journals on robotics covered an entire table. "Walking is tough," he said, rubbing his face. He had salt-and-pepper stubble and dark bags under his eyes. "I didn't realize it until I dug into the literature. MIT, Caltech, Chicago—they've all abandoned that kind of thing and gone all in on checkers. Checkers!" He groaned. "I found an article modeling upright posture and walking as a driven inverted pendulum. That I can do. But more than that, well, I don't know. He'll never be a star Little Leaguer."

"So, Robbie will be a klutz?"

"Don't call your brother that."

"He's not my—"

"Don't ever say *that*. Especially to your mother."

"But you said we should tell the truth. That science is about the truth."

He sagged. "Science, yes. But in human affairs... Not that lying is good, but sometimes..." He blew out a lungful of air. "Just don't ... don't say anything."

I was scared to say anything, and rightly so, after what happened with my grandmother, well before the cassette player could sit up or walk.

After my father gave our mother the cassette player, he did his best to keep Gramma away. He told her, "Anne needs to rest." And when my mother asked why her mother hadn't visited, he cleared his throat and told a lie—a lie as fat and pale as a maggot—about how Gramma was sick and didn't want to give whatever she had to the baby. "She still could call," my mother muttered. In fact, Gramma had been frenzied in her attempts to ring the house, but my father had disconnected the phones.

After three weeks, Gramma finally charged up the driveway and pounded on the door. "Anne? Anne, are you in there?"

"Don't answer the door," my father told us.

But Gramma persisted. Finally, my father opened the door. "Why, Ethel, were you knocking? We were all asleep." He glanced down our cul-de-sac, where our neighbors with poached-egg faces watched the old lady shouting on our porch. "Anne is still sleeping. I'll tell her you came by. I'll have her call you—though we've been having trouble with our phone line. That cold spell last week snapped a wire." My father was generally the worst liar I ever met, but this time he almost got away with it.

Unfortunately, my mother's mother was an old hen, so tough that you wouldn't cook her up and serve her to the pirate who kidnapped your family and sold them to coal mines. If she got her wish and was martyred to a pack of wild animals, they wouldn't be able to gnaw off a single limb. "Out of my way," she said as she shouldered past my father.

"Really, Ethel," my father said, racing after her, "it just about killed Anne, and the doctor says no one should bother—"

Gramma pushed past to find my mother sitting up in bed and cooing at the cassette player. My mother's face brightened. "Oh, Ma, I'm glad you came by! I thought you weren't feeling well."

Her pleasure at seeing her mother surprised me. In the past, whenever Gramma visited, my mother looked as if stomach acid were eating her from the inside. I was too young then to comprehend the chaotic dynamics, the strange push and pull of families.

Gramma stalked to the side of the bed and peered at the tape player wrapped in a blanket and gurgling. "What..." she said, "under God's good heaven, is *that*?"

I thought they had had arguments before, but I'd had no idea. The row that led to Satan being booted from heaven, the minor tiff that sparked the American Revolution, the teensy disagreements that kicked off the Thirty Years' War, the Great War, and the American and English civil wars—they had nothing on this fight. I slept peacefully only a few feet from a venomous lizard, but this fight gave me nightmares. It ended with my mother on the porch, clutching the tape player to her bosom, her face as red as a stop sign. Gramma was dead to her now. Did you hear me? *Dead.* Eventually, my mother, her face slick with tears and snot, went inside, slamming the door with a magnitude-six Richter-scale slam.

Out on the porch, my father stared down at his feet. "I don't know what you're up to, Alan," Gramma said after a silence stretched painfully thin. "I don't doubt that you love Anne, only your ability to do much about it. But hear me: the worse the lie, the worse the outcome, no matter what kindness you think you're doing her." She paused, and I thought she was going to make a long sermon of it. But she just fixed my father with a steely glare, like one of the pins my grandfather had used in his butterfly collection.

My father looked stricken. On more than one occasion, I had put my G.I. Joe action figure in the vise in the garage, pretending he had been captured by the KGB and was being tortured for nuclear secrets, and at that moment, my father looked a lot like that.

Shortly afterwards, Gramma moved east to be near her other daughter, and then she had a stroke, and I didn't see her ever again.

When I was ten years old, my mother suggested we take Robbie trick-or-treating. I went to protest to my father, but he had taken to long walks—"to blow off steam," he said.

I found Robbie in his room, watching a cartoon on TV. "What're you watching?" I asked.

Without turning, Robbie said, "I want to be a *real* boy." You wouldn't think a cassette tape player would have favorites, but he was drawn to *Pinocchio* as if by magnets.

I sighed. "Do you want to be Pinocchio?"

"Do you want to be Pinocchio?" he echoed back.

"Not me. You. Do you want to be Pinocchio? Like, for Halloween?"

"What's Halloween?"

"Halloween is when you dress up in costumes and go around and ring doorbells, and grown-ups give you candy."

"Why you dress up in costumes?" The subtleties of grammar were always tricky.

"People give you candy if you do."

"Why they give you candy?"

I changed the subject. "You could dress up like Pinocchio."

"I want to be a real boy!"

"No, you want to be Pinocchio. Then you can say, 'I want to be a real boy.'"

Jane and I gave him a long nose, a pointed hat cut out of paper, and a cricket—a rubber cockroach, really, from a novelty shop—on his shoulder. "Oh, that's so clever!" our mother said. "Let me get the camera."

She never took pictures of Jane or me in our costumes. I had dressed up as a murder victim, with a fake knife through my head. It wasn't original; at school, in Miss Brownlee's classroom, four other boys also had fake knives through their heads. Jane was in her Marxist phase (she tended to go through phases; Jesus had just been the first of many) and had dressed up as Trotsky. The scene played out as one might imagine:

US: Trick or treat!

KINDLY OLD LADY: Oh, what clever costumes! (To me) You look very scary. (To Robbie) And let me guess, you're Pinocchio! How clever. (Long pause, considering Jane) And you, dear, are...

JANE: Trotsky. Leon Trotsky.

OLD LADY: (after even longer pause) Who?

Unsurprisingly, Jane's enthusiastic explanation of Trotsky's role in the Fourth International dampened the Halloween spirit. Then it got out of hand in a different way.

ROBBIE: Trotsky. Leon Trotsky. Trotsky. Leon—
OLD LADY: Huh?
ROBBIE: I want to be a real boy!
OLD LADY: (smiling) Of course. And maybe if you're really—
ROBBIE: I want to be a real boy!
OLD LADY: —good, like Pinocchio—
ROBBIE: I want to be a real boy! (louder) I want to be a real boy! I want to be a real boy! I want to be a real boy!
OLD LADY: Is there something ... wrong?
JANE: Aren't all boys shouty like that?

Out on the street, people in costumes stared. I pulled Robbie's shirt up to yank out his batteries, and Robbie slumped. "Hold him," I said to Jane. I fumbled batteries back into Robbie, but he lay inert on the ground.

"We can't take him home like this," Jane whispered. "She's waiting. With a camera. She'd freak."

After several tries, I got the batteries into Robbie in the right order. He sat up and said, "Are we going to trick-or-treat?"

"I'm not doing this next year," Jane muttered.

My mother doted on Robbie, but even for him, her sands of patience ran out quickly. I'd overhear her say, "Not now, Robbie. I have a terrible migraine. It's like a nail being driven into my skull. Why don't you go bug your brother?"

And then came the inevitable *clump, clump, clump* up the stairs, and my bedroom door would swing open.

"Mama says go bug you."

"I have homework," I said.

"Why you have homework?"

"Because I go to school."

"Why you go to school?"

I sighed, swiveled around, and faced him. My first impulse was to pull out his batteries, but some other voice (it sounded like my father's, recorded deep inside me) said, *You need a better approach.*

I glanced over at Paul's terrarium. I remembered I needed to fetch some frozen mice to feed him. Simultaneously, an idea popped into my head.

"You know," I said, "Papa loves to experiment." *Papa* was Robbie's word, or rather, my father's word. It felt strange in my mouth.

"Why Papa loves to experiment?"

"It's his favorite thing in the whole world. And he loves little boys who experiment. Do you want him to love you?"

He whirred for a moment. "I want him to love me."

"Then you need to be in an experiment. Pull up your shirt."

I had seen my father stick a screwdriver into a recessed compartment in Robbie. Now I poked open that compartment and spotted a set of small dials all in a row, like buttons on a shirt, only labeled with letters: E, X, S, I, and C.

"Let's see what happens when we do this. Don't tell anyone." Taking my own screwdriver, a Christmas gift, I turned the X dial to the right, pulled down his shirt, and pushed him out of my room.

Later that evening, as he watched TV in his room, Robbie cried out in fear. I heard my mother stride down the second-floor hallway, calling, "What is it, sweetie?" I poked out of my own room and followed her into Robbie's.

Robbie cowered and pointed at the TV. "The bad person, the bad person!"

"Maybe you've had enough TV for today," she said, reaching for the switch.

"No, no, *no!*" Robbie shouted.

"My, we're having a temper tantrum today, aren't we?"

He shook his head and flung himself on the floor. When she picked him up, he screamed and kicked, connecting with her shin and making her swear. Robbie, of course, only repeated the profanity. It took quite a struggle to get him into his bed.

My mother closed the door and wiped at the perspiration on her forehead. "Do you know what's going on with Robbie?" She sighed. "Let me get your father."

As she headed downstairs, I snatched up my screwdriver and turned the X dial in the other direction. Then I made a breathless sprint back to my room, where I picked up a book.

My mother clumped upstairs. "Your father is off again on one of his walks. Robbie? You feeling calmer now?"

My reading was interrupted by my mother shouting. "Robbie? *Robbie!*"

I ran to Robbie's room. My mother was shaking him, an inert compilation of metal and plastic. She turned to me, wild-eyed, her hair flying. "Something's wrong!"

"I think he's sleeping," I said.

"Don't argue!"

As she flew out of Robbie's room, I rolled him over. The X dial was still turned up; I'd accidentally turned E down to its lowest setting. I reset both dials to the middle and was rewarded by the familiar whirr of Robbie's gears.

"He's awake!" I called out. "Robbie's awake now."

She ran back into Robbie's room to scoop him up in her arms. "I was so worried about you!" She cradled him, swinging him around the room in a slow, tender waltz. "I thought I'd lost you," she whispered. "I was so afraid I'd lost you."

I decided to be systematic, and in a notebook, I wrote the letters *E, X, S, I,* and *C.* *E,* I decided, stood for *energy.* Through my experiments, some of which alarmed my mother, I worked out that *X* equaled *excitability.* Next, I turned up the C dial. Robbie then got hold of a screwdriver, disassembling the oven and half the refrigerator, and my mother found him on the kitchen floor, surrounded by screws and nuts and coils of freon tubing. I wrote, *C = curiosity.*

"Maybe this is our reward for skipping his terrible twos," my mother said over dinner that evening. She glanced at Jane and me. "You both were awful at that age. I was tempted to give you away to a zoo. But Robbie has been so placid, I thought I had dodged a bullet." She fiddled with her glass. "Now he's making up for it with a vengeance."

My father pushed himself away from the table.

"You haven't finished your dinner," Jane said. "That's the rule."

"Different rules for grown-ups," my father said. "I'm going for a walk."

Later that same evening, Jane came into my room and flounced onto my bed. "I think he's having an affair," she announced.

My stomach squeezed at her words. "Him? Really? Have you tried to picture it?"

Jane made a face. "I know... Ick. Ick to the nth power. But he 'goes out for a walk' all the time now. He's not back yet, you know."

From downstairs came the sounds of our mother snoring on the couch. I pressed my face against my window. Rain lashed against the panes, and the windows of the garage laboratory were like the eyes of dead animals.

"I don't blame him," Jane said. "Why do you think I go to Lucy's so often? It's not as if I like her. Lucy and I have nothing in common. She whines about math being hard. She likes *ponies.*" She shuddered, then pressed her face against the window. "Do you think she's nice?"

"Who?"

"The other woman. The one he's having an affair with." Jane did have the ability to spin a whole tapestry of narrative from a frayed bit of thread. I shook my head. Jane stared out into the night. "I hope she's nice. I hope, wherever he is, he's happy."

I admit I got jealous of my mother's attention to pulleys and motors wrapped around a mewling tape player. So, the next time I changed Robbie's battery pack, I took a screwdriver and cranked both the C and E dials as far clockwise as they would go.

"What are you doing?" Robbie asked.

I gave him a tight smile.

That evening at dinner, Robbie came down from his room and stood at the table, peering at our dinners. "What is that?"

"Chains of amino acids," I said. I thought that remark clever.

Jane frowned at her plate. "Some kind of mystery meat."

"Beef," our mother said. "Definitely beef."

Jane flipped a gravy-strewn hunk on her plate. "If you say so."

"Can I have some?" Robbie asked.

"You have a special diet," our father said.

"Why?"

"Because you have a special digestive system."

"Why?"

"That's enough, Robbie," my father snapped.

"Jesus, Alan," my mother said. "First you treat him as if he could shatter, then you treat him with all the sensitivity of a rock."

My father slammed his fork down on the table and glared at my mother. "You always tell me how draining the kids are. I was trying to keep a burden off you. This is the thanks I get?"

My mother reached out her hand as if to touch him, but her fingers stopped short. "I didn't mean to sound unappreciative."

There was the familiar scrape as my father pushed back his chair.

"Where you going?" Robbie asked.

My father paused to wipe his smudged glasses on his shirt. He spoke to the air, as if he couldn't bring himself to look at Robbie. "A walk. Human stance and motion are like a driven inverted pendulum." As he grabbed his coat, I noticed how thin he'd gotten.

After the door had clicked shut, my mother looked at the three of us. "Well, who wants to watch TV?"

Late that night, as I listened to Paul scrabble in his terrarium and wondered for the gajillionth time if I could work up the courage to invite Becky over to admire him, I heard the front door click open. A glance at my illuminated clock showed it was almost midnight, and I heard my father's weary tread up the stairs.

In the morning, though, Robbie was missing.

"He's not in the attic, and he's not out in the garage," my mother said. "I even looked under the house. Do you think he went into the woods?"

My father shook his head, so hard that I thought it might just unscrew entirely and fall off. "I wouldn't panic."

"I'm not panicking. But I don't know where he is."

"Jane ran away all the time, but she just went to Lucy's house."

"But Robbie doesn't play with other children. You insisted. Remember?" She sank onto the couch, her face in her hands.

My father turned to me and Jane. "You two, I want you on your bikes and scouring the neighborhood."

"But it's raining," Jane protested.

"What about school?" I asked.

He furrowed his brow. "School is important, but we have to find ... Robbie." His gaze met mine, and I knew he meant, *For your mother's sake.*

I was tired of *for your mother's sake*, but I shrugged on a raincoat, threw my leg over the slightly-too-big ten-speed I'd gotten for my birthday, and wobbled down the street, splashing through puddles and wiping rain from my face.

I circled our block, then several blocks. At one point, Jane and I met coming from opposite directions. We stopped in the middle of the street and looked at each other. I didn't know about Jane, but my clothes were soaked and clammy enough to make an oyster call for a towel.

"This is crazy," she said.

"But what if she calls the police?"

We looked at each other, silently imagining that scenario, then pedaled off in opposite directions again.

By midmorning, the rain had stopped. Recess would be ending, and Miss Brownlee would be doing math. I liked correcting Miss Brownlee's math, and I was sorry I could not be there.

Back at the house, all I found was my mother still sitting on the couch. "Has Robbie returned?" I asked. She shook her head. "You don't need to call the police," I said. "I'm sure we'll find him."

She nodded. "I know you will, Johnny."

I was getting on my bike when she called to me from the front porch. "Johnny! Wait." I waited, gripping my handlebars, as she walked down the steps. "We should find Robbie. But..." She glanced around, looking very serious. "Johnny, I have to tell you something. Something I've never told anyone."

For a moment, I thought she was going to tell me someone else was my real father. Or that she had once murdered someone. Or that she had murdered my real father.

She said, "I know about Robbie." She gave me a sad smile. "I mean, I know your father made him in the garage."

It wasn't that my heart skipped a beat, or stopped. It was as if my heart had vanished altogether, leaving a black void in my chest.

She had been a mess after the baby died, she told me, and for a long time had wanted to believe Robbie *was* real. "I thought I was hallucinating, some sort of post-partum depression." When she came back to herself, the pretense had been established. "Your father, for all his faults, did this for me. If I suddenly said, 'I know it's all been a fake,' it would crush him." She lit a cigarette. "I've grown fond of Robbie, and I get carried away at times. Families are weird," she said, shrugging. "Now, go find him. For your father."

Some miles from our house, along a heavy metal fence, I spotted a small pile beneath a tree: Robbie, curled up and motionless. I slipped in fresh batteries, and he stirred.

"What were you doing?" I asked.

"I was following Papa." Apparently his circuits hadn't been damaged by the rain. Relief tasted like the sugary electric jolt when you bite into a frosted donut.

"Did you fall asleep here?"

"I followed Papa. Why does Papa come here?" He leaned against the fence, and I followed his gaze. It was a cemetery.

Robbie led me through the rows of gravestones. He stopped in front of a modest, almost tiny marker with a single lonely date on it:

Baby Boy Chant

"Papa comes here on his walks," Robbie told me. "Why?"

"Thank God!" my mother said as I pedaled up with Robbie balanced on the handlebars. She lifted him in her arms. "Oof, you're heavier than you look! But at least you're home."

"I'm home," Robbie said. "I'm home, I'm home, I'm home!"

She put him down, letting him run into the house as my father walked up wearily. My mother put her hand in his. "You know, Alan, he sounds just like you. He has your voice."

Area 50½

To study the tiniest of things, we must use the largest of microscopes. When I first heard the word *cyclotron*, I imagined an entire room of people on stationary bicycles pedaling furiously to generate electricity. (For my mother's birthday, my father had once created just such a stationary bike, complete with an attached generator. "You can power the TV with it," he said. My father was not very good at gifts.)

In fact, a cyclotron whirls subatomic particles around faster and faster in a magnetic field, then smashes them into other subatomic particles. Modern synchrotrons, the sleek heirs of cyclotrons, are city-sized rings of high-vacuum, magnet-clad pipes. They accelerate their tiny-caliber projectiles to nearly the speed of light, then steer them into head-on collisions. By tracking the shattered pieces that fly out, physicists deduce the workings of the smallest bits of the universe. As a boy, I loved to stack blocks and ram a toy truck through them, so it is no wonder that a career in physics attracted me.

I say all this to help explain just how unusual was the Edbert E. Enderson Accelerator Facility at my father's university. During the Great Depression, Mr. Enderson had attended my father's university, back then a combination Bible college and animal-slaughtering trade school. When war shook the world, he left college to enlist, but was rejected due to defective eyesight. Still keen to serve his country, he invented a compact flash cooker for hot dogs using electrical conduction: the wieners were electrocuted. The cookers proved so popular that Mr. Enderson got an enormous contract. After the war was over, he continued to supply the military. People said he could have filled a whole pool with hundred-dollar bills and gone swimming in it.

Mr. Enderson loved his old Bible-and-animal-slaughtering college, and he endowed the university with a large sum to "investigate through methods electric the age and origins of the Earth." The chair of physics proposed a particle accelerator, but there wasn't a plot of land large enough for a circular synchrotron.

Another former alumnus, known as the Sewer King, had willed the university his now disused private sewer lines. Convenience took precedence over reason, and the vacuum pipe and associated magnets were installed in the old meandering sewers. Instead of a neat circle, the kind of perfect geometric figure favored by Greek thinkers like Aristotle and Ptolemy, its design looked like a doodle by Salvador Dali. This made for a spectacularly inefficient machine, and experiments were only run for a few years before the university shut it down. Still, many in my town spoke of the accelerator as a beloved scientific achievement.

And I loved it, too.

My father was chief physicist at the accelerator, and he allowed me to explore the tunnels when no beam was running, which was most of the time. It was dark and cool and smelled of dirt and motor oil—favored smells for a young boy.

Shortly after I turned eleven, the last of the remaining accelerator technicians was let go, or quit, depending on which side of the lawsuit you stood on. So, my father recruited me to help maintain the increasingly creaky and recalcitrant machine. (I know you're proud of your own unusual employment history, but I think I have you beat.)

"You'll get Johnny electrocuted," my mother protested. "Your son, turned into a sizzling pile of charcoal. Imagine how you'll feel."

"I'll be careful," I said. "I'll wear gloves, promise."

"We have strict procedures, Anne," my father said. "We have a safety manual."

"If such a safety manual existed, I'm certain the first page would say, don't hire an eleven-year-old boy."

"Nonsense. John's been helping me for years."

My first job was to check all the steering and focusing magnets. As soon as the school bell rang, I would shoot out the door and beyond the playground into the woods, where I could pry up an unused manhole cover and drop down into the tunnels. I had second thoughts, though, when I heard things scuttling around in the dark shadows. Most of the time, it was rats. Most of the time.

I was in my bedroom, sullen winter rain tapping on my window, when my mother stuck her head in. "Johnny, you busy?" She didn't pause, but plunged on in the way she did when she was in a good mood, finding it easier to take up both sides of a conversation rather than to burden you with thinking up an answer. "Your father brought home a capital-I *important* visitor, but he's gone off to campus and forgotten the poor man. I was thinking of taking him shopping. You want to come with, sweetie?"

I had just been putting Paul back in his terrarium. Robbie, who had recently become fixated on Paul, had taken him out to play. Paul thrashed and hissed like a leaking tire whenever Robbie picked him up, and Robbie giggled when

Paul bit him. Jane, stopping by my open door, had scolded me for letting Robbie "torment" Paul. I said I didn't think either one had a deep emotional life, and Jane replied that was only because I was emotionally stunted myself. We had scowled at each other, and for a moment it seemed there would be a brother-sister tussle in parallel with the robot-venomous lizard one. But then we heard our mother coming up the stairs. With a sigh, I took Paul away from Robbie, and Jane had steered Robbie out of my room.

I closed the lid on the terrarium and said to my mother, "Okay."

"Tee-rific."

In the living room was a man as thin and vitrified as a test tube. "Professor Lyapunov," my mother said, "Johnny'll come with us to the store, though he's good at entertaining himself. Why, we could leave him home alone for days, a whole week, and he might not notice. He's like his father in that. Johnny, this is Professor Lyapunov."

"Hello, Johnny," Lyapunov said.

"Professor Lyapunov is from Russia."

"Originally from Russia. Now I am at Texas A&M, College Station."

"You poor man," my mother said. "Alan dragged me there once. This was before Jane or Johnny. As I remember, we had to drive out to the middle of nowhere, and then another hour before we got to College Station."

"It is isolated, yes," the professor said.

"Still, better than Siberia, I suppose."

"I have actually never been to Siberia."

"Why, that's the way it always is, isn't it? You never visit the tourist spots in your own home. There's some museum downtown, and we've none of us ever been."

"I went there on a field trip," I pointed out. "You came as a chaperone."

"Did I? And see what kind of impression it made on me? World-famous, it's called."

At the Higgledy-Piggledy, we shook the rain off our umbrellas, and my mother had me push the shopping cart. She turned to Lyapunov. "Look at all the choices. Sometimes it makes my head spin. I suppose this is quite different from Russia."

"Since I have lived in College Station for twenty years, I couldn't really say."

"How interesting," my mother said. "Johnny, steer us over to the butcher. I should cook up something in honor of our guest. If your father remembers to come home."

The sky continued to spit icy rain the next morning, so I went to school via the abandoned sewer-turned-accelerator tunnels. I was in Mrs. Jarczynski's fifth-grade classroom, along with Becky (and unfortunately, Steve Snoever). At recess, we all went outside and huddled under the eaves. I stood close to Becky, but not too close, because then I might have to say something.

But my mind was on something other than Becky. I had been halfway through the tunnel when I heard something scrabbling. My heart squeezing with fear, I had run the rest of the way through the tunnel to school, climbing up the old iron rungs to the manhole exit in the woods. My fingers still smelled of rust and old oil.

"I saw something dead this morning," Big Bruce suddenly said, taking us all aback. He was a hulking kid in our class who had been held back a year or two, or four or five, and he towered over us. This was the first thing he had said all year; mostly he just slept in his undersized desk, his massive head lolling. "It was a dead coyote. Something bit it in half. It had its guts hanging out and everything."

Another boy said all the coyotes were gone, that something had been eating them.

"I don't know," I said. "Nothing eats coyotes."

"Sharks," said Bruce. "They eat anything."

"We aren't near the ocean," I pointed out.

Big Bruce looked dejected.

After school, my father was giving Lyapunov a tour of the sewer-housed accelerator. "It's nothing like your cyclotron, of course, but it's the best we can do with few resources," he was saying as they turned a corner to find me wrestling a burned-out dipole magnet off the beamline. "Oh, hello, John," my father said.

"Hi," I said. "Hi, Professor Lyapunov."

"What are you doing?" Professor Lyapunov asked, his voice rising in puzzlement.

"Oh, this magnet got fried on the last run," I said. "We don't have any spares. I'm going to have to rewind the coils."

"Be sure to do your homework," my father said.

"Wait—your son repairs the accelerator?"

My father grinned. "Oh, yes, he's very smart."

"But he's a little boy! I am somewhat astonished," Professor Lyapunov said, no small admission from a man who likely had friends sent to the gulag under Stalin and had eaten barbecue with Texans in big hats and snakeskin boots. "The amperage—"

"I wear gloves," I said.

"Well, Alan, this is all, um, very interesting," Lyapunov said, "but I am feeling anxious to get to our subject."

"I thought you'd be amused by our local facility," my father said, rocking on his heels.

"Yes, it is impressive what you've been able to do with constrained resources, but I am wondering when we shall..."

My father's grin faded, and he put a hand on Professor Lyapunov's shoulder to steer him away. "Well, now, there's been a little hiccup."

I had a book report to write, so when I finished with the magnet, I went back to the beam splitter, where I had left my book bag. It lay there unzipped and flopped open, like a gutted fish. My books and crumpled sheets of homework were still inside. But I had saved a bag of corn chips from my lunch, as I often did as a hedge in case dinner was "delayed."

The chips were gone.

My father brought Professor Lyapunov home for dinner again that evening. He occasionally invited visiting colleagues home for dinner, at least when my mother was in a good enough mood. Robbie always got "put to bed" early to avoid uncomfortable questions. The dinner conversation followed a routine: the visitor would make small talk with my mother, but soon he (it was always men, as Jane pointed out) and my father would fall back on mutual jeremiads on the vagaries of their grants.

But this time, the tension between the two was palpable. My father sawed away at his food and shoveled it into his mouth, but Professor Lyapunov sighed and pushed his food around his plate, a Grand Prix race between a piece of pork, I think, and an underdone parsnip wearing a frayed veil of Velveeta. "Lovely dinner, Anne," he said to my mother, which taught me that Russians had no qualms about lying, "but I'm afraid I had a rather large lunch." Lyapunov turned to my father. "I called the airline. I am getting my ticket changed to tomorrow."

My father put his fork down and wiped his mouth with a napkin. "That's a bit hasty, Timofey."

Lyapunov spread his hands. "There is nothing for me to do."

"I'm sure we'll find... I'm sure it will get resolved. We have people looking."

"One more day, then."

I asked, "What kind of scientist are you?"

His pebble-gray eyes measured me. "Biology. To be specific, exo—"

"Do you research cancer? My father did an experiment on a Mexican bead-ed—"

"Ah, John, that's not relevant now," my father said. "You have homework."

Pouting, I clomped up the stairs to my room. I sprawled out next to the heating vent in the floor; sometimes I could catch voices that way. Lyapunov was soft-spoken, so I heard very little. But I did catch one word: NASA.

When I awoke the next morning, it was to stinging sleet.

"Can you drive me to school?" I asked my mother, but she waved a hand and turned over in her warm bed. My father had already left for the university.

I told myself I had imagined the noises in the tunnels, that it was rats. And Big Bruce was plain wrong about the half coyote; Bruce wasn't the brightest, after all. But down in the damp, squid-ink darkness of the sewer, I heard a noise again. My fear of the dark wrestled with my fear of being late, and pearls of perspiration clung to my skin. I pointed my flashlight down the tunnel.

Under the accelerator vacuum line was ... something. Pale, larval, it thrashed in the beam of my flashlight, and I saw the glint of an eye the color of tarnished silver. It made an unearthly noise, high-pitched, like a bat's call, and cold and blood-congealing. I dropped my flashlight. With a small *pop!*, the bulb burst, and so did my courage.

I backpedaled, only to trip on a cable and hit the floor with a hard, wet smack. So much for courage; I curled up, drew a deep breath, and bawled, hot, salty wetness in my eyes. I knew I was seconds away from getting bitten in half with my guts hanging out.

But nothing happened. I lay on the rough concrete floor, my eyes squeezed shut against the sight of the monstrous maw I imagined drooling above me. But I only heard the patter of feet running away down the tunnel.

When I returned, I came armed. It wasn't much: an X-Acto knife and a heavy hammer. Plus, I brought a flashlight and a spare. "Coyote, coyoteeee," I called out. "Here, coyote-eater..."

After a while, I got tired. The hammer was heavy, and two flashlights were clunky. But inspired by the missing corn chips, I put an open bag of potato chips on top of a quadrupole magnet. I also sprinkled some potato chips on the floor. Then I said loudly, "Well, I guess it's time to go home," stomped my feet on the floor as if walking away, and doused both flashlights.

I don't know how long I waited. I squatted, then knelt, then slumped to the floor, and I was finally on the cottony edge of sleep when I heard the crunch of a potato chip under a foot.

I thumbed on the flashlight. The sudden burst of light blinded me, so painful that I barely glimpsed a pale moon face shielded by an arm. It was smaller than I expected for a coyote-eating monster. Exclaiming *"Zeejust!"* or maybe *"Deezhooz!"*, it fled.

Blinking away the starbursts in my vision, I stumbled in pursuit. After a hundred yards, it ran into a dead-end side tunnel. I slowed and slid forward one foot at a time. Holding two flashlights, a hammer, and my X-Acto knife, my hands trembled. I told myself I had a venomous lizard as a pet; I could be brave.

At the end of the tunnel, I found it curled up, cowering in the beam of my flashlight. "Please," it said in a stilted, high-pitched voice. "I come in peace. Do not dissect me!"

"Who are you?" I asked.

The small figure uncurled tentatively. "My name is Krulltang," it said, each nasal syllable enunciated tonelessly. "I come from a planet around the star you call Epsilon Eridani."

Krulltang was no taller than me, but had pale skin and enormous, glittery eyes as dark as a moonless night. He wore a metallic jumpsuit, torn and soiled. His wrinkled forehead thrust upward, like a potato coming out of the earth, and I imagined a massive alien brain housed in his skull.

He told me his ship had been scouting Earth when it crashed. "Your radar interfered with our inertia-less drive," he said.

"Really? How?"

He gave a very human shrug. "That is not my specialty."

"What is your specialty?" I asked.

"There is no word in your language for it," he said. "You are very curious. And very small. You are a young of your race?"

I nodded. "My mother says I'm a bit too curious sometimes. Just like my father. He teaches at the university." Then I saw all the pieces lining up, like the metatarsal to the tarsal to the tibia to the femur... "Did you meet my father? Professor Chant?"

He shook his head. "Human names are strange to me. And humans at the university wanted to study me, dissect me."

"So, you ran away."

"Yes." He paused. "Have you any more food?"

I asked him if he could digest our food, if his biology had the same amino acids as ours. He stared at me for a moment, then said, "I am not familiar with your primitive Earth science."

"But you were studying us. Surely you studied our science."

"That is not my specialty."

"But what—"

"Please, Earth boy," he said. "I require nutrition."

"So, how did you get here? My father says interstellar travel is impossible."

Krulltang took another bite of the salami sandwich I'd brought from home, licked mustard from his fingers, and said, "Your Earth science is far behind ours. Only a few centuries ago, your 'wise men' believed your planet to be flat."

I frowned. "But that's not true. My father says Aristotle proved the Earth was round over two thousand years ago. The story about Columbus and people saying he'd fall off the edge of the Earth was made up."

Krulltang bit off another mouthful of sandwich. "You revere Ein-stein as a genius, and perhaps for an Earth scientist, he was. But he was wrong. Our ships travel faster than the speed of light." He leaned forward. "Of course, even we have limits. When we travel at the speed of light squared, all our matter turns into energy."

A tiny alarm chimed in my head. "What do you mean, the 'speed of light squared'?" I asked. "That doesn't make any sense."

"As I said, our science is far beyond your Earthly knowledge."

"But this has nothing to do with science," I said, heating up with indignation. "It's just, well... Speed is distance divided by time. The speed of light is one hundred eighty-six thousand miles for every second. But to say 'the speed of light squared' doesn't make any sense. Miles squared per second squared?"

"For a young Earth boy, you are clever," he said after a long pause, "but it is too advanced—"

"No, it's not. I asked my father to explain $E=mc^2$, and I didn't understand his answer, but I'm sure it isn't 'matter turns into energy at the speed of light squared.' Did you try telling this to any of the 'Earth scientists'?"

"No, I—"

"Well, I know my father would have gotten suspicious right away." I slid off the beam pipe. "If you don't tell me the truth, I'm going to go to my father. And to his friend Professor Lyapunov. He's the guy who wanted to dissect you, I think."

Krulltang fidgeted, and I started to walk away. "Wait!" he called.

I halted, but did not turn around.

He sighed, a long, whooshing exhalation full of regret, trepidation, and carbon dioxide. And he said, in a very different voice, a voice not stilted or mechanical or high-pitched, but baritone and very natural, "Okay, I'll tell you everything. Christ."

I turned to face him. He spread his palms out. "But you gotta promise, kid: don't turn me in." He pursed his lips and screwed up his face, as if he had to squeeze out the words. "I'm not from Epsilon Eridani. My name is Mike, and I'm originally from Maine. I ran away from the circus," he added.

"I thought people ran away *to* the circus."

"Not if you're in the freak show. Not if you've been labeled a freak your whole life and told the circus is your only option."

"Sometimes *I* feel like a freak," I said.

Krulltang, or Mike, whirled around and punched me, right in the face. Something exploded in my cheek, and hot stars shot across my vision. I sprawled backwards onto the concrete floor.

"Why'd you do that?" I whimpered, trying to not cry.

"I'm picking on somebody my own size. Listen, kid, you are not a freak. Do people stare at you, every day? Is it your *job* to be stared at, every goddamned minute of the day? To be laughed at?"

"I've been laughed at," I said, though it was close to a whine.

"Not every goddamned minute of every goddamned day of every goddamned year."

Mike told me he was tired of the circus life. In the freak show, he'd been dubbed "alien corpse from Roswell" and made to lie in a casket, then sit up abruptly, so people would shriek and run out. "Fun the first few dozen times, but day after day? It gets old." He said he'd gotten the idea to pass himself off as a real space alien. "By the way, thanks for the food. You got any smokes?"

Mike added that he could really use a stiff drink, too. He figured correctly that my curiosity would get the better of me, so I went home, sneaked a pack of my mother's cigarettes and a bottle of gin, and came back.

Mike immediately lit up and took a deep draw. "Oh, that's good stuff," he breathed. "Want one?"

"I'm eleven," I said, a bit indignantly.

"So? I was up to a pack a day at your age. What do you think stunted my growth?" He laughed. "Nah, kid, I just like to say that.

"I left the circus a few weeks back, a couple of towns over. Hitchhiked to the Army base at Fort Abattage. There'd been a meteor shower a few days before, so I made that part of my story. Then the colonel in charge there called up the university. They didn't believe my story at first, until they took an x-ray of me.

Then they got all excited. See, I've got a rare form of dwarfism, something called xenoplasia. Like, only three other people, ever, have had it. Not only do I look funny, my organs are all in the wrong place. My blood tests funny, too—it isn't A or B or O. And I got a bit of hydrocephalism thrown in," he said, tapping his head. "Every time I seen a doctor, which wasn't too often in the circus, I had to explain. None of them had heard of it.

"So, the university types kept bugging me about the space drive and all that stuff, like you did. Wanted me to speak the alien language. I told them I was kinda the space janitor. Made up a story about how my race had been enslaved by another race of aliens, and I'd escaped, and wanted political asylum."

He hefted the bottle of gin. "Don't normally drink this stuff, but when you're desperate... You bring a glass?" I shook my head. He shrugged and took a sip straight from the bottle.

"Anyway," he said, wiping his mouth, "I got a little carried away with my story. I hinted at an alien invasion—that the 'Tlekranites,' as I called 'em, were preparing to enslave Earth, too, just like my home world. Well, that made them piss their pants. I got so many questions that I came to regret that particular fib. Then they brought the military in, and they were bringing in this Russian guy, supposedly a hot-shot specialist in alien life, though since there ain't any such thing, how could he be an expert?"

"Professor Lyapunov," I said. "I've met him."

"I wasn't sure I could fool him, so I made another escape. I thought I'd lay low for a while." He took another swig, then proffered me the bottle. I waved it away. "That's my story. You going to turn me in?" When I hesitated, he added, "I know I did a lot of bad things. Fraud, lying to the government, and so on. I'm at your mercy here."

I shook my head.

"Finest kind," he said.

The rain had stopped, but parked in front of our house was a strange car with government plates, a plain blue Plymouth sedan as large as a gunboat. I had just reached our front door when a short man in an olive-green uniform with lots of ribbons on his chest stepped out. "Hello, son," he said and walked to the sedan.

I guessed that the Army man was looking for "Krulltang." My stomach did a gymnastic spin that could have placed in the Olympics.

I went inside and found Jane flopped on the couch. "Is *he* in trouble again?" I asked, meaning our father, trying to mask my anxiety.

"I don't know," she said. "They kicked me out of the kitchen. By the way, they know we listen through the heating ducts."

In the kitchen, I found my father and Professor Lyapunov.

"I am still skeptical," Lyapunov said. "There are superficial differences, yes. But the rest is just too similar. Even the number of chromosomes is the same. Why should that be?"

My father was about to answer, but I blurted out, "You mean Robbie?"

Professor Lyapunov smiled blandly at me. "Hello, John. Who's Robbie?"

"My brother."

My father warned, "John..."

"We keep him in the basement, so he doesn't frighten people," I added. "He's special."

"John!" To Lyapunov, my father added, "We don't even have a basement. John sometimes tells ... fanciful tales. Let's go where we can talk undisturbed."

After they left, I went upstairs and opened the door to my parents' bedroom. The lights were off, and I could hear my mother's slow, steady breathing. Slowly, holding my own breath as much as I could, I rifled through her purse and took another pack of cigarettes.

Down in the tunnels, I whispered, rather loudly, "Mike! Mike!"

He crawled from his hiding place under the beampipe. "You should call me Krulltang, kid, in case anyone catches us. Thanks for the cigs. Any more booze?"

I rolled my eyes as I handed the bottle to him. "You're as bad as my mother."

"Ouch. I don't want to know what's behind that. Got a light?"

I produced a soldering iron. As Mike pressed the tip of his cigarette against it, I told him, "There was some Army guy at my house."

"Damn. Can you get me some more food?" he said. "I'll have to hide out a bit longer, then make it back to the circus."

"Really? You'd go back to the circus?"

"You wanna hear what I miss about the circus? Elephants. Uh-huh. I like elephants. To elephants, people are all equally small; they could smash any of us like an egg, if they wanted to. To an elephant, people are all equally, you know, alien."

"I'm sorry pretending to be a space alien didn't work out," I said. "It sounded fun."

Mike leaned back and blew out a big puff of smoke. "It was less fun than I thought. I thought I would be treated special. Like a celebrity, instead of a monster. But the way they poked and prodded at me, I was like less than a monster. Just a piece of tissue to put under the microscope, or in their x-ray machine."

"Do you wish you were normal?"

He stabbed out his cigarette. "Do you know what's normal, kid?"

I looked down. "No."

"Neither do I. Don't feel sorry for me. Sure, I get tired of being pointed at and harassed and all that crap. And I'll tell you, it's a hell of life, being a professional freak. But you know what? If I were any different—if I were 'normal,' whatever the hell that is—then I wouldn't be me. I've decided that I'm the normal one, and everyone else who's abnormal." And he crossed his arms.

I got caught, of course. I was reaching into my mother's purse when something bit my fingers. I yelped, yanking out my hand. A small mousetrap dangled from my fingers.

My mother swooped into the room. "AH-HA!" she exclaimed. Then, "... John? I was expecting Jane."

My eyes welled with tears. "It really hurts!"

She pried the trap off my fingers and kissed them. "I replaced the spring so it wouldn't snap so hard." She examined the reddened marks. "You'll have a teensy bruise there, but nothing's broken. Just don't let anyone at school know. Or your father." She stepped back. "Now, how long have you been smoking?"

"I don't smoke."

She raised an eyebrow, then took my hands and sniffed, then inspected my breath and teeth. "Okay, you aren't smoking. But why are you stealing my cigarettes? Did you think I wouldn't notice? Don't think I don't know about the booze, too."

"They're for my, uh... Joel," I said, picking a name at random.

"Joel? Joel Guillaume? His father's a history prof? I should call up his mother—"

"That'd get him into trouble."

She gave me her best scary-mom dagger eye. "If he's drinking and smoking at the rate you're stealing, he *needs* to be in trouble."

I flopped down on my parent's bed. My mother sat next to me, her arm around my shoulders. "You'd better tell me what this is about."

"You can't tell anyone," I said.

"Cross my heart and pray to Jesus to rip my guts out if I do. Say, you aren't stealing to impress that girl you like, are you? Betty? Betsy?"

"I wish I were," I mumbled.

My mother followed me down the ladder into the tunnels. "I see why you and your father like to play down here," she said.

"Mike?" I called. "Mike!" We walked along to the quadrupole magnet, where he'd made a nest between empty cable spools. "Mike, come out. We know you're there."

With an exasperated sigh, he crawled out and looked up at my mother. "Greetings, Earthling," he said, in his affected monotone alien voice. "I am Krulltang, from Epsilon Eridani."

My mother barely kept from laughing. "Oh, you are, are you? What color is it? Your home star?"

He just stared at her.

She sighed. "Epsilon Eridani is a G-class star, yellow, like ours. You haven't been within ten parsecs of Epsilon Eridani, have you?"

"I had to tell her," I said. "She caught me stealing cigarettes. She made me tell."

"And the booze," she added. "Bad habits will be your downfall."

Mike slumped to the floor. "Goddammerung," he muttered.

My mother sat on the floor across from him. She tapped out a cigarette, lit it, and handed it to Mike. "I'd like to hear your story."

When he had finished, she smiled and said, "Say, you got any of that booze left you had my son steal for you?"

Mike returned with a bottle two-thirds empty. My mother took a swig and gave it to Mike. He downed a big gulp, then tipped it towards me. My mother grabbed the bottle. "I know my reputation," she said, "but I'm not *that* bad of a mother." She pulled her legs up and hugged her knees. "What are we going to do?"

"I imagine," Mike said slowly, "that you're going to turn me over to your husband and to the Army."

My mother shook her head. "You need to work on your powers of imagination. We have a lot of practice with powers of imagination in our family, don't we, Johnny?"

Towards evening, my mother drove our car to a quiet side street. She slowed the car to an arthritic ant's crawl by an old manhole cover. Mike slid into the back seat. He found himself next to Robbie, who chirped, "Someday I'll be a *real* boy!"

"What the hell?" Mike whispered.

I turned around in the front seat. "This is Robbie. He's ... something you get used to."

(On the few occasions that people outside the family met Robbie, most assumed he was a child with some horrible medical affliction, like a boy in a bubble, only one who needed machines to keep him alive. Such was the power of projection and assumption.)

We headed out of town, the sun turning the clouds to molten metal. "I can probably chance hitchhiking from here," Mike said. "Or you can drop me near a railroad."

"I've got something better in mind," my mother said mysteriously.

After about an hour, as I drowsily stared up at the black sky and the net of stars, my mother suddenly pulled off on a side road.

"What's that up ahead?" I asked. Silently, my mother pointed to a sign. "'Bartlett and Sons—The World's Only Two-and-a-Half-Ring Circus,'" I read off.

"I hope you don't mind. Unless you prefer the highway."

"Nope," Mike breathed. He rolled down the window and inhaled a lung-busting barrelful of air. "They have elephants! Elephants!"

"Elephants!" echoed Robbie. "I want to be a *real* elephant!"

It was nearly midnight when we rolled back up our driveway. My father threw open the door.

"Jesus, Anne, I was frantic! Where were you? What happened to dinner?"

My mother strode inside. "Oh, like you depend on me making dinner. Johnny and I grabbed burgers on the road, and Robbie wasn't hungry. Is Jane asleep, or over at Lucy's?"

My father fidgeted. "But where'd you go?"

She turned to face him, putting her hands on her hips and standing with her feet slightly apart. "The rains have stopped, the clouds have gone away, and it's a beautiful moonless night. We went to look at the stars. Out in the country, we could see the Milky Way, and I was naming the constellations for Johnny and Robbie. Isn't that right?"

Robbie began to hum "When You Wish Upon a Star," which we'd all sung on the drive home.

"It's a school night," my father said.

"School?" my mother said. "For thousands of years, the stars were our teachers. Science and stories, poetry and imagination all start in the stars." She reached over and ruffled my hair. "John might see them and imagine distant, advanced civilizations. He might realize how small and tiny we are in the universe. He might look at them and have his heart filled with unspoken beauty. Is that such a bad thing to show him?" She clapped her hands. "Okay, now, everyone to bed!"

My Neighbor Godzilla

Once, I asked my father for some plutonium. It was one of the few times I surprised him. He stepped back from the circuit he was soldering and wiped his glasses. Then he shook his head.

"Uranium?" I persisted. "Radium? A bit of americium?"

"Go ask your mother," he said. "She was the specialist in the actinides."

My mother was arguing with Jane. "No, you may *not* get a tattoo. Who do you think you are, a sailor?"

Jane had painstakingly inked on her belly a Disney-style princess with a flaming skull for a head. She gave our mother a cold stare, the kind that would make an iceberg reach for a sweater. "I bet when I grow up, everyone gets tattoos. Even old people like you."

"Great. We'll be a nation of sailors." My mother turned to me. "And you, Johnny, what do you want? A ring in your nose?"

I shook my head. "No. Just some plutonium."

"I'm fresh out, honey. Why, are you planning on building a reactor? No? Then, what?"

I hesitated.

My mother said, "We're through discussing this, Jane. You ... you go play with Robbie. I swear, you kids pay more attention to appliances than to your brother."

After Jane stomped upstairs, my mother sat on the couch and patted the seat next to her. "Sit down, Johnny, and tell me about this girl."

My stomach curdled a little bit. "Why do you—"

"Elementary, my dear son. One thing no boy wants to talk about in front of his sister is a girl he has a crush on. Betsy, right?"

"Becky."

"Well, blowing up Becky, or the school, or both, will get her attention, but not in a positive way."

"It's not her I want to blow up," I said.

"Tell me about it."

The day before, I had climbed to the top of the jungle gym. Up there, it was peaceful. I didn't have to pretend to play with anyone. A group of boys led by Steve Snoever were playing crippleball—our teacher, Mrs. Jarczynski didn't hold with crippleball, but when she wasn't on yard duty, they played anyway—and they had started to throw balls at a knot of girls. While I watched in horror, Becky had crumpled to the ground as if felled by a bullet.

By the time I clambered down to the playground, Becky was sitting on the asphalt, knees pulled up to her chest with her arms hugged around them, her mouth twisted as she tried not to cry. Standing behind her, Steve Snoever, a ball tucked under his arm, sighed and said, "Okay, I'm sorry."

Standing behind *him*, Big Bruce placed a thick hand on Steve's shoulder. "Say it like you mean it."

Playground rumors held that Big Bruce had been held back many years, maybe forever, a kind of Flying Dutchman of the fifth grade. Big Bruce had already broken three desks this year just by plopping down in them, and now he had a specially reinforced one. When Mrs. Jarczynski asked Big Bruce a question, she had to repeat it three or four times to get his attention. She had given up trying after Christmas break. Big Bruce was like a walking wall, vast T-shirts and ill-fitting sweatshirts stretched across his bulk. His pear-shaped head was topped by a tuft of ginger hair, and his eyes were brown and placid, like a cow's, or maybe like an African wildebeest. I had read that more people were killed by African wildebeest every year than by lions.

Maybe Steve, who looked small only when next to Bruce, had run across that fact, too. Steve shoved his hands in his pockets and said to Becky, "I'm, uh, sorry I hit you."

Big Bruce just stood there, staring off at the horizon. Maybe he was dreaming of lunch; he always brought a suitcase-sized lunchbox. Abruptly, he lumbered off. The earth didn't rumble with his steps, but it wouldn't have surprised me if it had. I wanted to say something to Becky, but I couldn't figure out what. I was going to ask, *"Are you okay?"* or maybe *"Do you need stitches?"* But when I opened my mouth, I blurted out, "Do you want help with math?"

Becky shook her head, still buried in her arms, as the recess bell rang.

Unexpectedly, after school, Becky ran up to me. "About help with math...?" she said, barely looking at me. I nodded. She smiled and skipped off.

I didn't walk home; I floated, my body a balloon. My only fear was that I would rise up too high, pop, and fall to earth as shreds of rubber. Still, maybe that would be enough.

It was, of course, for Steve Snoever that I wanted some lethal substance. Over dinner that evening, I dreamed up several pleasing scenarios, but then the phone rang, scattering my thoughts. My mother, who was in a good humor, went into the kitchen. Her voice was bright and cheery. When she returned, she lowered herself into her seat and took a bite of that night's Hamburger Helper before she said, "Well, Johnny, looks like you've got a job."

My own fork hovered in midair. "A job?"

"Tutoring."

I didn't listen for a few seconds. I saw a vision of Becky, with her cut-straight-across bangs and her blonde pigtails and her big glinting braces when she smiled. But then I noticed my mother looking at me inquisitively.

"Honestly, Johnny, I don't know how you do so well in school, the way you drift off. Okay, well, I'm married to your father, so I do know. I was asking if you know a kid named Bruce Gooseman? That was Mrs. Gooseman. Said her son is in your class, a friend of yours, and wondered if you'd be willing to help him out."

My stomach dropped like the one time I went on a roller coaster.

"*You* have a friend?" Jane asked.

"Jane, don't be mean," my father said without looking up from his physics journal.

"But he seems proud to not have any friends," Jane said.

"I know Bruce, sure," I said slowly.

"Then it's settled," my mother said. "She offered five dollars an hour, but I said for a school chum, you'd do it for three."

That's why, two days a week, I started riding my bike over to Big Bruce's house. The class was doing fractions: adding, subtracting, multiplying, and dividing them. (I myself had finished doing every problem in the book the first week, and during math class, I surreptitiously solved cubic equations.) Bruce, on the other hand, was struggling with basic arithmetic.

"Okay," I said, "here's a simple one." And I wrote it out:

$$2/3 + 2/5 = ?$$

Bruce stared at it for a long while. His head weaved for a bit, and I saw his eyelids droop down.

"Concentrate..." I urged.

At length, he sighed, reached out with an arm like a construction crane, and scrawled:

$$4/35$$

It was a long two hours.

Mrs. Gooseman walked me out the front door and handed me six dollars as the sun was setting. "Thank you, John, so much," she said. "I've been feeling a bit desperate. We tried other tutors, college kids, but they didn't relate well to Bruce." She paused. "Do you think Bruce made progress tonight?"

"It was a start," I said.

"I'm deaf in this ear," she said, tapping the left side of her head. "You'll have to repeat what you said."

"I said, I ought to get home before it gets dark."

She smiled at me, a small little smile, but with effort in it, as if that was all the smile she could afford on a tight budget, even though she wished she could be more generous. "You go on home. I'm sure your mother will be worried about you."

Two weeks later, we had a math test. Normally, I loved math tests, but for Bruce's sake, I dreaded it. There was no way he was going to pass. He was unable to focus and seemed to apply random arithmetic operations to numbers in the hope that he might get something right by sheer chance. Each time I went home, Mrs. Gooseman followed me out to my bike, paid me six dollars, and asked how Bruce was doing.

"There's some progress, I think," I said, repeating the lie when she turned her good ear to me.

"Oh, I hope so. Why don't you take these cookies home?" she offered, which only made me feel worse.

My feelings of guilt didn't stop me from eating the cookies. That's probably why I arrived at school the next morning with a rock in my gut. As we rustled into our seats, the sour looks on everyone else's faces suggested a similar feeling in their stomachs, although they were dreading the math test—all except Big Bruce. He caught me looking at him, and he made a funny face. After a moment, I realized he was trying to smile.

The math test came after morning recess. Right before recess, Mrs. Jarczynski had brought up the possibility of having a fundraiser to supplement classroom supplies. It turned out that Mrs. Jarcynzski was also "supplementing" her income and would later be dismissed for embezzlement, but we didn't yet know that.

Mrs. Jarcynzski asked for ideas. I raised my hand. "How about a science competition?"

Behind me, Steve Snoever muttered, "What a nerd."

Mrs. Jarcynzski shook her head. "No, John. For one, you'd have an unfair advantage."

Well, of course. That's why I'd suggested it.

She continued, "I was thinking we could have a waffle breakfast. Everyone has pancake breakfasts, but a waffle breakfast would make it unique, classier." She nodded decisively. "A waffle breakfast it is! This afternoon, we'll divide up into committees."

The math test was no harder than any other, though it was slightly longer; it took me ten minutes to finish rather than seven. The weight in my stomach didn't go away, however.

A day later, Mrs. Jarczynski handed out the graded tests. Big Bruce waited for me outside after the bell rang, holding his test. At the top, written in precise red ink, was a D+.

"Gee, Bruce..." I started to say, trying to think of an excuse. *"The test was unfair," "I didn't do that well, either,"* (though I had my test paper marked with *A++++ of course* crumpled in my back pocket), or *"Practice makes perfect."* But I kept my mouth shut. Even in my head, everything I thought of sounded awful.

Bruce made a face. He was smiling again. "This is the best grade I've gotten all year!" he said. "My mom's going to be so happy!" He started to lumber away, but then suddenly halted, even as the tide of fifth graders flowed around him.

"Mom said if I got a good grade, I could have a friend come for a sleepover." He paused for a long while, the way he often did. As I waited, I was thinking that a sleepover sounded like something girls did—Jane told stories of gossiping about boys and painting each other's toenails, though I assumed it was another of her sarcastic inventions—when I suddenly realized who Bruce meant by "a friend."

Late Thursday afternoon, I got my sleeping bag down from the attic and stuffed a change of clothes into my backpack. Jane was starting dinner, and my mother was on the couch, reading to Robbie when I walked by.

"Johnny, you look like you're hoping the governor will phone the warden with a last-minute stay of execution," my mother said.

"I guess."

"It's Big Bruce Gooseman," Jane said. "Back when *I* was in fifth grade with him, he didn't say anything all year. Not who I'd guess to be John's best friend."

"Sounds like he's shy," my mother said. "A bit like John."

"This one time, the teacher asked him to come up to the board, but he couldn't get out of his seat, so he scooted his desk—"

"Jane," my mother said, using a tone of voice that would leave a mark. "There's no call to make fun of someone, especially if that someone is a friend of your brother's."

"I just tutor him," I said quietly.

"*You* make fun of people all the time," Jane pointed out as the onions in the skillet behind her sizzled. "Last night, you went on about that woman in line in front of you at the Higgledy-Piggledy, how she—"

"She's a grown-up. That's different," my mother insisted.

"Big Bruce has been in fifth grade forever," my sister said. "Stuck in it like a woolly mammoth in a tar pit. He's got to be nearly an adult by now. So, *logically*—"

The clock twitched and read six. "I think your onions are on fire," I said to Jane, then sprinted out the front door.

Mrs. Gooseman splurged on a bigger smile when she opened the front door. "I'm so glad you could come, John! Bruce is very excited. Bruce, look who's here!"

Dinner was lasagna, made with hamburger and cheese, a change from the lasagna with anchovies and tofu my mother had scraped together the week before. ("Oh, I didn't feel like grocery shopping." This was why Jane often cooked: self-defense.) As we sat down, Mrs. Gooseman said, "Bruce's father is away on a business trip, so it's just us tonight."

Bruce began shoveling huge wads of lasagna into his mouth.

After dinner, Bruce and I sat in front of the TV, and Mrs. Gooseman brought us both bowls of ice cream, so big that they would have shamed the Himalayas. My stomach was already bursting, so although normally I would have been ecstatic at such a generous helping, I only scraped at it, the way a boy archaeologist might carefully remove layers of dirt from a buried relic. Still, I was secretly glad to see that Bruce, too, seemed nearly anesthetized by the food, because despite having worried about it all afternoon, I had not thought of a single topic of conversation. I've never had a talent for small talk.

(My mother had tried to help. "It's about *pretending* you're interested in the other person, even if you aren't. If you can pretend you're an explorer on Mars, or being hunted by a Tyrannosaurus, surely you can pretend to care about someone's boring life.")

The phone rang, and Mrs. Gooseman, washing dishes in the kitchen, picked it up. "Bruce, sweetie, it's for you?" she said, her words rising like helium balloons.

Big Bruce struggled to get up from the cheap vinyl sofa, sticky like old flypaper, and clunked out to the kitchen. I heard him say, "Uh-huh, uh-huh." He stayed on the phone for a whole rerun of *M*A*S*H*.

At last, Mrs. Gooseman stood in the doorway to the family room. "Bedtime, boys! I wouldn't want John's mother complaining that he didn't get enough sleep."

Bruce's room was small and dark, smelling of sweat and licorice. As I unrolled my sleeping bag onto the floor, Bruce sagged onto his bed, and the mattress springs groaned.

"My dad's not really on a business trip," he said abruptly.

I wasn't sure how to respond to that, so I said, "Your mom makes a good lasagna." I also considered recounting for him, verbatim, the episode of *M*A*S*H* he had missed. But that reminded me to ask, "Who was that on the phone?"

"Huh? Oh. It was that girl."

"What girl? From our class? Becky?"

Bruce slowly stretched out on his bed, reminding me of the way my mother would ease herself into cold water. "Yeah, um, Becky. She calls me sometimes. She just wants to talk." He gave a coagulated sigh. "Sometimes, I think my life kinda sucks, with my dad not being here and all. But then she tells me about *her* family."

He didn't say any more. After a few minutes, he began to breathe heavily. Part of me wanted to shake him awake and ask him about Becky's family. But I turned over a couple of times, the way my dog, Bessie, used to, and settled in to sleep.

I had almost drifted off to the cotton-fluffy land of dreams when a crackling thunder peal of sound jolted me awake. It was Bruce. His snores, which had started off mild, not much different from a gas lawnmower a block away, began to swell in intensity, rumbling louder and louder like an approaching herd of wildebeest. It was as if Bruce were practicing saurian roars for a scary movie about dinosaurs. His bedroom window rattled from the snores, and I swear, so did my bones. I tried wrapping my pillow around my head and stuffing my fingers into my ears, but the sound of his snoring penetrated my brain like a dentist's drill. I lay there for hours, wondering if Bruce could subcontract out to a shadowy government agency as an instrument of torture.

Abruptly, it stopped. The sudden, smothering silence that followed brought me to even greater wakefulness. It was so quiet that I could have heard an ant tiptoeing across the carpet. I strained to listen, but didn't even hear a whisper of breathing.

Somewhat panicked, I sat up, then crawled the few feet to Bruce's bed. My pulse surged in a quickstep march. Was he dead? What would his mother say? What would *my* mother say? I imagined Jane, her sarcasm thick as molasses: *"Great, John. You finally make a friend, and he dies on you."*

A few inches away, Bruce's voice whispered, "John?"

"Yeah?"

"What is it?"

"You..." It seemed weird to complain that he had stopped snoring. "Nothing. I was just having trouble sleeping."

"Yeah?" He wriggled and turned over with a walrus-sized flop, the mattress coils squeaking in protest. "I never get a good night's sleep, either."

The next morning, Mrs. Gooseman served both Bruce and me continent-sized helpings of scrambled eggs. Halfway through, I tried pushing it away, only see Mrs. Gooseman deflate a little.

"I suppose your mother is a wonderful cook. I never got the hang of it."

I wanted to say, *"No, my mother is a terrible cook,"* but that seemed to be even more insulting to Mrs. Gooseman's scrambled eggs. I pulled back the plate, stared for a moment at the little sea of yellow eggy water that had drained from the northernmost mass, and dug in again.

When I sank into my seat at school, I felt a curious lethargy. Normally, I lived for Fridays and the math quiz shout-out. In fact, I was so good at it that Mrs. Jarczynski had given me a handicap: I couldn't play until the last ten minutes. Even so, I would win handily.

But this Friday, as Mrs. Jarczynski read from her notes and called on students, the droning voices lulled me into a state of relaxation. *I can do this with my eyes closed,* I told myself.

Then suddenly I was jolted awake by the sound of the bell. I stood bolt upright, thinking it was a fire, but it was just recess.

"It was awfully nice of you to let someone else win," Mrs. Jarczynski said. "I think Becky really appreciated it." She walked past me and gently tapped Bruce's shoulder until he jerked awake. "Pay attention, Bruce," she said. "We've talked about this before."

"Yes'm," Bruce replied.

The rest of the day, I could barely keep my eyes open. I dragged myself home and up to my room and fell immediately asleep.

Monday morning, caught up on sleep, I walked to school clearheaded and happy. Then I saw Big Bruce, lugging himself into class, his eyes nearly swollen shut. I started to think, *Maybe Bruce never gets enough sleep.*

Before I finished that thought, the *clunk clunk clunk* of Mrs. Jarczinsky's sensibly heeled shoes distracted me. She paced back and forth in the front of the class. "Settle down, everyone! I want to—"

The bell clattered obnoxiously, trampling her words.

Finally, silence returned. Mrs. Jarczynski took a deep breath. "I have some bad news." Her voice wavered. She told us she had learned that Middling Avenue Elementary was having a *waffle* breakfast in two weeks—the week before ours. "No one would go to two waffle breakfasts in a row." She slumped into the seat behind her desk, pushed a leaning tower of homework papers to one side, and put her face in her hands. "We're ruined."

"I like waffles," Bruce offered.

Mrs. Jarczynski lifted her head to give a wan if surprised smile. This was only the fourth thing Bruce had said in class all year. "That's sweet, Bruce. But we need another idea, and quick."

I raised my hand. Mrs. Jarcynzski's smile, which was barely there to begin with, faded away. "I'm sorry, John, but I don't think a science fair would really work out."

The class erupted into laughter, *ha-ha* bouncing around like molecules of hot air. The balloon of amusement burst when Big Bruce twisted in his seat and shouted, "Shut up!" Even Mrs. Jarczynski was jolted.

That display of loyalty sent my brain to a new track, and a new thought. That was the thing growing up in my family: you learned early the trick of ideas popping up, like corn in hot oil. I said, "Why not some other breakfast? Something different?" Mrs. Jarcynzski opened her mouth, and I quickly said the first words on my tongue: "Omelets? An omelet breakfast?"

Mrs. Jarcynzski looked as if she was about to dismiss my suggestion when the creases in her forehead smoothed, and her mouth widened into a smile. "Why, John, that's brilliant!" (I have to say, it's addictive to get reactions like that.) She continued, "We can set up omelet stations where people choose their own toppings... Oh, people will line up for this. We'll beat Middling Avenue by a mile!"

Three weeks later, on a warm, windless morning, we held our omelet breakfast out on the playground. Our fifth-grade class had prepared feverishly. We re-painted the signs, and Mrs. Jarczynski drilled us in omeletting. Naturally, my experience shone through, so I became a front-line omeleteer. Bruce became my eggsman, the one who broke and beat and poured the eggs into the pan, made sure we were full up on fillings, and so on. This thrilled him to no end. "We're a team, aren't we, John?" he said, five or six times.

"My, aren't we talkative!" Mrs. Jarczynski commented. "If I had known it would fire you up so, Bruce, we would have held an omelet breakfast long ago."

Becky was bussing the picnic tables. Steve Snoever stood in the parking lot, directing traffic, blowing his whistle every second well before the first cars arrived.

I have a vivid memory of us all lined up and wearing shirts emblazoned with OMELETEERS. Mrs. Jarczynski brandished a bullhorn she'd swiped from the gym. "Let's raise lots of money!" she said, her amplified voice rolling across the schoolyard.

Bruce had been counting eggs, starting over several times, but then put a hand up to shield his eyes from the morning sun. "Look at all those crows over there." He pointed to the forest's edge in back of the school.

"I don't see anything," I said.

Bruce loped across the asphalt and onto the grass.

"Don't abandon your post!" Mrs. Jarczynski called over the bullhorn. "Don't abandon—"

But Bruce was halfway there and soon reached the tree line. The crows scattered into the sky, calling Bruce names. Bruce paused, then swung around and walked back.

"People will be here in ten minutes!" Mrs. Jarczynski said, still through the bullhorn.

"It was a coyote," Bruce said. "It was dead."

Mrs. Jarczynski lowered her bullhorn, revulsion crawling across her face. "I hope that doesn't turn people away."

"Half a coyote," Bruce amended. "With guts hanging out."

From the parking lot, Steve Snoever yelled, "They're coming!" He began blowing his whistle nonstop.

Mrs. Jarczynski raised the bullhorn. "Places, everyone. Fire up the stoves! Oil your pans!"

A trickle of people came from the parking lot.

"We have ham, bacon, mushrooms, tomatoes, bell peppers," I explained, "three kinds of cheese, onions, artichoke hearts, pineapple, Thousand Island and Russian dressing, bananas, M&Ms, and marshmallows." The class had voted on the toppings, an exercise in democracy that Mrs. Jarczynski regretted.

An hour later, the air buzzed with happy voices and the clang of steel utensil, the atmosphere redolent with the smell of eggs and cheese and ham (Russian dressing, not so much). The sixth-grade concert band was playing, and the cashbox sprouted a harvest of green bills. Mrs. Jarczynski's eyes were full of dollar signs.

Becky stopped in front of my station and smiled—a genuinely happy smile, the kind my father was no good at. "Hi," she said. She paused a moment, then said again, "Hi." She was looking at Bruce, not me, but she couldn't be faulted for that; he took up so much of the scenery that you could hardly not look at him.

A shadow fell between us. "Go on with your work, Becky," Mrs. Jarczynski said. "You can distract these boys later. I see a table out there that needs clearing."

Bruce said, "Nobody's using those tables."

"Becky doesn't need to be the center of attention right now," Mrs. Jarczynski said.

Becky slumped and walked slowly to the far end of the playground.

Mrs. Jarczynski shook her head. "I was just like her when I was her age. Totally boy-crazy." To me, she added, "This was a great idea, John. There's even a reporter from the newspaper, taking pictures! That'll show Middling Avenue. Waffle breakfast, indeed."

Bruce was breaking eggs into a bowl, then stopped. "Something's moving out there."

"It's those birds you saw, Bruce. Excuse me, the band wants to ask me something. Probably what to play. Some people have no initiative. Here, hold this," she said, handing me the bullhorn.

Bruce squinted, then turned to me. "What do you think it is?"

At first, I thought it was wind making the undergrowth shake. But the air was still, lacking the slightest wisp of breeze. I squinted. "Uh, Mrs. Jarczynski...?" I called.

The concert band had just struck up John Phillip Sousa's "Liberty Bell March," with the trumpets leading the way a little too fast, and the tuba oom-pah-pahing a little behind. The people at the picnic tables turned their faces, shining with eggs and grease, towards the band and away from the forest, so no one else saw what emerged from between the trees.

"Wow," said Bruce. "That's not good. *Really* not good."

Out on the grass field was something big—bigger even than the Cadillac the school principal drove. Its belly dragged on the grass as it lumbered towards us, a massive black tongue flicking in and out of its mouth, tasting omelets in the air. For a moment, it paused. Its beaded skin was a patchwork of yellow and black.

"Ernie?" I said weakly.

As the concert band moved into "My Sharona," Ernie heaved himself forward. I raised the bullhorn. "Uh, Mrs. Jarczynski?"

The squealing feedback made everyone flinch. Mrs. Jarczynski glared at me. *Don't you dare ruin this*, her angry eyes signaled.

My mouth was dry, but I managed to say, "Don't panic, but there's a Mexican beaded lizard who used to be my pet, but he's gigantic now, and he's coming for our omelets!" I waved the bullhorn towards the oncoming Ernie, who was building up momentum like a locomotive.

People panicked and screamed. Mrs. Jarczynski froze in horror. And Becky was wandering at the edge of the playground, head down, kicking at tufts of grass. She might have been crying. I didn't think she heard me. I knew I should run and grab her hand, but I was frozen, too, caught between wanting to save Becky and trying to think of what to tell my father about Ernie.

It was Big Bruce who moved. It was Bruce who ran along the line of stations, grabbing every plate with an omelet on it, filling his arms. It was Bruce who lumbered onto the playground, the scent of eggs trailing behind him.

"Omelets!" he bellowed. Boy, he could bellow magnificently. "Omelets!" Arms full of cooked eggs, he ran onto the playground.

Ernie charged onto the far edge of the asphalt, through the crippleball courts and among the permanent temporary trailer module classrooms. Bruce angled towards Ernie until the lizard caught the scent of omelets. Ernie swerved and followed, his thick tail thwacking one of the trailer classrooms, crumpling the sheet-metal wall. A couple of omelets dropped from Bruce's arms, and Ernie slowed to slurp them up, then surged after the boy. Bruce shot out from the classrooms, and legs churning, he sprinted towards the north end of the campus, leading Ernie away from Becky, away from all of us. Bruce's huge frame become smaller and smaller, until he was a tiny figure running across the grass, tossing plate after plate of omelet as a black-and-yellow monster lumbered after him.

Maybe it was luck, but I think Bruce was smarter than anyone gave him credit for. On the far side of campus was a concrete underpass, wide enough to walk through, but too narrow for a car—or a giant lizard. Bruce, omelets gone, but still smelling of eggs, led Ernie into the underpass, where the latter became wedged.

The lizard was wriggling there hours later when military helicopters flew in with steel cable nets to carry him away. My father, who was called upon whenever anything like this happened, said, "I think we're going to have to have a talk, John."

I biked over to Bruce's house. Mrs. Gooseman said, "That was some excitement you had at school, John."

I wondered if Bruce had told her how he had saved Becky. But I had something else to say. I gestured for her to turn her good ear to me. "I don't think Bruce is getting enough sleep."

"He has a regular bedtime."

"No, no. His snoring wakes him up. He doesn't get enough sleep, and in class, he falls asleep. He should see a doctor about this."

"Bruce snores?"

She must have listened, because he started doing much better in class. On the last day of school, he told me, "I'm going on to sixth grade next year! Maybe we'll be in the same class together. But sixth graders can be mean sometimes." He stuck out his hand, and we shook. "Thanks for everything," he said.

I wanted to tell him he was a hero—*my* hero—for saving Becky, for saving everyone. But the words felt so awkward, they wouldn't come out. And then I felt worse for saying nothing at all.

The Monster Island Affair

My mother grew up in Chicago. She once remarked that this explained the cold wind she felt blowing through her heart.

Her quip sounded familiar. After a moment, the dials in my head lined up. "That's from one of your blues songs."

"Very good, Johnny," she said, a crinkled smile on her lips. "You get a gold star. Now, where did I put those gold stars?"

She had grown up in Chicago, but she loved Delta blues. When she was in a good mood, or in a bad mood—not the kind that turned her numb as stone, but the kind that lit a black fire in her veins—she'd turn the kitchen radio to the blues station, her hips twitching side to side with the moaning guitar notes, and suddenly she wasn't washing dishes or chopping onion, she was standing at a cold crossroads at midnight, waiting for the devil to collect her soul. B. B. King, Muddy Waters, Robert Johnson... she loved those men and their wretched lives. Tales of misery satisfied her need to have her pain poked at though the grill of a radio. She listened to the blues nearly my whole summer vacation between fifth and sixth grade.

When our father announced that we were going to Plum Island for the summer, Jane and I looked at each other. We had spent the previous summer holed up in a motel outside of Calcium Dunes Missile Testing Grounds, trying unsuccessfully to stuff newspaper into the doorjamb to keep out the constantly blowing grit.

"Why is it called Plum Island?" I asked. "Do they have fruit orchards on it?"

My father frowned. "I don't think so, although there are some old forests there. No, it's spelled P-L-U-M-B. There used to a lead mine there, and the Latin word for lead is *plumbum*, which also gave us the word *plumber*, because the ancient Romans used lead pipes."

"Which destroyed their health and empire," Jane added. "Why not just mix lead paint chips into one of mom's casseroles?"

"If there's any cooking to be done, you can do it, Jane," my mother said. "I'm going to be on vacation."

My father shook his head. "You won't be anywhere near the mine ... although the, uh, facility where I'll be working is located in the mine. Proton decay experiment. There's actually quite a nice resort there, I'm told, with a pool. You all can swim and work on your tans. Maybe you might even meet some boys, Jane."

It took us three days of miserable driving to get there. (Bruce had agreed to feed my lizard, Paul, once a week.) Jane was carsick several times. "You smell like battery acid," I told her.

"Next time, I'm puking on you," she said.

Robbie, who was belted in between us, said brightly, "Next time, I'm puking on you and *you* and *you!*"

"Don't puke on anyone," our father admonished.

"Actually, I don't feel so good right now," Jane said. "If I could sit in the front..."

"Not a chance," our mother said. "I'm worse than you. And the back windows don't roll down. The only thing keeping my stomach settled is my cigarettes. Want one?"

"Anne," my father growled. He was hunched behind the wheel. When we stopped each night at some forlorn motel, we could hear the gristle crackle in his spine as he unknotted himself.

"You could have left me behind, Alan," my mother said.

"Who would take care of the kids?"

"Oh, be realistic. Like I watch over them now."

"You could have left us behind, too," Jane said. "I begged you to leave us all behind."

"We're a family; we stick together," our father insisted. It sounded like a threat. He glanced back at us, his face gleaming with sweat as thick as beef fat, and the car swerved from side to side.

"Oh, God..." Jane put a hand to her mouth. "Can you pull over?"

Plumb Island was an hour's ferry ride off the coast. Jane and I stood on the bow, tasting the salt air as sunlight skittered off the water. Jane turned to me, her long blonde hair whipping in the wind, and said, "No way it's going to be this good the whole time." And though I didn't want to agree, I nodded.

The island itself was long, narrow, and curving. To most people, it looked like a parenthesis, though when I looked at the map, I saw the fossilized skeleton of a therapod, its body drawn into an arc after death as the tendons along its spine dried and tightened. Or maybe it had been the caldera of an ancient volcano, blown to pieces in a spectacular cataclysm. I mentioned this last theory to my father. He said, "No, no igneous rocks," and he was right.

Four miles at its widest, and fifteen miles in length, Plumb Island had only one town: Port Brian, on its southern end. A dilapidated resort sulked on the edge of town with all the charm of an old dill pickle. We checked in, and my mother immediately stretched herself out on a bed. "Ah, that's the thing," she said. "Let me know when it's time to leave."

"Why do John and I have to share with you guys?" Jane demanded. "We need our privacy."

My father laid a suitcase on the carpeted floor and opened it. "We couldn't afford it. But there are three swimming pools. Not one, but three. And you've got your bikes."

"Where do we ride to?" I asked.

From the bed, my mother said, "Around and around and around until you wear yourselves out. Make sure you take Robbie. Or swim and swim and swim until you wear yourselves out." She flipped over and buried her face in a pillow.

That afternoon, Jane and I, with Robbie perched behind Jane, rode all the way around Plumb Island, from the barnacled ferry terminal at the southern end to the edge of the forest in the north. Then we returned to Floursack Mountain in the middle, the highest point on the island, maybe two hundred feet. We pedaled and puffed our way to the top, then watched a ferry pull out from the terminal and head towards the mainland, drawing a faint chalk line on the blackboard of the sea.

"Maybe someday, we'll be rescued from here," Jane murmured. "Centuries from now."

"You'd be bored at home and complaining," I said.

"I'm bored!" Robbie put in.

Jane looked at me. "You know the real reason we're here, right?" When I didn't answer, she rolled her eyes. "Dad's having an affair, and he's meeting her here."

"You're always saying that. Do you *want* him to cheat? Do you want a stepmom?"

She leaned forward on the handlebars. "I've read the Brothers Grimm. Step-mothers never work out well."

"You said Lucy's stepmom is nice."

"You're missing the point."

"I think the point," I said, putting my weight on a pedal, "is that you're nuts. Be careful, or the squirrels'll get you." And I raced down the hill before she could hit me.

After sleeping in our room for two days straight, my mother went out to the pool and slept under a parasol. My main chore was to keep Robbie out of the pool. "Why I can't swim?" he protested as I blocked him from approaching the water.

"You would sink to the bottom. You would short out. You don't want that, do you?"

"I don't want that," he agreed sadly. "But I want to swim."

I glanced around for my parents, then pulled a screwdriver out of my back pocket. But Robbie began shrieking, "Don't touch my dials! Don't touch my dials!"

"Okay, okay," I said.

"Take him biking," Jane suggested.

"He's so heavy."

"Do you want him jumping in the pool?"

With Robbie strapped into a child's seat, I pedaled to the top of Floursack Mountain.

"What's that?" Robbie asked. He pointed to an ugly insect silhouette on the horizon, and I heard a faint thwacking sound bouncing off the sky.

"A helicopter," I said. A big one, with two rotors, the kind used by the military. Churning the sky with its counter-rotating blades, it swung low over the forested northern end of the island, where I lost it in the sting of the sun.

I coasted my bike down the mountain. On the northern foot, where the scrub slope ended and the forest began, was a little blue shack, The Frying Fish, selling fried clams, fried oysters, fried fish, and fried scallops and mussels. Anything found in the ocean, they fried. We had stopped there the first couple of days. I liked it, but my father said the greasy food upset his stomach.

In my pockets, I found just enough change for some French fries. *Not a bad summer*, I was thinking, eating French fries on an island, when Robbie announced that he felt tired.

"Oops. Forgot to bring a battery pack. We gotta go back."

When we got back to the room, I rummaged around in my father's suitcase for an extra battery pack. The door opened, but it was only Jane.

"I saw her," she announced.

"She's out by the pool, right?"

"No, dummy, not *her*. The other woman."

I lifted up Robbie's shirt and pried out his batteries. "You're not still going on about that, are you?"

"I saw him get into a car with a woman. She looked Chinese, or some sort of Asian. Then they drove away."

"You're sure it was him?"

She put her hands on her hips. "He was wearing that stupid fishing hat he has. I'm sure."

"And I'm sure you're imagining things, something our family is all skilled at."

"I'm not," said Robbie. "I can't imagine anything at all."

I got bored biking around the island. There was an abandoned mine nestled in the far armpit of Floursack Mountain, but the only thing to see was a boarded-up entrance and a big padlock. I rode into the forest to find the helicopter, but there was nothing but old tin-sheeted warehouses, also padlocked. Back at the hotel, I wrote Bruce a postcard. I tried to write a postcard for Becky, but I had forgotten to bring her address, and besides, I couldn't think of any words that weren't as dumb as a bag of hammers. Giving up, I spent a day going through the tidepools, and I brought back a starfish.

"You killed it," my sister said.

"Let's look at it under the microscope," my father said.

I spent the rest of the days at the pool, at night climbing into bed smelling of chlorine. Jane found a piano in the lobby of the hotel and plunked at the keys. The previous summer, she had tried to be a long-distance runner, though she had only run for three days before, limping from blisters, she quit. This summer, she spent a whole week slaughtering notes until the hotel staff wheeled away the piano in the middle of the night.

My mother slept most of the day by the pool, thick white lotion slathered over her arms and legs. When she wasn't looking, I set Robbie's E dial down low and left him curled up on a chaise lounge next to her. My father vanished during the day—working on the proton decay experiment, he said. Jane whispered, "He's with *her*."

"Where's dad?" Jane asked our mother one day.

"Off somewhere, not waking me up," our mother murmured. "You could be with him, also not waking me up."

But at night, she seemed to come alive. "Is there someplace to go dancing?" she asked my father as we ate dinner at the hotel restaurant. "There ought to be someplace to go dancing." My father shrugged.

"Oh, you're such a lump. And you used to pretend to love dancing." She crooked a finger at the waiter. "Does this island have someplace where there's dancing? Music? Something resembling fun?"

"There used to be a midsummer gala," the waiter said, picking up the wine bottle and tipping it toward her glass. "But not for ... five years? Ten?"

She put a hand over her glass and turned to my father. "Maybe we should organize something."

"Yeah," Jane piped up, "we could put on a show. I could play the piano." The rest of us looked away.

We went back to our room, but my mother was bursting with energy. "I can't sleep. I was sleeping all day. Let's go out and look at the stars."

We walked along the darkened streets to the top of Floursack Mountain. The Milky Way stretched above us like sugar spilled on black marble. "I think that's Orion," my father said, pointing.

My mother tsked. "Orion's a winter constellation, dear. That one's Scorpius."

"You mean Scorpio," he said.

"No, Scorpio is the astrological sign. Scorpius is the constellation." She halted and wrapped her pale arms around herself in the cool summer air. "That bright star there is Antares, a red giant. It's six hundred light years away, fifteen times the mass of our sun, and it's dying. If you centered it on our sun, it would swallow up Mercury, Venus, Earth, even Mars."

"It could go supernova," my father said.

"Wouldn't it be fun if we saw it go supernova, right now?" my mother said.

Wordlessly, we all watched Antares, willing it to flare into new light.

The silence was broken by a distant clacking. "Helicopter," I said. Its black outline eclipsed the stars. "A big one. Does it look like it's carrying something?"

My father coughed. "I forgot my jacket. Maybe we should head back now."

The sun rose over the island, a golden scepter too bright to look at. I swam to the bottom of the pool and tried to stay down as long as I could. I imagined I had sunk to the bottom of the Marianas Trench, eleven miles down.

When I pulled myself out of the water, dripping, my mother called to me, "Johnny, I'm out of lotion. Could you be a dear and run and get some more?"

I had just stepped into the cool of our room when the phone rang. It was my father. "Is your mother there? Is Jane around?" His voice was tense.

"They're out by the pool. Robbie, too."

"Tell your mother to get in the car and drive down to the ferry. Don't bother getting dressed or packing. I'll meet you there."

"Why?"

"Just do it, John."

Hanging up the phone, I grabbed the lotion—I don't know why—and was halfway back to the pool when I heard distant sirens. I didn't think much of it, but then I heard the *thwack-thwack-thwack* of a helicopter. Standing in the shade, I looked up and saw it in the sapphire sky, like a giant locust looping over Port Brian and then speeding north.

The thwacking grew fainter. I sprinted the rest of the way to my mother. "Here's the lotion. And, oh, Dad said something about leaving early," I added. It wasn't exactly a lie, I reasoned, though my stomach felt the funny, squelchy way it did when I lied. But the helicopter had made me wonder what my father wasn't saying.

"He dragged us all the way here," she murmured. "We're staying put."

"I'm going to ride my bike, okay?"

She turned over onto her stomach. "Take Robbie with you," she said, her voice muffled by the towel she lay on.

"Where are we going?" Robbie asked as we got on my bike.

I wasn't sure, but I kept thinking about the *thwack-thwack-thwack* of the helicopter. I rode furiously north, towards the sirens and the helicopter, standing on my pedals to go as fast as I could with a robot on the back of my bike.

After a few short blocks, we left town on a cracked two-lane road, skidding to a stop next to old man heading the opposite direction with a slight limp. "What happened?" I asked.

He shrugged and spit on the ground. "I didn't see. Police turned me back. Said it was a tornado or some such thing."

I looked at the clear blue sky. "A tornado? You sure? They get tornados around here?"

He scratched his head. "Twenty years here, and this is my first tornado. But I've read tornados make an awful sound, chuffing and puffing like a locomotive engine bearing down on you, and that was the sound I heard." He shoved his hands into his pockets, then pointed with his chin towards Robbie. "What in heck is that?"

"My brother," I said, leaning forward on my handlebars. The man shrugged once more and continued into town.

I pedaled farther. A police car cruised slowly by in the opposite direction. Through an open window, the policeman said, "Show's over, kids" as he passed.

I coasted to a stop where The Frying Fish was—or rather, had been. The little blue shack was now just rubble, lumber and deep fryers smashed to pieces, just as if a tornado had torn through it.

By the time Robbie and I got back, my father was at the pool, fully dressed, hands on hips, elbows splayed out at perfect right angles. My mother and Jane, too, were stretched out in the sun, ignoring him. When I walked up pushing my bike, my father's face churned with agitation. "John, I told you to—"

"Was it because of the tornado?" I asked.

My mother said, "Tornado? They don't have tornados here. Hurricanes, sometimes."

"Tornado?" my father echoed. He looked up at the sky, the way he did when lost in thought, as if some answer might be skywritten there. *No tornados here,* I imagined, or maybe: *Surrender, John.* Then he straightened himself, a perfect parental geodesic, the shortest distance between child and adult, and said, "Yes. The tornado. A freak occurrence. I had told you... Next time, John—"

"You mean next time there's a tornado?" I said.

My mother guffawed so hard that her body lifted up off her chaise lounge.

"Don't talk back, young man," my father snapped.

"Oh, relax, Alan," my mother said. "He's got a point. If it's a 'freak occurrence,' we won't have another for a thousand years."

"Isn't it lunchtime?" Jane asked.

After lunch, I wanted to ride my bike some more, but my mother had decided she wanted to walk down by the shore and for us to go with her. "We can at least pretend to be a family for a little while." My father didn't disappear as he had been doing, but walked with us, clambering over wet rocks and lecturing us about the sea creatures we saw. He pointed out the barnacles and told us how Charles Darwin had studied them for years. "Mostly as a stalling tactic before publishing his theory."

"What theory?" Jane asked. He swiveled towards her, mouth open, and she quickly said, "Kidding, just kidding," before she bent down to poke at a sea anemone.

My mother looked out to sea, shielding her eyes with her hand. "Say, is that a tornado?" she said, before glancing back at us with a grin. My father looked slightly sick to his stomach, as if she were serving him up a meal of raw sea anemone, the arms still waving feebly. "Have a sense of humor, Alan," she chided him. "I mean, Jesus in a jumpsuit, don't take yourself so seriously."

The next morning, I gobbled my breakfast cereal and tore outside for my bicycle before my mother could tell me to take Robbie. Without him or Jane or anyone slowing me down, I headed across the island to the abandoned lead mine.

On the way, I paused at the ruins of The Frying Fish. Among the rubble, I found a crumpled menu. And there, below the list of fried seafood, I found what I had forgotten:

Now serving breakfast! Take-away omelets to order!

Here the gray asphalt road threading the island turned to dirt. I rode along it, sending a plume of dust up into the cool, quiet morning air. The trees were freshly cracked and fallen or pushed over, bushes flattened or torn up. The ground looked scuffed, as if a massive belly had been dragged over it. I skidded to a halt and looked for splay-toed footprints, but in vain.

At the lead mine, the entrance was still boarded up, but the lumber looked new. Though I didn't find any footprints, there were fresh tire tracks on the ground outside the mine, and an oil patch. Someone had parked there recently.

After lunch, as I lay out by the pool, I confided in Jane my theory: "Ernie is here."

"Who? From *Sesame Street*?"

"No, Ernie. *My* Ernie. The Mexican beaded lizard—the one *he* experimented on. You know, who escaped and nearly flattened my school."

"Oh, that Ernie." She stretched herself out on her towel after glancing towards the lifeguard, a slim boy of sixteen.

"I bet that's where *he's* going," I said.

"He's having an affair, I'm telling you," Jane said into her towel.

"No, he's going off to the mineshaft, where they're keeping Ernie, and probably examining and experimenting on him and everything."

"You know how crazy that sounds?"

"No more crazy than you insisting he's having an affair."

The sunlight punched down hard, like yellow fists, or golden pistons in a vast machine my father had made. I closed my eyes to slits as I walked to the pool, a fast, awkward step, my feet curled to minimize contact with the searing concrete.

I jumped into the pool. Cool silence enveloped me as I drifted down to the bottom. The pressure hurt my ears, but I liked the solitude down there. Up above, torsos and legs dangled from a shimmering quicksilver surface.

When I finally rose in a wreath of bubbles and broke the surface to gasp for air, I heard my sister call my name. "John!" she yelled.

I splashed to the edge. "You weren't supposed to jump in," Jane said, glancing over her shoulder. "Dad's just left. Get out. Now."

I elbowed out of the water. Jane didn't give me a chance to dry myself off, but grabbed my arm and towed me to the parking lot. We saw our father getting into a red economy sedan. Behind the wheel was a woman with black hair. "That's her," Jane said.

I squinted. "Is she pretty?"

"John!"

The car pulled out of the parking lot, and we ran to our bicycles. On Plumb Island, you could leave your bike unlocked, and it wouldn't get stolen. We pedaled after the car, our legs churning like eggbeaters. I was uncomfortably aware of the clammy wet nylon of my bathing suit against the hard seat of my bike.

Plumb-with-a-B Island was not big, and the speed limits were low. Even so, the car was soon three blocks ahead. Jane abruptly turned to the right. "Follow me!" she called.

The street went past the butt end of tourist shops and up the slope of Floursack Mountain. As we chugged up to the top, I looked to my left. I spotted the car as it sped out of town, toward the rubble of The Frying Fish, toward the boarded-up lead mine.

I caught up with Jane about halfway to the summit. The sky was laced with thin clouds, and surrounding the island was the steel of the sea, sparkling with rhinestones in the sun. "They're going to the lead mine," I said, panting.

"No, they're not," Jane said, pointing. I followed the arrow of her arm and saw the red car, a toy in the distance. It had slowed down and crept off the two-lane asphalt road, now disappearing down a dirt road into the shadows of the forest.

We coasted down the slope and into the forest. Sheltered by trees, the air was cool and dim. About a mile along the dirt road, we came to a handful of buildings, like tin shacks, but each about seventy feet long. I had noticed them before when I had ridden through the forest.

"What do you think's in there?" Jane asked. Now it was my turn to lift my arm and point. The red car that had carried our father away was parked fifty yards ahead next to one of the corrugated tin walls.

We leaned our bikes against a tree. Jane shushed me as we walked in a crouch along the corrugated tin wall of the shack. One door was open. Jane shook her head, and we circumnavigated the shack until we found another door. This one was padlocked. "We have to go back," I whispered.

Jane whispered back, her breath tickling my ear. "Have faith in your sister." She knelt down. Between her feet was a single chunk of brick. Just a bit of debris, but like a magic trick, Jane turned it over and smiled as bright metal flashed. A key. With all the deliberation of a World War II sapper, Jane eased the key into the padlock, turned it slow, slow, *slow*, until it clicked.

And then.

She slowly.

Opened.

The door...

The air inside was warm and humid. Light fell from a parade of bare bulbs down the center of the ceiling. From the far end, we heard the faint, brook-like murmuring of voices: our father, and the woman. There was the hum and intermittent gasp of machinery. Little rivulets of perspiration ran down around my ribs.

Most of the interior was taken up by a vast blue tarp, almost big enough to cover a basketball court, and it covered a high, long mound of sand or pale clay, almost reaching the ceiling, just below the pearl-string of light bulbs. An extension cord snaked over the bare, cold concrete.

The sound of metal on metal caused my heart to jitter, and Jane whispered, "Get down." I flattened myself against the pile of earth. It was moist and warm, and it stirred. I yelped and jumped back, and I would have yelled more if Jane hadn't clamped her hand over my mouth, because I finally saw what was under the tarp.

It was a woman—a huge woman. I thought maybe it was a giant inflatable figure, but then she breathed out, and I knew it was a real woman, flesh and sinews and skin and guts, lying flat on her back and naked beneath the tarp.

The sight of her plucked at my heart, like those blues guitarists my mother loved so much, causing something blunt and full of pain to ring inside me.

"Jesus, Marx, and Darwin," my sister whispered. She grabbed my hand, her fingers like pliers.

The Asian woman who had driven my father here said, "Did you hear something?" Her words were excruciatingly clear. I tried to hold still, but my heart beat so hard that my whole body vibrated.

My father said, "I don't think..." Then we heard his footsteps.

Jane nudged me. We sprinted for the door. The bulk of the vast woman and the tarp hid us from view. As we ran, my foot snagged on the extension cord. For a moment, it went taut, like a guitar string, and then pulled loose.

As we burst through the door out into the cool forest air, the hum of machinery stopped, leaving a dead, cottony silence, as if all the birds in a forest had suddenly stopped singing. I thought I heard the woman under the tarp exhale, a long, slow, sigh, and a sulfurous wind followed us, smelling like rotten onions.

And my father said, quite loudly, "Oh, boy."

I stood just outside the door, frozen as if in the middle of Antarctica. Jane had dashed ahead to her bike. She frantically flapped her hand at me to follow.

We grabbed our bikes and skidded behind the first shed. Peeking around the corner, we saw my father and the Asian woman rush outside. She *was* pretty, I decided.

"Please," my father said.

"I have no choice," said the woman, digging in her purse.

"But the major said if there were another incident—" Inside the shed, something smashed against the wall, causing it to bow outwards. Both my father and the woman jumped away.

A groaning noise came from inside the shed, and a huge pink fist smashed through the roof. "You don't call this an incident?!" the woman shouted at my father. She yanked open the car door and slid inside.

My father looked at the shed as the car engine cranked to life. He was being pulled in two directions; I could see him being stretched, like a rubber toy. Then he got in the car.

Jane grabbed the back of my shirt and dragged me back around the corner of the shed as the car passed. "We'd better go, too."

"Aww," I said. "I want to watch."

Suddenly, the side of the shed burst open, the corrugated metal walls peeling apart like the skin of rotten fruit, and a shoulder the size of a small car emerged. "They'll never forgive me if I let you get killed," Jane said, still clutching my shirt. "Though it might be worth it to see you squashed like a bug."

We got on our bikes and tore off down the road, following the dust raised by the car. About half a mile away, I stopped and looked back. "Come *on!*" Jane urged me.

But I had to look. I saw the giant woman dragging herself out of the shed, the way an insect crawls from its pupal case. Her deep voice, like the sound of boulders grinding against each other, rumbled through the trees: "AHHHHH..."

"John!" Jane screamed. The terror in her voice hooked my heart and dragged me away.

I had never ridden so fast in my life, pumping the pedals of my bike until my legs filled with lead. At the hotel, puffing and drenched with sweat, we threw down our bikes and ran to the pool.

We found our mother sitting up. "There you are," she said, folding up her towel. "Your father is frantic again for some reason, looking for you. He usually doesn't panic this easily. I said there wasn't any trouble you could get into. He said there's another 'tornado' alert."

"He's right," I said.

"We have to go," Jane said. "Now."

Our mother slid her dark glasses down her nose. "Now you two are in on it? What's going on?"

"We saw it," I said.

"The tornado? In *that* sky?" Shielding her eyes with a hand, she looked to the heavens.

My father called across the pool, "There you are!" His voice crackled with anxiety. "We're going. NOW." Holding Robbie against his chest, as if Robbie were a real boy, he gestured frantically with his free hand to us, as if he could sweep us away with his fingers, while from all around the pool, people stared at the madman yelling.

My mother sat there, tapping her toe. My father ran around the pool, his arms sagging under the weight of Robbie. "I thought we were meeting at the car!"

She crossed her arms. "Not until you explain what's really happening."

Sweat beaded on his creased forehead. "Will you please just trust me?"

"The last time I did, I ended up pregnant with Jane. I accept a lot of your cock-and-bull stories, Alan, but I have my limits. You've even got the kids in on it this time."

He looked at us strangely. "You are?"

Jane nodded. "We saw the, uh, tornado." His eyes widened.

"There's no goddamned tornado, Alan, but there is surely something funny..." My mother stood up, snatched up her purse, a broad leather bag almost large enough to carry Robbie in, and stalked off. We all followed her, almost in a perfect vee, like geese migrating.

Still in her bathing suit, she went to the car and unlocked the driver's side. "I can drive," my father said, but without a word, she held up a hand. He slumped, then slid morosely in the passenger's side, while Jane, Robbie, and I climbed into the back.

Hunched over the wheel, my mother revved the engine, and our old station wagon jerked backwards out of the parking space. She spun around 180 degrees and stepped on the gas. My head banged against the ceiling as we went over a speed bump. "Buckle up!" she yelled as we sped out of the parking lot. Ahead of us, a police car tore past, siren flashing arterial red, and she smoothly swung the station wagon around to follow.

"The ferry's the other way," my father said. My mother said nothing, but in the rearview mirror, I could see that her lips were tightly pursed. "Anne..."

"We're not going to the ferry," she announced. "We're going to see the tornado. Kids, you want to see a tornado, don't you?"

Jane and I exchanged glances. "I want to see the tornado!" Robbie chirped.

"Anne, please, this is not a good idea."

"Of course not," she snapped. "It's a stupid idea. But I like my stupid ideas, because they're mine, and not foisted on me as if I were some idiot."

We rocketed down the main street behind the police car. Each word from my father's mouth, begging my mother to turn around, seemed to crank her shoulders closer together, to ratchet her determination one notch tighter.

Overhead, a helicopter clacked. "Is that the weather copter?" my mother shouted, craning her head close to the window. Her voice was gay, almost cackling. She sounded like Margaret Hamilton as the Wicked Witch in *The Wizard of Oz.*

In front of us, the police car pulled sideways, lights pulsing, to block the road. My mother glided us to a stop, threw the automatic transmission into park, and slid out of the car.

The enormous woman from the shed was sprawled across the road, a mountain of bare, quivering flesh. Unable to stand, she must have dragged herself along the road. A dark stain trailed behind her. As we tumbled out of our station wagon, she shrugged herself forward a few more yards. She couldn't even lift her Winnebago-sized head, but rolled her face on the roadway.

My father stood in front of all of us, his arms spread wide. "We, uh, shouldn't stay here. It doesn't look safe."

Behind him, the enormous woman moaned, the way an ocean or a continent might. "AAAHHHH..." She sounded to be in pain, a pain that fractured her bones and squashed her internal organs as surely as gravity. Her eyes flickered open—they looked like boiled eggs—and she moaned again. "AAAHHH ... AAHHHLLAAANNN."

Her hand scraped forward, across the rough asphalt and toward my father. My father turned red, and my mother's forehead creased. It was a warm, sunny day, but she shivered a bit in her bathing suit and crossed her arms. "Is that...?" my mother began, frowning, a little V etched on her forehead.

"AHHLLLAAANNNNN," the giant woman said again.

My mother turned and faced my father. If you took liquid poison and froze it, you might capture the look on her face. "You," she said, and each of the words she snapped off, brittle and hard. "Son. Of. A. Bitch!" She raised a hand, as if she were going to slap him. He flinched, but didn't move, didn't protest; he was ready to receive her slap. That seeming admission caused my mother to sag.

"That's her, isn't it?" she said. "You dragged us all the way here... It *is* her. It's her."

Schrödinger's Wife

"Her name," my father said, "is Sophia, and she was dying." He told us the story as we drove home, only because my mother made him.

After we had encountered Sophia sprawled on the road, with the island police scratching their heads and helicopters clacking angrily, we returned to the motel room, packed, and left. My mother had insisted on driving.

"You shouldn't drive when you're mad," my father said.

"In that case, I might never drive again."

My mother didn't get out of the car, not even on the ferry crossing. "If I did, I might throw myself into the sea," she said as she drummed her fingers on the steering wheel. None of us got out, just sat crammed in the station wagon. The car smelled sour, with twelve hundred miles yet to go.

As my mother steered us off the ferry and onto the asphalt Mississippi of the interstate, she announced that our father would explain. Everything.

My father, sitting in the front passenger seat, squirmed worse than Jane or me. "I don't think the kids need to hear all this..."

"Yes, they do. No more secrets. Secrets will kill you. Light me a cigarette, will you?"

So, with an expression on his face suggesting the story was being extracted with dental pliers, my father spoke. "I... Well, I knew Sophia back in college."

My mother jabbed him with her elbow, swerving the car a bit as she did. "The *whole* truth, Alan. You didn't just 'know' her. She was your girlfriend."

"Yes," he said, his voice soggy with misery, "I had girlfriends before you. And Sophia was one of them."

"How like you to fall for a woman named Sophia," Jane said.

"Who's a woman named Sophia?" Robbie asked.

"Shh, don't interrupt," my mother said. "Go on, Alan."

"We dated for three years."

"You're still leaving stuff out." Over her shoulder, she called out to us, "She was the love of his life."

"I don't know I would put it that way," my father said. He stared at his hands in his lap, as if this were a test, and he, cheating, had inked answers on them.

"Explain why you broke up." My mother took the cigarette out of her mouth and tapped the ashes out the window. "Jesus in a three-piece suit, I'm having to interview you. Tell them the whole sad story, the way you did on *our* first date. For three hours."

"Okay, okay," my father mumbled.

As he explained, Sophia's father had died suddenly during her junior year. Her family finances a mess, Sophia had to abruptly leave Princeton and return home to Los Angeles. When my father decided to attend MIT for grad school, Sophia had broken up with him. "A few years ago," my father said, "she contacted me. She had stage four breast cancer and wanted to—"

My mother hit him again with her elbow, so hard I could hear the "oof" as the breath was driven from his lungs. "Whoa, whoa, whoa, mister!" she shouted. "You're leaving out part of the story."

"Anne..."

"Say it. *Say it!*"

He leaned forward and pressed his forehead on the dashboard. "I saw her before that," he said, his voice subdued, "when Jane was still a baby." He paused. When he spoke again, his voice came out strangled, as if the syllables were barbed wire and were catching in his throat. "We ... that is, I... Well, you could say we had an affair."

"'You could say,'" my mother repeated, her voice high and mocking. "'You *could* say...'"

"You could say," Robbie echoed cheerily.

"I broke it off! It was wrong, and I broke it off."

"Very thoughtful of you. Well, kids, any questions? For your thoughtful father?"

Jane leaned forward. "So ... do we have any half-brothers or sisters?"

When Sophia had contacted my father, she had meant to say goodbye. But he had the experimental serum, the same one I'd injected into Ernie. She had been reluctant. But when she was in hospice, pain eating her up like a shark, and the doctors had given her less than a week to live, she consented, and he smuggled in a syringe. "This was before we knew what happened to your lizard."

"His name's Ernie," I said. "And actually, Ernie was yours. Paul is mine. He's the control."

"Yes, yes." He explained that the drug was intended not to kill tumor cells, but to encourage them to differentiate normally as skin, lungs, bones. That part worked. But the out-of-control growth continued and accelerated, causing gigantism in both Ernie and Sophia.

He turned to my mother. "I was just trying to save a life."

"And you dragged us all the way here, so you could be with her."

He rubbed at his face. "After we captured, um, Ernie, and I learned he'd also been injected with the serum, we moved him to Plumb Island as well."

"Is Ernie okay?" I asked. "You didn't dissect him, did you?"

"No, we only took tissue samples." He paused. "If we could figure out how to control the gigantism…"

"There you go," my mother said as she flicked her cigarette out the window. "Always finding a way to turn betrayal into heroism."

My father's explanation left me feeling less enlightened and more dizzy, the way I did after a roller coaster. As the miles until home dwindled, I wondered what would happen when we pulled into the driveway. Jane, while both smug and horrified for having been right all along, instead focused on our father's treatment of Sophia. "He kept her *naked*, under a *tarp*," she kept saying to me, with increased intensity each time. "I mean, we all know he has the emotional sensitivity of a jar of formaldehyde, but I'd never have thought he'd keep a former girlfriend under a tarp … naked."

But when we arrived home, our mother got out of the car looking dazed. (When we'd stopped overnight, she had slept in the car, claiming my father would drive off without her, and he in turn had worried aloud that she would drive off without him, so that every stop, including gas and bathroom breaks, required tense negotiation over the car keys.) She staggered like a zombie into the house.

My father barked at Jane and me to unload the suitcases. After we dutifully dragged them inside, I fell upon my bed. I heard Paul scrabble in his terrarium, and my father turning on the shower, then I fell asleep.

I had a dream where Mrs. Jarcyznski had grown huge, and we all had to sit outside on the playground for math, when I woke up with my father shaking my shoulder. "John. John. Have you seen your mother?" Fuzzy with sleep, I struggled to sit up. His mouth tightened. "I can't find her. Help me look."

Jane went up into the attic while I crawled under the house. It was only when my father tried the door from the kitchen to the garage that we located her.

"I locked it," my mother said from the other side as he rattled the doorknob. "I changed the lock," she added.

"Were you planning this?" my father demanded.

"Don't bother calling a locksmith. I fixed it so it can't be picked."

My father paced back and forth in the kitchen. "There's a lot of dangerous equipment out there."

He was talking to himself, but my mother called out from behind the door, "And yet you encourage Johnny to play out here."

He stared at the door, as if willing himself into x-ray vision. "Why are you in the garage? Are you doing something out there?"

"It'll be a surprise!" she sang, stretching the last word into three notes.

She spent a week out there, refusing to open the door or to see any of us. My father pressed his ear against the door. "I can hear her moving around," he reported.

One night, I awoke and heard a floorboard downstairs creaking. Sliding out of bed, I tiptoed downstairs and found my mother rooting through the refrigerator. "Oh, hi, Johnny," she said when she closed the door, her arm full of sandwich makings.

My father was curled up by the door to the garage, hugging a pillow and snoring. "It'd be sweet," my mother said, "if it weren't for the other thing." She looked awful. There were bruise-like bags under her eyes, and her dark brown hair shot out in every direction.

On the tile countertop, which had images of mice and bunnies dancing among carrots and potatoes, she laid out cold cuts and slathered mayo and mustard on a slice of rye bread. "Good thing your father is a sound sleeper," she said.

"He's worried about you" was all I could think to say.

"Sweetie, it's not your job to play peacemaker," she said, humming as she sliced off big hunks of onion.

I handed her a small brown package. "This came in the mail for you," I said. "I didn't open it or anything."

"Good boy."

"It's from Upton, New York. That's where Brookhaven National Lab is, isn't it?"

"No flies on you, kiddo."

In front of her, she had a piece of paper, covered with her broad, looping handwriting and honeycomb drawings. "Those look like benzene rings," I said.

"Such a clever boy. Yes, I love benzene rings. So elegant, so useful." She lifted her left hand. "You know, your father had our wedding bands designed as benzene rings. He knew how much I love them." She shrugged and bit into her sandwich. "The last few days, I've been brushing up on my chemistry."

In the morning, I reported this conversation to my father. He took off his glasses and wiped them. "Well, if she has a project to distract herself with..."

At the end of a week, the door to the garage flew open, and my mother appeared, looking worse than before. The dark circles under her eyes had acquired a purple bruise-like color. Her singed, wild hair would have given Medusa a fright. And it was all accompanied by a whiff of sulfur and something worse, a repulsive metallic tang.

"Anne, what were you doing in the lab?" my father asked, adding hastily, "Not that I mind, but you haven't stepped through that door in years."

"Yes, and I was afraid I'd lost my touch. This was a challenging problem, the most perplexing in my career. It almost defeated me. And then, BOOM!" she shouted as she slapped her hand on the kitchen table, making us all jump. "I saw how to do it! In the end, it only took a few hours."

She held up a vial, which contained a few drops of a liquid with a faint green tint. "This is aurous trimethylated perchloric sulfide."

My father frowned. "Aurous? You mean—"

"Yes: gold." She put the vial close to her eyes and stared into the liquid. "It's not easy to get compounds out of gold, and this compound wasn't even designed for gold. And for extra points," she announced, as if submitting something to the state fair, "it's not just any gold. I used gold-196, which has a half-life of almost two hundred days. I've still got a few friends at national labs with access to obscure isotopes. And when it decays..."

"To platinum?" my father said.

"Most of the time. But nearly ten percent decays to mercury."

"Mercury!" my father exclaimed. He frowned. "But mercury compounds..."

"Are often deadly poisons," my mother finished, her voice sing-song as she caressed the vial. "And this is one of the deadliest. A single molecule can cause a chemical chain reaction that will shut down the central nervous system." Her long fingers twisted the black screw top of the vial. "In other words, all it needs is for one of those gold atoms to self-transmute to mercury..." And she put the vial to her lips.

My father tried to stop her, but was too late. All he accomplished was to knock her to the floor. "Are you crazy?!" my mother shouted from underneath him. "If you had gotten even the tiniest drop on yourself, it would have been fatal! What if one of the kids touched it? Christ at a carnival, Alan, sometimes you don't think." She pushed my father off her and wiped her mouth with the back of her hand. "Fortunately, I think I got it all."

I said in a choked voice, "Do you mean it won't—"

She seemed to notice me for the first time, and her eyes shimmered. "Oh, Johnny. What a terrible, terrible mother I am, letting you see that. No. I am a walking, talking, nucleo-chemical time bomb." She stood up and brushed herself off. "It may be ten minutes, it may be ten years, but I am dead, no matter what. Let's enjoy the time we have left together."

After swallowing the toxin, my mother seemed to relax and cheer up. The rest of us watched her as if she were a grenade that might explode at any moment, but she mocked us by singing show tunes and getting Robbie to sing along with her. The crazy whirl of feelings inside me slowly turned to numbness, and I would have questioned whether it had even happened if I didn't see the same haunted look on the faces of Jane and our father.

Summer was coasting to its end, and for the first time ever, our mother drove Jane and I to the mall to pick out new clothes for the beginning of school. Normally, I would have rolled my eyes, but I was too afraid to resist, as if by placating her, I might postpone the inevitable.

She even badgered us to play her favorite game. It was like Monopoly, only using the periodic table. "... three, four, five. Chlorine," my father said, moving his piece, a little Bunsen burner.

"That's mine," my mother said. "And I've got a vacancy. Gimme an electron."

My father sighed and handed it over. "I'm down to only three."

Jane rolled. "Ha!" I said. "That's my dysprosium. And my shell is only half filled."

Jane stuck out her tongue at me. "You're coming to the lanthanides," she said as I scooped up the die. "Whole lot of vacancies there."

"Is it my turn again?" my father asked. He landed on my germanium, but I had a filled shell, so he had to roll again. Then he landed on my mother's gadolinium.

"Five vacancies," she said, smacking her lips. "Five! Count 'em. You owe me five electrons."

"I'm out," my father said, pushing over the stack of electron chips. "If we really wanted to emulate electrons, we ought to have probability amplitudes. Then the electron could be half on germanium and half on gadolinium."

"Like Schrödinger's cat," I said. "Poor cat."

"Like this weirdo family," Jane mumbled. "Half genius, and half insanity. Half overcooked comedy, and half cold, black tragedy. Half love, and half violence."

"Sweetie," my mother said, scooping the pile of electrons toward herself, "all families are like that."

You skipped sixth grade, you've told me. Lucky you. My first day of sixth grade started pretty good, despite the butterfly-piranha chimeras churning in my stomach. I had just sat down in Mrs. Suzuki's class when I felt a feather-light touch on my shoulder. I turned around, and my heart sped up at seeing Becky.

"Hi, John."

"Hi," I said, desperately thinking of something to say. "So ... is Bruce in this class?"

Her smile faded a bit. "No, he's in Mr. Mavros's class." She brightened. "But at least he got out of fifth grade. Finally! All summer, he couldn't stop talking about how grateful he is for what you did for him."

My face grew warm. She looked shyly at her feet and said, "Maybe this year, you can help me with math, too, like you helped Bruce last year."

I have to admit, I had a funny, happy, squirming feeling inside.

After school, I ran home, so excited that I don't think I could have walked if a policeman had fastened a ball and chain to my ankle. I banged through the front door and skidded to a stop in the kitchen.

My mother lay on the linoleum, like a display mannequin that had been knocked over, arms stiff by her sides, eyes staring upwards at the ceiling, mouth slightly open. My father sat on the floor next to her, holding her hand. His eyes were red as raw beef from crying. "She was already cold when I found her."

I felt like I had walked off a cliff, like that moment before you fall, and fall, and fall, and the ground is rushing up to smash you...

I heard Jane tromp in. "Hello? Who left this door open? Why not just put out a sign saying, FREE TO THIEVES—" I felt her come up behind me. "Oh, shit." She pushed past me. "I thought she was bluffing. I thought she faked it. I thought..." And she trailed off. She shook visibly for a moment, her entire body trembling, as if shock and grief might burst her apart.

Still shaking, she staggered towards the phone. "No!" my father said. He looked up at us, his face slick with tears and contorted with emotion. "Not yet. Please. I'm not ready to let go. I don't want her taken away. Not yet."

He cradled my mother's head in his lap. "I'm so sorry," he whispered. "You deserved better from me." He said in a louder voice, "She was right about me. I didn't tell her, didn't admit it, but when Sophia first contacted me, she and I, we..."

"I don't want to hear this," Jane said, clapping hands over her ears. "La la la la..."

My father hugged my mother's body and wouldn't let us use the phone.

"It's going to be hard to explain why we didn't call right away," Jane said to me. "He could get in a lot of trouble."

"More trouble than when they figure out she was killed by a nuclear-powered toxin?"

Jane and I eventually fell asleep on the couch. When I awoke, the lights were still blazing, but through the windows, it was night. Jane was curled up with her head on the arm of the sofa. My father was sprawled on the carpet, taking slow, heavy breaths.

I smelled burnt eggs. Through the doorway, I saw my mother standing at the stove. I thought I was dreaming. Then she turned, and seeing me, took the cigarette out of her mouth. "You know, I'm suddenly famished. Feel like some eggs, Johnny?"

My father shuddered awake, opening his bleary eyes. He rolled over and saw her at the kitchen stove. "Anne!"

"Hungry?" she asked.

He scrambled to his feet and grabbed her wrist. "I thought you were dead!" he cried, feeling for her pulse. "You *were* dead. You were as cold as the floor. You had no pulse."

"You wish, mister," she said, laughing.

My father wanted my mother to go to the doctor, but again she burst out laughing, a bright spray of merriment that made him wince. "I'm not *sick*," she said, shaking her head.

"Poison control hotline? Bomb squad?"

"Why, Alan," she said, a fox's toothy smile on her face, "I almost believe you'll miss me when I'm gone."

We all rattled around the house like the last few nuts in a jar. Only Robbie was cheerful, regularly breaking out into the show tunes my mother had taught him. My stomach felt like it did the time I got food poisoning. More than once, I ran to the bathroom to throw up. More than once, I didn't bother to go to school.

Big Bruce even called to check in on me. "Just not feeling well," I told him. Bruce said he really liked Mr. Mavros's class and was learning a lot.

A few days later, my father came to my room and sat on my bed. "Listen, John," he said. "I've been thinking. Maybe you should consider going out for a sports team."

"I hate sports," I said. "You hate sports."

"Yes, but we're an insular family. We all sit around here like pickles soaking in brine. It would do you good to get out of the house, make some friends."

Now, as an adult, I realize he was right: I desperately needed friends. But at the time, all I could think was, *Really? Sports? That's your answer?*

"You think being the worst kid on the team, the one most likely to cause the team to lose, would help me make friends?"

He blinked at me. He took his glasses off, and his face looked naked, like a hermit crab pulled from its shell. "I'm sure there must be something you'd be good at. Maybe the chess team? Math team? Debate team?"

"We don't have those," I said slowly. "Budget cuts." In truth, I believed myself fundamentally unable to belong to anything: to a team, to our family, to the world.

A week later, Jane was the one to discover our mother dead. At breakfast time, I heard Jane cry out, and I ran down the stairs two at a time. Our mother was in the family room, face down, one hand stretched toward the TV. My father brushed past me and knelt down to feel for a pulse.

"Um, let's wait and see what happens this time," he said slowly. Checking his watch, he added, "I have a nine o'clock class to teach, but I'll come back right after that."

"You're just going to leave her here dead like this?" Jane asked, incredulous.

"I'm going to make some coffee," he said.

You know, I had a strange childhood.

It was hard to concentrate at school. "What's wrong?" Bruce asked at recess.

"You made a mistake in math," I wanted to tell him, but really, how could I? Would I start by explaining about Sophia and go from there?

When I ran home after school, my mother was still cold on the living room floor. "Can we call 911 now?" Jane asked, trembling with anger.

"Patience," my father urged.

And indeed, by dinnertime, my mother was up and around again. She had a red mark on her face where her cheek had been pressed against the bristly carpet, and she rubbed at it. "Why is everyone staring at me?"

When we explained, my mother said, "You're making that up."

My father, who sat at the kitchen table with hands folded, somberly shook his head. "You weren't breathing. No pulse."

"I'm not listening to this. I don't have to sit here and take it."

"Anne, you were dead. *Again.* I took your temperature this time. You had cooled twenty degrees."

"You're trying to make me feel guilty, when it's really all *your* fault. God-*damn*," she exploded, "you are cruel! Goddamn, god*damn*!" And she whirled up and swept her hand across the disorder of the counter, sending plates and silverware and pots crashing to the floor. "Why? Why are you doing this to me?!"

I stared down at our kitchen table. I wished I could shrink myself down to the size of an ant, to hide between the tight grains of wood, anything so I wouldn't have to listen to this.

"You took that poison," my father said. "You made it, and you took it—"

"It's always my fault, isn't it?"

He took a deep breath. "Anne—"

My mother put up a hand. "All right. Jesus and Mary in a Mercedes. Can we please stop talking about this? It's giving me a headache." She got up and walked away.

But two days later, she was dead again. Jane found her in the back yard. "John! John get out here, right now!" Her voice tugged at my guts, and I banged out through the screen door.

My mother was sprawled out in the scraggly flower patch, trowel in hand. "She hasn't gardened in years," I murmured.

My father was never skilled at reading faces, but when he got home that evening, even he could tell at a glance. "Where is she?" he asked, his mouth a tight pucker.

I pointed out the back door, where Robbie was sitting splay-legged, saying, "Why isn't Mama moving? Why isn't Mama moving?" over and over again.

My father went out the door, and I felt a gust of cool evening air. When he came back inside, he rubbed at his eyes for a moment, then let his shoulders sag. "I suppose I should start dinner."

"Are we just going to leave her out there?" I asked. Without answering, he lit the stove and started chopping onions.

The next morning, Jane said, if we weren't going to call the police or the mortuary, we ought to at least bring her inside.

My father shook his head. "She made this bed, so to speak, she has to sleep in it." He refused to discuss it further. Jane and I looked at each other, shrugged, and set Robbie up as a kind of scarecrow, to keep away birds or any other creature.

"You seem distracted, John," my teacher Mrs. Suzuki said when I slumped into my desk. "Is everything okay?" I shrugged.

Eventually, the last bell rang, and I slouched home. Jane met me at the front door. "We need the wheelbarrow. Oh, and a shovel."

I was still digging when she came out with an armful of her old dolls. "Mourners," she explained. "*He* may be in denial, but we might as well do this proper."

Jane finally declared the hole deep enough, and we rolled our mother into it. At the head of the grave, Jane said, "We remember our mother. She often wasn't a very good mother, but this is a funeral, and at funerals, you lie about people, so let's pretend she was good. I'm sure someday, we'll actually feel sad about her and not so angry all the time." And she gestured for to me to cover her with earth. "Ashes to dust, dust to earth, earth to … something…"

"Hydrogen to helium," I said, taking a shovelful of earth. "Helium to carbon and oxygen. Carbon to magnesium and silicon, silicon to nickel and iron. And then the whole thing implodes."

By the time we trudged inside, the sky had darkened to a livid purple, except for the painterly stripe of red and orange on the western horizon. Jane and I sat on the front porch and watched the autumn stars appear one by one.

"She did love the stars," Jane said. "So, that was nice, what you said, the supernova thingy."

I nodded and watched as a pair of headlights turned into our driveway. Our father got out of the car, his glasses reflecting the porch light, and Jane stood and crossed her arms. "Is she up?" he asked.

"Alive, you mean?" Jane said.

He nodded. Jane just stared at him, stone-faced. He pushed past her. A moment later, he returned. "Where is she?" he barked. When Jane didn't answer, he put his hands on her shoulders. "For God's sake, you didn't call—"

She slid out of his grasp. "No," she said, almost spitting. "But she was just *lying* there, in the flower bed. What if the neighbors saw?"

"She wasn't in line of sight," he said. "I checked."

"And you decided to punish her by leaving her—"

"What was I supposed to do? I know this is hard on you, honey, hard on both you and John—"

"But not on Robbie," I said, "because he only simulates emotion."

"He's not the only one around here who only simulates emotion," Jane snapped.

"That's a low blow," my father said. "That's really unfair."

Jane raised her voice. "Unfair? Do you know what's *unfair* around here? You—"

She was interrupted by the sound of the back door slamming. My father turned his head. "Robbie?"

No answer, but the floorboards creaked. My father yanked open the front screen door. Jane and I followed him inside. At the back door, we saw muddy footprints, trailing into the kitchen. "Hey, gang," my mother said from the stove. "What do people want for dinner?"

My mother kept shaking dirt out of her dress. "God dammit," she said. "It's gotten down in my underwear, too."

She leaned across the kitchen table. "Can't you do something, Alan?" she asked. "This is awful. Look, I promise, I cross my heart, I won't pull a stunt like this again." When my father shook his head, she said, "Can't you, like, irradiate me with neutrons or something?"

"I don't think that will work," my father said quietly. "One of those gold atoms, I'm guessing, is already in a quantum superposition. Half gold, half mercury. But because we can't observe it, the wave function doesn't fully collapse. And so, here you are..."

"Half alive and half dead," my mother said, bitterness on her tongue. A tear trickled down her face, leaving behind a thin, muddy track. "You won't do anything?"

"Anne—"

"All right!" she snarled. "You *can't* do anything. I'm *doomed* to this ... this twilight existence." She buried her head in her arms, rocking from side to side.

Then she lifted her face, her eyes red and her cheeks smeared with muddy tears. "I'm not going to go on like this." She stood up and yanked open the utensil drawer so hard that it came out and fell to the floor. Knives, forks, and mismatched spoons skittered across the linoleum. Snatching up a knife, she held it to her wrist.

My father stood, too. "Anne, there's no need to be dramatic."

"Oh, I think we're way past that point." Closing her eyes and grimacing, she pressed the blade against her wrist.

But as if it were a rubber joke knife, the steel blade turned upward, coming loose from the handle and clattering to the floor. My mother opened an eye. "Huh..." she said. "Huh."

The knives disappeared from the kitchen after that—all but the butter knives. I did see my mother sitting at the kitchen table, testing one of the butter knives against her forearm, but it just made pathetic pink tracks. Looking up, she said, "Look what that bastard has reduced me to." She paused. "You never were in the Boy Scouts, were you, Johnny?" I shook my head. "Too bad. Still... You know anything about knots?"

After that comment, all the rope and string disappeared from the house, as well as all the spare electrical cords. The remaining electrical cords for lamps and appliances were nailed down firmly.

I caught my mother trying to tug one up from the floor. "Little help here?" she said, then knelt down, popped the end of a cord from a socket, and bent her face down to it. "Maybe you shouldn't watch this," she said, but I couldn't look away as she put her mouth to the socket.

There was a sharp *crack!* and she flew back, almost halfway across the room. I ran to help her up, feeling guilty that I hadn't tried to restrain her. There were black smudges and red burn marks around her mouth.

"Ow," she said indistinctly. "'ell, tha' 'as s'ange."

The next day, she was dead again, lying on the living room floor, her hand clutching a glass, eyes open and staring through the ceiling to a distant galaxy. I stepped over her, turned off the TV, and went up to my room to do my history homework. A few hours later, I heard the TV come back on, and she was up smoking a cigarette and reading a book.

A few days later, she tried running a hose from the car's exhaust pipe to the interior. The engine blew a gasket. My father said to my mother, "And where will we get the money to fix that?"

Life felt underwater then, like we were all holding our breath. We hardly spoke; words were razors, and we might cut ourselves or one another with them.

At school, Becky, sitting behind me, whispered, "You okay?" Those words stabbed my heart. More than anything, I wanted to tell her, but how could I? I just shrugged.

"Bruce is doing really well now," Becky went on, her words soft and musical as a lullaby, the kind my mother never sang to me. "He even got a B on his last math quiz."

Part of me was jealous that they each had someone to confide in: Bruce, whose father's "business trip" had gone on for years, and his mother deaf in one ear, and Becky... I didn't know what grief she carried, but she had Bruce to talk to, while I had no one—yet another rock added to the cairn of sorrows weighing me down.

I was rereading *Tom Sawyer* when Jane knocked on my door. "You busy?"

I put my thumb on a page. "Why?"

Jane jerked her head upwards. "She's on the roof."

We went outside. My father squinted up at my mother as if she were an airplane high in the sky. He called up to her, "I thought you didn't want the neighbors to watch. I'm sure they can see everything now."

It was mid-October. It had rained all the previous week, and although the sky was now blue and clear, the roof was still wet and slippery, and she had to shift cautiously from foot to foot. Wearing a sleeveless yellow dress, one of her favorites, she shivered and clasped her bare arms.

"They aren't outside," she reported. "Jesus, I think I can see the university from here, Alan."

"That's good," my father said. "Now, why don't you just climb back inside the attic?"

"What did you do to me, Alan?" she called down. "I'm half dead, but I can't seem to finish the job."

My father stared for a moment at the weeds growing in our yard like a bad haircut. He called up, "I think that's just it. Quantum mechanically, you are between life and death. The cause of your death has already been established. So—and I'm guessing here—you can't die any other way." The corner of his mouth twisted into a superposition of smile and frown. "The wave function is a jealous mistress, and so it's become a hundred percent improbable that anything other than that poison will kill you."

"Oh, yeah?" my mother's voice floated down. "Let's see about that." She lifted one leg, like a soldier goose-stepping, and tilted forward.

"Anne, no!" My father's hands shot up in the air, and I felt my own heart nearly leap out of my chest as she toppled forward and off the roof.

But the back edge of her dress caught on the gutter, and with a sharp jerk, her plunge abruptly halted. She dangled there, swinging slowly back and forth, her bare legs pale in the late autumn sun, her ivory-colored underpants completely visible. "Oh, Christ in a Cadillac," my mother said. "Alan—"

"Yes," he said, his voice heavy with the burdens he'd carried all through the years. "I'll call the fire department."

Fission

As my father strapped me into a chair out in the garage, I asked, "Are you sure this will help?"

"Well, your mother's depressed."

Jane snorted. "Her problems are bigger than that."

"She's angry," I said. I left out, *"at you."* I left out a lot of things.

My father shook his head. "Depression is a misfiring of the brain. The brain is a soup of chemicals, neurotransmitters, regulating the firing of neurons. I don't know brain chemistry." He waved a pair of electrical cables. "But I do know electricity."

He had me watch sad movies, then zapped me—"just a little"—when I felt a twinge of sadness. But frankly, none of it felt as sad as what I had been living through. "Now?" he asked.

"No," I said. "Not sad. I like the guy playing the piano. And the fat guy. Don't we have a color TV?"

"The movie is in black and white." He leaned forward with the cables.

"I'm not sad!"

I felt sad when King Kong tumbled off the Empire State Building. When the Oxygen Destroyer stripped Godzilla's flesh in Tokyo Bay. When the burning castle fell in upon Frankenstein's monster. I suppose it says a lot about my life that I felt more kinship with monsters than with ordinary people. I was reluctant to tell my father any of this, of course.

With Jane, he tried a powerful magnetic field, placing a massive coil like a copper turban upon her head. "Whoa!" she said.

"Do you feel different?"

"No, it's hot. Ow! Get it off! It's burning! Can't you smell my hair burning?"

For his third trial, he wanted to try a combination of electric and magnetic fields. "Okay, John, you're up. In the chair."

I sighed and climbed in. My father picked up the paper and ran his finger down the TV listings. "Eight o'clock, channel seven," I said swiftly. *"Old Yeller."*

But before he could turn on the TV, the door to the garage slammed open. "What's going on here?" my mother demanded. A shower of dirt rained onto the floor.

"Just a little experiment," my father mumbled without looking at her.

"On the *kids*?" my mother shouted. "And ... is that *high voltage*?"

"It was for your sake..." my father protested.

"I don't care if it would save the Earth from a killer plague, or a killer asteroid, or goddamned killer hemorrhoids!" my mother said, waving her arms.

"Okay, okay. I've got another line anyway." He cleared his throat and cleaned his glasses on the edge of his shirt. Giftwasser College, he told us, just up the road, was shutting down their primate research facility and looking for homes for their experimental animals. "They're trying to place them all in primate retirement facilities, but so many research labs are shutting down, there's an excess of primates."

"A glut of gorillas," I quipped.

"Well, chimps mostly. I've got one already picked out..."

"Oh, God, Alan, no," my mother groaned. "No."

My mother had her own mad scientist experiments to perform. She tried hanging herself; the rope broke. She sat in a bathtub full of water and dropped in a hair dryer; a transformer blew two blocks away, darkening half our town. She found her father's old Army-issue pistol, but bought the wrong caliber of bullets. With her death entangled with a capricious, radioactive ion of gold, she continued to both live and die, just not on her own terms.

It also made for some very strange dinner conversation.

"Get this," my mother said. "I bought some Drano, but it turned out to be salt. Just plain table salt. Sure, it tasted salty, but how was I to know what Drano is supposed to taste like? I threw it up, and then I drove to the store and complained. The manager—this little rat-faced man with a little ratty mustache, so oily you could lubricate the car with him—he apologizes, says it's a one-in-a-million switch. The company that makes Drano also makes salt, it turns out. But then he gets this funny look on his face and asks how I *know* it's salt. So, I stare him down and tell him I may look like a frumpy housewife, but I have a PhD in chemistry. 'Oh, of course, ma'am,' he says, bleating 'ma'am' like a sheep. *Maaaam*."

"*Maaaam,*" Robbie echoed.

"That's right," she said, laughing. "*Maaaaaam.* That's exactly how he sounded."

Jane pushed back from the table, the legs of her chair scraping across the linoleum. "Ask to be excused first," my father murmured, staring at the dunes of instant mashed potatoes laced with canned green beans on his plate.

"Excused?" Jane snapped. "What's *her* excuse? I liked it better when you were experimenting on John and me. I liked the electric shocks better than the torture *she's* inflicting on the whole family." Jane's face had reddened, and her hair flew away from her face. Except for the color of her hair, she looked just like our mother.

"You haven't even touched your dinner," our mother protested. "I slaved over it for a good half hour."

"How do I know you didn't put Drano into it? Or rat poison?"

"Jane! You know I would never do anything to hurt any of you!"

"Oh, ha ha," Jane said. "Ha ha ha... That's supposed to be laughter, by the way. You haven't the faintest idea how you're hurting us, torturing us with the way you... How you try..."

Green nausea lurched up inside me, and I ran to the bathroom and vomited in the toilet. My eyes flooded with hot tears. I was kneeling there, panting, smelling stomach acid, when my mother came in and sat on the tile floor next to me.

"Oh, Johnny," she said, stroking my head. "Oh, Johnny..."

We sat in silence for a while. She reached up, wet a washcloth, and wiped my mouth. "I always hated throwing up," she said. "The loss of control. My body rebelling." She ran the cool, wet cloth across my forehead. "That's how I felt when I learned about your father and *her.* This uncontrollable, nasty, bitter rage burning my throat and my mouth and everything. I'm still out of control. I'm dead, then I'm not dead, and I can't stop it, and I can't hasten it." She leaned her head against mine.

In a small voice, I said, "It feels like everything is out of control now."

She put an arm around me. "I know, John. I know."

The week after Halloween, the chimpanzee arrived. My feelings were mixed. After all, it was my mother's attempts at self-destruction that had led to my father getting a chimp, but on the other hand, *we were getting a chimpanzee,* which seemed far more interesting than a mere venomous lizard.

"Come on out, little fella," my father said to the furry creature cowering in its cage. He proffered a banana. "Aren't you hungry?"

"Maybe it doesn't like bananas," Jane said. "Maybe that's just a stereotype."

I leaned in close to the cage. "What's his name?" I asked.

My father held up the shipping invoice. "Pankakos," he said. "Probably a pun, as the scientific name for chimpanzee is *Pan troglodytes.*"

"Pan-kak-" I tried out. "Pankoke..."

"Isn't 'troglodyte' an insult," Jane asked, "for someone considered subhuman?"

"It means 'cave dweller,'" my father said, "and, well ... chimpanzees *are* subhuman."

Jane put her hands on her hips and thrust out her chin. "Maybe chimpanzees think *humans* are subchimpanzee. After all, do chimpanzees torture humans for knowledge?"

My father's face reddened a bit. "Scientists don't mistreat their experimental subjects. It would ruin the data." He sighed. "But sometimes so-called animal rights activists will get a job at a laboratory and then make experiments look like abuse and mistreatment. In fact, little Pankakos's research lab was closed because of just such a drummed-up scandal."

Jane crossed her arms. "You're only making my point for me. He's probably expecting you to stick him with a needle, or to electrocute him at any moment."

My father sighed. "You're exaggerating, Jane."

"Well, you did electrocute *me*," I pointed out. "And he does look scared. Come on out, Pan...ko...ka..."

My father thrust the banana forward again, and the chimp shrank farther into a corner. "Stop shoving that in his face," Jane said. "I know I'd hate it if someone did that."

My father lowered the banana. "Well, maybe we should try some other foods."

I raised my hand. "I know! I'll make an omelet!"

But the chimpanzee just sniffed at the omelet. He shivered when we offered him a tuna salad sandwich, and screeched when I held out a potato chip. Jane rolled an apple into the cage. He picked it up, licked it with a pink tongue, and then threw it back at Jane. It barely missed her head.

At the back of the cupboard, I found a box of instant pancake mix, the just-add-water kind. To me, instant pancakes tasted like fried cardboard, but the chimp's eyes widened when I slid a plate into his cage. With long, hairy fingers, he picked one up, sniffed it, and put it in his mouth. Seconds later, they were all gone.

A second round of pancakes, complete with syrup, lured him out of the cage. "Why don't we call him Pancake?" I suggested. "Easier than Pan...koke..."

My father nodded in agreement, while Jane rolled her eyes. "Great. Another demeaning name."

Jane harangued my father about consent. "*We* could agree to being experimented on. But Pancake..." She made a face every time she said his name. "... can't."

"Well," my father said, "humans are unique for their ability to throw accurately, but also for language."

"And cars and TV," I added.

"Yes, but humans haven't always had cars or TV, whereas we have had language for a long, long time." He took a deep breath. "Grammar is a hard thing. I found that out with Robbie." He rubbed his chin. "I've read that not only do other primates not have language, obviously, but they also can't throw a ball. It occurred to me that the same skill in human brains that allow us to throw balls, rocks, and spears with great accuracy might be related to our ability to form complex sentences with ease. Think about it: throwing a baseball at a batter sixty feet away is an amazing—"

"I can't throw a baseball," I said, "and I talk just fine."

My father ignored this. "The primate intelligence research center at Giftwasser College was thinking along similar lines. They took a baby chimpanzee and taught him how to throw. He became surprisingly skilled at it. He also learned how to form sentences, complex sentences, with sign language. Isn't that right, Pancake?"

The chimp flashed a toothy grin, and his hands flew up birdlike, fingers weaving the air. Jane said, "Uh, do you *know* sign language?"

Our father frowned. "No, I don't."

Pancake repeatedly jabbed the air with a specific finger.

"Hey," I said. "Doesn't that mean—"

"Okay, kids!" our father said, hustling us out. "Better let me get on with my work."

My father soon gave up his attempts to learn sign language, discouraged by Pancake's fondness for obscene signs. Instead, he decided to teach Pancake to write.

The first step was a system of rewards. Out back, he set up a target. Jane and I demonstrated: whenever someone got a ball through the hole in the target, a bell clanged, and a little dollop of syrup was dispensed. Jane got three out of five. I got zero. Pancake rolled around on the ground hooting each time I missed.

"I still think your idea is wrong," I told my father. "Otherwise, baseball pitchers would be writing bestsellers."

The next step was to get Pancake to write with a thumb-sized piece of chalk and a fragment of slate. Jane and I wrote letters, our father rewarding us with syrup. "Oh, God, please," Jane said after a while, grimacing horribly as he thrust the bottle in her face. "No more. I think I'm going to throw up."

"You have to set a good example," our father said.

"You picked the wrong daughter for that."

At first, the endeavor seemed doomed. Pancake's letters looked more like a scattering of pick-up sticks, a cargo-cult version of writing. But when, by accident, he wrote down a legible, if palsied A or T, Pancake was rewarded. When he learned to copy out his whole name, he got a bottle of syrup. Then he learned to write all of our names.

After that, Pancake caught on quickly. I sometimes wonder what drugs he'd been injected with at that lab.

For Christmas, I got a model rocket kit. Jane got a shortwave radio and the copy of *Atlas Shrugged* she had been campaigning for, Robbie got a set of toy trucks, and Pancake got a catcher's mitt and a large marker. He promptly went around the house, writing his name on every surface, until it was taken away. The slate and chalk he was allowed to keep.

Pancake sulked, but a day later he wrote his first sentence on his slate:

JhON SMeLL POO

Chuffing, he showed it to my father.

"What a wonderful Christmas gift!" my father exclaimed. "Only a day late." He handed Pancake a bottle of syrup as a reward.

"Really, that's not even grammatical," I said, peering at the chalkboard. "And he spelled my name wrong."

"Yes," my father said, "but for a chimpanzee, it's positively brilliant!"

Pancake grinned and made an obscene gesture. "Weren't you going to experiment on him or something?" I asked. "Wasn't the idea to electrocute him, rather than me and Jane?"

My father sighed. "I wasn't electrocuting you, exactly, but..." He scratched his head. "Yes, experiment, hmm..."

My mother drifted through the house as if in a parallel dimension, in and out of life and death. Meanwhile, my father, having long before abandoned his original line of research, became increasingly obsessed with testing Pancake's narrative skills. He began by acting out—or enlisting Jane and me to act out—puppet shows. He first asked Pancake which character had done what: who had eaten the pie (the pig), or who had cried (the chicken).

Then he got more sophisticated. He asked who had *wanted* to eat the pie, but didn't (the horse), or who had felt sad (the lamb), or who had lied (the goat). The results thrilled him.

"It shows that chimpanzees have a 'theory of mind,'" he explained over dinner one night, while Pancake ate his meal (pancakes with peas mushed into them. Pancake was busy pushing out the peas with his fingers and dropping them under the table.) He explained that this meant Pancake understood that other creatures had thoughts different from his own, and he could imagine what those thoughts might be. "Many believe a theory of mind is what distinguishes humans from other species, but my study with Pancake destroys that assumption. I've started writing a paper—"

"Does Pancake know that your mind," Jane asked, "is using *his* mind to advance your own career?"

"Does a chimp even know what a career is?" I said, shoving my own set of unmushed peas around the plate.

"Don't slouch," my mother said, without looking up from her book. I couldn't see the whole title—something French, something French, *Perdu*. When we were younger, she'd had a rule of no reading at the table, mostly aimed at my father, but recently, she had sought a shield of her own. "Otherwise, you won't be distinguishable from an ape."

"Well, Searle says..." my father began, only to drift away in a foggy sea of thought. He pushed away from the table. "Hmm... I'd better look that up and make a note of it..."

"Can I be excused too?" I asked.

"Finish your peas," my mother said.

"How about half of them?"

"I'm not going to bargain with you."

Pancake scribbled furiously on his slate and slid it over to me, chuffing. It read:

JohN EET PEES DrINk POOs

"Ha," I said. "Ha."

Jane pulled the slate closer to her. "Hey, that's pretty sophisticated humor. He even seems to understand puns. 'Peas' and 'pee,' and then the connection to poo."

"When I was maybe four, that would have been funny," I grumbled.

"And you're so sophisticated now?" Jane arched an eyebrow.

"I'm sure your father will write a paper on simian comedy," my mother said.

"Better than torturing some poor creature," said Jane.

"Isn't grammar a form of torture?" I asked, and Pancake chuffed. "And sports," I added, but Pancake shook his head.

School returned, along with a cold snap.

"Did you get anything nice for Christmas?" Becky asked me.

"Uh, a rocket."

"That's cool."

I appreciated a woman who understood the appeal of Newton's third law. Then I realized it was my turn to move the conversation forward. "What about you?"

"I got some ice skates. Do you like to skate?"

"I tried a couple of times, but I just fell down and skinned my knees."

"Oh," she said, strangely crestfallen.

I later relayed this conversation to my sister, who punched me in the shoulder. "Moron. She was hinting that she wanted to go ice skating with you. You should have said, 'Why, yes, Becky, my dear, I *love* to go skating! Would you care to accompany me?'"

She put both her hands on my shoulders. "This is what you have to do. You have to invite her for your birthday." My birthday was a couple of weeks away.

"But we never have birthday parties. For good reason."

"Not here, dummy. Out for pizza or something."

I also invited Bruce, because honestly, I was scared for it to seem like a date. I wasn't completely sure what a "date" really was. I had only a hazy idea about holding hands, and maybe kissing.

On the actual day of my birthday, Becky came up to me at school. "I can't come," she said, on the edge of tears. "I ... I got in trouble."

"Oh," I said. I had trouble imagining what Becky could have done wrong. She was always so quiet and compliant.

Bruce came, and we managed to have a good time at the pizza place anyway. Jane came with us, announcing, "Since it's your birthday, I'm not going to tease you one bit."

"Is it true you have a pet monkey?" Bruce asked after eating an entire pepperoni pizza.

"It's an experimental chimpanzee. My father sticks electrodes into his brain and injects him with drugs and all sorts of things."

"Though sometimes he gets John and the chimp mixed up," Jane said, "'cause they look alike."

"Wow," said Bruce. "I wish I had an experimental chimpanzee."

He might have felt differently had he witnessed the scene when we got home. Coming through the door first, I saw my mother stretched out on the living room floor, dead. Robbie was in the corner, his gears whirring as he kept banging into the wall.

And Pancake had lifted up my mother's dress, his head poking under the fabric as if it were a tent. "Pancake!" I yelled.

He grinned at me—which, by the way, is actually a display of aggression in chimps—then pulled down the diaper he wore around the house and pissed on my mother's body.

I froze in horror for a moment, then grabbed a broom from the kitchen and chased him out of the living room.

My father came up behind me. "Oh, boy," he sighed.

My sixth-grade teacher, Mrs. Suzuki, talked to me after the bell rang. Her concern was sweet and gentle, and a dagger to my heart. If she had been tough and unsparing, I could have aimed all my resentment and misery at her.

She said, "Your performance isn't what I expected from you. All your previous teachers told me how smart and quick you are. I see glimpses of that John every now and then. But your work has been barely above average." She smelled of lilacs. Even now, when I smell lilacs, the memory of that conversation and of that year smacks into me, like wet flesh hitting concrete.

"Everything's fine," I said, my words barely audible.

But they weren't fine. My father had done nothing about Pancake. The man had carried my mother's inert form into their bedroom, rolled her into the bathtub, washed and dressed her, then locked the door; but for the chimpanzee, he made excuses.

"He's not a person. He doesn't understand what he's doing."

"You said he has a 'theory of mind,'" Jane said. She sizzled with anger, so electrified you could have charged a battery off her. "You got *Pankakos* so you could experiment with cures for depression—for *her* depression—but then you got derailed into proving that a chimpanzee communicating through writing is more than a parlor trick, that he has a theory of mind, that he understands what he's doing."

My own feelings were so combustible, I was afraid if I said anything, I might burst into flames. For the first time, I questioned where my father's loyalties lay. Yet neither Jane nor I had the courage to tell our mother. We dreaded the apocalypse that might spew forth if we did. To this day, I feel in my gut an icy ball of guilt for my complicit silence.

As spring rolled around, my father watched baseball games with his furry subject to further investigate Pancake's "theory of mind." My father cared for sports as much as I did, which is to say, not at all, but he was intrigued to see how Pancake would respond to the game.

At first, Pancake got excited whenever anyone threw a ball or got a hit, but gradually, my father introduced him to the concept of "his" team to cheer on. After that, Pancake made a show of laughing when his team scored, and blowing a raspberry when any other team did well.

"I've never seen you watch so much TV before," I said one evening.

"All in the name of science," my father said.

From the TV set came the crack of the bat and the staticky roar of the crowd. Pancake bounced up and down on the sofa. "He's just looking to you for cues," I said. "You know you have to leave the room."

My father got up and bent his head to me. "I tried that," he said in a low voice, "but he throws feces at the TV when the other team gets up to bat."

Leaning past my father, I said, "Hey, Pancake! Who's your favorite team?"

Pancake diligently wrote on his slate and held it up. "*I LIKe BreWerS.*"

My father grinned. "I told him the Milwaukee Brewers, uh, brew syrup." He pointed at the slate. "Look: subject-verb-object. He's quite good now." He rubbed his chin. "I wonder if I'd taught him German ... would he place the verbs at the end?"

Pancake smudged out the words on the slate and wrote some more, then held it up. "*JhON LIKe POO.*" When I turned from the room, I could hear him chuffing.

My father and Pancake played catch. It gave me a strange feeling to watch this. I had never played catch with my father, had never wanted to play catch with him, and would have given him an incredulous stare had he suggested it. But now, a baseball etched arcs in the air between my father in his black-rimmed glasses and the hooting, hairy chimp.

"It's exploitation," Jane said, waving a fork at my father over dinner. She vacillated between distrust and anger towards Pancake, and the same feelings towards our father. To Pancake, as he quaffed a bottle of syrup, she said, "You shouldn't be made to throw a ball for the entertainment of others."

Pancake swiveled his slate around to write, *I LIKe BALL ThrOW. (JOhN LIKe POO.)*

"Huh, he's learned parentheses," Jane commented.

Our father said, "Yes, I'm very proud of him. It's the first step to subordinate clauses, more difficult than throwing a slider."

"It's still exploitation, and you should be ashamed of yourself."

"He enjoys it," my father said. "He says so himself."

"He only parrots what you teach him."

"That's an interesting question of self-determinism," my father said. His face took on a dreamy, thoughtful look. "What is exploitation? Do I exploit a hammer when I use it on a nail? A knife when I use it on my steak? A tool has no will of its own, so it can't be exploited. Exploitation only happens when an agent—a human being, a chimpanzee—has a will of its own, and that agent's will is subordinated to someone else's."

"I don't think that's what exploitation is at all," Jane said.

"But here's my point: if Pancake could only parrot my remarks, then he is an agent empty of will. You can't simultaneously suggest his will is being subordinated to mine *and* label him no more than a mechanical echo." He folded his arms.

Jane turned red. "No, no, no!" she sputtered. "He's parroting you because he gets rewarded! Look at him, sucking on that syrup! The ... the opiate of the chimps, if you will."

My father chuckled, then resumed eating dinner and refused to say anything more.

Later that evening, my sister approached Pancake as he was watching a baseball game from the couch. "I've got something I think you should watch," she said, holding out the rectangular box of a VHS tape. It was *Planet of the Apes*, starring Charlton Heston.

Pancake loved it. He quoted it any chance he got. *IT A MADhOUSe*, he'd write, or he'd pound on the carpet and scribble, *YOU BLeW IT UP MeNIACs.* Then he rolled over, chuffing.

Jane's plan worked a little too well. The movie turned up Pancake's mischief dial. He stayed out of my room, because he feared my lizard, Paul, who hissed whenever he saw the chimp. But he threw feces at Robbie, and it splattered all over his chest plate. Robbie laughed. "Do it again!" And Pancake obliged, though he quickly got bored because Robbie seemed to enjoy it.

One day, we came home to find that Pancake had torn down all the cosmic ray detectors and laid them out in the backyard, spelling his name in letters big enough to read from passing jetliners. I could see my father going alternately pale and then red from conflicting emotions. He hadn't gathered cosmic ray data for years, but it was vandalism all the same. On the other hand, it demonstrated that Pancake possessed a sense of self to a degree never previously imagined in a chimpanzee.

My mother just lit a cigarette and gazed out at the backyard. "I know *I'm* not cleaning up that mess."

The school year was ticking towards its end. On a Tuesday, Becky handed me an envelope. It read, *For John* in a curving, somewhat uncertain script.

"Should I, uh, open it?"

She nodded, and clutching her book bag to her chest like a shield, she walked away.

Dear John, it read, *I'm sorry I couldnt come to you're birthday. Bruce said It was fun. I am having a party for my birthday. I hope you come.* It gave a date for the end of May, a month away.

I turned over the note. On the back, she had drawn little stick figures, and they were either banging their heads together, or they were kissing. My face felt warm.

Walking home, I decided to tell Jane. She would tease me, but she might also offer some hints. She had mysteriously alluded to kissing boys, but she was also a skilled liar. On the whole, I trusted her more than I did my parents.

Banging into the house, I dropped my book bag and got a soda from the refrigerator. When I came out of the kitchen, Pancake was sticking his hairy fingers into my book bag, his long, flexible lips pursed in concentration, as if he were fishing termites out of a mound.

"Hey!" I shouted. He hooted and ran off.

That night, I read and re-read Becky's invitation. I was pretty sure the two figures were supposed to be me and her. One had long hair, and I think the other one was holding a test tube and was supposed to be me. I would have slipped it between my mattress and box spring, but that was too obvious a hiding place, so instead I slipped it into my copy of *The Origin of Species*.

The next day as I was walking home from school, my mother pulled up in the family station wagon. "Get in," she said. "We were out shopping, weren't we, Robbie?"

"We were out shopping," Robbie repeated, as I climbed in the back.

"I thought I'd make a nice meal for the family for once," she said, turning onto our cul-de-sac. "I've been really horrible this year, Johnny, and I'm sorry for it. You're going to need years of therapy."

In the driveway, she filled my arms with paper sacks of groceries. Then she unlocked the door and gestured. "After you, young sir."

I stepped inside. Books and papers were strewn everywhere. And in the middle of the room, Pancake was squatting and systematically tearing pages out of books. From behind me, I heard my mother's sudden intake of breath.

"Excuse me, Johnny. I'm going to step away and say some words I'd like to pretend you haven't learned yet."

Pancake looked up and grinned. I saw the book in his hand: *The Origin of Species*. I tore after him, and he loped away, one hand clutching a wad of papers, the other knuckling along the floor. I chased him through the kitchen and up the back stairs, all the while yelling possibly the exact words my mother hoped I did not know. He ran down the front stairs, only to crash at the feet of my mother.

She snatched the papers. Pancake hooted and ran off. "I'm going to have a talk with your father," she muttered. "Here you go, Johnny." I was afraid she was going to ask me questions, but she just handed me the now crumpled note from Becky.

My heart struggled like a frightened bird in my chest. I jammed the note in my pocket and started up to my room. Glancing back, I saw my mother reading another crumpled piece of paper. She turned red-faced, as if she were standing in a pan of boiling water.

She marched into the kitchen, and I, as if leashed to her, followed. At the stove, a burner leapt to life, and she put the paper in the flame, watched as the fire turned it black.

At first, I thought she wasn't even aware of me. Then she said, "Don't worry, I'm not going to burn the house down. Not yet."

"You bastard!" she said when my father got home. Actually, she screamed it. "I knew I shouldn't trust you!"

"I'm not going to see her," my father said. "I just told you that. All I'm doing is recording my voice."

Jane and I stood on the stairs, looking into the living room. "What's going on?" Jane asked. She was normally bold and forthright, or "saucy," as my mother put it, but this time her voice was low and quavering.

"He's sending messages to *her*," my mother said, red-faced.

"It's more complicated than that," my father said. He'd heard from Plumb Island that Sophia was becoming more and more restive. The scientists didn't want to constantly keep her in a drug-induced coma, but when awake, she thrashed about and called out my father's name. They asked my father to pay a visit. He refused, but offered instead to send a recording. Perhaps the sound of his voice would be calming.

My mother picked up a cushion and threw it at him. Then she tried to lift a lamp, but the electric cord had been nailed down on account of her suicide attempts, so it crashed over on its side.

"Jesus, Anne," he said, cowering from the cushion strike. But she had already spun on her heel and stalked out. "Anne," he called after her. "Anne!"

That night, I woke to a rustling noise. At first, I thought it was Pancake, but when I turned on the light, it was my mother, with her arm thrust into Paul's terrarium. The venomous lizard had backed into a corner, hissing.

"You're scaring him," I said. I was too terrified to say she was also scaring me.

"Then why won't he goddamn bite me?" she asked, offering the tender flesh of her wrist.

My mother drifted around the house, a one-woman ship of the damned. She didn't respond when spoken to, didn't make dinner. That, we were used to, but we weren't used to her endless wandering at night, her footsteps going round and round and round.

At other times, it was hard to sleep after the arguments. At first, it was behind closed doors, but soon it burst out into the rest of the house, and my father looked like a man hunted. "Why?" she'd suddenly turn in the kitchen and demand of him, and he'd flinch.

"I didn't do anything, Anne," he pleaded. "I just saved her life."

"And would you do that for me? Would you save *my* life?! Or would you just stand by and munch on popcorn as you watched?" She grabbed the nearest thing, a box of instant mashed potatoes. When she threw it, it bounced off his forehead and broke open, a small snowfall of freeze-dried potato flakes drifting down.

"Of course I would," he said. "Of course. I would save you."

Late one night, my mother went outside in her bathrobe, backed the station wagon out of the driveway, and gunned down the street. She later said she was surprised when the speedometer trembled at nearly a hundred miles an hour—she had expected the gas to run out, or a belt to break—and she was looking for a convenient light pole or brick wall to plow into, when she realized she had automatically put on her seat belt. "Silly me," she muttered to herself.

"Why are you silly?" came a voice from the back seat.

She turned her head and saw Robbie. She later told us she thought, *He must have followed me out of the house.* "Oh, God! Robbie!" she screamed, and Robbie, thinking she was singing show tunes, burst into a rendition of "Seventy-Six Trombones."

At that high speed, turning the wheel slightly caused the station wagon to fishtail. A tire burst, and the car spun and rolled over and over, shedding rubber and plastic and metal, and came to rest in an empty field.

The paramedics who pried my mother out of the car said it was a miracle that she had only a bruise on her forehead, ascribing it to her seat belt. The inside of the car looked like a junk drawer: gears and belts and electric motors and a scattering of batteries. No sign of the little boy she insisted had been there. "Concussion," they decided, and they had to sedate her to get her into the ambulance.

Becky came to me at school. "I heard your mother was in an accident. Is she okay?"

"Oh, she's fine. She can't..." I stopped myself from saying, *"She can't die."* Instead, I added, "She can't drive for a while, though."

"Are you coming to my party?"

As my family was falling to pieces around me, I had clung to Becky, or at least the idea of Becky, like a drowning man to a piece of flotsam. I kept her invitation with its drawing of us kissing in my pocket during the day, and under my pillow at night. "Of course I am," I said. "Nothing could keep me away."

They kept my mother in the hospital for two days, not because of the bump on her head, but because of what she had said about Robbie. It was only with the bluff of filing a lawsuit that my father convinced the hospital to discharge my mother.

When they came home and stomped up the front steps, I had expected my mother to be the one yelling. Instead, it was my father's voice grinding in a low, angry gear. "When did you know? Why did you keep it up?"

"I told you, at the time, I thought it was sweet of you," she said, exasperated.

"At the time. Maybe you were doing it out of guilt."

He ignored this. "You knew all this time, but said nothing, just let me exhaust myself, week after week, year after year..."

As he said, *"You knew all this time,"* she glanced in my direction, and I thought she might say, *"I told Johnny."* Instead, she shrugged.

He continued, "You amused yourself seeing how long you could string me along?"

She whipped around and threw her hands in the air. "I was mad with grief. Literally *mad.* And you saw it. Dammit, Alan, for the first time in years, you saw me, and for the first time in years, you tried to do something about it. It almost made me love you again."

"By pretending."

"*You* started the pretense. I *went along* with the pretense. Isn't that what love is? Marriage? Family? Pretending in the face of all evidence that we aren't alone in this cold and brutish universe?" She was shouting and breathing hard when she noticed Jane and I staring. "Of course, my love for you kids is totally real."

"Don't drag them into it. I doubt they're fooled."

"Dad!" Jane cried.

Our mother turned, red in the face. "I've been fooling myself for years," she shouted. "I pretended you loved me, hoping it would come true. But I knew, days into our marriage, that you only loved *her*—if you can even love anyone but yourself."

Now his face turned red. I could see him swallowing the words he wanted to say, as if he'd become transparent, like the model of human anatomy I'd been given one Christmas, with clear plastic skin and all the organs visible inside, only he was wadding up his feelings and cramming them into the deepest gland beneath the liver and around the corner from the spleen. Then he shuddered into motion, a merely mechanical model of a human, and mechanically he walked up the stairs, and mechanically he went into the bedroom, and mechanically he closed the door behind him.

One afternoon, while I was doing my homework, Pancake waddled into my room and brandished his slate. *JOhN ThrOW BALL Me.*

"Busy," I said. "Doing human stuff."

Shortly afterwards, I heard a loud banging on the side of the house. My father was still at the university, teaching a late afternoon class, and sometimes Pancake practiced throwing a ball against the side of the house. But this sounded different.

I went downstairs. My mother was on the couch, watching TV, a drink in her hand. "Maybe you should play catch with him, John," she said. "I can't stand this racket."

"He'll just smear poo on the ball to throw at me," I said.

My mother groaned and rolled off the couch. "Think the hairy beast will listen to me?"

I followed her to the backyard. Pancake had a cardboard box at his feet. He reached into it, wound up his arm, and threw. Something clanked and shattered against the house.

My mother took the cigarette out of her mouth. "What's he throwing?" And then she threw the cigarette down and ran forward, swearing like a sailor. Pancake had the box of Robbie's parts and had been systematically demolishing them.

She was still in a white-hot fury when my father got home. "That ... that ... that *monster* has to go! It's him or me."

My father put up his hands. "Okay, okay, Anne. But I can't just drop him off at the pound. I'll arrange something."

"Tomorrow."

It actually took three days before he found a circus that would take him. "A circus!" Jane exclaimed. "How is that any better?"

My father said, "You'd prefer a lab? A lab where he's in a cage all day and gets given some experimental vaccine?" He inclined his head forward, glasses sliding down his nose. "Would a zoo make you happier? I don't have much room to maneuver here, young lady." He pushed his glasses back up. "Tomorrow afternoon, a truck will come for him."

"Good riddance," my mother said. "After that, we can put this family back together."

But the next morning, my mother was dead. Again. My father found her in the bath. He didn't want to leave her in the cold and soapy water, so he toweled her off and wrestled her into bed.

Pancake came in, saw her cold and lifeless in the bed, and began to leap around the room, howling and gibbering. My father tried to calm him down, but Pancake slapped at his face, knocking my father's glasses off. They flew into the master bathroom, and hitting the sink at exactly the wrong angle, they shattered.

"I have a meeting at two," he said over breakfast. He squinted without his glasses. "The animal transport truck comes at ten, and I'm going to go to the optometrist right after that."

MOM NOT GOODBye, Pancake wrote on his slate. *MOM ANgry Me*.

"What he'd write?" my father said, squinting. I read it aloud. "No, no, she'll miss you. She'll be sorry she can't say goodbye," my father said.

I barely managed to not blow milk out my nose.

Jane waved a hand. "I'm not going to be part of selling out Pancake," she said. "After school, I'm going to Lucy's and staying overnight." She pushed away her bowl and grabbed her book bag.

Pancake wrote on his slate and pushed it over. *JOhN ThrOW BALL Me*.

I shook my head. "I have to get to school, too." I fidgeted on my feet, wanting to ask Jane for suggestions for a present for Becky.

Pancake smudged out his previous request, then wrote, *NeVer See JOhN AgAIN*. I rolled my eyes. *PleASe SORRy MAke FUN JOhN*.

Sighing, I followed Pancake into the backyard. The early spring morning air was crisp and cool, and even in my black jacket, I shivered a bit. I threw a ball, which went way over Pancake's head. "Sorry!" I called as he scampered after it. He lobbed it back, a beautiful baseball-colored arc that landed right in my glove.

I threw it again, a little to one side. With one of his long, lean arms, he reached out and snagged it barehanded. He bounced the ball in his palm a couple of times.

"Throw it back. I gotta get to school."

Pancake grinned, baring his teeth, and chuffed. He leaned with his arm way, way back. Then he uncoiled the spring of his body and let fly.

All I remember is the ball coming in a straight line, the kind that would have made Euclid proud, as if Aristotle were right and Newton wrong, coming directly towards my face. Then an explosion of pain, followed by darkness.

When I woke, my head throbbed, and I felt like I was going to throw up. It was a good thing I didn't, because there was duct tape over my mouth, and my hands were duct-taped to the bars of a cage in the garage: the cage to send Pancake away in. My pants were wet, and I smelled urine; I must have pissed myself when the ball knocked me out.

Pancake was turning the key in the lock, and he noticed my eyes opening. He chuffed and grinned. I tried to say something, but with the tape over my mouth, it just came out as a muffled ooking. He took his slate and wrote, *MOM NOT MISS YOU*. Then he erased that and added, *I PUT RObbIe heR CAR*.

"Mmmff, mmmff, ook" was all I could get out.

Pancake chuffed some more. *They LIke Me beTTer. yOU SMeLL POO.*

I rattled the bars of the cage, but couldn't free my hands. He reached into the cage, slipped the slate around my neck, and knuckled into the house.

A few minutes later, my father came into the garage. He fumbled around for the light, then walked cautiously across the lab, almost stumbling over a large transformer. "Well, old fellow, I guess this is it," he said in a wistful tone.

I shook the bars of the cage. "Mmpf! Mmmph mmpff ook ook!"

"Yes, I know it's distressing."

How could he not recognize me? I looked down. I still was wearing my black jacket. Out of focus, I probably looked like a hairy beast.

My father continued, "I think everyone will mourn you in their own way, even John. Well, maybe not Anne. And I feel bad, I do. But in a way, well, you are the sacrifice made to keep the family together. It's a hard bargain, but I don't have any choice." He felt around until he found a big sheet of canvas with an address written on it. My father continued, "Maybe I don't have any agency. Maybe none of us do. Maybe it was all predetermined billions of years ago by colliding clouds of molecular gas... Well, there's nothing to be done now." As he spoke, he covered the cage with the sheet of canvas, like a curtain falling at the end of an act.

Interlude: Scattering State

I was seventeen when one of the circus clowns, Mr. Wuggles, asked me what I wanted to do with my life. I shrugged and told him I planned to stay with the circus forever.

Mr. Wuggles shook his head. His real name was Harvey Silbermensch, and he had a basset hound face, wrinkled and sad, yet his eyes held yellow flecks of love. "You can do better," he told me. "I know you don't think so, because…"

He started to choke up, as he always did when he thought about my origins. Of course, what I had told him and the other circus folk were lies.

In the dark of Pancake's crate, gagged, hungry, dehydrated, and having soiled myself, I came to believe my father had conspired with the chimpanzee. After all, he had betrayed my mother. Why not his own son? Many times, he had ignored or defended the beast's awful behavior. I concluded that he preferred Pancake to me—to any of us.

When the circus folk had uncovered the crate, they were startled to find a smelly human boy, taped to the bars, rather than a chimpanzee. They cleaned me up and gave me some food and water. Then they called the police.

The thought of going back home sparked fear and fury in me. If I returned, Pancake might straight-out murder me as my father looked on. Or I might murder both of them. When the tattooed woman took me to a Porta Potty to relieve myself, I kicked out the wire mesh in the back and slipped away, only to end up at a nearby competing carnival.

To stave off calls to the authorities, I invented a history of tragic loss followed by shame and degradation in foster homes and juvie halls. Many of the carnies and clowns had had their own ugly collisions with the system and sympathetically gave me shelter. Whenever someone started to question my background, I would again run away. Except for the brief time I repaired a submersible for smugglers, at gunpoint I hasten to add, I always landed at a circus or carnival.

I settled on a story that my immediate family had all perished in a horrible fire. My parents, I said, had been out in their shared home lab, hunched over a joint chemistry experiment, when, unable to keep their hands off each other (in my version, my parents were embarrassingly affectionate, always smooching in front of their kids), they had allowed one too many drops to titrate into the test tube, igniting a conflagration of biblical proportions. My three older sisters—two of them invented, to be consistent with my parents' fictional libidos—ran one by one into the fire to rescue our mother and father, only to be incinerated themselves. The last one, Jane, had hesitated. "Do something!" she had shouted at me, her eyes brimming with tears. "You're a boy!"

"I'm also the youngest!" I had shouted back.

Jane straightened her shoulders, threw open the door to the garage-lab, and was instantly torched. I'd felt the heat of her immolation on my face.

After the fire department doused the flames, they had found my parents burned to charcoal, but still embracing, and the ashen remains of my sisters stretched out in a line on the concrete floor, each with an outstretched arm, as if tagging the next.

Sometimes I hinted at a revolutionary invention of my parents, suppressed by nefarious forces, to justify my continued hiding. So went my story, which made even the strong man weep. At times, I myself believed it to be the truth, rather than a manifestation of my incendiary anger.

Recalling my tale, Mr. Wuggles blew his nose. "You're one of the smartest kids—no, one of the smartest *people*, period, that I've ever met. You got to go to college. Be a doctor or something."

I shuddered. "I can't stand the sight of blood."

"Then be a scientist. You light up every time you bring up a scientific fact. You helped design some of our amazing shoot-out-of-the-cannon tricks. And what about Cirque du Saur?"

Cirque du Saur had been my idea—you know, draw upon your obsessions. We outfitted the elephants and horses and camels and a few pigs with papier-mâché heads and armor, to look like Brachiosaurs and Stegosaurs, Ankylosaurs and Allosaurs, and so on. They trooped around the ring in the Parade of the Mesozoic. The clowns on unicycles dressed as killer Deinonychid raptors with scythe-like claws, and the trapeze artists put on leathery wings and spun through the skies as Pterosaurs. And I got to be ringmaster for a brief season, wearing khakis and a pith helmet, billed as *Boy paleontologist extraordinaire!*

Standing in the center ring, however, I was too distracted to enjoy the fake dinosaurs orbiting me. Instead, I scanned the audience for my family, for Becky, for Bruce. I even fantasized that I might spot the little blonde girl who'd insisted she wasn't lost. But I saw only unfamiliar faces and grasped once more how alone in the universe I was. My old scorching rage and grief, the feelings that made me kill off and weep for my family in my imagination, returned. You have gently asked me for details, but those memories still burn, like an arsonist torching my heart. All I will say is that Mr. Wuggles's nagging eventually got me to college, sort of, and then out into the wide and strange world.

Part II: The Romance of the Cyclotron

"If I have not love, I am nothing." —Paul of Tarsus

Crackpots Anonymous

Marcus Aurelius said time is a river that sweeps us along. My father thought time was a wall, one you might break through to the far side. For me, time is not a river, not a wall, but the rain. I came to this idea when I moved to Seattle after college. Every second, every hour, every day is a drop, and you think, *Oh, that's not much, it's just a drop.* Then another drop falls, and another, and they add up, entire years washed down to the ever-thirsty sea, and those opportunities to go home have slipped through cold, wet fingers.

A lot happened. A lot didn't. Mr. Wuggles had advised me to go to college, but the transience of circus life made my schooling more convoluted than the fractal coastline of Norway. My math and reading skills were so far ahead that the bearded lady, who tutored the children of the circus folk, let me teach. When I started the kids on differential calculus, though, she thought I would benefit from more formal schooling and enrolled me in a public school. (At my insistence, it was under my middle name, Calvin, which only muddled my records further.) The public school was a churn of dystopian normality and numb mediocrity. I corrected the teachers' mistakes, and I refused to play sports, and I got into a fight when I refused to play sports, and when the principal threatened me with expulsion, I rigged the school's public address system to broadcast from his office. I only thought to catch him drinking, or having an affair with his secretary, but... Well, it traumatized the entire school, and even though the principal was arrested and the girl was put in therapy, I was nonetheless expelled. But I was happier to be back at the circus. Sure, the other circus kids thought I was weird, but they were all proudly weird, too. I was just the weirdly smart one.

I did go to college, but as my transcripts had so many holes that you could use them to study topology, the only one that accepted me was a clown college. Floppy shoes, red rubber noses, and Maxwell's electromagnetic equations. After that, I found myself grown up, more or less. I went to Seattle for a job in an electronics repair shop, but the shop went abruptly bankrupt, and I needed income.

After yet another failed job interview, I rode the bus back to my apartment, wondering how I would make rent. Next to me, a small man with a bushy haircut wrote in a notebook. I caught glimpses of mathematical notations. "What are you working on?" I asked.

He looked at me shyly. "I've figured out how to divide by zero," he said.

"Really?"

"Yes, I'm the first person in history to do so. But," he said, his voice as sad as the *tap-tap* of rain on a window, "no one will take me seriously, because I don't have a formal math degree."

"You could take night courses," I said, but he shook his head.

"I don't have any money; I'm a missionary," he said, but I missed whether he was a Mormon or a Moonie or a Methodist. "I approached math professors at the UW, but they wouldn't even listen to me." He stood and pushed the Stop Requested button. "You have a blessed day."

When I was thirteen or fourteen, the carnival fortune teller, Esperanzita (whose real name was Jennifer), told me how to gauge a mark. "Everyone has a story they want to hear: they are loved, they are worthy, they are good deep down and not the selfish shits most people are." She affected a foreign accent for her clients, but dropped it when it was just me.

"But isn't that taking advantage of them?"

Esperanzita smiled. "Boyo, you still *are* good deep down," she said and ruffled my hair with a beringed hand. "They give me money to tell them that their life has meaning. Psychologists do the same, also for money; they call it science, but, really, I'm not very different. And I'm cheaper and faster." She leaned back and lit a cigarette. "Besides, I give them good advice. I tell a man his mother is happy in the afterlife, and to move on. If a woman's boyfriend is a creep, I tell her to get out. Many times, I've told a creep that *his* mother in the afterlife is cross with him for how he treats women." She examined the burning ember as smoke rose up. "I've done more good than harm," she said, then cackled. "See, even *I* want to feel better about myself."

Remembering that, I set about crafting a unique occupation.

I recruited clients through flyers I posted around the city, and met them in a coffee shop in the University District. We made introductions: Izzie, Roger, Tog, and Giorgio.

Right away, Roger said, "I don't like this." Roger was a bulky guy with a thick, fleshy face. He wore a snot-colored anorak and was always hunched over. I imagine if you x-rayed an oyster, holding its shell tightly closed, it would look something like Roger. "You promised that our discussions would be confidential."

I put up my hands. "I haven't revealed anything. But eventually, you're going to have to discuss your ideas with *someone*."

Roger jabbed a finger in the direction of Giorgio, a thin stick of a man with a cottony fringe of hair. "What if he steals my idea?"

"He's not going to steal your idea, Roger. Are you, Giorgio?"

Giorgio shook his head.

Roger folded his arms. "I'm not saying a word to anyone who doesn't sign a nondisclosure agreement."

"Fine. You can listen, then. Who wants to start?"

Giorgio scratched at his face. "Hey, wait a minute... What if *he* steals from *me*?" he asked, tilting his head towards Roger.

Roger snorted. I had to admire the precision with which that snort signaled contempt. Giorgio opened his mouth to reply, but I interrupted to take coffee orders.

As I returned from the counter, carrying a cardboard tray full of complex and expensive drinks and wondering if I had made another mistake, I walked past a table of students in their early-to-mid-twenties, around my age. Grad students, I guessed, their talk studded with physics jargon: "Lagrangian" and "variational" and "conserved quantity." It was like hearing someone mention an old flame, someone you'd had a bitter breakup with. But those people, those physics grad students, they didn't know me, so I just walked on by.

"Well," I said, handing out the coffees, "did you get started?"

"Not a word," Izzie informed me, puckering his lips and pulling an imaginary zipper across. Izzie had a mop of black hair and small, bright eyes, and you might have called Izzie "heavyset," which would be both a kindness and an understatement.

"Guys," I said, "you all came to me because you have insights, ideas that the world hasn't heard."

"I came because I saw your flyer," said Izzie. "Your flyer said you would help us communicate our ideas—the ideas other people laugh at."

I leaned forward, holding my hands out. "Exactly. This is a safe, nonjudgmental place to talk about your ideas, your insights."

Tog leaned forward, too. He was the youngest of them, not much older than me, with the long blond locks of a surfer dude. "You look like you're talking about a fish," he said, holding his hands apart in imitation of mine. "The one that got away. You know, the one that gets bigger and bigger in the retelling." Slowly he spread his hands to illustrate the growth of the imaginary fish.

"Can we stay on task?"

Tog's grin faded. "You said this is nonjudgmental."

"It is. I'm here to help."

"We're *paying* you to help," Roger groused. "Not that I'm seeing any results."

"I'm *coaching* you on how to present your ideas to the world. That's half the key. Einstein's ideas seemed just as crazy—"

Roger's head snapped up. "Einstein was a fraud!" he hissed. "The scientific elite knew it! The universities, the journals, they all knew it!" His voice rose in volume, even above the chatter and din of the coffee house. Heads turned towards us.

"Roger, this isn't helpful."

"It's the truth," he said. "People don't want to hear the truth! They just parrot what they've been spoon-fed on TV! And when someone tells the truth, challenges the official propaganda, and contradicts the lies they've swallowed their whole lives, their heads explode! *Ka-blam!*" He made exploding gestures with his fingers, and I regretted taking Roger on as a client.

A young woman with short, dark hair approached us. "Excuse me," she said. "Would you mind keeping it down a bit? It's great that you're enjoying your conversation, but we're trying to study." She gestured towards the table of physics students.

"Brainwash yourselves, more like," Roger muttered.

"I'm terribly sorry," I said. "We'll be more respectful with our volume from now on, won't we, guys?"

After the young woman sat back down, I said, in the *indoor voice* mothers and librarians recommend, "The point is, you have to sell your idea. A lot of seemingly bizarre ideas have become mainstream, because they were effectively communicated."

"Isn't that what we hired you for?" Izzie asked. "To communicate for us?"

"Well, not *for* you. I want *you* to get credit. So, we practice by explaining our ideas to each other. Okay?"

Roger grunted into the brown depths of his soy latteccino. "Only once everyone has signed a nondisclosure agreement." His elbows tight against his sides proclaimed, *"You might as well try Fort Knox; you aren't getting anything out of me."*

I sighed. "Fine. Who'd like to go next week?"

The next week, everyone signed nondisclosure agreements. I announced that it was Izzie's turn. Roger's right foot jittered as if he had soaked it in an espresso footbath. I told myself it was good for Roger to learn some patience and humility. Looking back, I may have had another agenda.

"So, Izzie," I said. "Share with us your idea."

"It's not so much of an idea as a concern," he said, twisting up his face.

"Ah, for God's sake," groaned Roger, "don't be such a tease, tubs. Tell us already."

Izzie looked around, as if he might be overheard divulging a secret. "Magnetic pollution," he said quietly, unhappily. Roger laughed out loud, a nasty, mulish hee-haw. Izzie threw Roger a poisonous look. "I've always been uncomfortable around TVs and microwaves. It's like bees under my skin. Being too close to a refrigerator, I can feel my lungs shutting down. I can't live near major power lines. Even those lights..." He pointed to the ceiling fluorescents. "... are torture. I only realized it when I spent time outside the city." His voice dropped. "Magnetic fields."

"You're *allergic* to *magnets?*" Roger said. He pulled his wallet from a back pocket and slipped out a credit card. "How about magnetic strips?" With a dopey grin, he waved it in Izzie's face.

"Oh, for Pete's sake," Izzie said, flustered, as he tried to bat away Roger's hand.

Roger said, "We can do a scientific experiment, right here. Everyone get out their credit cards and see if we make Izzie sick. Stop squirming; this is for science!"

"If you don't get that out of my face, I'll deck you!" Izzie said.

"I'd like to see you try, fatty."

No blows were exchanged, but the air vibrated like a taut metal wire. Izzie stood up. "Nonjudgmental? *Nonjudgmental?*"

"Hey, no one judged you as crazy or stupid," Roger said, "even though we thought it."

"Izzie," I said quickly, "Roger spoke inappropriately and rudely. But you're going to have to have thicker skin if you want to put your idea out there."

Roger muttered, "I'd say his skin is thick enough as it is."

"Knock it off, Roger." Yes, Izzie *was* large; he spread out across three chairs. But when Roger mocked him, I was rocketed back to my childhood, before my exile to the circus. There was a boy, Timmy, or Tommy. He was fat and pale, while Izzie was fat and dark, and he had been even more of an outcast than I was. And—this is hard to confess—I bullied him. Not often, but I called him names, just like Roger, and once, I hit him in his soft stomach, saying, "Bet you didn't even feel that." When Timmy ran off crying, I was afraid my parents would find out. For all her free-range parenting, this was exactly the sort of thing my mother would not tolerate. Years later, I lay awake at night thinking, *What kind of awful person am I?* Now Roger's snark set guilt sizzling inside me again.

"Listen, Izzie..."

"This is not what you promised," he said, like the hiss of a deflating ball, and he stalked out of the coffee shop.

Roger said, "Hope he paid in advance."

After everyone else left, I put my head in my hands. I was exhausted. Yet despite my cynicism and, let's be honest, contempt, part of me wanted to *help* these folks, wanted to *teach* them. It was unconscious, but it was my father's voice, the professor, speaking through me, as if recorded on tape. If I had understood that, I might have walked away.

I looked up to see the young woman from the week before. "Hey," she said.

"Sorry about the yelling. We're working on that. Really, we are."

"Yeah," she said, sitting down. "What else are you 'working on,' anyway?" She was around my age, with short, straight black hair that looked like a spray of raven feathers. Overall, she had a birdlike look; not in the fragile sense, but like a hawk, maybe a kestrel, with a sharply angled face and intense dark brown eyes.

I pursed my lips, hating the defensiveness rising up inside me. "You're a student at the university?"

"Grad student, physics," she said, and though I had guessed it, my heart sped up as if I'd injected raw espresso grounds straight into a vein. "My name's Ada, by the way."

"John," I said. "So, you're in grad school, PhD, postdoc, tenure track and all that, right? But some people who aren't on the academic route nonetheless have, or think they have, ideas outside conventional thinking."

"Crackpots," she said. "You're talking about crackpots."

I shifted in my seat. "Well, I use the term 'outsider science.' Sometimes 'alternative science,' or 'dissident science.' And, yes, most of them are probably wrong. Academics don't have the time to listen to them. And I don't blame the academics for that. My father was a physics professor, and my mother, my mother... Anyway, academics don't have the time. But I do."

"Let me guess," Ada said. "For a fee."

I shrugged. "There's a price for everything. Even if you aren't the one plunking down dollars for your education, someone else is. It's not like I lie to these guys. In my way, I'm trying to educate them. If one of them learns something, that's a success."

Ada fixed me with her most hawklike stare. "Wow," she said. "Just wow."

I started to stand up. "Sorry if we bothered you."

She shook her head. "I was curious. That's why I'm in grad school: curiosity. You know, rubbernecking, looking at the crazies." She laughed.

"Don't say 'crazies,'" I snapped, so sharply that I surprised myself.

Her face paled. "You're right. That was cruel of me. That was... I'm sorry." She lowered her head, then looked up again. "But now I *am* curious. About dissident science and everything. Do you mind if I sit in sometime?"

"Only if you're willing to sign a nondisclosure agreement..."

The following week, it was Tog's turn. Giorgio drifted in, followed by Roger, who plopped down and asked in a mild tone, "No Izzie, I take it?", as if he and Izzie might exchange Christmas cards.

I shook my head. I had called Izzie, but he hadn't picked up.

Ada hadn't shown either by the time Tog slid into the last seat. I felt a squishy mixture of disappointment and relief that I wouldn't be embarrassed in front of a normie.

Tog pulled out of a paper bag his model of an atom, whiffle balls tied together with pipe cleaners, although he seemed confused about the difference between atoms and nuclei. Roger snorted in derision, and the meeting quickly degenerated into sarcastic comments. We had scheduled an hour. For the last fifteen minutes, we sat in painful silence, until Roger groaned, and we all left.

I was angry with Roger, and I was angry with myself, so I almost didn't hear my name being called as I headed for the door. It was Ada, who flagged me over to her table.

"I'm sorry I couldn't join your group," she said. In front her were scattered pages of handwritten equations. "I was hunting down every obscure table of integrals in the library." She turned to her study group. "Everyone, this is John. John, this is Lalita, Ezra, Harald, and Zhong-hao. We're a bit stuck with this problem."

"What is it?" I asked.

"Some math," said Harald, a pasty-faced guy with wispy blond hair and a faint accent: German, or maybe Scandinavian.

Perhaps it was because I had just been dealing with Roger, but the patronizing tone reignited my anger. "I know math. Like calculus, differential equations, group theory, complex analysis..."

They looked at Ada, who shrugged. "The problem is straightforward, but it's got an integral we can't evaluate," she said. "I thought I was good at integrals, but this one is kicking my butt."

"I thought we should tackle it numerically..." Ezra said.

"Professor Ko despises computers," Ada said. "Says they rot your brain."

"They can be a useful tool," said Lalita. "Maybe he wants to see if we'll try."

"Let me see it," I said. My father used to wake up me up in the middle of the night to make me recite integral tables, and in college, I had solved differential equations while riding a unicycle, but I didn't say that aloud.

Ada pushed her open book in my direction. "It's pretty arcane," she said as I ran a finger over the page. "I must have tried a dozen different substitutions, and looked through all the integral tables. Even this Russian table of integrals—"

"Gradshteyn and Ryzhik," I said, naming the authors. I didn't know why they looked surprised; the book was infamous. I squinted at the integral. "Approximate it," I said.

Ada blinked. Harald said testily, "That's the same as numerical evaluation."

Ada blinked again and asked, "You mean with a polynomial?"

"A gaussian. You know, a bell curve. If you need a fancy name, it's called 'method of steepest descents.'"

Harald frowned. "I still think—"

"It's a standard technique," I said to Ada. "Of course, I work with crackpots, so what do I know? I gotta catch my bus."

The next week I arrived early, but Ada had arrived even earlier. She was sitting where my group met, reading Shankar's textbook on quantum mechanics.

"You were right," she said. "I looked it up. A standard technique, like you said. Can I buy you a coffee to say thanks?"

While she was at the counter, Roger strutted in. The Man Who Hunched now had a wondrously straight spine. I wondered if his berating of Tog and Izzie had juiced up his confidence. I had to push down hard on my own desire to make him feel lilliputian. It was not a good impulse, I knew, but it kept chittering in my ear.

When Ada came and handed me my coffee, Roger raised an eyebrow, but said nothing.

Ada sat down and said to me, "So, you're very well read."

"I'm sure you mean well, but that came across as patronizing."

She reddened. "I didn't mean it like that. I guess I didn't ask about your background."

I asked, "My credentials, you mean? If I have a proper degree in science?"

Roger snorted his own contempt for credentials.

"Now you've got me feeling awkward," she said. "It's not so much a matter of credentials ... but what *is* your background?"

"As it happens, I do have a bachelor's degree. In physics." I carefully did not mention where I had gotten my degree.

Tog and Giorgio arrived, shaking off the rain, and Roger leaned forward. "I'm sure you find this pretty girl interesting to talk to, but we're paying for your time." He tapped his watch and gave a smirk to Ada. "Have fun with your homework."

Ada straightened up. "John said I could sit in." She unzipped her backpack and pulled out a handful of papers. "I brought a nondisclosure agreement. If you find this acceptable, I'll sign a copy for each of you."

Roger harrumphed and snorted, a high, merry snort with overtones of untamed horses and mocking children. But he couldn't find anything wrong with Ada's nondisclosure agreement. At last, he looked up and said to me, "She's here to make fun of us."

Ada said with a straight face, "I'm just here to observe. I won't say a word."

She reached for the nondisclosure agreement, but Roger kept it tightly clenched in his fist. "I don't like this," he said at last, rocking from side to side.

I said, "If you want to put your ideas out there, it means being vulnerable. Izzie, remember, struggled with being vulnerable. He didn't handle it well."

"Izzie was a crybaby," Roger muttered.

"If we're going to be name-calling, you're a scaredy-cat. At least Izzie opened up. You say you have these important ideas, but you won't open your mouth. You say it's because someone might steal them, but I think you're more afraid someone will criticize you, will *mock* you, the same way *you* mocked Izzie and Tog."

Roger glared at me. Finally, he blew out a long, gusting, symphonic sigh. "All right," he muttered.

"Then why don't you begin?" When he started by launching into a tirade about "the system," I admonished, "Stick to the science."

"I know, I know," he said. "Gotta avoid offending anyone. Gotta be politically correct. Say the wrong word, and they'll crush you like a walnut." He clenched his fist. "Einstein was wrong, of course—and this has nothing to do with him being Jewish!" he hissed. "Newton was wrong, too, and he wasn't Jewish." He folded his arms, as if he had proven something.

"Go on," I said.

He took a deep breath. "You know how NASA, and the Russians, too, sometimes lose space probes? It's because both Newton and Einstein were *wrong*. Wrong about gravity."

"But if that's true," I said, "then how is it that we can predict the path of cannonballs and comets? How is it that NASA has put so many satellites into orbit, even sent men to the moon?"

"Fudge factors. I ought to know. I was a civil engineer. You know how we figured out how to make roads? We tried a bunch of things, found what didn't work, and kept trying until we found something that does. NASA had a lot, and I mean a *lot*, of failures before they succeeded. That was them figuring out fudge factors. The NASA engineers all know the theory's a load of hooey, but they don't want to upset the university egghead types."

Giorgio cleared his throat. "Well. Roger, in your opinion, is it all, I guess, random?"

Roger waved away Giorgio's question. "Once you learn how to build a road, it always works. No, there's a theory, all right, just not Newton or Einstein. You know what tipped me off? Go ahead, ask me."

I asked. It took a lot of effort to ask without sarcasm.

Roger answered with a grin, as if he'd already proved his point. "You ever watch the water go down the toilet?"

Tog, who was drumming his fingers absently on his thighs, laughed aloud.

Roger sneered. "What's so funny, *dude*?"

I interjected, "I guess you'd better explain the connection."

"Vortices." Gravity wasn't so much pulling, Roger explained, but pushing us to the ground as something—"substance R," he called it—swirled into the Earth. Momentum was the turbulence of vortices in the wake of an impulse. It was hard to follow, especially when he broke off to mock Newton and Einstein.

I put my hands on my temples and said, "So, does your theory predict, for example, the orbits of the planets better than Newtonian theory?"

"The vortices sweep the planets along."

"Yes, but Newtonian physics predict the positions, very accu—"

Roger lifted his rounded shoulders and let them drop. "All I find in the textbooks are circular arguments. They assume Kepler's laws and write down figures that fit them."

Ada stirred again. "Excuse me," she said. Roger rolled his eyes. "I'm sorry, I know I said I would be quiet, but... That's not true. Astronomers take very careful and precise measurements."

"That's what they tell you," Roger said.

"I *know* these astronomers. I don't think you do."

"Did you watch them take the data? Did you take data yourself? Did you ask them if they 'corrected' it to fit the theory better?"

Now Ada folded her arms. "Astronomers don't 'correct' data to fit a theory."

"That's what they tell you, missy. What will happen when your professor says, 'We can't publish this data; it doesn't agree with high-and-mighty Newton and godlike Einstein'?"

"Roger!" I said. "You're getting ridiculous."

"It's those theories that are ridiculous! Have you even *read* them? In one breath, Einstein says the laws of physics don't depend on velocity, and in the next, he says going fast will make your clock run slow. It's complete gobbledy-gook."

"That's not—"

"Of course it is!" Roger said. "But you can't see it, because you've been brainwashed! You sold out to fit in, just like everyone else at the universities."

"Sold out? I don't go to a university. I wasn't even accepted to graduate school. If anyone would be ripe to reject the status quo, it's me."

"Maybe you're that desperate to be accepted! Maybe you still think," and his voice took on a singsong, mocking tone, "'If I clap my hands and click my heels and believe, they'll let me in.'"

"That's a whole lot of supposition," I said. I suppose I didn't say it as calmly as it looks written here.

Roger stayed in his seat, as fixed as a mussel on a rock. He gave me a cold, mollusky sneer. "I notice you don't deny it. I notice you don't deny anything."

I stood up. "That's it. We're done, Roger. You're out. You're on your own."

He unstuck himself from his seat. "See? When I challenge you, you just throw me out. You *are* brainwashed, and you can't see it."

I thought he might throw a punch. I stood up and braced myself. I had a learned a few things from the carnies that my father could never have taught me, such as how to defend myself.

Roger said, "You're a sad person. You want to be accepted, so you believe everything they tell you. I feel sorry for you." Then he banged out of the coffee shop and slammed the door.

"Some definite anger management issues there," Tog mumbled.

Giorgio said to me, "I thought you handled that as well as you could. Still, poor Roger."

I wished I had coffee left, so I could spit out a mouthful. "Poor Roger?"

"After the first meeting, he told me his wife died. A year ago, I think. He must be tremendously lonely. Even so, I promise I won't be as infuriating next week." He raised his cap to all of us, and he and Tog left.

Ada was still sitting there. I felt embarrassed to have lost my temper in front of her. She glanced over at her group, who had already settled at a nearby table.

"I hope you don't lose face with your friends by being with us," I told Ada, deciding not to add, *"with us crackpots."*

"Oh, we have plenty of eccentric professors," she said. I slipped into my raincoat. Ada grabbed her own coat and followed me out the door. She said, "I hope it's not a sore spot, but you said you weren't accepted to grad school?"

I nodded.

"Where did you apply to?"

"I applied here. I applied everywhere. And I got turned down everywhere."

"Were your grades..."

"My grades were fine. My GRE scores were okay, too—better than okay. It was because I went to a clown college."

"Well, I only went to Montana State myself, and that's not so—"

"No, I mean, I went to *clown college.*" I sighed. "I got shipped off to a circus when I was twelve. It's a long story," I added when her eyes widened. "There were kind folk who tutored me as best they could. I got into the Midwestern College of Circus Arts. They have a physics major, dynamics being an important part of juggling, tumbling, being shot out a cannon and all that. Now imagine putting that on an application for grad school."

As I told her this, I felt a pang, missing my clown college. I had loved my classmates. They would come to my dorm room to ask if a particular twist or tumble was physically possible, and even when I said no, they would try anyway; sometimes I had to revisit my calculations. Half of them had run away from home, half had been thrown out of their homes, but all of us—nerds and gays and teen moms and smartasses like me—we stuck together. They kept me afloat during my senior year, when in the midst of applying to grad schools, I received word that Mr. Wuggles had died of a sudden heart attack. I was named valedictorian, but the acclaim felt like a knife to my gut. Maybe I had moved to Seattle because I had a dark cloud over me, and the cold rain felt like my entire life.

"Oh," Ada said, shivering in the drizzle.

"You should go inside," I said. "With your friends."

"We're studying for a major test in stat mech," she said. "My brain will be so fried. Afterwards, I was thinking of going to see this Bulgarian science fiction film at the Neptune Theater. Do you like science fiction?"

"Not so much. Too close to my life."

Ada tilted her head. "Someday I'm going to have to find out what you mean by that."

The group met on Wednesdays. I thought it appropriate, as its namesake, Wotan, chief of the Norse gods, had sacrificed an eye to obtain true perception. If the myth wasn't exactly like that, I prefer my version. Maybe I wasn't all that different from my clients.

On the weekend between, Tog phoned to say he wouldn't be coming to the group again. He started to explain, but got sidetracked into a story about one of his co-workers, and never found his way back.

I was feeling down, and I would not have been surprised if Giorgio hadn't shown. But show up he did. It was just the two of us, I told him. I asked him what he did, and he told me he repaired shoes. A dying profession, he admitted, as most people today wore cheap shoes of plastic and rubber. But he liked working with leather, stitching and repairing shoes. He'd spent five years as an apprentice, honing his craft, doing the same tasks over and over until his fingers knew them of their own accord.

Science was the same way, I told him, though most people didn't appreciate that. Science students learned techniques, be they mathematical or experimental, and applied them over and again to different situations. Even the habit of self-questioning, the heart of scientific discovery, was something one mastered through practice.

"That's a nice way to put it," Giorgio said.

I bought us coffees, and we sipped them in companionable silence. Finally, I said, "So, Giorgio, what's your thing? What insight or idea brings you to me?"

Giorgio smiled shyly. "Look at all these people, all this life. It seems amazing to me. Almost miraculous. Doesn't it to you?"

"You think life is a miracle?"

"In a metaphorical sense, I suppose, but not scientifically. But when I think scientifically about life, I think about how amazing and unlikely life is. The universe is mostly cold, empty, and sterile. Yet here, in this tiny spot, we have life abundant and overflowing. I believe life did not start here on Earth, but came from somewhere else. Maybe from Mars, or maybe from Venus in her youth, before she became a furnace. But probably from outside our solar system."

"If you have trouble believing life started here on Earth, because it's so improbable," I said, "isn't it just as improbable that it started somewhere else?"

"That's a good point. I would say it's more likely to have started elsewhere because there is simply more 'elsewhere' out there." He took off his glasses and wiped them on his shirt, a gesture that reminded me of my father. "What do you think? Don't you find it plausible that life started elsewhere?"

"Oh, I find it totally plausible that life started elsewhere. But I find it equally plausible that life started here."

"I don't know." Giorgio lifted his head. He looked up through the ceiling of the coffee shop, through the notetaking service on the second floor, through the gray rain clouds over Seattle, to the stars and planets light-years away. "I like the idea of life starting elsewhere."

Gently, I said, "You don't... Science isn't based on what we like, what we want to believe. Often, it is exactly what is hardest to believe. That's another one of those talents that you have to learn: accepting that which is hard to believe."

"I see. And do you think you've mastered that talent, John?"

"Of course. But perhaps I'm flattering myself."

"It's not self-flattery that comes to mind when I think of you, John. Quite the opposite."

"Hmm?"

"One thing I've noticed about people is that while some find it hard to believe bad things about themselves, other find it hard to believe *good* things about themselves. You might be one of those."

"I don't know. I have a high self-regard for my intelligence."

"I don't mean intelligence. I mean that pretty girl, the one who's been hanging out here."

"Ada?"

"She clearly likes you, John."

I shook my head. "I don't think so." But then I remembered her invitation to go see a movie with her. Had she been asking me out on a date?

Giorgio put a hand on my shoulder. "John, I've been married three times, so I know. She likes you." He stepped back. "If you can believe life arose from a dirty pool of sludge, why do you find it so hard to believe she might like you? Close your mouth. Go and find her. Ask her out."

I found Ada where I thought I would, in the library, near tables of integrals. "How was your stat mech test?"

"Brutal, but I passed." She brushed aside a raven lock. "Your dissident scientists?"

"I think that's finished," I said. "A failed experiment."

"Edison said, 'I know ten thousand things that don't work.'"

It's hard to explain, but her words hit me like a lightning bolt. I knew what Frankenstein's creature felt when the doctor shot him full of electricity. That was the moment I came back to life. That was the moment I began to fall in love with her.

"Here's another experiment," I said, my heart racing. "How about I buy you a cup of coffee?"

Giorgio was right about me. I expected her to say she had a homework set to finish, an exam to study for, a boyfriend. But he was right about her, too. She said with a grin, "It's about time."

Over coffee, she asked me about my life story. I grimaced. "When I write my autobiography, you can buy it. How's that?"

"Okay, you don't have to tell me anything personal," she said, rolling her eyes. "That's why a lot of us went into science, isn't it? So we don't have to talk about the personal stuff?"

"You're in science, not me. I'm just a guy in a coffee shop who talks—*talked*—to people with ideas outside the mainstream."

"But you do have a degree in physics. Even if it's from a, um, less-than-esteemed institution. And you know *way* more than most people with a BS in physics."

"BS is what I'm good at."

She tilted her head to one side, giving me that kestrel look. I tried not to feel like a mouse in a field. "You're deflecting like crazy. And I'm not asking anything really personal, like about your family, or who gave you your first kiss..."

"The bearded lady," I said. "'Sweet sixteen and never been kissed,' she said, and gave me one. That was all she gave me, seeing how she was married to the sword swallower and all, but she meant well."

"And then, after all that deflecting, you say things like that."

"Why do you want to know, anyway?"

"I'm curious. I grew up in a curious family..."

"I've come to realize my family was the most curious of all."

"And that's another one. Are you going to tell me about your family?" I looked away, and Ada sighed. "I was starting to say, that's why I became a scientist: because I'm insatiably curious about the world and how it works. I'm curious about people, too. Many physicists are not; they seem more comfortable with particle accelerators. And now you're smiling."

"Well, yes, I know what you mean about being more comfortable with particle accelerators. I'm probably one of those people. I used to work on a particle accelerator."

"In college—your, hmm, clown college?"

"Fourth and fifth grade. It ran through a disused sewer line in my hometown." I saw her start to smile, and added, "Yeah, I know how it sounds. But I can take apart and put back together dipole and quadrupole magnets, momentum separators, stripping foils..."

"That's not what I was smiling about," she said. "I was smiling because there's someone I want you to meet. He might have a project for you."

The Manhattan Poetry Project

T he someone Ada wanted me to meet was Huey Osmont Hile. If the name sounds familiar, it's because he won the Nobel Prize for predicting the accelerating expansion of the universe. His paper was never formally published, only a curious preprint that almost sunk his case for tenure—until astronomers, peering at the farthest galaxies, determined that he was right.

"Hate to bite the Swedish king's hand that gave it to me," he told me later, "but that prize ended up more curse than blessing." Hile detested being a celebrity. He desired only to sit at his desk, working through equations. But the university wanted to parade him around "in lipstick and a control-top girdle," as he put it. "My job, to put it bluntly, was to bat my eyes at rich people, get them to give the university money. I felt like an expensive call girl."

Within minutes of meeting me, Hile brought up grad school. "Your Miss Zachary speaks highly of you," he said, referring to Ada, "and mentioned your unusual background."

"It runs in my family."

"Yes, it does. You're Alan Chant's son, aren't you? We were grad students together at MIT, and then postdocs. I knew your mother, too. I haven't heard from them in years. How are they?"

I hoped my face didn't reveal the green acid that filled my stomach when he said my father's name. "We don't talk much these days."

"Families can be complicated." He coughed, then turned to grad school. "I extracted your application file. It's true that your schooling was off the beaten path." As he said that, in my head, the sound of a steam calliope played. "But your GRE scores should have countered that. I could make some phone calls."

I shrugged. I wasn't sold on the idea of a PhD; after all, it hadn't brought either of my parents happiness or clarity. But Hile was so eager, I couldn't piss on his generosity. "Thanks, Professor Hile."

"Ozzie. Or H_2O. Most people call me that." He stood up. "I may have to twist some elbows, since it's late April. In the meantime, I have a proposal for you. Come with me to Los Alamos National Lab for summer research. I think I can find an interesting project for you."

And so, off I went to New Mexico.

I didn't have a car, but received another surprise: Hile offered to drive me from Seattle to Los Alamos. He liked driving, he said. He had put himself through his undergraduate days by driving a delivery truck, and when he was on the road at dawn, the edge of the sky turning a delicate abalone pink, he felt young again.

We headed out east at four in the morning, had reached Snoqualmie summit by dawn, and arrowed out towards the great washboard plains of eastern Washington. Hile, who had struck me as a shy and retiring man, soon made it clear why he was willing, even eager, to drive with me to Los Alamos.

"I made a similar trip with your father, oh, over thirty years ago." This time, the mention of my father only caused a dull, throbbing ache, like a cut beginning to heal. "We had finished grad school and landed postdocs at Los Alamos. Your mother came out for a week—Anne and your father were dating then—and she took it as her mission to take us to all the bars in town. Santa Fe was smaller and rougher then, but not only could Anne drink everyone under the table, she could drink them through the floor and all the way to China... I suppose I shouldn't be telling you this."

"It's not anything new to me," I assured him. I noted my own reaction to Hile's reminiscences. The sting had dissipated, perhaps because his nostalgic memories of my parents struck me as mythical as my spurious tales of losing them to a chemical fire.

"When she wasn't around, your father and I stayed up late working. We'd get kicked out of our office and go back to our apartment to continue. Your father came up with the most fantastic ideas—crazy stuff. But just as quickly, he'd figure out the fatal flaw and move on. I think that's why Canterbury liked him so much."

"Canterbury?"

Hile glanced over at me, and I could tell he was about to launch into a long story.

The subject of physics teems with violent imagery. We split atoms, establish the universe with an almighty explosion, illustrate the precepts of motion by firing cannons. Perhaps this is because governments have long employed masters of mechanics and engineering for weapons of war, from Archimedes to Leonardo da Vinci to Werner von Braun and Edward Teller. Others have been forgotten, among them Hieronymus Canterbury.

Canterbury was born in Hungary, but he fled to England as the Nazi floodwaters rose in Europe. His original name is lost, the records destroyed in the

Blitz. "Good," he was reported to have said. "Let the old burn away." He was an eccentric polymath, having taught himself Japanese at age nine and differential calculus at ten. At age eleven, he built his own rocket, blowing off his right eyebrow and left pinkie. If I had met him, I wouldn't have known whether to hug him like a long-lost brother, or punch him in the face out of jealousy.

At MIT, Canterbury was one of my father's professors, and he changed his life. Decades later, he changed mine as well.

"Canterbury came to Los Alamos shortly after the end of the war," Hile told me. "His radical ideas at first endeared him to the lab. People were considering all sorts of things—nuclear-powered aircraft that never needed to land, that kind of thing. But Canterbury dismissed such projects as 'tiny potatoes.' He wanted to use timed nuclear explosions to send messages to interstellar civilizations, a kind of gamma-ray Morse code. He had a fondness for conspiracies, like he believed in the Roswell aliens, and he was convinced that Schrödinger had gotten his wave equation from a secret source." At my puzzled look, he explained: "Schrödinger kept diaries—mostly for his, er, romantic conquests—but the diary for that year, the year he discovered his famous equation, went missing. Canterbury thought this meant there had been some sort of a cover-up.

"But Canterbury and your father... Can I tell you something? I struggled to keep up. Their conversation whirled around me, making me feel like Dorothy in the cyclone."

"But you won the Nobel Prize," I protested. "You didn't end up at some ass-water state university, like my father."

"Just goes to show, there's luck involved. I'm not saying I'm not smart. But I'm not that lightning-quick kind of guy, the way your dad was—is—or Canterbury."

We rode the gray river of the highway, wound our way through Oregon, threaded across Idaho, and careened over Utah. At the shore of the Great Salt Lake, we saw a flock of white birds rise and wheel in two great arms, like the negative of a galaxy, until a black cloud of insects drove us back into the car.

As we drove through Colorado and its towering pillars of angry red rock, Hile told me about Canterbury's plans to colonize Mars, arguing that the vast land areas would be ideal for growing crops. Finally, we reached the dry bones of New Mexico, where I always felt like I was in a vast frying pan, waiting for some god to turn on the stove.

The Rio Grande cut through New Mexico like a giant scar. On the eastern side lay Santa Fe, full of rich tourists, poor Hispanics, and struggling artists. Dotted across the landscape were the even poorer Pueblos, people who had been there a thousand years or more, seen by Anglo tourists as local entertainment.

From Santa Fe, we headed north, passing several pueblos and their gas stations and speed traps, dropping down to cross the muddy Rio Grande, and then climbing up and up and up. As we reached the top, the view was spectacular, especially in late afternoon, when shadows threw into relief the weather-gnawed geology, when clouds drifted across the landscape like airborne jellyfish, trailing dark tentacles of rain. There, perched on the mesa, lay the sleepy town of Los Alamos, and the infamous national lab burning with dark secrets.

Hile never came out and said so, but it soon became clear why a Nobel Prize winner in physics took an interest in a young man from a clown college. He guessed that being my father's son, I would both have a high tolerance for off-the-mainstream ideas while retaining critical faculties. Damn him, he was right. With his stories about my father, he set a hook in my mouth as if I were a fat silver trout in a lazy mountain stream.

I forget my original project. My first days were spent in safety training. When I finally showed up at the building where I was supposed to work, it had been closed down: contamination from tritium. Later, I wondered if Hile had engineered it. He shouldn't have been able to do that, but he *was* a genius.

I found myself exiled to an old, musty building, number 18, a couple of miles north of the main lab. The concrete floor was as bare and gray as a cold winter's sky, and the only contents were a single desk much older than I was and a row of file cabinets standing at rusted attention. Hile arrived with my nominal supervisor, a round-faced Chilean woman, and sat on the desk.

"I've convinced Dr. Gutierrez here to let you go through some old files," Hile said, gesturing at the rusted cabinets. "They contain notes from Canterbury and his lab assistants. Since he left in a hurry and a huff, they never got cataloged. You're... Well, you're the perfect person for this task, John. To pull the pearls from the swine, to salvage the treasure from the wreck."

And then he left me alone among the file cabinets.

I counted eight file cabinets. Two were empty, like shells popped open by starfish and left on the bottom of the sea. One had rusted shut, but by rocking it back and forth, I felt the contents shift and rustle. The rest opened readily with a modicum of force.

First, I determined the chronology. The earliest files came from December 1945, when Canterbury had arrived at the lab. The last were from 1950. Hile told me Canterbury had left Los Alamos for MIT in early 1952. I looked at the corroded cabinet. *1951?* I wondered.

The notes were jumbled, in a Cuisinarted blend of English and Hungarian. I found a Hungarian dictionary and set to reading the notebooks. It was all there: Mars, Roswell, quantum mechanics. *What was Schrödinger hiding down those Austrian trousers?* he wrote.

At the same time, Ada and I were writing to each other by email. These were the early days of the internet: simple and quiet, a few databases and a couple of bulletin boards where people were quaintly polite to one another. Scientists were early adopters of email, having invented it to avoid talking on the phone.

Guess what? Ada wrote. *I'm going to Socorro to the VLA.*

Me: *The Vermont Liberation Army? Oh, wait, you mean the Very Large Array.*

(The Very Large Array was a radio telescope observatory: hundreds of huge radio dishes all pointed in the same direction in the sky, like so many monstrous chicks looking upward to be fed.)

Ada: *Ha, very funny. Well, not very. But points for trying. <smile>*

(Emoticons were still very primitive; they had barely pulled themselves onto land and had only just developed lungs.)

Ada: *This is last minute. The postdoc got sick, so I'm going in his place.*

Me: *I don't have a car, but I could take a bus down and visit.*

It took me a whole afternoon to work up the nerve to send that last email. I hadn't had much luck in asking out women. In the circus, the snake lady's daughter had a crush on me, but I'm ashamed to say the girl's vertical pupils unnerved me.

Ada: *I won't have a car, either. But Socorro has, like, twelve people in it. It's tumbleweeds and roadrunners, and a lone post office where coyotes receive their ACME supply shipments. How about if we meet up in Santa Fe instead? I get to the VLA—the array, not the army—in ten days. How about in three weeks? – A2Z*

"A2Z" was her signature, a pun on "Ada Z" (say it aloud and fast). I had tried to come up with something to match H_2O and A2Z, but really, "JCC" didn't have the same ring. Now I was tempted to sign JWHAD—John Who Has a Date.

As the summer ticked by, I worked my way through the files, summarizing ideas and transcribing entries that seemed important. But I felt foolish. I had come to Los Alamos to work on cutting-edge physics, to model implosions or measure the tensile strength of exotic plutonium alloys. But Hile had me reading four-decade-old notes. It didn't matter if he had been Hile's professor or my father's; I knew a crackpot when I saw one.

I went to lab colloquia, heard about high-temperature superconductors, and the puzzle of supernova mechanisms, and the tricksy behavior of superfluid helium. If it was something super, it was a subject at the lab. Afterwards, I trudged back to building 18. All the exciting science, all the current discoveries were a tantalizing two miles away. I felt like a hungry man who watches a cooking demonstration and is sent away without a bite. It felt like exile once more.

I also became more curious about the cabinet that was rusted shut. I tried to pry it open with a crowbar, but only managed to buckle the sheet metal. So, I bought a hacksaw and started sawing away—destroying government property, perhaps, but no one burst in to arrest me. No one cared.

It took two days to get the cabinet open. Inside were more cheap notebooks filled with Canterbury's cramped hand, like the scribblings of a seismograph. But the cabinet contained something else. I opened a notebook not written in Canterbury's hand, which I knew well by that point, and on the first page was written in block letters: NATHAN W., SUMMER 1951. It didn't contain equations or scientific notes. In it were poems.

In the winter of late 1950 and early 1951, Canterbury invited poets to spend a summer at the laboratory. He sent out dozens of invitations, to famous poets and to novices (though he was cagey as to the exact location; the existence of the laboratory was still a closely guarded secret). In the end, eight came.

Canterbury had helped lay the groundwork for interpreting messages from extraterrestrial intelligences, should we ever receive one. This built naturally upon wartime decoding efforts. But Canterbury became distracted by and obsessed with poetry. Like any text, poetry is a linear sequence of symbols that repeat, both regularly and irregularly. Yet good poetry, *great* poetry conveys much more than information. It carries unspoken emotions and contexts beneath the skin. It stabs at the heart.

Maybe Canterbury hoped to weaponize poetry, or to use the knife-in-the-guts power of poetry for propaganda. Mathematics had mapped out the dance of the planets and stars, the beating rhythm of electrons, the rules of genetic inheritance. Maybe he sought a new continent to conquer. Maybe he didn't know what he wanted.

He instructed his poets to write new poems. He measured the poems, the frequency and positions of words and imagery, and fed them to his equations and the lab computers. He suggested that the poets try new schemes, new approaches.

"A new structure, like a sonnet?" asked the youngest, a precocious nineteen-year-old woman from Smith College.

"Or cheap theatrics," said one of the older poets, named John like me. I pictured him as a weedy man with a scraggly beard, wiping his black-rimmed glasses on the edge of his shirt, but tense, as if perpetually standing on a ledge. "Not good poetry."

"All poetry is theater," said Anne, who was the second youngest at twenty-three, but married. "All life is theater."

Canterbury transcribed the discussions, but I wondered if he'd put words into the poets' mouths, the way Plato placed whole philosophies in the mouth of his martyred mentor, Socrates.

"Can you really mechanize beauty?" asked Miguel, who wrote about his parents working in the fields while sending him to college. "Shackle poetry to theorems and a few lines of math?"

"We've mechanized death," said Randy, the oldest poet, with a beard like a prophet's, and everyone was silent for a while.

"What you mean, then," Nathan said, "is that since death and poetry are two edges of the same knife, if we can mechanize death, we can make a machine for poetry. If the bomb doesn't kill us, poetry surely will."

Canterbury filled several notebooks with his efforts and even enlisted the lab's early computers, until an administrator found out and made him stop. Canterbury wrote across the top of his pages, *Thirteen (Mathematical) Ways of Looking at Poetry*; a man too concerned with thinking himself clever. There weren't actually thirteen analyses, and I'll only mention a few:

- Claude Shannon's entropy of information. Entropy is a measure of messiness. Somewhere between the frozen regularity of a crystal (zero entropy) and the helter-skelter run-in-all-directions randomness of hot air (maximum entropy) is *useful* information.

- Fourier analysis, the idea that everything is built upon layers of regular rhythms. Timing plus math exposes the hidden heartbeat. For example, the pattern of mass extinctions, including that of the dinosaurs, suggested the existence of Nemesis, a dim star periodically disturbing the outermost edges of our solar system, raining Olympian bolts of destruction upon the Earth.

- Schrödinger's equation, which ejects Newton's clockwork particles in favor of Fourier's overlaid waves, interpreted by the feverish probability of a gambler gone mad. Who wouldn't see poetry in that?

- Thermodynamic phases. Ice, water, and steam are composed of the same molecules, but at different temperatures, in different arrangements or phases. Canterbury tried to diagram the "phases" of a poem and the places where they changed. (Hile had applied this idea to the universe, and I couldn't help but wonder if Canterbury had inspired him.)

All of this was dry and mathematical, although you should know that to a physicist, a mathematical proof is like a sonnet, elegant and terse and beautiful, like the sun after a spring rain, only with a better metaphor.

It wasn't just mathematics, however. Canterbury had his poets write poems for him. Poems every day. He had them in his file cabinets, complete with scribbled annotations and numbers, the same numbers he fed to his hungry equations.

I met Ada at the bus stop on the edge of downtown Santa Fe. We awkwardly hugged, and I brushed my face against her hair. It was a warm summer day, the sky a robin's-egg blue dome, and we walked toward the central square. On either side, blocky buildings with faux adobe facades hosted shops for tourists. We walked close, occasionally bumping against each other in shy courtship.

My head was full of poems and Canterbury's cramped mathematical equations and the scent of Ada's hair. If I had written about that moment, I would have written about the Casimir effect: two metal plates with a vacuum between them will feel a pull towards each other, because the vacuum is not empty, but a stew of particles blinking into and then being annihilated out of existence. Those ephemeral charged particles, for a fraction of a second, pulled on the metal plates, and in turn, the plates pulled towards each other, towed by invisible, unseen forces. And in the same way, the small distance between our bodies was not empty, but churning with thoughts rising and disappearing and pulling at us.

Well, there's a reason why I'm a physicist, not a poet. I almost confessed these ideas to Ada, but instead, I said, "So... Radio astronomy?"

Ada looked up at me, her face happy and open. "Yeah. I like the idea of eavesdropping on the universe. I also like the grand scope of radio astronomy. With optical telescopes, you squint at smaller and smaller points in the field of view. But with radio astronomy, you embrace the entirety of the sky."

We stopped in front of a storefront that had laid out silver and turquoise jewelry, and she talked about mapping the radio source at the center of our galaxy, Sag A*, pronounced "Sadge-A-star." Sagittarius was the constellation of the archer, a centaur, half man and half horse, and weren't we all half one thing and half another? He aimed his arrow at the heart of the poisonous Scorpius, but his own heart, at the center of our galaxy, was an enormous black hole hungrily devouring any stars that strayed too close.

"And your summer work?" she asked. "You're rather cagey about it. Is it some sort of secret?"

"I don't have a clearance. It's just ... complicated." I wanted to come across as a serious physicist to her, someone solving difficult differential equations or carefully measuring minute magnetic fluctuations. I wanted her to think I had put my fascination with dissident, outsider science behind me.

"Oh, did H_2O put you onto some weird project? That would be like him." She took my hand. "Don't worry, I won't interrogate you. At least not by email, if you're worried about being monitored." She paused, looking thoughtful. I was thinking mostly about her hand in mine. "And I won't suggest that we send each other coded message by email, the way Feynman did during the war."

Physicist Richard Feynman had worked on the top-secret Manhattan Project during the war. He and his girlfriend—later wife—mischievously sent each other puzzles, codes, and other things designed to test the limits of censorship.

"His girlfriend was dying of TB," I said. "Maybe they felt they had less to lose."

"If I were dying, would you tell me more about your work?" Ada asked.

We stopped in front of a store displaying kachina dolls. "If you were dying, there might be more important things to talk about than what's in a few old rusty file cabinets."

"Old rusty file cabinets, eh?" Ada said. "You slipped up."

"All it takes to get me talking is a pretty girl. A pretty, *smart* girl. I mean, a pretty, smart young woman. I mean, a *smart*, pretty—"

"Maybe you would be *smart* to stop right there." But she didn't let go of my hand.

At the restaurant, I ordered a red chile Colorado, so spicy that I could only eat a couple of bites, while Ada had a blue corn tamale. We talked about family. Mostly, Ada talked: her father was a professor of theology, of all things, and her mother a psychologist. She had a sister two years younger, studying to be an elementary school teacher, and a much younger brother.

Then she fixed me with her hawk stare. "You?"

"Well, I have a father, and a mother, I guess, and a sister, about three years older. And then there was my... Well, and there was, uh... I'm not really in touch with them."

"What happened?" Ada asked, her voice gentle.

I took a long time to answer. "A lot."

She reached for my hand and squeezed. I wanted her to keep holding my hand, but she let go and forked another bite of tamale.

"I'm not trying to be mysterious," I said.

"I know. Whenever you're ready."

We splurged and ordered sopapillas with honey for dessert. Ada had half of hers and gave the other half to me. As we headed back to the bus stop, we held hands again, and I felt lightheaded, although it could have been because Santa Fe was at seven thousand feet. Los Alamos was, too, of course, but that was the story I told myself.

As we waited at the bus station, Ada said, "So, any particular reason your parents named you John? I mean, obviously, I was named after—"

"Lady Lovelace, the poet Byron's daughter, friend to Charles Babbage and his difference engine. I figured."

"In college, my father originally majored in electrical engineering. He thought he'd be part of the coming computer revolution. But on a whim, he took ancient Greek, got hooked, and... But he still had a soft spot for Ada Lovelace." She bumped against me, a nudge. "What's your story? Or is that top secret?"

"Well," I said, "my mother's family was religious, though my parents weren't. My mother, apparently, thought it would make *her* mother happy to give me biblical name, only not too biblical. The way she told it, I'm not named for John the disciple—"

"The disciple who loved Jesus," Ada said.

"Okay, sure, I guess... Or John who wrote the Gospel of John, and it wasn't even after John the baptizer, the guy in camel skins who ate bugs. No, she claimed I was named after the John who wrote the Book of Revelation..."

"John of Patmos. *Apocalypse* in Greek: revelation, or unveiling. My Greek isn't like my father's, but I picked up a little."

"That's me: the author of the apocalypse," I said. "That's how my mother saw me."

"Oh," she said. And then, "Here comes my bus."

"Mine's in about thirty minutes," I said as her bus pulled up, wreathed in the scent of diesel. "So much for simultaneity," I added: a physics joke. Ada laughed, and her laugh was like a little helium balloon tugging my heart upward.

The bus wheezed to a stop. Ada faced me, tilting her head to one side. "Oh, for goodness's sake..." She stood on the tips of her sneakers, leaned in close, and kissed me.

You probably remember what your first kiss was like. Mine was just like that.

She rocked back on her feet, gave me a wry smile, and ran to her bus. Halfway there, she turned and called, "That wasn't so bad, was it?"

My reply was "Uh, um, no!"

She waved and got on her bus.

Canterbury wanted to unleash the power of poetry, but one man's unveiling is another woman's apocalypse. As the summer came to a close, I found that he hadn't made a breakthrough in poetry. You can assign a word a number, like ASCII encoding for computers and email, but how do you assign it a value? How do you weigh a metaphor, or measure an image? Moody, ephemeral poetry defied mathematical analysis, but could still cut like a stiletto. Canterbury pressed the poets for poems; more data for his analyses. They balked and complained, then wrote at night under the clear New Mexican skies.

He was getting nowhere. So many of his ideas had come to naught. He was terrified of having no legacy. He wrote, *Feeling desperation, much perspiration, desert desolation.*

Then he added something I hadn't seen before: *prob. pump. Must fetch from NTS.* NTS was lab-speak for the Nevada Test Site—as in, nuclear weapons tests.

Canterbury spun out many fabulous tales. In addition to Schrödinger's missing *journal de amor,* Canterbury seemed obsessed with why Lise Meitner, co-discoverer of nuclear fission, never won the Nobel Prize. Sexism and antisemitism didn't explain it for him. He thought it had to be a conspiracy. He thought Meitner knew something or had discovered something, and to keep the spotlight off her, she was denied the Nobel.

In Canterbury's imagined cover-up, Meitner had discovered something hidden in quantum mechanics. Something no one else had found. There was no evidence for this. Still, Canterbury chased after quantum mechanics as if it were a magical Macguffin. *Nonlinear?* he wrote in the margin of one notebook. *Nonlocal? Non-real?*

Whatever crazy theories he had about quantum mechanics, he managed to design, have built, and get deployed at the Nevada Test Site something he called a "probability pump."

I emailed Ada, suggesting that we meet up in Santa Fe again. She wrote back, *I'm so sorry, John, but I have to head home to Montana. My father's had a relapse.*

I stared at the computer screen. I didn't know what she meant by a relapse. She'd said nothing about her father being ill. Both of us were keeping secrets in our back pockets. I felt the way Canterbury must have in 1951: the lazy summer days slipping away, and what had felt like victory threatened to turn into a cold, damp loss.

There were sketches of the probability pumps in the notebooks: cylinders you could cradle in your arms like a babe, only these babies were batteries, filled with exotic metastable materials, charged up by the aftereffects of a nuclear explosion.

As the summer of '51 wound down, Canterbury wrote, *I have convinced them to take a leap. Well, "convince" is a stretch, for I have not been fully forthcoming with them. Yet what is poetry but a stack of lies measured out to unveil the truth?* [Another apocalypse.] *What are our equations, but dressing the rough beasts of nature to make them look well mannered and buckled to the plow? Also a lie, of a kind. Perhaps I am lying to myself.*

Canterbury did more than write equations and run computer programs. In desperation, he carried out an experiment involving one of his probability pumps. Later, I guessed more about the devices, but even that summer, I figured it was something quantum mechanical. The machinery of the subatomic world is not springs and levers and gears but fuzzy probabilities, as indifferent gods roll dice uncountable times a second. And nuclear explosions were massive fireballs of quantum probabilities rising in smoke and ashes into the stratosphere.

Canterbury wrote, *Exposure: fifteen minutes, while they worked in silence. I left the room and went for a walk. Coward. When I returned to the sound of scribbling pens and pencils on paper, I asked how everyone was. Sylvie said the room felt hot and stuffy, and could someone please open a window?*

In the weeks after their exposure to the effects of the probability pump, the poets wrote, and wrote, and wrote. Some, like Nathan, reported themselves unable to sleep due to the poetry pouring out. I found fat folders of poems, labeled in Canterbury's handwriting, *Post prob. pump.* When I read them, my heart squeezed and started to pound. I felt perspiration on my temples and in my armpits. I had to put the poems down and go outside into the diamond sunlight refracting on the high plateau.

I don't remember any of the lines, only how they lit my heart afire. And I don't have access to the poems anymore.

Canterbury wrote, *I have succeeded, but I don't know what I mean by success, and I don't know what I have learned. The poets all feel it. Randy pesters me to know more about the "device" (I had assured them it wasn't radioactive, which is true, and yet not the whole truth), and I no longer know what to tell them. Is this how the Lord felt after the days of creation, reveling in the earthly beauty of Adam and Eve, yet wondering what darkness He had unleashed?*

I had no training in poetry. In the circus, the poetry was in motion, not in words. Yet their words lashed at me, stung like maddened hornets, cut like broken glass. Sylvie wrote about her dead father, bloated in her memory like the corpse of a seal; Anne wrote about witches flying high across a blackboard sky; John wrote about searing adulterous passions locked away like old history books. And Nathan, a shy man passing from youth into middle age, who lived with his parents, who early in the summer had written tightly controlled verses with tightly controlled images, suddenly strode boldly across the page— *You write like a colossus,* Sylvie had written on one of his poems—afire with sex and resentment and longing and wonder. They weren't even separate coherent poems, just page after page of searing verse. He wrote about a bird fluttering in the backyard, only it was really the boy who had kissed him at age twelve; about water in a pothole turned to ice, only it was about his father's emotional abandonment; and about a lamb being taken quietly to slaughter to serve as dinner for a man whom the poor farmer owed money, but instead, it was the babysitter who had molested him at age six.

Then the poems stopped. Canterbury wrote on August 10, 1951, *Found Nathan. Hanged himself. Face turned purple, bowels evacuated. How unpoetic is death. On a scrap of paper, he wrote only this: "It's too much, and too little."*

He also noted, *This is the sixth anniversary and a day of Nagasaki.*

After that, I sat at the desk, staring at the long-abandoned paper wasp nests in the corners of the ceiling. Every time I started to open up the papers, I saw my mother, sawing at her wrist with a knife, sticking her tongue in an electrical socket, jumping off our roof, and my heart beat so fast that I thought it might explode.

I turned to the last pages. Canterbury wrote, *Project disbanded. Poets departing. Investigation promised. Threats made by management— "How could you?", etc., "What were you thinking?", etc., endangering nat'l sec., etc., career ending, etc. I used to think a career was more important than a life, as if I had never seen the Nazis march in. Forgive me. I hope the other poets forgive me. I hope the other poets survive.*

Reading this, I got a cold feeling on the back of my neck. Canterbury never wrote out the full names of his poets, but rereading notes from the beginning of summer, I found:

John B., 34
Miguel I., 29
Randall J., 37
Sylvie P, 19
Anne S., 23
Nathan W., 33

I did something I shouldn't have done: I carefully cut out the page with the names of the poets. It bore no mathematics, nothing that could be construed as classified. (In my defense, I shouldn't have had access to anything classified.) I thought myself safe.

To go from Building 18 to the main site, I had to exit the secure area, walk a dirt road, and then go back in, flashing my badge. I had done this scores of times. But this time, as I walked through the gates, red lights flashed, and a bell rang. I stood stock still, a rabbit seeing the shadow of a hawk.

The guard came out of his hut. "Let's see what you got in your bag, son." He carried a Geiger counter. "That was a radiological sensor. Probably a false alarm."

But as he passed it over the items in my backpack, the Geiger counter suddenly crackled and spat and clicked at the list of the names of poets: a radioactive set of names.

Although the page of names was taken away, I nonetheless looked up biographies of famous poets in the Santa Fe library. The back of my neck felt radioactive when I made the connections.

I never found any published poems by Nathan. He had no close family and died un-mourned and unnoticed. Ignited by Canterbury's experiment, he had burned too bright too quickly. The other poets were luckier, for a while, anyway, until the flames burned them up, too, leaving only bitter fame.

Later we figured out that Canterbury, ever eccentric, had devised an ink with minute traces of plutonium. As for why, we never figured that out, aside from some sort of magical thinking. But it turned out that *all* the notebooks were contaminated.

The lab's doctor examined me and took blood samples. "Actually, you should be okay. The alpha radiation won't pass through your dead skin cells. As long as you weren't licking the pages, you should be fine. You *weren't* licking them, were you?"

"You're not in trouble, John," Hile told me. "But those documents have been taken to a safe storage bunker."

"What did Canterbury *do*?" I asked. "In his notes, it's as if he held ... like a séance, or a performance, or *something*. He exposed the poets to one of his probability pumps..."

Hile held up a hand. "You shouldn't talk about *that* outside of a classified area."

"But I don't have clearance. I can't get into a classified area."

Hile nodded. "Well, then—I hate to say this—you shouldn't talk about it at all."

He got up and started to walk away.

I said, "Professor—H_2O—*Ozzie*—they all *died*."

"Everyone dies, John," Hile said, his back still to me.

"A couple of the names I didn't recognize," I said, "but the other ones—it was like Nathan—they committed *suicide*." I paused. "Was that because of the, um, that gadget?"

He glanced over his shoulder, and I saw a flicker in his face. "If you're asking that question, John," he said, his eyes downcast, as if talking to himself, "do you still wonder why you shouldn't talk about it?" Then he went out the door, closing it behind him.

Love and Death-Rays

The pull of science is love. As a child, I was obsessed with dinosaurs: their enormous bodies, their tiny brains, their tragic fate. Other scientists I've met have been seduced by stars and rocket ships, by savage storms and upheaving continents, by mold and cellular division and multiplication. We each fell in love with something beautiful, terrifying, awe-inspiring... something greater than ourselves.

But as you have lamented to me on many occasions, science is lubricated by money. Scientists become accountants and hucksters. We beg for money in proposals and hope someone with test-tube eyes and a good bank account will care enough to pay. We squeeze out every penny and lie awake at night, wondering how we'll cover the salaries of students and postdocs full of coffee and dreams of discovery.

Investments in science lay the groundwork for a better, more prosperous society, and for us to be ready should another Manhattan Project be needed. But as economies falter and the lash of war becomes distant, the urgency fades, and budgets lose impetus.

This explains why, about two weeks before I was to begin graduate school, Huey Hile admitted with embarrassment that he didn't have grant money to support me. "I'm really sorry, John."

To be sure, I had assumed a Nobel Prize winner would have grant money flowing out of their pockets.

"I guess I can be a TA," I said.

Hile looked stricken. "The department has filled its teaching assistant slots. You're on a waiting list, but..."

I slouched out of his office, feeling as if a Pachycephalosaurus had head-butted me in the gut. I was so upset my legs buckled, and I leaned against a bulletin board sprouting a thick crop of posters and flyers. When a bent staple scratched my forehead, I looked up to see:

SCIENTIFIC/TECHNICAL HELP WANTED
If you are buzzing with ideas for the FUTURE,

SKILLED in science, electronics, chemistry, and machinery,
this may be the JOB for you.
PHOENIX

And a phone number.

"What's this job you found?" Ada asked over sushi.

At the beginning of the quarter, we were both back in Seattle. I hadn't heard from her for nearly five weeks, but we took up again as if it had only been a long weekend. I had asked, "How's your father?", but she looked away, saying only, "The doctor thinks it's in remission now, but we don't really know yet." She spoke like someone being dragged over broken glass, so I changed the subject to my search for employment.

I showed her the flyer. "They asked me to bring a resume and a letter of recommendation. I went back to Hile, and he immediately wrote one out. He even showed it to me."

"Really? What'd he write?"

My face grew a bit warm, as I was embarrassed to boast. "Um... 'Mr. Chant is one of the most talented and resourceful young scientists I have ever met. You should hire him.' The end. I guess he felt bad about not having money for a research assistantship."

"H_2O is a nice guy, but he doesn't gush easily." Ada studied the flyer. "This looks like the ads *you* put up, for your 'dissident scientists.'"

I shrugged and took the last piece of unagi. "I suppose it could be sketchy. But I'm scrambling to find any work."

The server came by. "Something else?"

Ada scanned the menu. "Scallop sushi? Sounds different."

"Sorry, out of those," the server said.

"Then another dragon roll." After the server left, she said, "You know, I've never had scallops. Most of my past boyfriends were either Jewish or vegan."

I admit, I got a little tingle when she said "past boyfriends." Did that put me in the category of "current boyfriend"?

A week after I sent off Hile's letter and my resume—which I spent several days writing and rewriting, trying to make it sound more normal, and failing—I got called in for an interview.

I traveled by bus to a nondescript two-story office building in Ballard, one of Seattle's cheerfully quirky neighborhoods. I found a door labeled PHOENIX. A stout, mahogany-skinned woman let me in, introducing herself as Cristina Hernandez, the office manager.

"It's a compact operation," she said as she gave me a tour of cramped offices and a small lab with back-to-back technicians soldering electronics.

"What exactly does Phoenix do?"

"Mr. Pigeon's vision is to seek out, evaluate, and monetize underappreciated intellectual properties—patents, inventions, that kind of thing."

"Mr. Pigeon?"

"Mr. F. L. Pigeon—he's the owner and head."

We sat down and went over my resume. I remember sweating as I stammered out my life story.

She nodded. "Mr. Pigeon appreciates people who don't follow the usual well-worn path." She slid some drawings over to me. "To give you an idea of what we deal with, why don't you take a look at this and let me know what you think? I'll be back in thirty minutes." She stood up.

Before Ms. Hernandez was out the door, I blurted out, "It's some kind of backpack accelerator, a particle accelerator." The design impressed me. Accelerators took up huge amounts of real estate. Cyclotrons lurked like Grendel in concrete caverns, while the largest synchrotrons burrowed under and around entire towns and crossed international borders. This design shrank one down to the size of a suitcase. "Aside from the problem of the power supply—which would need to be the size of a truck to meet these specs—the radiation would kill whoever was wearing it. Unless that's the point?"

I looked up at Ms. Hernandez. Standing behind her was a tall man wearing a blazer that, despite his size, looked a size or two too large. He had burnished red hair like copper coils and a darker, close-cropped beard, his hands in the pockets of his blazer.

"John, this is Mr. Pigeon," Ms. Hernandez said.

Mr. Pigeon didn't take his hands out of his pockets, so I didn't offer to shake.

"Let's talk in my office," he said. He was one of those tall men who nevertheless had a high, tenor voice.

I followed him to another small, cramped room. Clearly, Phoenix did not try to impress you with cathedral-sized office spaces. I decided I liked that. Small and scrappy fit me.

Mr. Pigeon sat down behind a narrow desk devoid of photos or trinkets. Beneath the beard, he had a soft, dumpling face, but his dark brown eyes looked hard as polished stones. On a shelf behind him, a small cage contained a pair of white mice, pressing against the wire mesh to look at me, like fans hoping to spy a celebrity.

"You know about accelerators," he said. He was studying my resume, and Hile's letter, too. "Many physics students focus on quantum gravity or black holes, wanting to be the next Einstein. Accelerators are not nearly as sexy, but they are practical." I caught a sweet whiff of approval in this last statement.

"I've got my impractical streak, too." That elicited a slight smile. Above him, the mice scrabbled in the pine shavings, twitching their pink noses. "Do your mice have names?"

"They're rats, smarter than mice. But no. They aren't ... pets." I glanced at him, and he shrugged. "Years ago, when I was getting my PhD, I worked on rats. For a while, they were more real to me than people."

"What were you investigating?"

"Neurobiology. But I left the program halfway through. I suppose I keep rats as a reminder of unfinished business." He stood up. "My company trades in overlooked technological potentialities. This calls for someone with high technical skills, critical judgment, and an eye for the unconventional. Do you fit that description?"

"I don't think I fit any description," I said, more to myself, but Mr. Pigeon nodded and thumped the blueprints on his desk.

"You efficiently and correctly characterized these plans, seizing upon the key points with impressive speed. What I need, Mr. Chant, is for you to do the same for other designs."

"You want me to evaluate inventions, the good and the bad. Like a patent clerk, I guess, like Einstein in 1905."

Mr. Pigeon nodded. "Yes, while he was revolutionizing three fields of physics."

He offered to hire me and told me the pay. For a struggling grad student, it sounded like a fortune. He said I could work part-time while taking classes.

"Well, Mr. Chant?"

I nodded. "This I can do."

My first year of grad school started at this time. Ada was in her second year, already fretting over the qualifying exam, an exam so fiendishly difficult that if it weren't administered by professors, it might qualify as hazing. As for myself, I felt disconnected from the program. At first, it was just me getting used to a normal university. At my undergraduate clown college, most of the faculty, even the physics instructors, wore red rubber noses, and we students were expected to be able to solve difficult math problems while juggling bowling pins and wearing big floppy shoes. This probably explains why I got a B- in electromagnetism. So, by comparison, my UW courses were so tame that I sometimes fell asleep, only to lurch awake and blurt out a mistake the professor had made on the blackboard. At clown college, we honked horns whenever someone, whether professor or student, made a mistake, and everyone laughed good-naturedly. But at the UW, saying aloud to a professor, "You left off a factor of two pi there" often only earned a glare in my direction.

More importantly, I had no official employment at the university (though Hile had dredged up funds to cover my tuition), so I didn't get a desk. I hung out in Ada's shared office instead. As time ticked by, other students dropped by to ask me about integrals and other knotty math problems.

"You've got a reputation," Ada told me.

"How did that happen?"

"I boasted about you."

"What, the integrals? They're just party tricks." In truth, I knew Ada would make a better researcher than me. She had better focus, concentration, and follow-through. I was quick, but she was deeper. I tried to tell her this, but she always changed the subject.

On a weekend afternoon, when heavy rain had washed away our plans to go hiking, we sprawled on the floor of my small apartment. "I should finish my homework," Ada said, opening up her notebooks.

"Galactic evolution?"

She shook her head. "Actually, I'm switching to nuclear experimentation. Stellar reaction rates. Professor Ukoma talked me into joining his group."

"Yeah, funny, he talked to me, too."

"Someone might have mentioned your experience with accelerators," Ada said. "Anyway, at the last moment, I swapped out galactic evolution for nuclear astrophysics."

"But you love radio astronomy."

She sighed, as if over a lost crush. "I know. But I have to think about the future." She stared out the window at the gray skies.

"Do radio telescopes work in the rain?"

"Hmm... Why?"

"Let's build our own."

"Our own radio telescope?" Ada said. "You should know, I really suck at soldering."

I opened my mouth to say I had learned to solder at age nine, but closed it again. "Practice makes perfect," I said instead.

Ms. Hernandez introduced me to two other evaluators: Serge Kreminsky, a barrel-chested, middle-aged white man with a broad face, tiny glasses, and graying hair; and Junie Johnson, a Black grad student in electrical engineering at the university, her hair woven into tight cornrows. Serge said he used to sell insurance, but had a long-time hobby with ham radio.

At Phoenix, we were assigned files—sketches, blueprints, patents—to evaluate for practicality, possible uses, and potential improvements. We even had funds to build working models of inventions. Serge told me he often went to junkyards, where he could find all sorts of parts nearly for free. "I picked up the habit from the show," he said.

"Show? What show?"

Serge and Junie looked at each other. "We also answered an ad, but not for Phoenix," Junie said. "For a TV show." She described it as "some kind of unscripted competition." Nowadays, she would have called it "reality TV," but this was before *Survivor* and *America's Top Model* created the archetype.

Mr. Pigeon had pitched a program called *Iron Genius* to a network. The idea was a cadre of amateur inventors who would be given a pile of spare parts to invent solutions to overcome various challenges that got harder and harder.

It occurred to me that *I* could have been a contestant. After all, inventing something out of junk at a moment's notice was a family skill. But I was also shy and didn't relish the idea of being on TV, so I shook off the idea.

"For this job," Serge told me, "Mr. Pigeon doesn't want us to only evaluate inventions. He encourages us to improve them, take them in a different direction. I don't think he cared about *Iron Genius*. For him, it was a way to recruit below-the-radar inventors."

He broke off as Mr. Pigeon himself came into our shared office. "Some files for you," he said, sliding them across my desk. "Since you're new, no hurry."

I flipped through them. "I'll finish them by tomorrow."

He eyed me. "Somehow, I think you're as quick as you claim. I'm sure Professor Huey Hile is glad to have you as his student. How is Hile these days?"

"He's good. Busy, of course. Really, really busy. Saw him yesterday."

"So, not too busy for the son of his old friend, Professor Alan Chant."

Up to this point, my conversations with Mr. Pigeon had been genial. But when he said my father's name, his words felt probing, cold and cutting, like a knife made of raw iron, and my stomach became queasy.

"Uh, I'll get started on these, Mr. Pigeon," I said, spreading the pages across the desk. I had to look away, surprised at the hot wetness in my eyes.

Mr. Pigeon returned his hands to the pockets of his blazer. "I look forward to your report."

Ada had offered to make dinner: her first time cooking for me. I thought up some quips about cooking over a Bunsen burner, but when I showed up at her third-floor apartment, I found myself still in a disjointed mood. After giving me a light kiss, Ada furrowed her brow and said, "Is everything okay?"

She had put on a nice dress and earrings, and a faint floral perfume lingered from when she had brushed her face against mine. The table was set with candles, and she had classical music playing.

"Brahms?" I asked.

"Not even close," she said. "Mozart. Although perhaps I should have gone for late Beethoven quartets. Maybe I misjudged—"

"It's not your fault."

She poured a glass of wine and handed it to me. I stared at the glass.

"You don't have to drink it. Don't feel pressured." She reached for it, but I swung it away.

"I've never had any problems with alcohol," I said. "But, well ... my mother did." Ada stood very still. "Today at work, Mr. Pigeon brought up my father. I guess he pieced together the connection with Hile." Even as I told her about it, the wet pressure at the corners of my eyes returned. "Hile talks about my father, of course, tells stories about him, but they're old friends. But when Pigeon said my father's name, it upset me, more than I would have thought. There was something ugly..." I blinked away the tears forming. I had thought I had finally buried my grief, but I could feel it bubbling up at the back of my throat. "I'm sorry, you wanted to make a romantic evening, and I've spoiled it."

Ada gave a half-smile and took a half step towards me. "Our families have a strong grip on us. I know that." Another small step. "And I also know how I feel about you."

I swiped at my dripping nose. "Gah, this can't be very romantic..."

Another step, and her body brushed against mine. I could feel her radiating warmth. "Do you know when I fell for you?" she asked. "You chided me for being unkind. Towards your 'outsider scientists.'"

"The crackpots."

"You told me not to call them crazies. You cared about them, even if they were crackpots. You saw them as human beings, even if flawed. And that's ... the moment I fell for you."

But then she leaned away. "I'm sorry," she said. "I'm making you uncomfortable."

"No," I said. "I mean, I am, but not because... Well, yes, because I'm not used to... I wasn't expecting..."

"Me wanting to kiss you?" My face must have been a question, because she nodded. "But not if you don't want me to."

I wanted to tell her when I'd first fallen for her. But that's not what happened next.

I woke up happy, with Ada asleep next to me. I wondered if this was what love was like. I had had infatuations and crushes before, of course, but they had all been as imaginary as a hobbit.

I tried to dress quietly, but she opened her eyes. "You have to go?" she asked sleepily.

"Yeah, sorry, gotta finish my quantum homework."

She lifted her head, and I leaned over to give her a kiss. It seemed so natural, so easy, and I didn't want to leave. I wanted to crawl back into bed and stay with her forever. Stalling, I sat on the edge of the bed and gestured to a picture on the wall. "I never asked you about that."

"Mmm?" She craned her neck to see. "Oh. That's Sanjusangendo Temple, in Kyoto. My favorite place in Kyoto, anyway, one of my favorite places. There's a walkway, thirty-three paces long, past a thousand and one statues of Kannon."

"Statues of cannons?"

"Kannon." She gave me the English spelling. "The bodhisattva of compassion and mercy, an incarnation of the Buddha. They had archery competitions there, shooting arrows as those thousand and one Buddhas of Mercy watched." I could hear the twang of bows and thwack of arrows hitting targets as she talked. "That must take some nerve."

Thinking of competitions, later at lunch, I asked Junie and Serge, "So, who won? The TV show? I don't really watch TV, so I missed it."

"Oh, *Iron Genius* was never broadcast. We never finished," Junie said, "not after the alligators and sharks."

"After the *what*?"

Serge leaned forward. "You have to understand, this was a very unusual production. Or so I assume." He shifted upright, taking a bite of a chicken salad sandwich. It was raining, so we ate at our desks. "Maybe they're all like that. I haven't been on any other."

I looked at Junie.

"Me neither," she said. "It was fun, kind of, but weird."

The show was built around a series of challenges, she explained. The first challenge was to lever a flipped car off a trapped person, in this case, a dummy.

"But when we began to work," Junie explained, "the dummies all start scream-ing. *'Mama, mama, help me, I'm dying!'* Really loud. And there was also blood, fake blood, spurting everywhere."

"Very unnerving," Serge said. "A couple of us quit on the spot."

"Remember Dave?" Junie said. "The radio control hobbyist? He kicked at his dummy until its head flew off and the screaming stopped."

"Wow," I said.

"The second challenge," Serge said, "was to make a nonlethal deterrent. Like for crowd control. Then we had to demonstrate our invention."

He looked over at Junie, who added, "On sasquatches. You know, Bigfoot, or I guess Bigfeet, in this case. Very tall actors in hairy costumes. They had this smoke machine going, and all these sasquatches came out roaring at us."

Serge said, "Most people made some sort of glue, but Penelope, she's a food chemist, so she had an advantage. She built this gun—"

"A diarrhea gun," Junie said, scrunching up her face and laughing at the same time. "It shot out this stuff that looked just like diarrhea, and it smelled *horrible*. But she said it was harmless and nontoxic."

"I remember that one of the actors playing a Bigfoot, he threw up inside his Bigfoot mask," Serge said.

"I think a couple of them did. I know *I* felt like throwing up."

I pushed away my half-eaten sandwich. "And now I don't feel like finishing lunch. Thanks a lot, guys."

Although I signed a nondisclosure agreement, a real one, with Phoenix Corpo-ration, I shared what I could with Ada. I got a lot of mileage from Serge and Junie's tales of *Iron Genius*. "Oh, how *disgusting!*" Ada said about the diarrhea gun. "Although, I did have this one boyfriend who was a biologist, who always said everything about our bodies is normal and for a reason."

"I wonder one day what stories about me you'll relay to a future boyfriend."

Ada put her arms around me. "Sorry! I do talk about my exes too much." She kissed me lightly. "But biologists aside, a diarrhea gun is just weird. You sure you want this job?"

"It pays better than a teaching assistantship. And I'm not working on a diarrhea gun. Not yet. Besides, weird is all I've ever known." Over time I had slowly told her my tale—my true story. Just like I'm telling you.

"Well, there's unconventional, and then there's weird."

We were sitting at her kitchen table. We had eaten dinner over the kitchen sink, because the table was covered with sketches for our homemade radio telescope, small enough to fit in a car. The rain had intensified, tapping out secret messages on the windows of her apartment. "So, absolutely nothing weird in your life?" I asked.

She smiled. "Besides building a personal radio telescope?"

"You never got into mischief as a kid?"

"No, my sister was the one who rebelled. Okay, well, I did have this weird hobby: I made up imaginary languages and alphabets. Too much Tolkien, I guess. I tried to teach them to a boy I liked, you know, so we could pass secret messages, but he didn't understand what I was going on about."

"How many did you invent?"

"I guess two or three mostly worked out, and word lists for half a dozen others. I also went through a phase of collecting dictionaries in different languages—not only Greek and Italian and German, but also Hebrew, Chinese, Japanese, Swahili, Navajo..."

"Okay, so, how do you say, 'You're beautiful' in Swahili?"

She wrinkled her nose at me. "I didn't actually *learn* those languages. At most a few phrases."

"How about 'I like you' in Chinese?"

"*Wo ai ni,*" she said promptly.

"Wow," I said.

"*Wo,*" she corrected. "You have to get the tone right. It dips down, then back up." She bent over the drawings of our radio telescope. "Actually, I spent more time on writing systems."

"Alphabets?"

"Alphabets, syllabaries, even ideograms like Chinese."

"And you taught them to your boyfriends."

"No, I *tried* to teach one to *a* boy I liked. Then I learned that he liked another girl, so I gave up." She shrugged. "I guess I was weird."

"By my standards, that's pretty normal."

"Was your childhood really that strange? It's not like you were raised in a secret cult of assassins." She squinted at me. "Tell me you weren't raised in a secret cult of assassins."

"I wasn't raised in a secret cult of assassins. Though, I suppose someone raised in a secret cult of assassins grows up thinking it's perfectly normal. You learn at your mother's knee how to asphyxiate someone with a newspaper, and how to combine ordinary kitchen ingredients into deadly poisons."

Ada put down her pencil. "Ugh, I don't want to even think about how to combine ordinary kitchen ingredients into poison."

"I'd only poison somebody to protect my loved ones. Well, loved *one*. You."

"Talking about poisons isn't very romantic, just so you know." She glanced at the picture of Sanjusangedo. "But the real question isn't 'Would you kill for someone you love?' It's 'Would you *die* for someone you love?'"

"Would you?"

She nodded. I felt I ought to say, *"Me, too,"* but it would sound like I was trying to win points with her—which I was.

"I suppose the Kannon of Mercy would approve," I finally said.

"So, what happened after the sasquatches and the diarrhea gun?" I asked Junie and Serge. The clouds had blown away, and it was a beautiful fall day beneath a sapphire sky. We sat at picnic table in a tiny park a block away from the Phoenix offices. "Did the challenges get worse after that?"

"Just different," Junie said. "The next one was to find a treasure chest in a garbage dump—a really stinky garbage dump."

"You won that one," Serge said.

"Ground-penetrating radar," Junie said, grinning. "I'd previously made one for friends in geology going down to Antarctica, so it was easy to whip up another. But Serge won the challenge after that."

"I simply won a war of attrition," Serge said. To me, he said, "The challenge was to build a killer-robot killer. We had seventy-two hours to build remote-controlled robots to fight against a killer robot with rotary saws for hands."

"Course, there was a twist," Junie added. "In this case, just as we started, a bunch of puppies and kittens were released on the soundstage floor, scampering between us and the killbot."

"Though those puppies and kittens were fake—just toys—and Junie here figured that out first."

"And the alligators and sharks?" I asked.

"That was supposed to be the next challenge: attach a 'grenade launcher,' really just a paintball gun, to the head of a shark or gator. Not as dangerous as it sounds: they'd gotten vet students or someone to pull the teeth of the gators and sharks they had in a tank."

"But then the SPCA caught wind of it, and they did not like it at all," said Junie. She finished the lunch she'd brought, prepackaged spinach salad, and got up to toss the flimsy plastic container in the garbage can.

"Even though gators and sharks lose and replace teeth all the time," said Serge. "Still, the production got shut down. I don't see how it could have played on TV anyway. Too weird. Then Pigeon offered the two of us jobs, said he liked our inventiveness."

"I think that was the plan all along," said Junie, sitting back down.

"Maybe," said Serge. "We never did get to the death-ray challenge."

"Death-ray?" I asked, intrigued.

"The contestants, we had this pool," Serge explained, "betting on what the final challenge would be. Most of us put money on 'death-ray.' I know I was getting this mad-scientist-slash-supervillain vibe, especially with the sharks and gators. The exception was Penelope, you know, the inventor of the diarrhea gun. She bet on zombies."

"I told her, a zombie is just a slow-moving, brain-eating death-ray," Junie said, "so really, we were all in agreement."

Later I realized that deep down, I also thought of neutrinos as a kind of death-ray. After all, my father claimed a neutrino had killed our dog, Bessie. At college, I learned more about the shy, tiny particles. In the subatomic world, protons and neutrons are the nine-hundred-pound (really: gigaelectron-volt) gorillas. Electrons, by contrast, are light and nimble, weighing barely one two-thousandth as much as a proton. But neutrinos are tinier still, weighing less than a *millionth* as much as an electron. You might wonder how one could possibly weigh such a tiny, squirrely particle, especially as neutrinos travel at nearly the speed of light. Yet their ghostly nature makes them the perfect assassin.

Thus, when Hile brought up research topics, I blurted out that for my undergraduate senior thesis, I had investigated ways to determine the infinitesimal mass of the neutrino. "Hmm," he said. He tapped his foot and stared up at the ceiling, as if looking for an escaped birthday balloon. I opened my mouth to downplay my suggestion, to say it was probably a psychological reaction to the death of my childhood dog, that by reducing the murderer from a near-mythic ghost to a number in a table with a lot of other numbers, it might assuage my grief. I hadn't come up with that; my undergraduate quantum professor, Ellen Boghassian, had suggested it. But Hile looked so deep in thought that I didn't dare disturb him.

He returned his gaze to me. "Long-baseline interferometry?"

I nodded.

"'Give me a place to stand and a long enough lever...'" Hile said.

"Archimedes," I said. With his brilliant, insatiable mind and a penchant for devising machines of war, Archimedes had been the Edward Teller (architect of the hydrogen bomb) of his day. Among the legends was that Archimedes had used mirrors to focus sunlight on the sails of invading ships, setting them afire with an ancient death-ray.

"It's good to keep Archimedes in mind when it comes to starting research. To tackle any problem, you need leverage," Hile said, a satisfied look on his face.

"I've barely started classes," I said, trying and failing to keep a note of panic out of my voice.

"Never too soon to start," Hile insisted.

Ada noticed me staring at the picture of Sanjusangedo and the thousand and one statues of Kannon. She cleared her throat.

"If you're thinking about compassion and mercy, want to come with me to feed the homeless?"

What I wanted was to look good to her, and maybe to Kannon as well, so I agreed to help the following weekend at the Street-Wise Shepherd Outreach Center downtown. The organization gave clean clothes and food to the homeless, and a couple of days of the week, there was even a barber available. I was assigned to ladle out soup, while Ada chatted with the guests as she handed them premade sandwiches. She knew several by name, and they beamed when she talked to them.

Afterwards, as we sat on the bus back to the U-District, Ada asked me my thoughts. "Was it what you expected?"

"I didn't know what to expect," I said, "so I'm glad I didn't come with any preconceptions. So, what made you want to work with the homeless? A sense of pity?"

"Not pity," she said. "Compassion."

"Isn't that the same—"

"No. Pity is looking down on someone. Compassion is more ... leveling. It's putting yourself in someone else's shoes. In ancient Greek, the word for *compassion* literally translates to 'someone felt in their guts for someone else.' Sorry, I'm a real language nerd." She laughed. "You talked to some of them, right?" I nodded. "Everyone has a different story. Some have mental health issues, others substance abuse issues, and others are just plain unlucky. Some don't want to follow any rules. Life has a lot of rules, you know?"

Although I had never thought about myself as a rule-follower, I am. Scientific research is about figuring out the rules of the universe: where an apple will fall, when the moon will shine in the sky, what medicine will cure a disease.

Academia likes to imagine itself stacked with iconoclasts, but in reality, it's also full of rules and expectations. My courses were kicking into high gear, and we had our first exams. I was disappointed to score in the low eighties, until I found out the average was in the forties. "How did you do?" one classmate asked me. I put my hand over the big red 82 on my paper and said, "Oh, about average, whatever that means," and she laughed. That made me think of Ada laughing, and her kisses, and her hands on my face and on my body.

I worried about Hile's expectations of me. He had outlined an absurdly ambitious research project. He wanted to recast his Nobel-Prize-winning prediction about the expansion of the universe, originally written using the language of thermodynamic phase changes, into a full quantum description. As he talked about the relationship between temperature and imaginary time, I began to feel extraordinarily stupid. Maybe he thought I needed to be humbled. Maybe this was how *I* sounded to other people.

I piled up papers and books and wrote out dozens of pages of notes, but the next day, it looked like cuneiform, like the tracks of a chicken dancing in the mud. It didn't help that my mind was (and still is) chaotic, a rebellious adolescent seeking affirmation while simultaneously doing the opposite of what was asked.

I tried to make excuses. He waved it off. "I know you have a lot on your plate, John." I had told him I'd found a job, but I never explained what kind of job, worried he would think it was strange.

At Phoenix, we often worked together, so one day Junie Johnson brought me a design for a "sonic scalpel," using powerful ultrasound to cut through tissue, cartilage, and bone. "The electrical stuff is straightforward," said Junie, leaning on my desk, "but I'm not as strong on ultrasound."

"I'll have to look up some stuff at the library," I said. "Hmm... These notes make approximations I'm not sure I would trust."

"You taking a class on this?"

"Not yet," I said. My classes were working through Lagrangians and least action principles and a whole beauty pageant of particles as we systematically marched through the standard physics syllabus, while for Phoenix, I had to jump from one peak of knowledge to another, skimming the literature for barely enough information to pry open my understanding. Personally, I found the contrast enjoyable. Ada, who had a tidier mind, shuddered; she needed to master the foundations before moving to the fringes.

I would dash by bus or by bike from the nondescript office in Ballard to classes on campus, frequently scribbling out my homework at 2:00 or 3:00 a.m. as I listened to the rain, and then hastily rewriting it to be more legible before turning it in. Occasionally, Serge and I would run to a junkyard to get spare parts with which to build a working model of some of the designs we were examining.

And also, when we both had a free moment, I grabbed coffee or a quick lunch with Ada, both of us poring over notes. She was as busy as I was, maybe even more so, studying nuclear astrophysics and beginning to carry out experiments in that field. On weekends, we began to gather parts for our home radio telescope with trips to junkyards. There was a bit of the boyfriend-girlfriend thing, too, and I found myself thinking, *So, this is what happiness is.*

Junie and I handed Mr. Pigeon a report on the sonic scalpel. "It won't work," I said. "You can't get the focus narrow enough to cut neatly."

"You figured out the math?" Mr. Pigeon asked.

"We built and tested a demo," Junie said. "We can show you."

In the tiny lab, we had set up cheap hunks of beef and big bones. The room was redolent of blood. "Look at these cuts," I said. "Not the precision work one wants."

"And it just fractures bone, instead of cutting it," added Junie.

"You don't think it can be improved?" Mr. Pigeon asked.

I shook my head. "No, our experiments match the math, and the math says you can't focus much narrower."

Junie put a hand on the working demo of the sonic scalpel we'd rigged up. "This would work better as a torture device than as a tool for surgery," she said.

Mr. Pigeon put his face close to the nest of wires and coils. "I could probably find a buyer for that," he murmured.

Junie made a face. "Tell me you're joking."

Mr. Pigeon straightened to his full height and smiled broadly. "Of course I am." Looking down again at the would-be scalpel, he said, "Time to move on," and handed us a thick file. "New project. I want both of you working on this."

Junie flipped through the first pages. "Defenses against hypersonic missiles," she read. "I don't see any plans."

"Just specifications," Mr. Pigeon said. "I want you two to come up with a proposal. Your own design." Junie and I glanced at each other. "I've gotten a contract from a client who in turn is fishing for a Department of Defense grant."

"Hypersonic missiles aren't a thing," Junie said. She plucked at her hair, the way she did when she was perturbed.

"Not today. But the client thinks it could be one day, and wants to be ready to step up to the Pentagon."

"What approach do you want us to use?" Junie asked, flipping through the file. "Rail gun, microwave, laser..."

"Evaluate the options and rate the best ones."

"Basically, you want *us* to invent this hypersonic missile defense."

"Exactly." Mr. Pigeon slipped his hands into his pockets.

Back in our cramped office, Serge waved off any suggestion that Mr. Pigeon was dissing him by not putting him on the project. "I've got my hands full, and he knows it." He glanced at Junie. "So, I'm guessing rail gun?" To me, he said, "For the killer robot challenge, she mounted a rail gun on her rambot. Took out a leg of the killbot, too."

"Hey, I know magnetic fields," Junie said. She sat down on her desk and massaged her temples. "Though I have to say, I feel a bit uneasy about this."

"What's wrong with missile defense?" I asked.

"Any defense is only a few steps from an offense," she said. "A scalpel can become a shiv, or a sonic scalpel a torture device. I don't want to work with weapons, and I told Mr. Pigeon that."

"Don't worry, it won't be used to shoot down UFOs," Serge said with a smirk. Junie made a face at him.

"What's this?" I asked.

Junie sighed loudly. Serge said, "She's a UFO conspiracist."

"Am not!" Junie sighed again. "On *Iron Genius*, each of us filled out a form with our hobbies and interests. That became sort of everyone's call sign. Serge, the ham radio enthusiast. Penelope, the food chemist. Dave, the radio control hobbyist. Eun-jeong, the ex-Marine. I've always been fascinated by the idea of alien astronauts visiting ancient Earth and being mistaken for gods, but then I got labeled as the 'UFO conspiracist.' I was steeling myself to be pegged as 'the Black engineer,' like some kind of mythical beast, but 'UFO conspiracist' is way worse. Thanks a lot, ham radio enthusiast Serge. Now John will think I'm crazy."

"I doubt that," I said. "I once met a guy who pretended to be a space alien, and then had to flee government scientists who wanted to dissect him. I met him in a sewer, which my father had turned into a particle accelerator."

Junie stared at me for a moment, then burst out laughing. "Oh, John! You sure know how to make a gal feel better."

While Junie started working up specs for a rail gun defense against hypersonic missiles, I sauntered through the back files of Phoenix, looking for inspiration. One particular set of plans, though it had nothing to do with missile defense, caught my attention. It was a modification of a nerve induction device—a "wireless taser," the drawings called it—intended to inflame pain-conducting nerves in the victim. It was based upon a paper claiming certain microwave frequencies could resonate specific nerve cells. Now *this* was a torture device. "Kannon forgive me," I whispered.

Of course, it was so horrible that I couldn't just put it aside. In the campus library, I found a big atlas of the nervous system. I wondered if instead of pain, one could induce sleep or lethargy, but there aren't specific nerve cells for that. There are pain neurons, of course, and nerves that transmit touch and heat and cold, as well as nerves that stimulate muscles, both voluntary and involuntary, and so on.

I stopped at mirror neurons: neurons in our brains whose task it is to model the behavior of others. They activate when we watch a sports match, or a horror or adventure movie, or when we listen to a sad song and tears form in our eyes. Some biologists think mirror neurons drive our theory of mind, our understanding that other people have agendas and ideas separate from our own.

Digging deeper, I found experiments suggesting that mirror neurons are particularly sensitive to terahertz radio frequencies. You know how easily I spark off ideas; it was part of my childhood. And from the dark mines of my subconscious came the raw clay of an invention.

As we were lying together in bed one Saturday night in October, Ada asked, "Why haven't you tried to contact your family? If not your father, maybe your sister? She didn't send you off to a circus."

"Oh, I'm sure she was happy to see me go."

"I doubt that. Siblings fight and get on each other's nerves, but they don't really want bad things to happen to each other."

I said nothing for a while.

"Sorry. I know it's a sore spot for you."

"Maybe ... maybe I'm thinking how lucky I am to be in bed next to a naked girl."

She pushed at me. "You *are* lucky, buster, and don't you forget it." She kissed me to prove it. "I don't mean to be pushy. But family, even when troubling, is important."

"You ever take apart a golf ball?" I asked. "You know, saw one in half, and find out it has all the complicated wires and stuff wound all the way through it?"

"Yeah, of course."

"That's how my chest starts to feel whenever I think about my family." I pressed my face against her, breathed in her scent. "I'm sorry it's so hard for me to talk about."

"Well, to be fair," Ada said, almost in a whisper, "I don't tell you much about *my* father. It's because his prognosis is still uncertain. The doctors say he's clean, but then want monthly scans. I'll try to share more with you."

"I guess that's my cue to say *I'll* share more of my family stuff with you?" I felt her nod in the dark. "Okay, deal."

She stretched her body, pressing herself against me. "And, well, there is another thing I haven't shared with you. I don't know why I kept it secret... Well, I *do* know why."

"What did you keep secret?"

She took a deep intake of breath. "Want to go to church with me in the morning?"

As we sat in the pew, I whispered, "When you said you had a secret, I thought you meant, like, you had a tropical disease, or you're an international bank thief."

"But this is worse, right? Be honest."

"No, just ... less expected."

The service was nice, I guess. I had only vague memories of church with my Gramma as a little boy, and how hard it had been to sit still and be quiet. I thought of church as a place where people came to frown. But this was different. The building was full of light, and the organ thundered, and the choir wove their lines together like ... well, like angels. My inner response was, *This isn't so bad.* I was careful not to say it that way to Ada.

She introduced me around to her friends, who ranged from my parents' ages to white-haired ladies in their nineties. I was deathly afraid that they would ask me some subtle theological question, like what did I think of the Nicene Creed, or what was my stance on the Arian heresy, but they were very polite. They didn't even tease Ada about having a boyfriend. Maybe she brought a lot of young men around to church.

Afterwards, she treated me to lunch, "for being a good sport." At the restaurant, I pulled off the tie I had found in the bottom of a drawer and asked Ada, "So, why didn't you tell me about your, uh, secret life? And are we going to hell for, you know, last night?"

She rolled her eyes. "I think that second question pretty much answers the first one, doesn't it?" she said coolly. "I mean, look at your life: you poked a dinosaur in the eye, your pet lizard turned into a monster, you met a giant woman and a pretend space alien, you had a robot brother your father invented, and your mother... But despite all that, you can only conceive of Christianity as being solely about not having sex?"

When I blushed and looked down, she lowered her voice and added, "Did I say that last part too loud?"

"Maybe," I mumbled.

"I hope I haven't shocked you too much."

I raised my head. "I supposed I should have guessed, your father being a professor of theology and everything."

"And I suppose I was being too subtle with my hints," Ada said. "I told you I first fell for you when you told me not to call your clients, those crackpots, those alternate scientists, crazy? I mean, you knew they were wrong, but even in private, you had compassion for them. It's like Jesus, who saw the divine in prostitutes and lepers." When I winced, she added, "I don't mean to get carried away. You're not in any danger of being crucified by the Romans."

"Just by our professors," I said.

Our food came, and we ate in silence, until Ada said, "I can tell you want to ask me several thousand questions."

I shrugged. "Okay, sure. For one, you told me most of your ex-boyfriends are Jewish."

"A lot of guys who are loudly Christian aren't very deep. Often not even very kind. What else?"

"I'll think of something," I said. She was right: I did have a lot of questions. But despite her assurances, I was afraid of offending her. So many good things in my life had gone wrong that I had come to expect a meteor crashing down, or a plague that turned everyone into zombies, or self-righteous Libertarians.

When I said nothing, Ada said, "I see I killed this conversation. Like one of those death-rays." She chattered away, probably to fill the silence. "Why on earth would they want a death-ray?"

"Ratings, I guess? I don't know how television works."

We finished the last of the pad thai. As Ada looked over the bill, I said, "Can I ask one last question? Though this may be a death-ray for … us."

Ada sat still. "Shoot. Shoot your death ray."

"Okay, here goes… Do you really believe all that?"

"All what?"

"God, Jesus, the world made in six days, floods, Jonah and the whale…?"

"Literalness makes sense for science," she said. "Not necessarily for absolutely *everything* else."

"What does that mean?"

"Well, you're asking, isn't the story of Genesis, of God moving over the waters, and Adam and Eve, and the snake and the apple, and so on just a fairy tale? Isn't the story of God loving us, given how cold and cruel and unforgiving the universe is, just a fairy tale?"

She said this calmly, but I thought of her father, marked for death by cancer, and my own mother trying to die and unable to, and I nodded.

"But isn't *love* a fairy tale? Touching and kissing and sex, just a trick of our genes so they can propagate themselves, using chemicals to fool us into the fairy tale of *love*? If we had kids—this is just science fiction for the moment—and we cared for them, saw them grow up, cheered them when they had their own kids... Isn't what we think of as our *love* for them a fairy tale, a tale to get us to propagate those genes?"

"But those chemicals, the ones you say fool us, those are real," I said in protest.

"Yes, but is the *idea* of love real? Other chemicals make you hallucinate. Because the chemicals are real, would you say the hallucinations are, too?" Ada leaned forward. "My point is, if you say you're against fairy tales in general, just how far are you willing to go? It's understandable to say, given the cold indifference of the universe, that the evidence for a loving God is scant. But then, if you truly want to have the courage of that conviction, shouldn't you also say, 'I don't really mean it when I say, "I love you," it's only a biochemical impulse'?

"What's it going to be? Are you arguing to give up the fairy tale that's *inconvenient* for you, the one about how the destitute and the sick, the prostitutes and the lepers are just as worthy as the healthy and the rich, but *not* the one that's *convenient* for you, the one that gets you laid? Hmm? How's that for a death ray? Have *I* killed off our relationship yet?" She fixed me with her hawk stare.

I said, "If we were playing chess, I would tip over my king."

She gave me a sweet, satisfied smile. That smile was heroin for my heart. I would have done anything for that smile.

Under the Volcano Lair

A century after Isaac Newton introduced his laws of motion and gravity, and calculus, Pierre de Laplace said that if at a given moment, you knew the exact position and velocity of every particle everywhere, you could predict the future of the universe, right down to me writing this sentence. Laplace was wrong. Not only does quantum mechanics tell us the universe is one big gambling den, chaos theory points out that even the tiniest error will inevitably multiply and devour predictions like a zombie plague.

Science is nonetheless resilient. Like a martial artist, we have flipped randomness over our shoulder and tamed it as a calculational tool. Of course, this assumes the house doesn't cheat, that the odds are not fixed, that the universe does not have a bias.

Even Hile, a hard-nosed materialist, ascribed some events to luck. "I remember when I took my qual," he told me. All graduate students have to take a qualifying exam in their second year, to demonstrate their mastery of the key concepts and skills. "One of the problems no one got right, not even your father. But I remembered the answer from an obscure book I'd casually flipped thought a few months before."

"Is that luck?" I asked. "I'd call that hard work."

"There's an element of being at the right place at the right time. My work on the expansion of the universe"—for which he'd won the Nobel Prize, a detail he elided— "was done on a whim. Your father was working on strange quarks, had great ideas, but they led nowhere. I've done a lot that led nowhere, too, but the expanding universe work happened to be solvable *and* timely. It's like the guy who opens a gas station, and the next year, they build an interstate next to it. He worked no harder than the guy with a gas station far from the interstate, but he gets much richer."

To myself I thought, *Hmm, a Marxist analysis of scientific progress.* Jane would have loved it.

I was thinking about Jane in her Marxist phase as Ada and I looked at pictures of ourselves dressed in Halloween costumes from the week before. "You know, my sister once dressed up as Leon Trotsky," I told her.

Ada snorted. "Did she have an icepick stuck in her head?"

"No, she just went on about the Fourth International. To this day, I don't know what that was. And I don't want to know," I said, when Ada started to explain.

In the pictures, I was dressed as a cow, and Ada wore a cardboard pie around her waist. We had gone to a Halloween party as a "pie-on" and a "moo-on," the subatomic particles the *pion* and the *muon*. Strangely enough, we won the prize for best couple's costume.

"You still think about your sister, don't you?" Ada asked in a quiet voice. When I did not reply, she said, "Not pushing, just noticing. I'm a scientist; I'm supposed to observe."

"You sound just like me when you say things like that."

"Exactly," Ada said smugly.

In mid-November, I walked into our shared office at Phoenix, only to find Junie putting her personal items into a cardboard box.

"What's going on? You didn't get fired, did you?"

"She's quitting," Serge said, not looking up from his desk.

Junie hoisted the box up into her arms. "I'm not leaving you high and dry, John, don't worry. My notes are on your desk."

I followed her out to the parking lot, where she placed her belongings in the trunk of her compact Toyota. "What happened?"

She gave me a tired smile. "Nothing. Mr. Pigeon didn't get creepy or racist on me or anything. But I keep seeing how this work could turn in a bad direction, like the death-ray we joke about, only for real. I mention this to Mr. Pigeon, and he says, 'In what bad direction do you see it turning?' Like maybe he's *interested* in the bad direction." She looked up at the sky as a few fat drops began to fall. "I'm planning to finish my PhD this spring, but I find myself lying awake at night, asking myself if this, Phoenix, is the right thing to do or not."

She fished in her purse for car keys. I asked, "What are you planning do? After you graduate?"

Junie shrugged. "Probably industry, although I'd also like to teach. My advisor, she's got connections, so I've got some choices."

"Do you think I should quit?"

"I won't think badly of you for staying. I've just got a feeling this isn't for me." She unlocked her car door. "You take care, now."

A few days later, I arrived at the Ballard office building to find two new people occupying both Junie's old desk and mine. Mr. Pigeon appeared in the doorway, rocking back and forth on his feet, hands in the pockets of his slightly oversized jacket. "I've hired these two to replace Miss Johnson," he said, after giving their names, which I promptly forgot.

"Are you firing me? Where am I supposed to sit?"

"Off-site," he said, and gestured for me to follow him out of the office.

As he quick-stepped down a flight of stairs, I said, "You mean, like, work from home?"

"Not your home," he said over his shoulder. "I can't guarantee its security. I want you to work at my residence."

We walked half a block to his car, an older-model BMW. It had a few scratches and dents, but nonetheless had been washed and polished until it gleamed. He drove us to Wallingford, another Seattle neighborhood, to a tall, skinny blue clapboard house. Propped up against the sky, it rose slightly higher than the houses around it, as if someone had added half a story just to spite the neighbors.

Because he was the CEO (or president, or generalissimo, or something—I never have grasped how businesses actually work), I had expected a sprawling house with huge rooms of dazzling white marble and polished gold fixtures. Instead, the inside of the cramped house was all dark wood, as if it had been hauled out of a bog, with carpet the color of dirty lemons. Stairs led up the second floor, but Pigeon walked past them into a spare kitchen with faded yellow linoleum. Out the window, as the clouds cleared, I could see Mount Rainier, the dormant volcano sixty miles south of Seattle. Over time, I noticed Pigeon gazing at Rainier. I later wondered if he thought of it as a metaphor for himself: an incandescent power lying dormant and out of sight, waiting for the moment to awaken and reshape the landscape with fire and ash.

Pigeon pulled a bottle of amber liquid from a cabinet and poured it into a small glass. I caught a familiar sharp scent, earth and overripe fruit. Walking out of the kitchen into the dining room, I spotted in a corner a cage inhabited with small white furry bodies. "More friends, I see. Never alone."

"I suppose not," Pigeon said.

Next to the stairs leading up to the second floor was a wooden door. Now I noticed the vacant eye of a video surveillance camera mounted on the wall, watching everything. Pigeon opened the wooden door, revealing a second steel door, and unlocked it with a key.

A lonely bulb lit the steep staircase down. At the bottom was another steel door. Pigeon's fingers stabbed at a keypad, and the door opened. Beyond it, fluorescent lights buzzed overhead. Pigeon walked quickly behind a desk with a large monitor; this was in the early days of personal computers, and he had splashed out for a top-of-the-line model. The desk was covered in manila folders, and behind it were rows of shelves also stacked high with folders.

I turned and surveyed the room, probably with my mouth open. In addition to the files, I counted four, five ... ten ... fifteen cages with white rats.

"For your PhD, did you have them run mazes?"

"Something like that," Pigeon said. "They are very intelligent."

"I hope you aren't training them to replace me," I said, then added, "Sorry, sometimes I don't censor myself."

Pigeon looked at me coolly. "You have a very interesting mind, Mr. Chant. I like that about you." He handed me some keys and a slip of paper with the keypad code. "You'll be working solo. And your project is shifting. The hypersonic missile defense was, in fact, only a preliminary investigation. What the client really wants is an asteroid defense system."

"Which client?" I asked.

"SSSS-Corp.," he said, enunciating each S. "Super Science Saving Society." He shrugged.

"And this ... SSSS-Corp. thinks the Pentagon will shell out for an asteroid defense system? Or NASA?" Another thought occurred to me. "Is this why Junie quit?"

Pigeon nodded and jammed his hands into his jacket pockets. "I approached her a week ago. She felt I had deceived her, both of you, by not revealing the full extent of the project up front. She was also uneasy with the secrecy SSSS-Corp. demands. If you, too, decide to quit, I will respect that."

"But you're banking on the fact that I won't be able to resist working on an asteroid defense system," I said.

Pigeon just smiled.

When I got to Ada's apartment, I was soaked through from the rain. "Sorry, I'll try not to drip on everything," I said.

"Poor thing," Ada said, bringing me a towel. "Want me to make you some hot tea?"

"I can make it myself and finish dripping on your kitchen linoleum." I glanced over at the pile of books and notes on her table. "I see you're knee-deep in homework."

"Yeah, that Intro to Cosmology course is really kicking my butt. How's your research going?

"Um, not so well. I found in a paper by Hawking how to write the wave function for the universe as whole, and when I showed it to Hile, he nodded, but now I don't know what to do with it. I talked with Professor Athanasiou, you know, who teaches stat mech, but he pleaded to being an experimentalist." I walked over to the pile of electronics under an unlit lamp and toed a transformer.

Ada sighed. "I know, I know, I promised we could work on the radio dish. And I keep putting it off."

I shrugged. "It's just something fun to do together."

"I feel like I'm neglecting you," Ada said, then suddenly burst out laughing. "Sorry, you look like a wet cat." She reached out and fingered my shirt. "You really are soaked through. Your jeans, too. Aren't you cold and clammy?"

"Not like an actual clam," I said.

"I'd be a terrible girlfriend if I let you catch pneumonia and die. So, it's out of purely noble motives that I'm getting you out of these wet clothes," she said as she began unbuttoning my shirt.

"Don't you have homework?" I asked, though I didn't stop her.

"Building a radio dish antenna isn't the only fun thing we can do together."

The next afternoon, I rode my bike to Pigeon's house in upper Wallingford. I was trying to get the key into the lock when the door lurched open. I expected Pigeon, but instead it was an old man, his head bald as an egg and covered in liver spots. "What do you want?" he demanded. "You one of those religious types?"

I flashed on going to church with Ada, but since that was much too complicated to explain, I said, "I'm working for Mr. Pigeon, he hired me..." When the old man glared at me with turtle eyes, I added, "He gave me keys, and the combination to the basement."

With a sigh, the old man, dressed in a blue flannel robe and slippers, shuffled aside. I asked, "Is Mr. Pigeon around...?"

"*Mister* Pigeon? You mean Freddy—that's his name, *Freddy*. Well, Freddy's not around. Freddy's probably out at a bar somewhere, dreaming his little dreams."

I froze for a moment, then slid past the old man. "Well, then, I'll just go the basement and get to work..."

"His lair, you mean," he called after me as I hustled down the stairs. "That's what it is: his *lair*."

A few hours later, I was putting the folders back when I heard a key in the lock above. I went up and found Pigeon in the cramped hallway. "I left my notes on the desk," I told him. "By the way, there was this old ... um, older guy here." And then... I get myself into trouble from time to time, as you may have noticed. It's like a little monkey in my brain whispering, *Do it, say it, do it, say it.* So, I said it: "He called you Freddy."

For the first time, Pigeon lost his composure. "God *dammit*, Duke..." He sighed and said to me, "Ignore him. He'll sabotage you if you let him."

From upstairs came the old man's voice: "Not as much as you sabotage yourself."

Pigeon shouted at the ceiling, "And he's not nearly as deaf as he pretends to be!" To me, he added, "If only I could figure out how to weaponize him."

At Thanksgiving, Ada flew home. As I drove her to the airport in my rented pickup, she said in a low voice, "I haven't told them about you." My pulse sped up, although I had already guessed she hadn't. "It's not that I'm ashamed about you; in fact, I'm bursting to tell them. I have this speech, about how supportive you are and how happy you make me. And I know this is weird, but with all our worries over my dad's illness, I felt *ashamed* of how happy I am with you, when he could be dying. And I want to have a happy Thanksgiving, now that things are better..."

As I pulled up to the terminal, she began to cry. I wanted to hold her, but the airport cops were waving for the cars to move on, and she got out, red-faced, and waved to me from the sidewalk. Then she lugged her suitcase inside the terminal, and I slowly drove away, back to the U-District.

I had told Ada I had plenty of homework to do, as well as trying to understand Hawking-Hile wave equations, but I found myself unable to focus. To my surprise, I soon found myself at the Street-Wise Shepherd Outreach Center. I spent a few hours handing out clothes and chatting with the guests, even though I was still terrible at small talk.

At my apartment, I was hunched over my desk, working on equations, when the phone rang. I glanced at the clock. Nearly midnight. I picked up the receiver, and Ada spoke quietly.

"They've all gone to bed, but I wanted to hear your voice," she said. "It's snowing here. Really piling up."

"I'm imagining the flakes drifting down."

"I miss you." This she said almost in a whisper, like a secret.

I said I missed her, too, and told her about going to Street-Wise Shepherd. I finished, "You should probably get to bed."

"Not yet. It's a comfort to hear your voice." Her tone turned tense. "We're a bit on edge. The doctors say they're hopeful, but they want to keep scanning my father for any recurrence. Lung cancer is the most likely to metastasize, and..." Her voice trailed off.

"You should go to sleep."

"I want to hear your voice a few minutes more. Tell me something."

I was going to tell her of my struggles in research, how I felt akin to medieval alchemists trying to draw magic out of opaque elixirs of pseudo-scientific jargon, how I wondered if they ever felt fraudulent the way I did. But before I could, Ada said, "Tell me about your first crush."

"My first crush? That'd be Becky... Wait, actually, it was when I was about six, and I was digging in our backyard for dinosaur bones. A girl about my age shows up and asks what I'm doing, and I tell her, and she says, 'Like a paleontologist?' Pronounced it perfectly, better than I could. I was so impressed that I immediately crushed on her. The next day, her family moved away, and I never saw her again. I didn't even think to ask her name."

I was going to ask Ada about *her* first crush, but I could hear her breathing getting slow and regular. "You sleepy now?"

"Yeah. Thank you, John. I love you." Then she hung up, before I could say, *Wo ai ni.*

On Sunday, I picked up Ada from the airport. She hugged me, hard, as if to break my ribs, and on the drive home, she was talkative, telling me about her sister, Andy—short for Andromeda, after the galaxy, I hoped, and not the sacrificial maiden. "Do you find you get along better as adults than as kids?" I asked.

"Mmm, we were pretty tight as kids, but now we've gone our separate ways. We've drifted apart. We had this terrible fight when she drove me to the airport."

"About what?"

Ada sighed. "She invited her boyfriend to Thanksgiving. Frankly, he doesn't treat her well. He makes these jokes at her expense. Little poison needles, like. Mom and Dad and I were exchanging glances, and for a while I thought my dad would take him outside for a little talk. But later, Dad said, 'Well, Andy's a grown-up,' although he looked unhappy." She turned towards the passenger window, fogging it with her breath. "She's always had bad luck with boys—men, now, I guess. Anyway, on the way to the airport, I tried to talk to her about it, and she got defensive and said Mom always runs down all her boyfriends, and I'm the same. By the time she dropped me off, we had stopped speaking."

Then she turned and put a warm hand on mine. "Andy's always been jealous of me, even though she's prettier than I am"—I snorted at that—"and she is. But if I started talking about *my* new boyfriend and how kind and smart and good-looking he is, it would look like I was showing her up. So, again, I didn't tell them anything. I know, I know, I'm the world's worst girlfriend. It's, you know... *Arggh*. Family dynamics."

We chugged along the interstate in heavy traffic. I said, "One, I'm pretty sure my family dynamics could beat up your family dynamics without breaking a sweat. Two, I'm also pretty sure somewhere out there, some woman is poisoning her boyfriend with arsenic, or maybe polonium, so you couldn't possibly be the *worst* girlfriend."

She leaned over and kissed me. "Thank you for understanding," she said softly.

My research for Hile stayed firmly on pace to nowhere. Hile's original equations predicted the rapid, inflationary expansion of the Big Bang, but I could only get a slow, gentle swelling, like a Minor Burp. To make things worse, the numbers for the asteroid defense system didn't look promising. For small rocks, I could work up a scheme. But the call from SSSS-Corp. specified that the defenses must work up to extinction-level events, asteroids and comets on the order of ten kilometers across. The kinetic energy of such a bolide is enormous, billions of times larger than the largest hydrogen bomb. I began to understand Junie's concerns. The amount of sheer power needed to destroy it or even just nudge it aside would itself be enough to eradicate whole countries. My stomach began to ache.

After a couple of hours, I decided to take a break. Pigeon had told me I could use the kitchen and any food or coffee or tea in the fridge or cupboards. The kettle on the stove was steaming when a voice came from the second floor: "Hey! Hey! A little help?"

At first, I ignored it, assuming Pigeon would respond, but then the calls came again: "God dammit, won't you come help? I can hear you in the kitchen."

I went to the foot of stairs. "Isn't Mr. Pigeon home?"

"No, *Freddy's* not here. Can you come and help me?"

I turned off the stove before tromping up. In the second-floor hallway, I called out, "Hello?"

"Here. In the bedroom. On the right."

I pushed the door slightly open. "What do you need?" I asked, just as the stench hit my nose.

"I shit my bed, all right? I made a mess, and I can't clean it up."

His expression was so miserable that I couldn't look at him, so I just stared down at my shoes. "Um, Mr. Pigeon wants me to—"

"I don't care what Freddy wants; he left an old man alone to shit himself. You the kind of guy who leaves an old man to stew in his own shit? God dammit."

"Just a second." I went downstairs, found some dish gloves under the sink, and came back up. "Duke, right?"

"Oh, so Freddy let slip that much information. Yeah, I'm Duke—or the *other* Mr. Pigeon. I prefer Duke. Can you *puh-lease* clean me up?" I stepped into the room, and he saw the gloves. "I'm not toxic waste; don't believe what Freddy tells you."

"Hey, I used to shovel out elephant dung when I was at the circus," I said.

The old man was silent as I lifted him out of bed and stripped him of his feces-sodden pajamas. "Circus, eh? Maybe you're not as dull as most of Freddy's little friends."

I got him showered, put his bathrobe on him, and sat him in a chair. Then I stripped the bed, threw the sheets and the pajamas into the washing machine on the first floor, and returned with a mop and a bucket to wipe the wooden floor. I used a liberal amount of bleach, in part to cover the smell.

As I worked, Duke pointed out spots I missed. "I'm getting to it," I said, a bit curtly.

"You sound just like Freddy—can't stand criticism. No wonder he likes you."

I swabbed furiously at the offending spot. "He finds me useful."

"Oh, no, I know how Freddy ticks. I bet he sees you as a surrogate son. He wants to show he can be a better father figure than *his* old man. He still resents me... Christ, why'd you drop the mop?"

I'd dropped it because when Duke said "Freddy" still resented him, it was as if the old man had reached into my chest and squeezed my heart. I wondered if somewhere my father was complaining to another young man about *his* ungrateful son.

"Sorry," I mumbled, picking up the mop. I wrung it out and glanced at the clock. Another hour had passed by. "Listen, I have to go. When does, uh, Freddy get back?"

Duke shrugged his thin shoulders. "Who knows? Could you microwave me some dinner? I don't want to wait until morning to eat. There's chicken pot pie in the freezer."

Feeling the vise of time, I ran down the stairs, tearing open the cardboard package. *Microwave on high five minutes, perforate the crust, microwave on medium three more minutes...* As the microwave hummed, I stepped into the hallway and waved at the video surveillance camera. "Hello? Can you hear me? Duke, the old man... Mr. Pigeon's, uh... Duke needs help. If you're watching, can you tell Mr. Pigeon?"

The dark cyclops eye stared impassively.

Back in the kitchen, I waited impatiently for the microwave. When it dinged, I plopped the chicken pot pie on a plate with a fork and ran it up the stairs.

The old man looked at the lonely pot pie, then at me. "Am I allowed to have a glass of water?"

Thump-thump down the stairs, then back up. Duke had eaten only a small forkful. "Where am I supposed to sleep?" he asked.

The question confused me. "On the bed?"

"Without sheets?"

"Where does, um... Where do you keep the spare sheets?"

"How the hell would I know? Freddy likes to control everything, haven't you noticed?"

I opened every closet, cupboard, and drawer. "I can't find any," I told him. "Your sheets are still in the washing machine."

"My pajamas, too," Duke pointed out.

I closed my eyes. I had homework to do. I had planned to make dinner for Ada before she headed off to the nuclear physics lab. "Let me make a phone call first," I said. Maybe she would forgive me for having a feeling in my gut for an old man.

On the weekend, Ada wanted to make a romantic dinner for me. "To make up for being the worst girlfriend ever," she said.

"Also the best girlfriend ever, since for me, *N* equals one," I pointed out. "You top all categories."

Her menu included a mushroom risotto, fish in a creamy sauce, and steamed artichokes. While she cooked, I took some of her dictionaries and was reading aloud words in other languages that sounded funny. "Here's one: 'selling price' in Japanese is *urine.*"

"Let me look at that." I held the open page to her as she stirred. "That's pronounced 'oo-ree-neh.' What are you, twelve?"

"Hey, here's another one!" I said, and despite her disapproval, soon got her laughing.

"Stop," she said, "you're going to make me burn the risotto!"

"Don't worry," I said, "I don't know what risotto is supposed to taste like." She was stirring it and pouring in white wine when the phone rang. "Here, take over for me," she said, before picking up the phone. "Hello?" Then she took the phone into the other room, closing the kitchen door behind her.

After fifteen minutes, the risotto turned gluey, and the water steaming the artichokes had dried up, and the pan had begun to burn. I turned everything off. It was nearly forty-five minutes before she came back.

"Sorry," she said. "Andy."

"Everything all right?" I asked quietly.

She inspected the pans on the stove. "I think I ruined dinner," she said. I could see her hands trembling. "No, I guess, not really, everything is not all right." She turned to scrape the risotto into the garbage with the wooden spoon before I stopped her.

"It's okay," I said. "I don't mind." I steered her to the table. "Sit down. Do you want to tell me about it?"

"My father... A scan... It's spread to his bones and his liver. Maybe elsewhere. They're debating between more chemo and radiation therapy. Andy said the doctors are not optimistic. She gave me a bunch of statistics, but I can't remember them."

"I'm sorry." I put my hand on hers and squeezed. She began to cry, and I put my arms around her and kissed her wet cheeks, hoping that was the right thing to do.

I read everything I could on quantum wave functions. Even down in Pigeon's basement, as I tried to figure out how to deflect an incoming asteroid, in my mind I saw the wave function of the universe rising and falling like the cadences of a poem.

My head felt full and fuzzy and stretched in too many directions. I wandered upstairs, wanting a clarifying cup of tea, only to find Duke with a coat over his pajamas and wearing rainboots instead of his usual worn slippers, sitting on a chair in the kitchen.

"There you are," he growled. "I'm late for a doctor's appointment. Let's go." He saw me glance up at the video surveillance camera. "Heh. Don't bother.

There's no one there. Freddy's paranoid. He's scared someone's going to steal one of his precious ideas. He'd like you to think he has a squad of goons at the snap of his fingers, but he doesn't. C'mon. Or are you worthless, too?"

"I don't have a car."

Duke dangled a set of keys. "Freddy's got a couple. We can take one of his."

Because we arrived late, we had to wait two hours for another open slot. To pass the time, I tried to make conversation with Duke. "Have you lived all your life in Seattle?" But he groused, "I grew up in an orphanage. Didn't Freddy tell you? He likes to tell people all sorts of things about me."

"To be honest, he doesn't bring you up."

Duke snorted. "He used to claim I wasn't his real dad, told people I was hard on him because he wasn't really my son. But now he just pretends I don't exist."

We sat for a while. Duke hummed to himself, a tune I thought might be the theme song of a long-forgotten TV show. "You know, for a while, Freddy demanded he be called Red instead of Fred."

"Like his hair," I murmured.

"Nah. It was after his mother died. I suppose he wanted to be a different person, one with a still-living mother. But poor Louise found herself in the wrong place at the wrong time." Duke shook his head, then slumped and fell silent.

It was evening, and rain was coming down hard and cold by the time I parked in front of that tall, skinny house in Wallingford. The steel door to the basement was open. I helped Duke up to his bedroom, then went down to the basement. I found Pigeon at a desk, his face lit green by the pixels on the computer screen, and I caught the scent of the glass of whiskey next to him.

I said, "I took Duke to his doctor's appointment."

Pigeon didn't say anything. Didn't even move.

"I said, I took Duke to his—"

"Don't worry about Duke," Pigeon said, so quietly that I could barely hear him. "Ignore him."

"Kind of hard to do that," I said. There wasn't any more I could say. I went upstairs, got on my bike, and rode home in the rain.

Ada sometimes came over to my apartment, although it was smaller and danker than hers. As she drank coffee and pored over cosmology at my tiny kitchen table, I sat on the old gray carpet and began soldering some circuits. "What're you working on?" she asked without looking up. "The radio telescope?"

"Oh, another little project."

"Homework? Research?"

"Finished E-and-M. Clearing my mind with a little light circuitry. Like a sorbet between courses, only with soldering."

In fact, I was trying to work out an invention using the stimulation of mirror neurons. My idea was to stimulate one's own mirror neurons, making you hypersensitive to the tiny, unconscious telltales we all give off. In short, to make one able to read minds, or a better poker player.

"How's work? For Mr. Pigeon?"

"Huh?" I looked up from the circuit with the terahertz frequency generator. "Oh, fine." Although I was sweating over the asteroid defense plans, the checks from Phoenix never bounced. Not having to worry about food and rent was surprisingly addictive.

Even so, the day before, when I had let myself into the house on upper Wallingford, Freddy Pigeon and Duke were having a shouting match upstairs. I hustled down to the basement, but couldn't avoid overhearing snatches: "—old parasite—" "—puffed-up drunk—" "—*mean* old parasite—" "—always looking to blame others—" "—no sense of gratitude—" "—goddamn *bastard*—" before I pushed the heavy steel door shut.

When Pigeon came down half an hour later, I stayed bent over my work as if I had heard nothing. I noticed he had a glass in his hand and caught the familiar sharp whiff.

Pigeon saw my glance and followed it down to the glass in his hand. He said, "My mind races so fast with so many thoughts, I sometimes need to slow it down."

"Slow it down?" My stomach felt so tight, I could have played a drum solo on it.

"You have a quick mind, John. Very quick. Surely your thoughts must overwhelm you at times, shouting at you for attention. Ordinary people don't understand this." He said this as if he were talking about a parking lot or a cloudless sky.

"I don't think there are 'ordinary people.'" It came out of my mouth, but in my head, the words were Ada's.

Pigeon shook his head. "It's easy to be impressed with your fellow humans when you're young. In time, your views will change." He cleared his throat. "I have read your reports. I appreciate the depth of your technical analysis, but I believe you're being too pessimistic."

"Sorry," I said. "I've gotten stuck. Listen, Mr. Pigeon, I was wondering if from time to time, I could evaluate some of your other projects, like I used to do. Thinking about something different might get me out of my rut." I went on quickly. "I've been learning about Monte Carlo methods and simulated annealing, and that's how my mind works, I think."

"Interesting. I was going to suggest you work more systematically, but a random walk can be surprisingly productive."

As I so often do, I blurted out my first thought. "Professor Hile says luck is part of success, that it was luck that led him to his Nobel Prize."

When the words came out of my mouth, Pigeon froze for a moment, and I flashed back to what Duke had said about Freddy's mother—*in the wrong place at the wrong time*—and with a cold horror, I thought I had touched a raw spot.

Then Pigeon unfroze and gave me a smile, a simply horrible smile, as if he had only read about smiles in books. "Is that so? Does Professor Hile think we make our own luck? Imagine that. What luck will you make?"

Despite Pigeon's approval, I worried he might fire me for not solving the problem of asteroid defense. Although my nondisclosure agreement prevented me from discussing any details, I vaguely confessed my worries to Ada.

She hugged me. "Oh, John. We'll add it to the list."

"You got a list? What else is on it, besides, um, your father?"

"The qualifying exam, for one," she said. "And then there's, you know, research. The nuclear physics lab has been very kind to let me squeeze in some time for runs, but it's all on off hours. A lot of graveyard shifts for me. Sorry."

"Can't it wait until after your qual?"

"There's a window of opportunity I want to take advantage of. Professor Ukoma said the same thing as you, but I was able to convince him. I have to get some runs in." She put a hand on my arm. "I'm going back to Montana. For Christmas."

"I see."

"I'm the world's worst girlfriend, I know," she said, crossing her arms. "Please just be patient, a little longer. If we get through Christmas, I will tell them."

"It's okay," I said.

The last weeks of the quarter limped by. Wet snow fell. I squeaked out passing grades in my courses, by which I mean, Professor Shirakova, bless her Russian heart, said with a sly grin on her face as I picked up my final, "Congratulations, John." I looked down at the score: 72. "No one's ever broken seventy before on one of my finals," she added.

Ada got an easy A in nuclear astrophysics, an A-minus in stellar atmospheres, and a B in introduction to physical cosmology. "Well, I did put in a lot of graveyard shifts on my experiment," she said.

A few days before Christmas, Ada flew to Montana. She called me late at night, after everyone else was asleep.

On Christmas Eve, I went to midnight services, pretending to myself I was going with her and that she had just stepped away for a moment. I thought I might stick out like a leprous thumb, the nonbeliever, but the church was packed with people in their heavy coats and scarves and wool hats, singing about lights and angels and shepherds, and with light and joy in their faces, they wished me, a stranger, Merry Christmas. I'm a terrible singer and hate the sound of my voice, but I did enjoy the beauty of the music, and I imagined Ada hundreds of miles away, listening to the same carols and hymns. The preacher got up in the pulpit and said, "We always imagine the Holy Family in a freezing stable, but we know it couldn't be too bad, because the shepherds who came left praising God. If it had been a terrible situation, the shepherds, no strangers to poverty and bad sleeping arrangements, wouldn't have left a woman and her newborn child in a bad way; they would have said, 'Come with us, we'll set you up.' The shepherds, like the poor everywhere, would have taken care of them."

And he was right. The folks in the circus weren't rich, but they had showed me what care they could. Other times, when I had gotten lost or my car had broken down, it wasn't someone driving a Mercedes wearing an expensive watch who had stopped to help, but a working-class family in a clattering old Volkswagen bus, or a young black woman driving a dented Chevy who gave me aid, or the Latina who picked me up, all of fourteen, on a dark and scary highway and bought me coffee and pie at an all-night diner. I never even asked their names.

I don't know if the universe has a point—the theological term Ada introduced me to is *teleological*—or is just a random roll of the dice. And even luck can roll both ways. The same event might contain the seeds of good luck and bad.

It was by luck, as I was leafing through the non-asteroid defense projects, that I spotted a word: *ügyes*. It's Hungarian for "clever," one of Hieronymous Canterbury's favorite compliments. Looking more closely at the page, a photocopy of an old document, I recognized the handwriting as Canterbury's.

That afternoon, down in the basement of the house in Wallingford, I shuffled through more files and found other pages in Canterbury's hand. Most were photocopies, though there were a few faded originals. My headed pounded with the implications, and I found I couldn't focus. I put the files back, shrugged on my rain jacket, and headed home.

Everyone has different strategies to ward off stress: meditation, deep breathing, physical exercise, visualizing a calm, safe space. Me, I do calculus in my head and think about inventions.

As my bike whizzed along the Burke-Gilman trail, I realized my "mind-reading" invention was unlikely to work. Theory of mind means we understand that other people have independent thoughts from our own. In practice, however, we still project a lot of our own thoughts and feelings onto others. Theory of mind is crucial to a functioning society, because we automatically try to understand and work with the thoughts and agendas of other people. But an overactive theory of mind also may have led humans to see gods and spirits in animals and trees and fire and wind, to feel the wrath of the sea and the loving embrace of the sky. I resigned myself to putting aside the stimulation of mirror neurons as yet another unripe idea.

I didn't share any of my thoughts on theory of mind to Ada over dinner in her apartment (I cooked), especially as it touched upon religion. But as we washed dishes, our hands immersed in warm, soapy water, I glanced over at the picture of Sanjusangendo and the thousand and one Kannons of Mercy. And a thought struck me, with the force of an arrow shot from a taut bow. Another thought, another invention.

The next day, it rained even harder. I wore a Gore-Tex rain jacket, but by the time I reached Wallingford, even having taken the bus, my pants and shoes were soaked, and my legs and feet would have made an oyster reach for a blanket.

I found Pigeon in the basement. He had a glass with ice and viscous brown bourbon, and I felt a stab of irritation.

"It still won't work," I said.

Pigeon looked up.

"The asteroid defense. It requires too much energy."

He looked at me with his cold pebble eyes. "Surely there's a way to make it work. SSSS-Corp. has invested a lot in this. In me. If we succeed—when *you* succeed—they will shower us with the fruits of their appreciation."

"I got all the fruit I need. That isn't the problem. It's the laws of physics. It doesn't matter what their accountants or lawyers say."

Pigeon snorted. "Accountants or lawyers," he muttered. "Bunch of lizard people."

I realized then that he was quite drunk.

He leaned on the desk and looked up at me. "Did I ever tell you how I acquired this house? Before I started Phoenix, I made money in real estate, acquiring properties with interesting features. This one once belonged to smugglers."

"Drugs?"

"Exotic animals." He walked slowly over to a bookshelf.

"There's a door behind it, isn't there?" I asked. "It's colder over there. Some sort of sub-basement?"

He nodded, swinging open the bookshelf. "Given your perceptiveness, perhaps I should lay my cards on the table." He unlocked the door behind the bookshelf.

As we descended the cold stairwell that smelled of clay, Pigeon said, "You strike me as someone with ambition, Mr. Chant. Well, I have ambition, too." He unlocked the door at the bottom, letting in warm air. I caught a sharp whiff of formaldehyde, overlaying some musky animal scent.

Bright lights hung from the ceiling. To the left and right, the walls were stacked from top to bottom with cages of white rats, the room alive with their rustling and soft chittering. But it was the far wall, directly across from the stairwell, that seized my attention: shelf after shelf of glass containers that glinted in the harsh fluorescent lights, at least a hundred of them. A tangled thicket of wires ran among the containers, each filled with some thick, translucent fluid. Several chugging pumps bubbled air into the fluid. I squinted; in the very center of each container, bristling with wires, I saw little pink-gray blobs.

"Are those...?"

Pigeon leaned against a table. Only then did I notice several bloody, decapitated bodies of rats lined up neatly.

"My brain runs fast, faster than most people's," he said, a shy grin of triumph on his face. "Much like yours. But even my brain, on its own, is not powerful enough to carry out my ambitions. Some years ago, I realized what I had to do." He turned and gestured at the wall of glass and bubbling fluid and bits of tissue. "I built myself a better brain."

A Sum of Histories

When I worked with outsider scientists—crackpots—many objected to the weirdness of modern physics. Some argued that the randomness of quantum mechanics or the malleable space-time of relativity was a conspiracy to dethrone Man (they disliked feminism, too) from his central place in creation. I allow that, in the future, scientists might overturn quantum mechanics or relativity for new theories. But we won't simply turn the clock back and say Newton or Aristotle had been right all along, or replace Newtonian forces with vortices, as Roger from my crackpot group advocated. If and when we unveil a new conception of the universe, it will be even stranger than quantum mechanics or relativity, and it will leave us humans feeling even more alienated and alone in a cold, incomprehensible cosmos.

"I have a plan," Pigeon continued. "I've never shared it. But you, you'll appreciate it." He pulled a silver flask out of a pocket and took a slug. It smelled pungently of loam and apples.

Back in grad school, Pigeon explained, he had wired together the brains of four white lab rats and taught them to win at tic-tac-toe. Rather than congratulating him, his professors had kicked him out of the PhD program, for the sin of violating regulations regarding animal experimentation.

Exiled from academia, he had moved into a cheap, rat-infested apartment—and with the brains of twelve rats he'd trapped, he taught his invention to pick out good real estate investments, including the house in Wallingford. Building an aggregate of twenty-five brains, he'd mastered the stock market. The money from that, he had used to start up Phoenix, although he admitted his company had been on the brink of failure when SSSS-Corp. propped him up with an investment. In fact, he claimed, the latest iteration had pointed Pigeon to SSSS-Corp., prompted him to hire me, and had nudged him to develop the sonic scalpel.

"But the sonic scalpel was a failure," I pointed out.

"Was it?" He took another swallow from the flask.

"Unless you plan to make a fortune from a torture device." Although the room was warm from the bodies of the rats and the cerebrospinal fluid in which the brains were bathed, I shivered slightly.

Pigeon's eyelids fluttered. "It's not just to make a fortune. And as the saying goes, to make an omelet..."

My mind conjured the scene of a gigantic Ernie chasing Bruce across the playground, lured by plates full of cooked eggs. "In my experience, making omelets brings out monsters."

"Monsters? Even though I have to cozy up to SSSS-Corp., my goals go beyond their asteroid defense project—far more than making money. Real estate, stocks, technology, those are stepping-stones. No, surely you can see, the biggest frontier is *here*." He tapped at his forehead.

"You want to build the same thing with human brains?" I blurted out, feeling slightly sick to my stomach.

Pigeon waved the thought aside. "Oh, God, no! Not human brains. Though I've reached the limit of rat brains, so I'm thinking of moving on to something else. Dog brains. Or pig brains; pigs are smart. Maybe monkey brains... But definitely not people brains."

Pigeon turned to me with a frown. "But now you tell me the asteroid defense can't work. That will make those lizard people at SSSS-Corp. very unhappy. Let me tell you in confidence, I was going to eventually betray them. I'm not a villain. But their cash keeps Phoenix afloat. If we can't give them asteroid defense, I'm going to have to go to plan B."

He gestured to me. "Come on, I want to show you something." He went up the stairs, staggering a bit, to the basement. In the corner was a video cassette player. "You ever hear of TIM talks?" he asked as he clumsily pushed a cassette into the slot.

"Sure," I said, "but I don't remember what TIM stands for."

Pigeon paused. "Hmm... 'Transgressive something something...' Doesn't matter." He pushed the button on the VCR.

The TV screen flickered to life. A plump thirty-something woman with black hair pulled into a bun paced back and forth on a stage. "There's no sound," I said, leaning forward.

As Pigeon fiddled with the volume, he said, "This talk is titled, 'How Fringe is Fringe Science?' But that's a cover. Ah." The volume leapt up loud, and the woman was talking about astronomical alignment at Stonehenge, and in Mayan temples, and muons revealing a void beneath the Great Pyramid. An electric buzz ran through me. There was something familiar about her.

"This," Pigeon said smugly, "is Dr. Wimplemaker. Dr. Sharon Wimplemaker. She has several books and multiple TIM talks, but behind all this, she's near the top of C-QUARK."

"C-QUARK?" I asked. My brain was churning. I couldn't place the name Sharon Wimplemaker, but her face and her voice made my brain resonate like a brass bell.

"It's a secret organize, er, organization, so of course you haven't heard of it. The Committee for Questions on Advancing and Revealing Knowledge. What I've heard," and here he smiled, "is that they control which scientific theories become accepted and which get ignored. Which are mocked, and which win prizes."

"Isn't that through experiments?" I asked. Turning from the video to look at Pigeon, I noticed beads of perspiration on his forehead, despite the cool temperature of the basement. "Experiments validate or invalidate theories."

"That's what you're told in school," Pigeon said. "Classic Popperian dogma. But who controls which experiments get published, and which rejected by referees? C-QUARK."

"I don't think that's how it works."

Pigeon wiped at his forehead. "C-QUARK has immense troves of ideas, theories squelched, observations buried, inventions locked away. And I want... I want you—want you to work—"

Suddenly, Freddy Pigeon bent over and vomited onto the bare concrete floor, a thin yellowish liquid. The cold air filled with the smell of stomach acid.

"You don't look so good, Mr. Pigeon," I said, backing towards the door, "so I'll let you, um, recover, while I consider your suggestion." Before he could say anything, I ran up the stairs, both flights, two steps at a time, and fled.

I didn't know what to tell Ada when she eventually noticed something was bothering me. Surely the confidentiality clause in my contract included a roomful of rat brains in glass jars wired together. On the other hand, not mentioning it was like neglecting to say you'd seen a ten-car pileup on the freeway, or a grizzly bear rampaging through a frozen yogurt shop.

It never became an issue. Ada talked to her sister late in the evening, slept for an hour, then went to the lab. Usually I walked her there, then fetched her before sunrise. She yawned both ways. After a shift, she went home, slept two hours, got up and drank a quart of coffee, and went to class. I could have sprouted a rhino horn from my forehead, and she wouldn't have noticed.

We, meaning mostly me, had finished the home-built radio telescope, and one evening, we hung it out her window. The galactic center was below the horizon, so we couldn't raise Sag A* and the static cry of its supermassive black hole. But we caught the faint whine of a pulsar, the corpse of a dead star humming at hundreds of cycles per second as it whirled at close to the speed of light. Both of us were blue with cold when we finally brought the antenna dish inside and closed the window.

"Okay, now I need to head to the lab," Ada said, teeth chattering.

"No, you're taking a hot shower and going to bed, young lady," I said sternly.

"Okay to the shower," she said, raising herself up on her toes to kiss me, "but then the lab." She wrapped her arms around my neck. "You take such good care of me."

When she was in the shower, the phone rang. I hesitated, thinking it was her sister, Andy. But it kept ringing, so I picked up, trying to invent an excuse on the spot. A late-night study group, I decided I would tell her sister, with Ada in the kitchen making coffee. But it wasn't her sister. My gut twisted as I recognized the voice of Freddy Pigeon.

"I wanted to follow up about C-QUARK," he said. "As I was saying, I want you to go work for them."

"Why are you calling here?" I asked in a low voice.

Pigeon continued as if I hadn't said anything. "You'd still actually be working for me, of course. You will infiltrate C-QUARK and access their files."

"I didn't give you this number." My temples began to throb with anger.

"Of all people, you shouldn't be surprised at my resourcefulness. Now, we need to put together a strategy—"

"You're drunk," I said sharply.

There was a long silence. Freddy said, "It's in the evening that my thoughts tend to race the most..."

"I don't care about your excuses," I snapped, my heart pounding like tympani. "Don't call me here. Ever." I slammed down the phone.

Ada peeked out of the bathroom, wrapped in a towel. "Who was that?"

"Wrong number," I said.

The next morning, I wanted to strangle Freddy Pigeon. Ada would definitely not approve of me strangling Pigeon. Nor would Jesus or Buddha. So, I had been working on a better way. I had a half-built device, what I had started to think of as the "cannon," stashed under my bed. It would be finished soon, and I was looking forward to impressing Ada with my cleverness.

When I let myself into the house in Wallingford, Pigeon was not home. I had opened the door to the basement when I heard a faint call. Upstairs, I found Duke sprawled on the bare floor of his room. "I fell," he said weakly, "and it hurts something awful. I maybe broke something."

"I'll call an ambulance," I said. "Is there a phone up here?"

"Don't," Duke said, his turtle eyes watery. "Letting strangers into the house, especially authorities... He'd never forgive us."

Duke wanted me to drive him to the emergency room. I didn't think that was a great idea and said again that I'd call an ambulance, but he pleaded with me. For someone who constantly belittled Freddy, he was shockingly terrified.

He weighed so little that I was able to clumsily carry him down the stairs. "Ow, you're hurting me!" he whined. He smelled of ointment and salty perspiration.

"You're the one who didn't want an ambulance with professional EMTs who have a stretcher," I said. "I never took a class on 'carrying an old guy who's probably fractured his hip.'"

Duke turned his face away from me. "God, you're as bad as he is. Same smart mouth. No wonder he hired you. *Don't drop me!*" he shouted, and I almost did.

On the ground floor, I staggered over to the couch to deposit him, while I searched through the pile of keys in the kitchen for car keys. I was at the door, telling Duke I was getting a car and would be back for him in a minute, when Freddy Pigeon walked in. He eyed Duke on the couch, then turned to me.

"What's going on here?"

"Duke fell, and I'm taking him to the emergency room," I said, while at the same time, Duke said, "We're eloping. What does it look like?"

Pigeon turned to me. "I told you to ignore him."

I spread my arms wide. "Even when he's fallen and broken something? And you're not here? Even when he's crapped himself, and you're not here? Even when he has a doctor's appointment, and you're not here?"

Pigeon scowled. Duke said, "I'm always raining on his parade. Stop worrying about your parade, Freddy."

Pigeon muttered, "I'll take him to the hospital."

"Wait," I said, putting a hand on his arm. "Are you sober? Are you safe to drive?"

Pigeon battered away my hand, much more savagely than necessary, and planted himself between me and Duke. "How dare you!" he said, his high tenor wobbling in fury. "How dare you impugn me—"

"I'll impugn you all I want after last night!" I shouted back. Pigeon was tall, but he was also soft, and the carnies of my lost childhood had taught me how to throw a punch and how to sweep a leg. I was so angry that I was ready to put those lessons into action.

Now, however, Pigeon shrank back. "Last night?" he said, his voice softening.

"Hoo, boy," said Duke from the couch. "Here we go..."

"You called me last night, called me at—"

"What did I say?"

"He doesn't remember," said Duke. "A blackout. He does that."

"Shut up," said Pigeon.

I wagged a finger at him. "It wasn't what you said, you... It was *where* you called me."

But Pigeon had stepped back and was rubbing his eyes. "Duke's right," he said. "I don't remember a thing." He took his hand away from his eyes. "Go home. I'll pay you for today. Go home. I'll take care of Duke."

"That'll be a first," said Duke.

I don't know about curiosity being felicidal, but it certainly has taken me to unexpected places.

That brief glimpse of Wimplemaker continued to nag at my brain. At the library, I tracked down articles mentioning Dr. Sharon Wimplemaker, all of them on fringe ideas and outright conspiracy theories. The few pictures of her were not helpful; most were at a distance, or her face was partially obscured. Then I found one about aliens visiting Earth; it even had a picture of Dr. Wimplemaker standing over the alleged corpse of an alien from a crashed UFO.

I was thinking about what Junie Johnson would have said about this, when a synapse in my brain went *bing!* and I recognized the alien corpse. It was Krulltang—or Mike from Maine—the would-be alien I'd met in my father's sewer-turned-particle accelerator.

Wimplemaker was giving a talk down in Portland. Without telling Pigeon, or Ada for that matter, I took a bus down to Portland and sat in the back of the hall.

Wearing a simple blue turtleneck sweater and large glasses, Wimplemaker came on stage and began to talk about dark matter and possible connections to astrology. (I forced myself not to giggle.)

As I half listened, my thoughts drifted into hazy memories. My Mexican beaded lizard, Paul, scrabbling in his terrarium. My sister's haughty disdain. The smells of acetone and vinegar. Flasks lysing DNA out of cells. An electrophoresis machine, a notebook of interpretations, and the humiliations of second grade.

With an electric shock, I sat bolt upright. Sharon Wimplemaker was none other than my short-term second-grade nanny, Shahra.

My breath caught in my throat. For years, I had been haunted by two things: my dream of the curse of the dinosaurs, and Shahra's DNA prediction of a lonely future for me. Even with Ada, I sometimes woke up in the middle of the night and brushed my fingers against the warmth of her body, just to reassure myself she was real.

After the talk, I waited outside in the drizzle. A lone figure wearing a long, beetle-blue coat walked across the parking lot.

"Shahra!" I called. "Shahrazad Sattari!"

Her head snapped around. Despite the large, wire-rimmed glasses, I recognized the face framed by black hair as definitely Shahra's.

I pushed back the hood of my rain jacket. "I'm taller now," I said, "but it's me, John. John Chant. Anne's son."

She squinted, and then her mouth fell open in a perfect circle.

We retreated to the back corner of a coffee shop, where we could talk quietly, shedding our wet coats as well as the lost years between us.

"My God, Johnny, you're the last person I expected to run into."

I gave her a grim smile. "By the way, *Sharon,* congratulations on getting married, is that right? What does Mr. Wimplemaker do? Or is he also a Dr. Wimplemaker?"

"Ah, that. The name is assumed. I found that in my line of work, not drawing attention to my Persian heritage is an advantage."

"What exactly is your line of work? I don't mean this fringe science stuff. I mean C-QUARK."

She shook her head. "I see that sad, perceptive little boy has grown up into a perceptive young man—I hope no longer sad." She leaned forward. "How did you hear about it?"

"I was put on your trail by a very interested party, a guy named Fred Pigeon. With a business called Phoenix."

Shahra leaned back. "Oh, him. Yeah, I know about him. Fringe inventions."

"He wants me to, quote, 'infiltrate C-QUARK,' unquote. He appears to think it's a real thing, your secret committee. He believes you have secret stockpiles of suppressed theories and inventions. He hasn't told me what he wants, but it's probably not the engine that runs on water."

"You don't believe it's real? C-QUARK?"

"Now that I know you're involved, I'm sure it isn't."

My former nanny laughed softly. "Then why did you seek me out? Just to reminisce?"

"I saw you in a picture with Krulltang, or Mike, a little person who pretends to be an alien. It was in an article about an alleged autopsy on a real alien."

Shahra's eyes widened. "Mike Crutcher? The actor?"

"He's an actor?"

"That TV show—you know, the one they said was *Star Trek* meets *Goodfellas*—he played the main alien. We took that picture as a joke."

I shrugged. "I don't watch much TV." I sipped my coffee. "Did you know I met him, Mike, back home? A couple years after you left."

"Yeah, he mentioned that. He has a soft spot for you. That's partly why he agreed to help me out with that article. Though it was mostly your sister."

"Jane?"

"Yeah. He's filming her book."

One of Jane's fleeting phases, after wanting to be a revolutionary leader, and before trying to be a self-taught musician, was to be An Author, with capital A's. She had filled several notebooks with an analysis of the feudal and implicitly oppressive economies of mythological societies. "Where does magic come from?" she had asked me once when I was ten. I ignored her. I was the rare bright boy who wasn't into fantasy or science fiction. "It must come from *someone*'s labor." She had scribbled out an ersatz epic where children who fled or fell into or were kidnapped into fairyland were forced into slavery, toiling to create pixie dust, the source of magic. That was Jane: a Marxist in Elfland.

I had assumed she'd never got anything published. She had always been starting grand schemes and never finishing them, just like the rest of the family.

Shahra/Sharon gave me a phone number for Mike Crutcher. Before we said goodbye, Shahra said, "Listen. Fred Pigeon wants you to infiltrate C-QUARK. But I—or rather, C-QUARK—could use someone on the inside of Phoenix. You."

"Why? C-QUARK isn't even a real thing."

She sighed. "C-QUARK isn't, but Project Papercut is." She never told me the source of the funding, but admitted that the mandate of Project Papercut, and its front, C-QUARK, was to corral potentially dangerous ideas and information. "We don't 'fix' the Nobel Prizes, which is a stupid yet useful rumor to have going around. But among all those crackpot ideas and conspiracy theories, there are occasionally very dangerous inventions. And it happens that Fred Pigeon has of a whole stash of those."

I pursed my lips. "You mean, like Canterbury's notes? That's what you're after, isn't it?"

Shahra sighed and took off her glasses, waving them around like a conductor's baton. "Can I count on you to not rat me out to Pigeon, Johnny? ... Johnny? Can I count on you?"

I was distracted by her use of the word "rat," wondering if she had any idea about Pigeon's experiments. I managed to say, "Sure, okay. I'm tired of secrets, though. Secrets tore apart my family."

"I'm real sorry about what happened to your folks, especially Anne. But yes, we want Canterbury's designs. And anything built from those designs. One thing in particular."

Despite my repeated questions, she wouldn't tell me what that one particular thing was. I said, "That's stonewalling, that right there. That's why you aren't getting much from me. You want something, you gotta share something. You've told me almost nothing except that you're using a fake name. Look, Freddy Pigeon, I doubt he can do anything, good or bad. He's a miserable alcoholic."

"It's those miserable alcoholics you have to watch out for, John. I think you know that."

"Also, his father makes him miserable. They make each other miserable."

"What about *your* father, Johnny? Maybe you should go see him."

I called Mike "Krulltang" Crutcher, though getting past his agent wasn't easy, until I mentioned having met Mike in a sewer-turned-particle accelerator.

"John!" Mike shouted over the phone. "How the hell are you? Did you grow any taller?"

"Yeah," I said. "I'm nor— I grew a couple of feet."

Mike in turn gave me a number for my sister.

"Ohmigod, John!" Jane said over the phone. "I can't believe it's really you!"

There was an awkward, crackling silence. "And I can't believe you published a novel," I blurted out.

"I self-published it, actually," Jane said, "under a pseudonym, and it would have been forgotten if Mike hadn't stumbled upon it."

Mike had been thumbing through a pile of cheap used books when he came across hers. While the book didn't bear her real name, it did list our hometown—not a place he was likely to forget—and this seized his attention like a steel-toothed trap. He had managed to track her down, and they realized they had me in common. After that, Mike mentioned the book in an interview, sales picked up, an agent contacted Jane, and it became a Big Thing.

"In the beginning, he talked about you a lot, but after a while, he figured out how painful a subject it was and dropped it."

I heard a sound in the background, like a mewling cat. "Just a sec," Jane said. I heard rustling sounds. "Snack time."

"Snack time?"

"For Billy-boy. Three months old. I'm pretty sure there's no one in the family with that name, which is why I chose it."

"You have a *baby*? When did you... I mean, did you...?"

"Oh, no, I'm not married," said Jane. "I *think* I know who the father is, but that's not really very important to me."

"Oh," I said. And then I ventured, "Speaking of parents..."

"We finally buried her."

"So, she..."

"Well, her condition got worse and worse, and she was spending *most* of her time dead. She was the one who suggested it. 'No point in you having to dust me once a week,' she said, 'no point in you having to answer awkward questions.'"

"Oh."

"She's in that big cemetery on Highway 314, just outside of town. You can go visit."

"Oh," I said again. "And *him*?"

Jane didn't answer at first. From the noises, she was doing something with the baby. "He's still around. The same as always, only more so. I hardly talk with him. What is there to say?" I heard loud sucking sounds, and she spoke so softly, I almost couldn't hear her. "He hated what happened to you."

"Could have looked for me," I said, surprised at the bitterness in my mouth.

"*She* was falling apart, literally, and I ... I was a *mess*. I made both their lives a holy hell." She sighed. "He *did* look for you. He'd lost the packing slip, so when he wasn't propping up mom and me, he drove across the country, snooping around circuses. I told him to put up flyers, but because he is who he is, he built this device using cosmic ray muons to x-ray circus tents, trying to see if there were any boys hidden beneath the big top. Just a sec..."

There was another pause as she did something, then her voice returned. "I went with him a couple of times. It crushed him, the way he failed you. I kinda wished he'd seen how he failed me, too. Then, typical for him, he got distracted trying to perfect his muon tomography machine." She sighed, but then her voice brightened. "Listen, we're not far from you. Most of the filming is in sound stages in Vancouver, with some location shots in the British Colombia forests. Mike suggested we drive down to Seattle—well, he has his own driver—and meet you for lunch. That way, you can meet your nieces."

"There are *more*?"

"You sure you want me to join you?" Ada asked.

"I'm going into the valley of the shadow of my childhood," I said. "I need you with me."

Mike said to meet them in a restaurant he knew in Seattle. It was one of those places that strives to play it cool and casual, but was really much fancier than any place Ada and I could afford.

I almost didn't recognize Jane at first. When I had last seen her, she had been a waif of a young teenager, perpetually exasperated with everyone. Eleven years had added flesh to her frame and sorrow to her face. For a moment, she held back, but she must have glimpsed my old self, for she threw her arms around my neck.

"I don't remember you being this sentimental," I said, "especially about *me*."

Mike rambled up, wearing an oversized ball cap that shadowed his face. He was hunched over a bit, but when he got close, he lifted his face and broke into a big grin. He positively strutted over, shot out his hand, and we shook.

"Well, well, look who's all grown up now," said Mike Crutcher, formerly Krulltang of Epsilon Eridani. To Ada, he said, "I see little-now-big John has good taste. Wowser! Don't mind me, miss, I was a circus freak for much of my life, and bad habits die hard."

Jane embraced Ada, and Mike gestured to the restaurant host, who ushered us to a semiprivate table in a far corner. A waiter surreptitiously came over and placed a stiff cushion on a chair. Mike clambered up and looked around as we all sat down.

Jane said, "I told John I wouldn't embarrass him in front of his *girlfriend*, even though I was always going to be the scandalous one in the family." She looked down at Billy-boy, gurgling in her arms. Off to the side, a silent au pair tended to her daughters, Katya and Serena, four and two-and-a-half. "No father, you see. Okay, well, there *was* a father. It wasn't immaculate conception; it happened in the usual sweaty, noisy fashion... Ah, there, John's turning red, mission accomplished. But it was just no one I wanted to keep around."

Ada made faces at the baby. "The only scandal would be an unloved child," she said.

Jane said, "Or one who's undernourished, or undereducated, or placed in a literal or figurative box, but that's my inner Marxist talking."

I asked, "Are you a Marxist again?" To Ada, I said, "Jane went through phases, you see. First she was into Jesus, then into Marx. In between, she was into the Grateful Dead, or the Moody Blues, someone like that. I forget what else."

"You were into dinosaurs," Jane pointed out.

"Not quite the same."

"He broke the sewer, digging for fossils in the backyard," Jane told Ada.

"You have this thing about sewers, don't you?" Mike said, signaling to a waiter. To Jane, he added, "We met in a sewer-turned-cyclotron—"

"Synchrotron," I corrected.

"He did mention something about a *particle accelerator* in the sewers," Ada said.

"Finest kind," Mike said. "I was pretending to be a space alien. I mean, pretending to be a real one,—not in a movie or any such thing, I hadn't gotten into acting yet—and a friend of John's dad wanted to dissect me. John and his mom helped me out of that unpleasant fate. Sorry to hear about your mom, by the way, John."

The waiter came and took our orders. Mike said, "I didn't want to impose on your reunion with your big sister, but we're wrapping up shooting, and who knows when I'll be back in these parts again. I told Jane, I gotta see him." He paused. "It *is* good to see you, kid. Jane here told me you've had some hard times."

"I guess."

"What circus was it?"

"I actually ran away *from* the first circus I was sent to, then ended up at another one." Both Ada and Jane were looking at me intently. I said, "I took advantage of *their* kindness. I told them lies, because I was too bitter to go back. Whenever someone got suspicious, I ran away again. Whenever I got spooked, I ran again, to this circus or that carnival. So, really, Jane, it's my fault you couldn't find me, that dad couldn't find me. I didn't want to be found. I was so angry, and I felt so betrayed." I left out the tales I'd told of familial combustion.

There was an awkward silence that didn't fit the joyful mood of a few minutes before, like when an ancient and beloved teacher farts in front of the class.

At length, Mike shattered the silence by hitting the tabletop with the flat of his palm. "Ain't that life, kid? We don't get found when we want to, and we get found when we don't want to, and... Well, you're all geniuses, I think; you can figure out the rest." He paused and looked all around the table at us with his dark silver eyes. "But at least for the moment, in *this* moment, we've found one another. I don't think you get much more than that. Ah, here's the chow. Let's eat, I'm starving."

As we were saying our goodbyes, Ada said, "Tell me again, what are you doing up in Vancouver?"

Jane looked at me. I said to Jane, "I haven't gotten around to telling her. I had to start with, 'You know my sister who you're always telling me to go find? I found her.'" To Ada, I said, "It's not a secret, or at least not a *family* secret. But Jane, under a pseudonym, wrote this book, and it's being made into a movie—"

"Miniseries," Jane interrupted, "and tell her the name."

"*An Illegal Immigrant in Fairyland.* By Janet C. Plainsong."

Ada put her hands to her mouth. "Oh my goodness, I *loved* that book! Wow, John, your family really is overflowing with talent."

I shrugged. Jane said, "John doesn't read books."

"I read a *lot* of books, just not fiction."

"You should read it," Ada said. "It's really funny—like the time when the 'giant' comes out to menace the children who've been enslaved to make magic, but it's only giant relative to the tiny fairies, so the giant is actually smaller than a human child, and the heroine—her name's Nan—she just pushes it over. But it will also make you cry, like at the end... I shouldn't spoil it for you."

"Ooh, I like her, John," Jane said.

I was surprised how lifted my spirits felt after meeting up with Jane and Mike. It gave me enough confidence that a couple of days later, when I met with Hile in his office, I asked, "Say, what do you think happened to Canterbury's notes?"

I had shown Hile where I was blocked in my research, unable to produce the Big Bang the way he had, and he hmm'ed for a while, then said, "Ah! Here's your problem. You're treating this as a one-particle system, but in fact, it has a huge number of particles—all the particles in the universe, in fact," as if I should say right back, *"Why, of course, I see it all now! How could I have been so stupid?"* Instead, I brought up Canterbury.

On the blackboard, Hile had crossed out some terms in my equation and was writing in others. "Mmm, probably stored in a lead-lined vault, I imagine. Plutonium-239 has a half-life of twenty-four thousand years, so it will be a while before anyone else reads them."

"What about the ones that weren't radioactive? I mean, I wrote a report. Who read that? Did it just go into some classified file?"

"If you're worried your time was wasted, John, it wasn't. Nothing we do is wasted. Not everything leads to a better coffee maker or cures cancer, but it has a ripple effect, nonetheless." He turned back to the blackboard, adding the next term. "I don't know if anyone at the lab will *read* your report, but even so..."

"Speaking of curing cancer, I remember my father had this experimental drug... He tried it on a Mexican beaded lizard, and on a, um, friend of his... Do you know anything about this?"

Hile's hand hovered over a minus sign. "No, I haven't been in contact with your father for years. I suppose I should reach out." He normally wrote equations fast and easily, but now he erased, rewrote, and erased again. After a few minutes, he dropped his arm. "Well, I'm blocked. I suppose I'm discombobulated. I had a break-in at my house a few days ago, despite a *very* expensive alarm system. Let's pick this up next week, shall we?"

While I divided my time between classes and working for Pigeon—who insisted I continue to work on anti-asteroid defenses, no matter how impossible it seemed—Ada was spending eight-hour shifts in the middle of the night, measuring cross-sections for rare isotopes, only to spend another eight hours studying for the qual, falling asleep in class in the few spare hours she had. As my monkey brain could only stay still for a short time before leaping to another tree, I admired her ability to focus for such long periods. But I also worried about her burning out.

My own research for grad school was not going well. I barely understood what was happening in my small life. How could I ever understand the quantum evolution of the entire universe?

The end of the quarter barreled down upon us. Although the qual was scheduled right after spring break, Ada said she was going home. Her father's cancer hadn't responded to treatments at the hospital in Bozeman, so he was coming to Seattle, where the Glen Spinoza Cancer Treatment Center was one of the most advanced in the world in cutting-edge regimens. Ada would fly to Montana and drive with her family to Seattle.

"You'll be completely wrecked for the qual," I said, then regretted it.

"What else can I do?"

"Nothing, I know," I said, hugging her. "I'm sorry."

"I'm sorry to leave you behind again. I..." She wiped at her nose. "Someday, our time will be about *us*. I want that, John."

I kissed her. "It's okay. I made my own plans for spring break."

Working for Pigeon had boosted my bank account, which I used to buy a ticket. My hometown streets were wet with recent rain, the trees bare of leaves. It was eerie returning to a place I hadn't visited in years, to see people digging out their gardens for spring planting and taking grocery bags out of the trunk and children stomping in puddles. Who had told them everything was normal? Where was the sign—JOHN, STAY OUT. THIS MEANS *YOU*, MISTER—that I expected? I cruised by my old school, where I had formed a crush on Becky, where an omelet breakfast fundraiser had lured out a gigantic venomous lizard. I drove by Big Bruce's old house, where I had been unable to sleep. Finally, having exhausted those memories, I turned onto our cul-de-sac. On the hill behind our house, where Jane and I used to play in the woods, a shiny new subdivision had sprouted up. That seemed like the most unreal part: some of the best memories of my childhood, erased and paved over.

I parked on the street. An unfamiliar car, looking unloved and uncared for, sat in the driveway, the windshield plastered with red-brown leaves.

Finally, I got out of the rental car. It took me a good five minutes to ring the bell. I kept staring at the peeling yellow paint.

After I rang a second time, my heart swinging like a clapper in my chest, the door finally opened. While my father was the same age as Hile, he looked much older, as if twenty years and not ten had passed. His sandy-brown hair had gone white, and he was thinner and slightly bent, like a used paper clip. Only his old black-rimmed glasses, smudged with fingerprints, were unchanged.

"John," he said, his voice papery and thin. "Jane said you might come by. I wasn't sure, but she said you would."

"Uh-huh," I said.

He didn't exactly invite me in, just walked away with the door left open. A lot of invitations are like that.

We didn't talk much. The living room still had the same furniture I had grown up with, only more worn and musty-smelling. After my father poured me a glass of iced tea, he plopped down into an easy chair and stared at the stains in the carpet. I wasn't expecting an apology, but an acknowledgement would have been nice.

"Jane has three kids now," I said. "Who would have guessed it? Jane, a mother."

"Three? I thought it was two. Oh, yes, she told me. A boy, isn't it? I've only met the girls. She said she would come by sometime, but she's busy in LA, or New York, or some place like that." He seemed curled into himself, the way the feet of the Wicked Witch of the East curled up when Dorothy got her shoes.

"I'm in grad school now," I blurted out. I had not wanted to give him the satisfaction, but sitting there, I had no other conversational gambits—I had foolishly been expecting him to shoulder the burden—and so it burst out of me. "Physics. University of Washington. With your old friend, Huey Hile."

"Ozzie?" A brief flicker of life. "How is he? He won the Nobel a couple years back."

"Nine years ago. He asked about you. I wasn't sure what to say."

My father looked out the bright square of a window, not at me. "Not much to say."

"Are you still teaching? Research?"

"Something like that," he said, like sandpaper against wood.

"Hile took me to Los Alamos last summer. I came across some notes by your old professor, Canterbury." When he said nothing, I added, "Hieronymous Canterbury."

My father gave a long sigh. "Canterbury was borderline crazy," he said at last.

"Hile said Canterbury was fond of you," I said. My father grunted. After a while, I said, "I remember a lot of crazy things in my childhood. Remember when I broke the sewer line? And Ernie, that Mexican beaded lizard, who got huge, and got taken to Plumb Island? Remember Robbie? You made Robbie."

"Course I made Robbie," he said, looking out the window.

"And there was that box, that time travel box, the time window you made."

Now my father turned to look at me. His blue eyes looked watery behind his thick black-rimmed glasses. "Time travel is impossible. It's science fiction."

"But I went out to the garage and turned it on, and this eye, a dinosaur eye looked out at me, and it stuck a claw through the window and burned out your machine."

He had let his gaze fall to the floor. His lips moved, but no words came out.

I stood up. "Let me take you out to dinner. Can I stay here tonight?"

I had trouble sleeping in my old room, still furnished with childhood books and a dried-up terrarium. I went downstairs and out back, where Jane and I had (temporarily) buried our mother when she was (temporarily) dead. But the hillside above our backyard, once our private fiefdom, was lit up by the sodium streetlamps of the new subdivision, and I saw people moving in their windows, back and forth, as if run by clockwork.

Then I went into the garage, and the sights and smells brought me fully back to my childhood. I felt eight years old again.

My father had groused, "I don't know that it's safe to stay here, John. People have been breaking in."

I remembered what Jane had told me. "Into the house?"

"The garage. I hear them breaking in and rummaging around out there, but by the time I get downstairs, they're gone." He frowned. "Can you buy me a new lock?"

Like Jane, I had thought he was imagining it. But then I saw that the rusted old padlock had been battered open, the latch splintered. When I went inside the garage, his old home lab, it looked like a tornado had spun through it. For hours, I went through the piles of junk in the garage: ancient oscilloscopes and voltmeters and piles of soldering irons like robot cigars. Under a stack of old bills, I found sketched plans for Robbie. I wondered if I would come across plans for myself.

I was about to go back to bed when I came across a flat wooden box and opened it up. Nestled inside was a single remaining vial of the bubble-gum-pink serum, the very serum that had cured cancer in Ernie, the Mexican beaded lizard, and given him gigantism; the serum that had cured the cancer of my father's old flame, Sophia, and given *her* gigantism, too.

Behind the serum box, I found the singed ruins of the time window, about the size of an old-fashioned boxy cathode-ray-tube TV set. Even twenty years later, it smelled of smoke and burnt metal. I unscrewed the housing. The screws were rusted, so it took a good forty minutes to get them all out. Inside, nestled among wires and bars of exotic metals and minerals, I found an egg-shaped bronze device, like an oversized football. A probability pump. I recognized it from Canterbury's drawings.

Shortly before spring break, before I had gone on this trip, I had gone to church with Ada. The gospel reading had been the parable of the prodigal son, a prat who demanded from his father his half of the estate, and then went off and spent it on partying and wanton women. Standing in my father's garage, I found myself the prodigal son in reverse: long banished to a far-off country, and only now coming home to seek my inheritance.

I picked up the probability pump. It felt slightly warm to the touch, like plutonium. In its place, I put a lead brick and closed up the sooty ruins of the time window. I told myself it was my right. So much had been stolen from me. I also plucked out the last remaining anti-cancer vial. With so much on my ledger, what was a little pink serum?

On the way out of town, I found her grave, marked Anne Jael Sallis-Chant, with her birth date. There was no other marking—no Treasured Wife, no Beloved Mother, not even a date of death.

Spring was coming after a long, wet winter. The grass was emerald green and springy. The sun, a brass watch on an invisible fob, swung from the sky. I stretched myself out on her grave. Fingers of sunlight kneaded my muscles, and I thought to myself, *This is peaceful.*

A murmuring rumble came from the gravestone, and I put my ear to the cold granite.

Someone there?

"It's me. It's John. Johnny. Jane told me you were here."

Oh, Johnny. You came to visit. How are you?

I told her I was in grad school. I told her about meeting Hile, going to Santa Fe and Los Alamos. She had to ask me a couple of times to speak up; sound doesn't carry well through six feet of earth. I told her about Ada, how brilliant and beautiful she was, how kind she was. I related an edited version of how I had run into Shahra again, and Jane, and came home after ten years away.

I wasn't a good mother, was I, Johnny? I tried to do my best, but it wasn't very good.

For years, I had carried a knot of anger and resentment, a bruise on my heart. I had nursed that resentment with the bitter milk of loneliness, and scripted many a speech denouncing her selfishness, her disastrous parenting. But now she was a shrunken memory, whispering from a grave.

"Don't you feel claustrophobic down there?" I asked.

It's cool and dark and comfortable. Your sister made sure I had a well-sealed casket. Sometimes I wonder how the world is turning up there. But I can't do anything about it now, and that is wonderfully freeing. I feel peace now, real peace.

I asked if there were any messages I should pass on.

No. But I do miss my blues, Johnny.

I had time before my flight. I went into town, bought a compact disc player, and placed it against her headstone, so the sounds would transmit down. I rigged up some small solar panels to recharge the player's batteries. "How's that?"

Wonderful. You're such a good son, Johnny. I'm sorry I let you down. I was so wrapped up in my sorrows... I'm sorry about what happened to you. I'm sorry I let it happen.

And so was I.

Introduction to Physical Cosmology

After a long drive from Montana, Ada had checked her father into the Glen Spinoza Cancer Treatment Center. "I'm wrung out," Ada said, flopping herself onto my ratty couch, "but it's a relief to have him nearby. Now we have to argue with the insurance company. They don't want to pay for anything."

"Can I ask, what's the prognosis?"

With dark circles under her eyes, she looked haunted by death herself. "It's spread everywhere."

I took a deep breath, feeling as if I were standing on a high dive towering over a pool. "Remember I told you about my pet Mexican beaded lizard, Paul, and his brother, Ernie? And my father's ex-mistress?"

"Mmm?"

"At our house, my father's house, I went out to the garage, his lab. It was a mess. But I found it." I showed her the vial of pink serum.

She recognized what it was and stiffened. "And, what? Make my father a monster? Imprison him on some island?"

"Well, he wouldn't be dead."

"It doesn't sound like life to me," she said, her voice cold and tense like naked steel.

"I know, I *know*, but... I feel so helpless. You must, too." I knelt down to put my arms around her, but she shook me off.

"Helpless? Do you know what I've been doing these past few months at the nuclear physics lab?"

"Measuring reaction cross-sections for the CNO cycle?"

She huffed. "Okay, yes, that is what I *told* you I was doing. I was actually working on something else."

Ada had been spending the last few months secretly synthesizing astatine-211, a potential radioisotope for cancer therapy. Bonded to monoclonal antibodies, it would, like tiny assassins, take radiation directly to the cancer wherever it was in the body. But astatine-211 was difficult to synthesize, and the one lab in Russia producing it had shut down. On the sly, Ada had been using accelerator beam time to make it, a few thousand atoms every night. She had delivered a lead vial containing the precious isotope to the Glen Spinoza Cancer Treatment Center the day before.

"And Okuma never figured it out?"

"Well, he did, like a month ago. The accelerator techs knew something was up a lot sooner, but they liked me and said nothing. Okuma was mad for about fifteen seconds, then said his father had died of cancer when he was a boy and that he understood."

"Oh," I said. Then: "Will it work?"

She sank back on the couch. "I don't know. The doctors say it's his last best chance." She craned her neck to look at me. "Better than turning him into some sort of *kaiju*."

"I was only trying to help."

She spread her arms wide. "I know. Come here."

She fell asleep while still hugging me, and I covered her with a blanket.

When I went down to Freddy Pigeon's sub-basement, I found him extracting brains from a batch of rats. "Rita is composed of over two hundred brains," he said. I looked away as he wielded a stainless-steel scalpel, though I heard the snick of the blade as it sliced. "Two or three components die each day, so I have to constantly replace them."

Queasy from the smell of rat blood, I asked, "Rita?"

"Rita is what I call the current version of my ... apparatus. I name the iterations after famous neuroscientists, such as Santiago Ramon y Cajal, Carl Wernicke, Donald Hebb, and in this case, Rita Levi-Montalcini."

"Oh, yeah, she won the Nobel Prize a few years ago." (Probably you recognized those names immediately.) "Nerve growth or something." I almost asked, *"Do you think that was C-QUARK's doing?"*

"Perhaps I could train you how to maintain Rita. How to—"

"No, thanks," I said. "I can solder, weld a bit, wind magnets, and I even know how to calibrate a gamma-ray spectrometer. But dissecting rats for their brains? That's where I draw the line." I looked away from his gloved hands red with blood. "I'm going upstairs."

Half an hour later, Pigeon came up from the sub-basement, smelling of disinfectant. "Still stuck?" he asked. "Perhaps you need an influx of new ideas."

I took a deep breath and said, "I doubt even Hieronymous Canterbury would have a wacky enough idea to solve this."

Pigeon gave me a sharp glance. "Of course you figured that out. However, I wasn't thinking of Canterbury, but C-QUARK." He told me Wimplemaker would be giving a series of talks in the Seattle area the following week. "This will be a perfect opportunity to contact her."

"I'm not going to be some sort of secret agent for you," I said, crossing my arms. "I'm good at inventing, not spying." It would only make things worse to admit that I'd already been in contact with Shahra.

Pigeon rubbed at his face. "Rita predicted you'd be reluctant."

"You discuss me with your rat superbrain?"

He gave a weak smile. "Rita advises me on all my plans. Rita encouraged hiring you, predicted that Miss Johnson would quit, even saved Phoenix by leading me to SSSS-Corp." He took a silver flask from his jacket, unscrewed it, and sipped. I resisted asking if Rita had any thoughts on his drinking.

When I was a child, my Gramma talked about praying to Jesus for guidance. Back then, I imagined it like a séance, or a fortune teller, only with a Bible instead of a crystal ball. Now, I imagined Pigeon, stretched out on a couch, pouring his heart out to his collection of rat brains in their bubbling fluid. I felt vaguely sick.

I said I wanted to make some tea. When we clumped upstairs into the kitchen, Pigeon said, "I should go check on Duke."

"The governor paroled me!" Duke yelled from upstairs.

"I'm glad he's better," I said.

"Not really. He got kicked out of the rehab center. I—"

"You would have left me there forever!" Duke shouted.

Freddy took a deep breath. "He was terrorizing the nursing staff. It's not just me who finds him impossible." He lowered his voice. "Other places won't take him. He needs constant attention, sabotages my time, and for obvious reasons, I can't bring in outside care."

Duke called out, "Are you boys horsing around? Don't make me come down there!"

Freddy kept his voice quiet. "I can give you a raise—a substantial raise. I'm under pressure from SSSS-Corp. If you would simply go to Wimplemaker's talk..."

My insides felt twisted up, like a wound rubber band. "Listen, Mr. Pigeon... I appreciate the work you give me. But to pretend with this, um, Wimplemaker that I'm something I'm not... I'm stressed out enough. I got classes, I got homework, and my girlfriend's father is dying..." I immediately wished I had said nothing.

Pigeon's face homed in on me like a radar dish imitating sympathy. "I'm sorry to hear that. Heart disease, cancer...?"

I shrugged. "Yeah. Cancer."

Pigeon nodded vigorously. "I had noticed you were distracted lately. Now I understand." He started to turn away, then stopped. "I showed you Rita, but I never fully confided in you, did I?" He took a deep breath, as if about to confess a murder, or that he forgot to pay the phone bill. But then Duke yelled down, and Pigeon sighed and trudged up the stairs, and I went back to plotting how to kill an asteroid.

Those days, I saw little of Ada; she spent most of her time studying for the qual in her father's room at the Glen Spinoza Cancer Treatment Center. When I asked her if the astatine-211 was helping her father, all she said was "We don't know."

A couple of times each week, we grabbed lunch together, but we said very little, because what could we say? Ada's father was in the shadowlands. I remembered my own mother shuttling between life and death, and how I'd felt no more substantial than a smudge on a lens, and at the same time as if my guts were full of granite and lead bricks. But it wasn't the same, because love and grief trapped Ada with her father in the bardo, while for my family, it had been betrayal and rage and shame.

The phone in my apartment rang. I thought it might be Ada, but it was Shahra.

"What's up, Johnny? I'm giving a talk in Seattle in a few days."

"I know, Pigeon keeps bugging me to go."

"I thought I'd come a day or two early, to see you."

"Should I feel special?"

"What's with the hostility? I thought we got along back then. Were you upset that I left? Your mom fired me, you know."

"She fired you because she didn't need you anymore, because I got kicked out of that school—because you made up stories, got me to make up stories, too, and in the end, those stories hurt people. What's your story now? That C-QUARK, whatever that is, will dictate whether or not string theory gets the Nobel Prize? I mean, really. String theory."

She laughed. "It's not string theory that keeps me up at night."

"So, what does?"

"What Pigeon might have."

"What Pigeon has is a lot of crazy ideas. Even if you get ahold of Canterbury's notes," I asked, "what are you going to do with them? Who is C-QUARK working for? The CIA? The American Physical Society?"

"We just want to bury them. Those ideas."

"It's hard to kill an idea," I said. "I'm pretty ignorant of history, but even I know that."

"We're doing our best to protect people."

"Everyone thinks of themselves as the hero of their own story," I said. "Doesn't mean they are."

"Are you, Johnny? Are you the hero of your story?"

I wasn't so sure.

When next I went down to the sub-basement, I found a cage with three dogs in it. One was a pit bull, and the other two mongrels. They barked and whined and nudged at a metal bowl. Next to the cage was a big bag of dry dog food. I poured some of the food into the bowl. All three lunged for it, and the pit bull bit one of the mongrels, causing it to screech in pain.

Back upstairs, I found Pigeon in the kitchen at the microwave. "Why are there dogs down in the sub-basement?"

"Those three had been branded as unadoptable by the shelter," he said as the microwave beeped, "and were scheduled to be put down." He opened the door and took out a pot pie.

"And you thought, what, they'd make good company for Rita? Give Rita a robot arm and teach it how to throw a ball?"

"Pit bulls are not the most intelligent breed of dog, but they are plentiful in shelters." I winced when he said this. Pigeon put the pot pie on a plate with a fork. "Excuse me, I have to take this to Duke."

A few minutes later, Pigeon thumped down the stairs, more forcefully than I would have thought necessary. In the kitchen, he yanked open a cabinet and grabbed a glass. It slipped out of his hand and shattered in the sink. Sighing, he raised his face to the ceiling. "He complained that I didn't bring him water," he said, his eyes closed.

"I'll clean up the broken glass. You take him his water."

"He'll just demand something else," he said, exasperated.

I wrapped the shards of glass in an old newspaper and was putting it in the garbage under the sink when Pigeon returned. "The thermostat is set too high. An hour from now, he'll complain it's too cold." He leaned over the sink to look out the kitchen window. Mt. Rainier was visible on the horizon. I imagined him thinking either, *Volcanoes have no parents to sabotage their plans for eruptions*, or *Maybe instead of dog brains, I can start with Duke's.*

"Did you ever have a pet dog?" I asked.

Pigeon pivoted abruptly, his reverie shattered like a dropped glass. "A pet...? No. My mother was allergic to dogs. And cats."

"I had a pet dog. Bessie. Sometimes I thought she was the only one who really loved me. She got cancer—from a cosmic-ray neutrino, my father thought—and we had to put her down." I frowned. "I'd hate to imagine *her* brain in a jar, being trained to do tricks."

"Well, no one loves *these* dogs."

"So, they don't matter?"

Pigeon took down another glass and a bottle and poured himself a drink. "You are a sensitive and empathetic young man. Empathy is a noble thing, but I can't help but wonder, if we felt empathy for everything, for the whole universe, wouldn't we end up paralyzed?" He gestured with his glass towards the ceiling, taking a sip. "Of course, I have trouble mustering much empathy for my own father."

He looked over at me. "Speaking of cancer, rumor has it that C-QUARK's files contain a cure."

"Oh, yeah, I know about it. It has kind of huge side-effects."

Pigeon poured out more of the amber liquid. "The gigantism? I heard they fixed that."

When I got back to my apartment later, my phone was ringing. It was my sister. Jane asked how things were going, and I told her.

"I know it's hard on you," she said. "But think of what it must be like for poor Ada."

"Yeah, I know. I just wish—"

"Listen, remember what it was like with mom, you know, being dead every once in a while? How crazy that made us all? Did you tell any of your friends?"

"I didn't really have friends."

"You had Big Bruce," she said, "and there was that girl you liked, Becky." I was surprised Jane remembered Becky's name. "Would you have told any of them? Did you?"

"Bruce had problems of his own. Becky, too. I didn't want to burden them."

"*Quad erat demonstrandum,*" Jane said.

I wanted to tell my sister how I loved Ada so much, but was terrified of losing her to her slow-motion maelstrom of grief for her father. But in my head, that sounded selfish and heartless, so I did not work up the courage to say anything.

I found Freddy Pigeon in the sub-basement, staring at his jars of rat brains.

"What does Rita have to say?" I asked.

Pigeon swung around to face me. "We're trying to find a way out of our situation." His words were slurred. "You've left me in a pickle, Mr. Chant. You insist that the asteroid defense cannot work. When I told this to the herpetominids, they were quite upset." Despite being quite drunk, he said *her-peh-TAW-meh-nids* fluently.

"The herpe-who?"

Pigeon gave a barking laugh. "The lizard people. SSSS-Corp. They claim they're from the Earth's core, but really, only a hundred kilometers underground." He waved his arms, raving. "I *told* them their plan was shaky. So many things could go wrong. Suppose we miraculously design a workable asteroid defense; they then want to send the plans back in time. If it could be done at all, it would require a probability pump, which I don't have, despite lots of effort and money."

My heart thumped when he said "probability pump." That shocked me almost more than his ranting about herpetominids.

Pigeon blew out a big, wet sigh. "I suppose they *needed* some exaggerated sense of optimism to stay in hiding for tens of millions of years. But because there's no asteroid defense, they are furious." He leaned forward, burying his head in his arms. "They watch the house. I see them everywhere. Their masks, they're good, but they can't hide the fact that they have no necks."

Upstairs, I found Duke sitting at the kitchen table, half his body wrapped in bandages and plaster, not quite a full-body cast, but close. "Say, when Freddy gets drunk, does he ever talk about really crazy things?" I asked.

"More crazy than usual? Yeah, all the time."

From out in the front room came the sound of rats rustling through the wood shavings in their cages. "Poor bastards," Duke said.

"Because they live in a cage?" I asked.

"I know what that's like," said Duke. "Except Freddy takes better care of his rats than he does his old man." He leaned forward. "You know he used to experiment on 'em? Rats, I mean."

"Yeah, he mentioned that," I said slowly. "Back in grad school." I did not know if Duke had any inkling of what was in the sub-basement. Or that his son imagined himself conspiring with an underground civilization of lizard people to... What? Change history? Save the dinosaurs?

"Goddamn rats," Duke suddenly said with vehemence.

"You don't like them? They give some people the willies."

"Nah. It's... I doubt Freddy told you about his mother. Ooh, boy. It's a punch to the gut. But it'll help you understand. See, as a lad, Freddy wanted a pet.

He pestered us, but Louise, she was allergic to dogs, cats, you name it. But it turned out she wasn't allergic to rats, so we got the boy one. Only Freddy's a daydreamer, so of course he forgot to feed it and to clean the cage. One day, he and I got into it. Freddy, he knows how to push my buttons, so he brought up how he thought he wasn't really my kid, and I blew my top, and Louise stepped in, playing peacemaker as she always did. Except this time, I smacked her. Only time, too... But anyway, Louise, she picked herself up like nothing had happened, took the cage with the rat, and drove off to return it."

He paused to swipe at his eyes. "On her way to the pet store, someone ran a red light, T-boned her car, killed her instantly." He sat in silence for a long while. Finally, with a strangled voice, he said, "The boy always blamed me for that, but if I'm honest, in my heart, I've blamed him. If you want to know what hell is like, it's this. Him and me, tied together, each believing the other responsible for the worst moment in both our lives." He sagged in the chair, as if being slowly crushed.

Before I could think of anything to say, the door to the basement opened. Duke looked away, brushing at his eyes again as Freddy staggered in. Seeing Duke at the kitchen table, he muttered, "You shouldn't come down the stairs by yourself."

"We were plotting a coup," Duke said, his voice still hoarse.

"You could fall again."

"Fracturing my hip and putting myself through excruciating pain is a cry for attention," Duke said. "What's your excuse?"

"I'm taking you upstairs," Freddy said.

"In your condition? We'll fall and both break our necks." Duke turned to me and said in a stage whisper, "Avenge me!"

"God!" Freddy exclaimed. "See what I have to put up with?"

A few days later, Ada sat for the qualifying exam. While she was huddled over her papers at the university, I went to Shahra's talk, where she brought up at least six kinds of nonsense. Afterwards, Shahra beamed when she saw me. "Hi, John. Want to grab some dinner?"

She picked a Nepalese place near Greenlake. "Let's get some momos," she suggested as we sat down. "Love those Himalayan dumplings. And let's get their fiery sauce."

"Do I call you Dr. Wimplemaker in public," I asked, "or can I just call you Shahra, real quiet?"

"Are you going to help me out? I can make it worth your while."

"If I cared about money, would I be in grad school?" I pointed out.

"It's not money I'm offering. I have connections. I can get you and your girl-friend faculty positions after you graduate. It wouldn't be Harvard or Caltech, or even the U-dub, but I have influence at some medium-sized midwestern state schools. As good as your father's university, or even a bit better." She sipped her beer.

I sat still for a moment, stunned like a bird that had suddenly banged into a plate glass window. You had to hand it to Shahra: she correctly guessed my strongest temptation.

"You'd start off as research faculty, for a couple of years, to make it look natural," she said, "but then get voted in as assistant professors. After that, tenure would be up to the two of you."

It was as if she had x-rayed me, revealing the tiny spot in my brain where I secretly imagined a lifetime with Ada. The devil himself couldn't have offered me a better deal. Most likely Shahra had known other naïve young men experiencing their first love.

I shook myself. "What, you aren't going to offer us Nobel Prizes?"

"Ha."

"So, what do you want? Scoop up all of Canterbury's designs? I'm not even sure where they are."

"A list of what Pigeon has would be nice, but that's not the real prize." She took a piece of paper out of her purse and slid it over to me. My heart jolted, and my mouth felt dry. It was a photocopy of a design: a probability pump. "I see you know what this is," Shahra said, stuffing the paper back into her purse.

"I ran across a mention of it at Los Alamos last summer."

Shahra spoke quietly. "Canterbury claimed Lise Meitner first came up with the idea. A machine to shift around probabilities, the working fluid of quantum mechanics. Teller and Oppenheimer dismissed probability pumps as impossi-ble." A waiter plopped down a plate of momos. Shahra ate one and continued, with a hand over her mouth as she chewed. "But Canterbury made them work. A dozen were built and charged up at the Nevada Test Site in late 1949."

She told me two pumps had been discharged in experiments, then the pro-gram was shut down, and the remainder were locked in a deep underground vault—except three of the "pumps" in the vault were fakes, replacements to hide the theft of the real ones. One of the missing real ones, the Soviets got their hands on. Another was thought to have been passed to Cuba, to China, to North Korea, or maybe to Israel or France.

"The last missing pump was presumed lost, but rumors kept rumbling that Canterbury had it. It wasn't in his effects when he died. Most think he sold it, but money meant nothing to Canterbury, only his dreams. The few physicists who've heard of probability pumps don't believe it's possible. But you do, don't you?" Shahra paused. "Pigeon may have gotten hold of one, from the same source as Canterbury's notes."

I shook my head. "No. Pigeon doesn't have one."

Shahra eyed me like a cobra eyeing a mongoose, or maybe the other way around. "You know this?"

"Freddy said something recently, when he was drunk, about needing a probability pump, like he didn't have one."

Shahra pondered this. "Canterbury wouldn't have left it to just anyone. He'd have left it to someone he trusted." When I didn't respond, she said quietly, "Like a former student. Like your professor."

"Hile?"

"It's possible that Hile is the source of Canterbury's notes in Pigeon's possession. Maybe not everything got transferred."

I frowned. "Hile said something about his house being broken into."

Shahra nodded, taking another momo. "Pigeon knows a man named Trinh who carries out the occasional dirty job. And on Trinh's rap sheet is breaking and entering."

In my head, I was replaying my conversations with Hile. "You know, Hile once told me luck played a part in his winning the Nobel Prize."

"Interesting," said Shahra. "Maybe he persuaded luck to be on his side. Maybe he used a probability pump on himself, came up with the accelerating expansion of the universe, and won the Nobel."

"Now that you say that, Freddy may believe the same thing. We were talking about Hile, and he said something about making luck. But Freddy doesn't have a pump. He expressed frustration about this. He was also raving about a lot of other wild stuff. So, what do you want from me?"

"Hile may still have the pump. But if it's not at his home, then it's probably in his office. It wouldn't be so easy for Pigeon's man, Trinh, to be sneaking around a busy physics department. Even late at night, there are grad students around." She paused. "On the other hand, no one would pay attention to a grad student late at night..."

"You want me to *break into* Hile's office?"

"I have a friend who can give you the tools, show you how to do it."

I put my head in my hands.

"Please, John. You don't know how dangerous this device can be."

"I do, I do." The vibrations from the poems in the locked file cabinet, and those poets' sad fates, still ricocheted around in my heart. "While I'm thinking about it, let me ask a couple of questions."

"Shoot."

"Since you know about weird stuff, maybe you know about the anti-cancer serum my father was testing, that made a pet lizard *and* his ex-girlfriend grow monstrously large?" Shahra nodded. "Pigeon said C-QUARK has a cancer cure without that side effect—without gigantism."

"I'm sorry, John," Shahra said. "That's not true. This is about your girlfriend's father, right?" She saw me wince. "You may not believe me, but I don't enjoy snooping around your private life. Just part of the job. I'm sorry about that, and I'm truly sorry, but the side effects of that serum haven't been fixed."

"And I should believe you? Should I believe this fairy tale about getting us faculty positions?"

She blinked at me. "I'm many things, but I'm not *cruel*," she said. "If I could help you, I would. I will." She pursed her lips. "You said you had two questions?"

"Oh, the other one's not important." I decided at the last minute not to ask her if she'd ever heard of herpetominids.

After we finished eating and Shahra had paid the bill, she said, "Will you think about it?"

I looked away. "You're asking a lot. Ada... She wouldn't forgive me for doing something wrong just to help our careers."

But I was more tempted than I let on. In fact, I had started to think about a plan to give the probability pump to Shahra. You see, I already knew where it was: in my apartment, hidden under my white briefs.

When I got home, I discovered that Ada knew, too. The probability pump was sitting on my kitchen counter as she tapped her fingers and sipped a mug of coffee. "What's this?" she asked. When I didn't answer right away, she said, "And don't say it's a prize from some math competition when you were in fourth grade."

"I *did* win a lot of math competitions in fourth grade. Umm, why were you snooping in my underwear?"

"Like you never peek in mine? I was just stopping by to tell you how the first day of the qual went. You weren't here, I got bored, and ... I found this."

I sighed. I wanted to deflect, to bring up Shahra's offer, but I couldn't see how to make that conversation go well. "Remember how reluctant I was to talk about Los Alamos?"

"The poets? The ones you aren't supposed to talk about?"

"The serum isn't the only thing I took from my father's house."

Her eyes moved upwards, the way they did when she was doing integrals in her head. "A probability pump? The thing that changes probabilities, that made those poets famous?"

I nodded. "And other things. Apparently, one's unaccounted for."

"How do you know that?"

"Pigeon, or someone, was looking for it. Rumors are going around that Hile has it. Someone broke into Hile's house, to look for it I guess. Now I think my father was right, that: someone *did* break into his garage to search for it."

She struggled to sit up. "Will Pigeon, or whoever, realize you have it?" I shook my head. "What makes you so sure? Let's hide it somewhere safe."

"There's nowhere safer."

"The nuclear physics lab—I can put it in a locker there, and no one would suspect."

"Pigeon doesn't know. No one does. Trust me."

She crossed her arms. "It's hard to trust you when you don't tell me things. I know, I know, I didn't tell you about synthesizing radio-astatine, so I'm the pot calling the kettle black."

But I did know. I had completed my invention. Call it penance for the weapons designs I had analyzed for Phoenix. Call it my personal entry—no, my *anti*-entry into *Iron Genius's* death-ray challenge. I called it the "cannon of mercy." I had designed it to stimulate the mirror neurons, enhance empathy, and induce compassion. I hoped to impress Ada with my combination of gee-whiz science and Jesus-worthy awareness of the suffering of others.

Or so was the theory. Theories had to be put through experimental testing. So, when Ada had gone off for the first day of the qual, I tested the cannon of mercy on myself.

Even at the lowest setting, with a single second of exposure, the first few hours were miserable. I threw up repeatedly as my mind replayed, over and over, all the ways I had ever been unkind or cruel to people. It was a surprisingly long list.

For a while afterwards, people were transparent to me. It wasn't mind reading, not by a long shot. Instead, I could acutely read emotions, see beneath the skin. When Shahra told me there wasn't a side-effect-free cancer cure in C-QUARK's file, and when she made the offer for faculty positions, I could see she was telling the truth.

The aftereffects of the cannon also made it hard to look Ada directly in the eye. I wondered if they would wear off. (They did, slowly.) When she sighed and said, "Okay, we'll do it your way for now," the naked concern in her voice socked me in the gut.

The next morning, when she stopped by to kiss me before her second day of the qual, just a light kiss, I tasted her love and affection and guilt and worry and pride and self-doubt, all on her lips.

I skipped class that day, staying in my apartment with the lights off, the shades drawn, and no TV or radio. I didn't even open a book. I just lay in the dark, looking up at the ceiling, praying to Jesus or Kannon or whoever was listening for Ada to pass the qual. And when thoughts of all the worries of the world pressed in on me, I put my pillow over my face and screamed out all the compassion, all the feelings in my gut.

Unable to get up, I finally called Pigeon and said my girlfriend was sick, and I was taking care of her, and I didn't want to expose anyone—him, Duke, or Rita, for that matter—to whatever bug it was.

A week later, the physics faculty determined that Ada had passed the qual. In truth, Hile, back from DC, told me that technically, she *hadn't* passed, but had been just under the qualifying mark. At the faculty meeting, Ada's advisor, Professor Ukoma, spoke forcefully, explaining her family situation, pointing out her grades and independence and leadership among the students. Hile shouldn't have shared this with me, but the aftereffects of the cannon, slowly wearing off, revealed his shoulders sagging beneath an unseen weight. He told me, "We looked carefully at her exam. The problems she did solve, she solved brilliantly. Luckily, this convinced the rest of the faculty. Okay, Shirokova was against it—don't tell anyone—but she's a hard-ass with every case."

Hile paused. "I have to go on another emergency trip, John. It's very last minute. I'm not sure when I'll be back, or when I'll have a chance to communicate. I have every confidence in your abilities." I never did learn if it had to do with Pigeon, or Canterbury's notes, or the probability pump. But I *saw* he was saying goodbye.

Stunned, I wandered the halls until I found Ada sitting in the student lounge. She was holding the letter from the faculty. Her face was gray, her eyes unfocused. I sat down next to her. "Hey," I said. "What is it? Didn't you pass?" I asked, pretending I didn't already know.

She shook herself and the letter. "Oh, I passed, I guess." She swallowed. "The results of the latest scan came in. The radio-tagged antibodies, with the astatine I made—it's not slowing the cancer. It hasn't had any effect."

I reached out to touch her shoulder. I was trying to figure out how to bring up Shahra's offer, trading the probability pump for faculty positions, or maybe tell her about inventing the cannon of mercy, anything I could spin as good news. Or just tell her I loved her. But in the shadow of her father's mortal illness, I couldn't see how to do that. The words tasted sour in my mouth before I could say them.

Ada shook off my touch. "I need to be with my family," she said. "Sorry, John." She rose swiftly and left, her distress a knife to my heart.

I didn't hear from Ada for two days. Not hearing from her was agony. Even worse was replaying over and over the fear and grief I had heard in her voice and seen in her body. I went to the department, but completely failed to focus on my research.

When I got off at the bus stop, Shahra sidled up next to me, wearing dark glasses and a headscarf. Anxiety radiated off her like alpha particles from polonium. "Have you thought about my offer?"

"It's not so simple to steal from a Nobel Prize winner, you know."

"But you're considering it."

"I need more information from you. Like, what university are you talking about? How are these positions going to magically appear?"

Shahra told me the school, then added, "I have to keep a few cards close to my chest, John."

I started to walk away. In truth, every time I imagined handing over the pump, the thought of Ada's disapproval stabbed me in the gut. I hoped it would fade enough that I could actually make the trade. In my mouth, I could taste the future for Ada and me, and it tasted sweet.

She sprinted after me. "You're sure Pigeon doesn't have it?"

"He *wants* one for, um, some fantasy project."

Shahra put a hand on my arm. "It's just that, starting from nothing, Pigeon made money in real estate, in stocks. When his tech company was about to go belly-up, last-minute investors rescued him. He sure has had some lucky streaks. You see why I think Pigeon has the pump."

"He doesn't, but... This is going to sound weird, but then, maybe not. Freddy thinks himself a genius, but not enough of a genius, so he, er, *built* another brain. Out of a couple hundred rat brains." I paused. "He has it in glass jars in the basement of his house, his resident genius. *That's* the secret of his success."

"Jesus," Shahra said. "That's a new one. Jesus..."

"He plans to upgrade it to dog brains; he's already collecting dogs from shelters. After dogs. it will be monkey brains. He said he's ruled out human brains, but will he actually stop at monkeys? I don't know."

"So, what does he want the probability pump for?" she asked. When I shrugged, Shahra eyed me. "I appreciate you telling me about the brains, but I gotta say, I think there's something else you aren't telling me."

I didn't want to tell her a crazy-sounding story about herpetominids, or Pigeon wanting a probability pump to send asteroid defense plans back to the Cretaceous to save the dinosaurs from extinction. Maybe I should have, to deflect her from guessing that *I* possessed a probability pump.

Instead, I shook my head and said, "I need to get home. I'm expecting an important phone call."

"Okay, John, I'll let you go. But you have to tell me the rest of the story, next time!" And she sashayed away.

I, however, was rooted to the spot. Across the street, I had spotted a woman in a heavy trench coat. She wore an obvious wig and had a sour face. But that wasn't what caught my attention. She had rolls of flesh under her jawline, so thick that she appeared to have no neck.

She caught me staring, rotating her whole body a few degrees to glare back at me for a few moments. Then she walked away. No one around her paid any attention, but under the influence of the cannon of mercy, like an x-ray, I could *see* that her gait was subtly nonhuman, like a cross between a lizard and a chicken.

I shook my head. When I looked again, she had disappeared. Maybe the cannon had excited my imagination, too.

On the morning of the third day, the phone in my apartment rang. I was afraid it was going to be Shahra again, or even Pigeon, but relief flooded through me when I heard Ada's voice.

"John, oh, John, it's so good to hear your voice."

I heard background noises. "Where are you?" I asked.

"At a pay phone at the hospital. I just stepped away—I can't talk long. I need to get back. It's ... it's not good." Her voice sounded like ground glass. "They're infusing him with the last of the radio-astatine, but after that it's just going to be ... palliative care."

"What can I do?"

"There's nothing. There's nothing anyone can do." Her voice was a husky whisper. "Just pray for him. I know you don't pray, John, but if you do, pray for him, for all of us. Do that for me, will you? Please?"

"I will," I said. I wanted to believe we could have a future together. I feared that future was slipping away—even if Pigeon didn't change the past. "I love you, Ada."

But she had already hung up.

I went to class, but the lecture flowed over my head. I didn't write a single word in my notebook. Afterwards, I trudged to Hile's office and pressed my face against the glass. Inside was only darkness.

When I got back to my apartment, the red eye of my answering machine was blinking. I hoped it was Ada, but it was Pigeon's tenor voice.

"You have not come to work for several days. I had chalked that up to discouragement with the project and your personal woes, but then," and here his voice tightened, *"you have been spotted consorting with Dr. Wimplemaker."*

The mysterious Mr. Trinh had filled him in, I guessed. But then I had the wild thought, *What if that woman I saw really was a herpetominid, and she—it—told Pigeon?*

Pigeon's words were tightly wound with rage. *"I told myself this was resource-fulness, that you were acting on your own initiative. Nevertheless, I have, in moments of ... weakness ... confided in you too much."* Underlying his anger, I detected deeper feelings, cold and dense as lead bricks. I caught a whiff of decay, like meat that had gone bad. *"Have you betrayed me? After all I did for you?"* He paused for a long time. *"There is too much at stake, the herpetominids... Goodbye, John."*

His voice sounded truly sorrowful. I would say, *"as sorrowful as if he had just watched a beloved puppy get kicked to death,"* but Pigeon would have just scooped out its brain and plopped it in a jar.

After the message finished playing, I looked in the basket where I kept my keys for the house in Wallingford. They were gone, along with the keypad code, which in retrospect I should not have written down.

My body rang with alarm. I went into my bedroom and yanked open my underwear drawer. The probability pump was gone.

Anger surged through me. *Pigeon*, I thought ... or maybe C-QUARK.

When I got to the tall, skinny house in Wallingford, the door was a few inches ajar. "Hello?" I called out, clutching the cannon of mercy in my arms, its metal housing cold. I stuck a reluctant foot in the crack between the door and the jamb and eased it open wider. Warm air washed over me, and I smelled something fetid. I stepped inside.

I found Duke sprawled on the stairs. His right leg was at an uncomfortable angle, and he had a bloody bash on his head. I smelled shit; he must have voided his bowels. I tried to find a pulse, but my fingertips throbbed with the frantic rhythm of my own heart.

The door to the basement was open. *What am I doing?* I squeezed shut my eyes and focused on my anger, but all I could do was to imagine Duke's fear and pain.

With each step down, I shook. I felt as if I were lowering myself into liquid nitrogen, that I might shatter into a thousand pieces at the slightest touch. My heart fluttered like a trapped bird, panicked, with nowhere to fly.

When I reached the sub-basement, the scents of ammonia and the sea washed over me. I saw Shahra grimacing and holding a baseball bat, her black hair unraveled from its bun and sticking out at all angles like a witch, her glasses nowhere to be seen. Facing her, Pigeon gripped the sonic scalpel, keeping Shahra at bay. I also saw that Rita had been smashed, glass and wires and fluid and brains scattered across the concrete floor. It was only a bunch of disembodied rat brains, dreaming of cheese and making rat babies; while still vibrating from the effects of the cannon, I vividly imagined life leaking out from those lonely scraps of tissue.

"It's me!" I called out from the doorway.

"Johnny?" Shahra said without turning her head. "Go away."

"So, he *does* know you," said Pigeon. "Conspiring against me."

"This is between me and you, birdie. You were on my radar long before John came along."

"Then why'd you bash Duke?" Pigeon snarled.

"He had a gun."

"He did *not*."

"Well, I thought he did." Shahra feinted with the bat at Pigeon, and Pigeon brandished the sonic scalpel, which hummed loudly. It was then I noticed that Shahra, who was left-handed, was holding the bat with her right hand; her left arm was cradled against her stomach.

"He needs an ambulance," I said. "Duke's hurt real bad."

"Once I'm through here," Shahra said sharply.

"Nice friend you have, John," Pigeon said, venom in each word.

I inched into the room, keeping the cannon behind myself and out of view. I had to swallow before I could speak again. My stomach was doing backflips, trying to signal that I should run out of that sub-basement, and my brain was beginning to side with my stomach. "I don't have many friends, *Freddy*," I said, "so I guess I can't be choosy."

"Your pretty girlfriend just you being lucky?" Freddy Pigeon said, with overtones of jealousy and self-pity.

I was standing awkwardly with the cannon of mercy behind my back. Then it slipped out of my grasp and clattered to the floor. Pigeon's gaze flicked towards me.

Shahra took advantage of his distraction and batted the sonic scalpel out of Freddy's hand. He slipped on the cerebrospinal fluid flooding the floor and fell, cutting himself on the shards of glass. Shahra raised the baseball bat high. I could read the red anger and fear flowing through her. Freddy Pigeon held up a bleeding hand.

I dropped to my knees, grabbed the cannon, flicked on the power switch, and turned the amplitude to its highest setting. My skin tingled and my hair stood on end from the surge of powerful electric fields. I pointed the cannon in the direction of Shahra and Pigeon, then squeezed the trigger. The air crackled with electric potential.

Seconds later—it felt like an eternity—the capacitors in the cannon blew, filling the basement with the acrid scent of ozone and burnt electrical paste. My fingers, scorched and stinging, dropped the cannon. It hit the concrete floor and broke apart.

Shahra's eyes went wide, and a high keening sound came from her throat. She dropped the baseball bat as if it were on fire, and it splashed into the lake of spinal fluid. She put her hands to her face. "Jesus, Johnny, what did you do?"

Freddy Pigeon wrapped his arms around his midsection and vomited, adding an acrid stench to the air. Shahra swore at length. "Even when I just *think* about hurting—ow!" She scrunched up her face. "It's like a wasp in my head, stinging when I think about—*goddamn!*"

Freddy, on all fours, panted. "You invented ... a ... weapon."

"A cannon. A cannon of mercy," I said. "I weaponized empathy."

Freddy looked at me, his eyes red and swollen, and then barked with laughter. "That ... is genius," he said hoarsely, then turned toward Shahra. A sly, vicious, and knowing look crept over his face: how to use the situation. "At least I don't ... have to think about ... if I killed the old man."

Shahra screamed, as if she had touched a high-voltage wire. "It was self-defense! I thought he had a gun!" Tears streamed down her face. "And what about you? You've sold blueprints for weapons. Ever think about the people—"

"Shut up!" cried Freddy. He knelt close to the floor, his clothes wet with cerebrospinal fluid.

"—the people *you've* hurt and killed?"

Freddy curled up in a ball, whimpering like a beaten dog.

"Hey, guys," I said. "Trying to torture each other like that, I mean, come on."

"Johnny," Shahra said, taking short, shallow breaths, "can you make it stop? Just make it stop."

"I can't," I said. "Maybe it fades with time. I'm not sure."

Freddy Pigeon was rocking himself. I crouched down by him. "What about the probability pump?" I asked. "Where is it?"

"The ... pump?" Pigeon moaned.

"You took it from my apartment."

"You ... had it? Didn't know. I guess ... your father..." He squinched up his face, perhaps thinking of Duke.

I turned to Shahra. "Then *you* took it?"

"Took what? Wait—*you* had the probability pump? All this time?"

I stood up. "But it's gone—"

And in that moment, I understood.

"I'm taking your car," I told Freddy, my arms full of the pieces of the cannon. "I need to go, right away." As I ran up the stairs, I called, "And call an ambulance for Duke!" My stomach sloshed when I passed the old man. My imagination played a raw scene of Shahra's bat coming down, so real I could feel the crack of Duke's skull. But that sickening stew of empathy was overpowered by the lash of my need to find Ada. I closed my eyes and ran outside.

Evening had begun to shroud the sky. I spotted Freddy's beat-up Audi. It was a stick shift, which I had never been very good at, and for the first hundred feet or so, it lurched down the street, the clutch grinding.

With all haste, I drove over to Ada's. I circled twice, trying to park, my mind going crazy with scenarios. In my panic, I finally parked in a red zone, then flew out of the car and up the stairs to the third floor.

I let myself into her apartment. No one was there. I started with her underwear drawer. Nothing there, so I searched under her bed and in her closet. Only then did I notice her bookbag by the front door. I unzipped it. Where books on stellar structure and particle detectors normally would be, I found the probability pump. It felt cool, ordinary, an empty shell, like an insect's discarded husk. Whatever charge it had was gone.

I sat on her couch for an hour, then carried the probability pump the five blocks to my apartment; no point in driving. The baleful red eye of the message light on my phone winked at me.

"Hi John, it's me. I... It's wonderful news. My father is better. The radio-astatine finally worked. The doctors don't believe it. They want him to stay here, but he wants to get out. We're going out for dinner, to celebrate. It's like a miracle! Except, well... I'll tell you later." She paused. I could hear some noises in the background. When she spoke again, it was in a lower voice. *"I'm going to tell them at dinner, tell them about you. Come to my apartment, around eight. I'll introduce you. John, I'm so relieved."*

But at eight o'clock, her apartment was dark, and no one answered when I knocked. I considered waiting inside, but it would be awkward to be sitting on the couch when they finally came in. *"Don't call 911, that's no burglar, that's my boyfriend."*

So, I stood outside the entrance to the apartment building, but it was cold, the kind of damp chill that seeps into your flesh no matter how wrapped up you are, so I walked back to my apartment. Overhead, the clouds had been blown away, and stars shone like jewels. Cars drove down the street, music and laughter leaking out.

In my apartment, I paced restlessly, a caged animal. At nine o'clock, I circled around to Ada's, returning at ten o'clock, then at eleven.

When I stood outside just before midnight, I saw a light in the window. I ran up the stairs and knocked, quietly at first, then insistently. The door opened a crack. "Hello?"

"Ada?"

The door opened more. The young woman wasn't Ada, but looked a lot like her. "She's..." She glanced over her shoulder, then stepped outside, shutting the door behind her. She wasn't wearing a jacket, and she shivered in the cold. "Are you a friend of hers?"

"John," I said. "John Chant." When she looked blank, I added, "Yes, I'm a friend of hers." I wanted to say, *"I'm her boyfriend."*

"I'm Ada's sister. I have to... I'm so sorry." By the yellow porch light, I could see her eyes were red and puffy, and she was saying something. I asked her to repeat it, but I still didn't catch what she was saying; there was static in my ears like a bad radio station.

Ada's sister said, "We were going out for dinner, a big celebration with the good news about my father's health, a miracle really, and Ada said there was something she wanted to tell us all. We went to a seafood restaurant, and Ada said she had never had scallops, and she ordered them..." Tears ran down her face, and she choked down a sob. When she was able to talk again, she said in a voice so quiet that I could barely hear it over the roar of the cold sea in my ears, "At the hospital, they said it was an allergic reaction—a severe allergic reaction.

The scallops... She didn't know; none of us knew. The paramedics tried for thirty minutes..."

She broke down crying again, and only then did I understand what she had told me about Ada, as if the words had traveled a long distance and finally reached me; as if someone had pulled my heart from my chest and thrown it onto the hard, frozen ground.

Eventually, she said, "Please, we're all in shock right now." She glanced over her shoulder. "I need to be with my family now. With Ada's family. I'm sure you understand." She stepped inside, closing the door behind her.

I walked to Freddy's car, kicking aside litter. There was a parking ticket on the windshield. I tossed it into the street, drove to my apartment building, and parked in another red zone.

My apartment was unspeakably lonely. Despite the dishes in the sink, the shirts and socks on the floor, the books in a tottering tower on the desk, it looked staged, as if no one had ever really lived here, as if it were all a diorama in a museum.

I took the radio telescope and put it in the trunk of Freddy's car, next to the shattered remains of the cannon. Heading south to Tacoma, I crossed at the narrows, drove by Bremerton and through Port Gamble, passed Poulsbo and on to Sequim, where I gassed up. Shortly before dawn, I reached La Push at the edge of the Pacific and parked down by the beach. Across the sea was Kyoto and the temple of Sanjusangendo and the thousand and one statues of Kannon. I walked to the shoreline and threw the pieces of the cannon of mercy into the ocean.

At the car, I mounted the radio telescope, and slipping on headphones, scanned the sky until I found a little whistle, a pulsar: a dead star casting its song of grief and loss once more.

Part III: A Tiny Piece of Infinity

"We dream, we wake on the cold hillside, we pursue the dream again. In the beginning was the dream, and the work of disenchantment never ends." —Kim Stanley Robinson

Barriers

You have told me about the losses in your life, so you know the feel of the cold vacuum of grief in your gut, the numb terror of absolute absence. It's one thing to imagine a dinosaur stalking outside and to dig for bones in the backyard, only to break the sewer and embarrass yourself in front of a new crush. It's another to have a door slammed in your face and locked shut. Ada's family didn't know I existed, so I never found out where or when her funeral was held.

Instead, I grieved in unhealthy ways. I hung up when Shahra called. I acted as if Pigeon had never existed. Two years later, I found out Duke had survived Shahra's attack only when I read his obituary: death from a stroke. The one person I opened up to was my sister, Jane, now that we had reconnected. With everyone else, I felt like a golem, animated clay without a soul. But when I talked to Jane, some valve inside turned, and I sobbed to her for hours on the phone as she listened patiently.

Some secrets I still kept from Jane. I didn't tell her about the probability pump sitting sullenly in my apartment, or how I hated it, hated myself for bringing the pump into Ada's orbit; she had used it to trade her life for her father's. If I had told Jane, the guilt would have exploded me like a critical hunk of plutonium. I took a sledgehammer to the pump, but the exterior was so tough, designed to survive a nuclear explosion, that I barely scratched it. But I couldn't bring myself to get rid of it; Ada had used it to trade her life for her father's.

I wished I could see Ada again. I had only one photograph of her—she had detested having her picture taken—and it was us together in our winning Halloween costumes as joke subatomic particles. It was painful to look at that picture, to see me pressing against her and simultaneously feel her absence. But I wanted to see her smile, see her laugh, see her hawk look as she intently discussed nuclear reactions powering the wind from the sun. If only there were some way to open a window to the past.

When I had a brief school break, I rented a car and drove cross-country to my father's house, my old home. Maybe it was the gallons of Mountain Dew I drank to keep awake all night, or maybe it was just the blunt hammer of grief, but as I drove through the darkness, I thought about black holes. A romance has sprung up around black holes, but in reality, a black hole is just a void where a star used to be, a hunger that consumes gas, planets, other stars. A supermassive black hole sits at the heart of our galaxy, a cold rottenness feasting on the Milky Way from the inside like a parasitic larva, only that black hole won't pupate into something else. When it has swallowed the entire galaxy, it will remain a mouth that can never be filled.

It was a relief when the sun rose, even though I was driving nearly directly into that molten copper penny, and I was free to dwell on things other than black holes, like the divergence theorem, and various kinds of infinity, until finally I turned onto our cul-de-sac and pulled into our driveway.

I spent a few listless hours with my father. After we had shared the latest news about Jane and her kids, we sat in near silence. His breath whistled in and out of his nose. I stood and asked, "Do you mind if I take some stuff from the garage?"

I thought he might ask what I wanted, but he only shrugged. "They stopped breaking in, whoever it was," he said raggedly. "Nothing of value there."

I took the wreckage of the time window, the burnt coils and capacitors, and put it in the trunk of my rental. Underneath, I found some old, yellowed preprints, scientific papers by my father, and took them, too.

Back in Seattle, I read his papers. He proposed modeling space and time not as a grid ticking off miles and years, nor the elastic coordinates of Einstein's general relativity, but as a barrier, like a hill between *here* and *there*, between *now* and *then*. To get from *here* to *there* and from *now* to *then*, you had to climb the hill before going down the other side. For time, this barrier was asymmetric: downhill towards the future, but to get to the past, you would have to climb up an impossibly steep hill.

It was a novel ideal—okay, a borderline-crackpot idea, the kind my father specialized in, the kind that Canterbury loved and that I had embraced myself. I checked against a list of my father's publications, but these papers were not in his c.v. I wondered if they had been rejected as too speculative, or if he had even submitted them. I wondered if C-QUARK had had a hand in suppressing them, because, in those papers, he argued that one could use quantum effects to tunnel through those barriers, making separation in time and space vanish like smoke.

In the quantum world, particles tunnel through those hill-like barriers like a spooky, subatomic John Henry. Actually, it's not spooky or magic at all, but sloppy accounting. In classical, non-quantum physics, if you don't have the energy to climb that hill, you are trapped.

But in the quantum world, space and time and velocity and energy are uncertain. For short ticks of time, the energy needed to climb over a hill is sufficiently vague to have a chance to sneak through with less.

This may sound wild, but without tunneling, stars would not shine, could not manufacture oxygen, iron, gold. Without tunneling, plants could not efficiently photosynthesize. If the universe were run by a sharp-eyed accountant, it would be a dead and dull place. Luckily, quantum mechanics shrugs and only cares that the books balance in the end, forgiving countless minor miracles in the interstices of time and space.

Major miracles, however, such as skipping across space or peeping into years past, require significant perversion of nature's accounts. The energy needed to tunnel back in time is so enormous, you have no chance to do it, unless...

Unless you can bend the probabilities themselves.

I felt a bubble of understanding percolate to the top of my skull. My father had used the probability pump to deflate the barrier of time. But he had abruptly stopped. Perhaps when his young son had poked a dinosaur in the eye and nearly burned the house down, my father had gotten scared and decided not to pursue such a dangerous research path.

I felt a little deflated myself. The probability pump I had was fully discharged. With a nuclear test ban on, no more would be made. Maybe if I quit school, searched around the world, I might find one of the missing ones. But certainly, they were locked up tight. And the past, and Ada, were also locked away forever.

Hunched over my father's preprints and puzzling over quantum tunneling, I noticed I had stopped obsessing about black holes and their insatiable appetites. In addition, it prodded me to think more about the research Hile had assigned me: quantum tunneling of the state of the universe.

Unfortunately, I still could not make it work, and Hile was on indefinite leave. I received a few cryptic postcards from him. It seemed he was either working on a hush-hush project for the government, or on the run, or maybe both. I asked Ukoma and Shirokova, but neither knew any more than I did.

With the itch of panic beneath my scalp, I looked into other advisers and projects. Ukoma welcomed me to work with him, but the thought of working on astrophysical nuclear reactions, Ada's topic, felt like grabbing a hot iron.

Shirokova suggested a research direction, but despite my respect for her, I found it so soporific that I fell asleep just reading the background material.

I was well into my second year, passing my classes, but without enthusiasm. With my heart hollowed out, I had fitfully started a letter of resignation from the program. That's when Professor Athanasiou knocked on the door of my shared graduate office.

Petros Athanasiou was a recently hired assistant professor. A short, slender man who'd look like a young teenage boy if it weren't for his perpetual dark five o'clock shadow, his pleasant demeanor hid intense tenacity. I'd had him for statistical mechanics, and I knew he did research in materials under extreme conditions.

"Hello, John, how are you?" he asked, but without waiting for an answer, continued, "Have you had any contact with Professor Hile?"

I shook my head. Pushing aside one of several stacks of books, he settled himself on the edge of my desk and said, "Hile had promised to help me wrestle with some ideas for tunneling in materials. I've got experiments, I'm getting data, but I'm having trouble making sense of it." He spread his hands. "He was on the search committee when they hired me, and he sounded so enthusiastic—he *promised.*"

"I'm stuck on tunneling, too," I said. I pointed him to a blackboard where I had scratched out equations. Athanasiou walked so close to the blackboard, I thought he might get chalk on his nose. I said, "I can't get it to tunnel at the right rate in the early universe. The Big Bang expands too slowly."

"Don't tell the creationists," he murmured.

"H_2O, um, Professor Hile, he said I made a mistake, that I wrote a single-particle equation, but I never figured out what he meant."

"Oh!" he said. "That I understand. Is this the time evolution of the universe?" He chalked a big X through a plot on the blackboard. "This part, in the early universe, right after the Big Bang—you need coherent tunneling. Later, it's incoherent, so a single-particle approximation works. But not here, not in the beginning."

When he explained it, the world clicked into place, like finding the missing piece of a jigsaw puzzle—except I find jigsaw puzzles mind-numbing and mathematical arguments exciting.

A class of particles called bosons are easily swayed by their peers. If one boson marches in a certain rhythm, other bosons like to march in sync with the first boson; they adopt the same wave function. That's how lasers work: photons, particles of light, are bosons. Inside a laser, one photon bounces back and forth between two mirrors. That photon recruits other photons, until a huge number of photons are racing from mirror to mirror and back again, all in the same quantum state, until released in a beam of coherent light: a laser, or maybe a death-ray.

According to Athanasiou, Hile had said that coherent, synchronized particles enhance tunneling through a barrier. When particles are coherent, sharing the same wave function, that coherence effectively reduces the barrier and increases the probability of tunneling.

Don't worry if you're not following. I barely understood at the time, although I pretended I did. But I did notice a lovely conclusion: in the early universe, the coherent dance -step of particles to the same quantum tune produced not a death-ray, but the sudden, spectacular tunneling of our universe into existence.

Athanasiou wanted to squeeze coherent tunneling out of electrons—literally. Electrons are not bosons; they classify as fermions, and fermions famously would not be caught dead wearing the same quantum wave function as another fermion.

Now, electrons chilled close to absolute zero partner up and behave like bosons. But Athanasiou thought superconducting pairs of electrons a cheat. He wanted to encourage electrons to tunnel through a barrier at room temperature by applying extreme pressure, forcing them, if not into the same quantum wave function, then into the next nearest one. Hile had sketched out the calculations, if you could call six pages of algebra a sketch, and concluded that it would work. Or could work... Might work.

"It's your project, if you want it," Athanasiou told me.

The project appealed to me. The pressure needed—millions of times greater than atmospheric pressure, far greater than the pressure in the deepest trench of the oceans, as much pressure as found in the molten center of the Earth—could only be produced using a diamond anvil. Professor Athanasiou's lab contained a huge mechanical press, in which an electric motor the size of a small car drove a series of tough, tractor-wheel-sized titanium gears, multiplying the force by thousands, pressing down on a bit of industrial diamond, which focused all that stress into a tiny, pinprick-sized point.

In the same way, I focused my own stress and grief and darkness into the experiment, setting up the electrical leads, devising ways to multiply the pressure to insanely crushing levels. Then, systematically, week by week and month by month, I cycled through a long list of materials, to see if the pressure induced coherent tunneling in any of them. During those long hours, I did not think about black holes. I even went hours without thinking about Ada. It was almost like peace.

After a year and a half of work, a blink of a bloodshot eye when it comes to research, I found a class of materials that exhibited coherent tunneling of electrons. It required center-of-the-Earth-scale pressures, so no good for practical applications, unless you're a lizard person living at the Earth's core.

"Ah, but you've shown that coherent tunneling can occur," Athanasiou said.

He was so happy, he sent me to an American Physical Society conference in Sacramento, California. It was a huge conference complex downtown by the river and the railroad museum. I was to give a breathless twelve-minute talk on my results.

I checked into the hotel, then walked down to the conference registration table. "Hmm, what's your name again?" the woman at the table asked, peering at a list of participants.

I felt a trickle of sweat in my armpits and a sick feeling in my stomach.

Then the woman asked, "Are you sure it's for this conference?" She pointed to a banner that read, Postmodernism Meets Modern Science.

"Oops," I said, my face turning warm.

The woman smiled. "You aren't the first one. You want that table over there."

I lined up behind a stout middle-aged man with a shiny bald pate, a big bushy beard, and thick glasses. He was half a head shorter than me, and his faded jeans were held up by colorful suspenders. I leaned around him to check the banner along the front of the table: American Physical Society Division of Condensed Matter.

"Thank God," I muttered. The man in front of me turned to face me. "I had gone to the wrong registration table," I explained. "Whatever postmodernism is."

He leaned out to looked down the corridor at the other table. "Oh, it could be interesting. I have a friend who's giving their plenary talk."

We reached the front of the line and received our identifying badges, mine labeled, J. CHANT, U WASH, and his with B. BECKER, RIKEN.

I pointed at his badge. "RIKEN, that's in Japan, right?"

"Yeah, I'm one of the few *gaijin*, foreigners, employed there. I'm Baka," he said.

At first, I thought he was pronouncing 'Becker' with his strong Southern accent, but then he explained. His first name was actually Buford, which he didn't care for, but in Japan, he'd acquired the nickname *baka*, which means "fool" or "crazy," because he was always doing outlandish experiments, so much so that even the normally ultra-polite Japanese muttered *"baka"* when he was around. "I think of it as unique honorific," he said.

"I'm John," I said. "My mother told me, when I got in trouble, that it was after the John in the Bible who wrote the Book of Revelation. You know, the apocalypse and all that."

"Sweet," Baka said, a grin on his face. "The fool, and the end of the world. We should get a drink sometime. Hey, maybe after Codd's talk."

"Codd?"

He nodded. "Erstmann Codd. He's the one giving the postmodernism plenary talk this afternoon." He handed me a flyer advertising the event.

The APS conference didn't start until a day later. I had intended to practice my talk, but as usual, my curiosity whispered in my ear and wouldn't shut up. The flyer from Baka gave a short bio of Erstmann Codd: Princeton undergrad, PhD at Penn State, served a brief time as faculty at some obscure university in Louisiana, then landed at a Stanford-based think tank. Among his publications were *The Physics of Mayonnaise* and *The Inequality Equation*. My brain was going all Jiffy Pop, so I gave in and went down to the main auditorium.

I spotted Baka Becker and plopped into an empty seat next to him. He nodded, just as Erstmann Codd bounded onto the stage.

"Hello, Sacramento!"

I was startled when people cheered and whistled. Later, I learned that Erstmann Codd was a kind of science celebrity, with popular TIM (Transgressive, Iconoclastic, Metamodern) Talks. In his TIM-Talk videos and in person, he jumped onto the stage like a rock star, and after drinking in the crowd's vocal accolades, he began to pace back and forth. With his broad chest, thick black beard, pale bald head, and a voice that boomed like Yahweh himself, he was a commanding presence.

Codd started his talk with a riff on inconsistencies in language and how that mapped to inconsistencies in mathematics. Although usually I'm the fast talker, Codd's lightning patter made even my head hurt. He cited Gödel's theorems, chaos theory, and the random nature of quantum mechanics. I did not see how it all fit together, but the crowd seemed rapt. I glanced over at Baka, whose face was shining with joy.

"I'm not sure I'm following all this," I confessed in a whisper to him.

"Oh, you shouldn't take it literally," Baka said, chuckling. "More of an extended pun. He's both poking fun at postmodernism and writing a love letter to it."

After the talk, Codd came up to Baka, who said enthusiastically, "Great talk! Complete nonsense!"

"Thanks," said Codd. "I tried."

Baka introduced me, and Codd shook my hand with a beefy grip. We all went out to dinner at a Chinese restaurant overlooking the river. They made for an odd pair: both bald and bearded, but one short and soft with glasses, and the other tall and buff with eyes like obsidian.

Codd asked me what I was working on, and I told him about electron tunneling under extreme pressure. "Sweet!" Baka said with enthusiasm, while Codd said, "Ah. Stamp collecting. A good thing for a dissertation, I suppose, solidly non-transgressive. Good if you want a career."

"And this postmodernism thing," I said. "Is it good for a career?"

"In the humanities? Certainly. It's the big gorilla." He grinned. "But in the physical sciences? It's like lighting yourself on fire. Though history remembers the ones who lit themselves on fire."

He had other things he was working on. The postmodernism stuff, he admitted, was mostly word games. But he had developed a thermodynamic model of economics. "Can't create work without creating entropy," he said. "My Marxist friends all hate it, but it's true. What I mean by that is—"

"'The poor you will always have with you,'" I said, surprising even myself by quoting from the gospel.

"For on the fly, not bad," Codd said, grinning, "even if Jesus is passé and God is dead." He started to talk about how heat engines required a large difference in temperature to be efficient, and how economic entropy had to always increase.

"Entropy?" Baka said, his chopsticks draped with *dan dan* noodles, his glasses spattered with spicy sauce. "Sorry, I was distracted, thinking about tunneling."

"He means," I explained, "that there has always been an exploited class, and as a law of a kind of physics, nothing can be done. Very convenient," I added, echoing the version of Ada in my head, but the sarcasm got lost.

"Exactly," Codd said, nodding so vigorously I worried his head would fly off. "You get it!"

Two days later, I stumbled nervously through my talk. Baka Becker was in the front row, grinning like a crazy fool. To my surprise, I got several questions, until the session chair had to cut off the discussion.

Baka followed me out. "That was sweet," he said. "You've got me thinking of at least a dozen experiments I can't wait to do."

He started to tell me, ideas rushing out of him like water from a breached dam, when a small older woman approached, even shorter than Baka, leaning heavily on a cane. Her gray-streaked hair was in a sensible bob cut, and her eyes, like hungry ravens, missed nothing. Despite her small stature, her presence grabbed me like a fist. Baka shut up and stepped aside.

"Lillian Galbraith," she announced. "Interesting talk." She asked me several probing questions, mostly about how I had calibrated the measurements and whether I had considered doping material with nitrogen (I had, but hadn't had time to implement it), and nodded at my answers.

And then I flew back to Seattle and continued my research.

Along the way, I passed the qualifying exam. I had forgotten all about it, until a fellow grad student opened the door to Athanasiou's lab and said, "Hey, John! They're starting the qual!"

I followed him to the big hall, was handed a list of problems, and sat down and wrote out my answers. I got an average score, which apparently disappointed my professors, but nonetheless, I passed. And then I went back to the lab and continued crushing various materials with the diamond anvil.

A year after the APS conference, I wrote my dissertation: "Pressure-induced coherent tunneling of electrons in room-temperature materials." Writing a dissertation is normally a grinding, tense affair, the climactic linchpin of a graduate career. But I felt so disconnected, almost disassociated from my body, that I observed myself as surprisingly neutral, as if it were simply another experiment that would either succeed or fail.

I barely remember my oral defense. The word "defense" makes it sound like a sports competition on a broad, grassy field, as titans so massive they block out the sun clash and grapple. The actual defense was more sedate. Athanasiou gave an introduction, including an oblique allusion to Hile. I explained the concept of coherent tunneling, showed pictures of the mechanical press and the diamond anvil, wrote out a few equations, and showed a dozen plots of data. After I finished, a few questions were raised politely, and I answered in somber tones. Then they shook my hand and congratulated me. It all seemed so anticlimactic.

At first, I wasn't sure what I would do next. I applied for postdoc positions everywhere. But all the rejections for grad school still hung over me like an evil spirit, and I still considered myself far outside the main streams of physics. Deep down, I did not believe I would get an offer.

I was surprised when I did.

Long ago—back when pterodactyls flew across volcano-reddened skies—a fresh-ly minted PhD might become a professor straight out of grad school. But that was when science barely knew the world is round, that it orbits around the sun, and that germs cause disease. Furthermore, you were likely to die young from the Black Death, or from one of a hundred religious wars over eggs or haircuts, I think, leaving no time to dawdle.

Today, science is so stuffed with facts, it can't squeeze through the library door, and a mere four, or six, or eleven years in a PhD program only gets you a few bites of the vast pie of knowledge. Thus, it's become traditional to spend a few years in postdoctoral research positions.

I left Seattle to spend a year as a postdoc at Cal State University Los Angeles, working under Professor Lillian Galbraith.

I hadn't realized it when I'd met her at the APS conference—in fact, I didn't think to mention it to Professor Athanasiou—but Galbraith was a giant in applied material science. She wanted me to use coherent tunneling to improve the coupling between optical photons and semiconductor devices.

I spent a year enthusiastically trying to coax results out of all sorts of materials. Well, the first nine months were enthusiastic. Then I grew wary, then discour-aged, and finally outright despondent.

Despite a reputation as a stern taskmaster, Galbraith did her best to buoy me. "You already know, John," she said, as I handed her the latest plot that absolutely failed to show any improvement, "you have to go down a lot of research alleys just to find out which are the blind ones."

"Yeah, well, I feel like I'm getting mugged in a lot of those alleys."

Galbraith laughed, which she seldom did, and for a moment, my other failures didn't matter.

Meanwhile, I was going down my own blind social alleys. Jane had gently told me I needed to move on from Ada, and although I didn't admit it aloud, I knew she was right. But LA is a lonely city, and after each disastrous date, I went home discouraged and wondering if I would forever compare every woman I ever met to Ada.

I tried sports (tennis, soccer), hiking, and a cooking class. I even posted personal ads, before dating apps became the major way of meeting people. I felt not like a pioneer, but embarrassed. I was disconcerted by how everyone in LA described themselves as looking like this or that movie star, which led to some strange conversations. On one phone call, when I declined to name which celebrity I thought I looked like, the woman at the other end said, "Well, you know, to make a relationship work, you have to be vulnerable."

The other thing I discovered about LA was that everyone is a screenwriter. I asked my barber, "Have you written a screenplay?" He said, "Yeah, I wrote this one about a barber, who's really an ex-assassin, who gets pressed into doing one last job... Why, are you an agent?"

Even Galbraith's secretary, Edie, had written a screenplay, about a secretary who discovers that her company is handling alien technology.

"I wouldn't know how to begin to write a screenplay," I told her.

"I took an evening class," Edie said. "One trick I learned is to put the answer to the big question, who done it or whatever, in front of the audience's nose from the beginning, only you distract them until the big reveal. *My* villain is the guy coming out of the heroine's boss's office, in, like, the first scene. You think the sinister mastermind is the boss, but then you learn it was this innocuous other guy all along."

I said, "Oh, like Dorothy and the ruby slippers? The way home was on her feet, the whole time? In *The Wizard of Oz*?"

"Never saw it," said Edie.

But I didn't care. I realized the answer had indeed been sitting before me the whole time.

Less than a month later, I was able to demonstrate coherent tunneling for Galbraith, not with electrons, but with bosons that had been there from the beginning: let there be light! With the right setup of laser cavities on both sides, I could get a few photons, enough to be detected, through a millimeter of lead—or half an inch of plastic. "Staggeringly simple," Galbraith said. "But often brilliance is simply noticing what no one else has." She tapped her cane on the floor. "Start writing it up. Hmm... Since the enhancement is so large..."

"A millionfold," I told her. "At least."

"... let's give it a new name. *Super*-tunneling. Like superconductivity."

"But superconductivity causes electrons to ignore imperfections in the material. Here, the effect, the *supertunneling*, is sensitive to imperfections in the material." In fact, I felt deeply disappointed by this.

"No matter. You've demonstrated the principle. Good work, John." I admit, her praise tasted sweet. Galbraith paused, then added, "I'll extend your postdoc another year. You can get another paper or two out in that time."

As it happened, I didn't need that extra year. I got an offer for a faculty position instead.

A Confederacy of Quarks

The job offer came from Louisiana University of the South at Renderville, or LUSR. I got a phone call from a voice that boomed so loudly, I had to hold the handset away from my ear. "Dr. Chant? I'm Bud Boudreaux, chair down here in the physics department of Louisiana University of the South at Renderville. You might not have heard of us, but we're up and coming, and you seem to be up and coming, so I thought we might join forces. I'd like to set up an interview with you."

"Interview? For a postdoc?" Before Galbraith had told me I had another year, I had sent out my curriculum vitae, hunting for the next postdoc.

"For a faculty position, son, professor of physics and all that. Assistant professor, but from there, it's just a short step to tenure."

My interview was a thirty-minute conference call. (Most faculty interviews last one or two full days.) They asked about my education and training. They asked about my recent papers. "You have any questions for us, son?" Bud Boudreaux asked.

A week later, Bud Boudreaux called me again and made me an offer. My feelings were as mixed as if you had dumped my insides into a Waring blender and turned it on high. I had won the lottery, the lofty goal of many graduate students. Yet I almost turned it down. The temptation Shahra had offered in the desert had been faculty appointments for me and Ada. The irony of landing a position without Ada left me hollow and depressed, and I wondered if it was some elaborate scam. But Galbraith beamed when I told her the news and encouraged me to accept.

Three months later, as I got into my car to drive from Los Angeles toward Louisiana, I felt an impulse to instead drive straight west into the cold arms of the Pacific Ocean.

Renderville is the seat of Mouffetteenoyee Parish, the ground so saturated with water that any tree taller than twenty feet will topple over, and any building higher than two stories will sink. When I got out of my car, the air was thick with humidity, overlaid with a scent I couldn't identify.

I wandered into Wunderkine Hall, home to the Department of Physics, and found the main office. The décor would have been considered outdated back in the 1950s. "Hello?"

A woman stuck her head out of an office. "May I help you, sir?" (I was to learn later that people in Louisiana say 'sir' a lot, though it can range in implication from politeness to a nasty threat.)

"I'm new faculty here? John Chant?"

"Oh, hello, Dr. Chant. I thought you were coming tomorrow. I even ordered a cake. Well, we can have that tomorrow. Welcome to Renderville. It's not LSU over at Baton Rouge, but we do what we can. I'm Sally, chief administrative assistant here in the department office. Elsewhere on campus, you can just refer to me as 'Sally From Physics,' and everyone will know who you're talking about." Sally was a middle-aged white woman dressed in a casual pantsuit that was mostly gray, but with a few splashes of bright acrylic colors, blue and pink and yellow. She wore half-moon glasses, had big waves of dark curly hair, and came across as a cheerful, fun aunt, although I'd never had one of those.

"I guess I should... Uh, is Dr. Boudreaux in?"

Sally's face fell. "Bud isn't here anymore. Such a shame."

"What happened?"

She glanced away. "Well ... you're likely to find out sooner rather than later. He's off to the ... facility down at Possumtown."

"Facility? Is he sick?"

"No, he's..." She looked around as if spilling a secret, though I later learned that the whole story had been the main topic of conversation on campus and in town for months. "... in jail."

"Jail?"

She nodded. "A cheating scandal. Betting on football. We take football very seriously here."

"Oh. Say, is there something in the air, or am I imagining it?"

Sally lifted her face and sniffed. "You know, once you live here long enough, you forget about it. This town was once home to the largest hog-processing plant in Louisiana. That's why we're called Renderville. I'm told it stank something awful. The prison used to be here, too, but a judge in the 1950s ruled that it was cruel and unusual to force prisoners, even those on death row, to breathe such foul air, so the prison moved to Possumtown. I grew up in Baton Rouge, so I only heard about it. The plant closed about forty years ago, but the stench was so steeped into the soil that it never went away. Folks here petitioned to get the prison back, said it would be good for the economy, but Possumtown managed to keep it—the prison, I mean. We got to keep the smell."

I asked, "Is there a vice chair or someone..."

"You mean Dr. Sonny? Sonny Soleil? He's... Well, he's in jail, too. Same scandal." She let out a long breath. "I'm afraid it took out about a third of our faculty. That's why we were in a bit of a rush to hire you." She brightened. "But you seem like a real nice young man. I checked you out. I told Bud you were a good choice, and he agreed, although frankly, he had other things on his mind. The authorities let him finish the hiring before they took him away. Sonny they took away months ago."

"I guess that makes you de facto in charge."

Sally From Physics laughed. "De facto, that's me. Although it's more like, de too much to do, de too many responsibilities. I'm only here in the morning. In the afternoon I'm in the office of the Dean of Inhumanities. He also left, but he sneaked away to Uruguay before they could arrest him. The former assistant dean is also at Possumtown."

"Dean of—did you say 'Inhumanities'?"

"Why, yes. Our university has three colleges: Agriculture and Engineering, that's A&E; Humanities, like English, history, languages, and the arts; and then Inhumanities, which is everything else. We're in the College of Inhumanities."

"They didn't say that in my interview. I'm glad I didn't end up in the College of Axe-Murdering."

"Love your sense of humor, John. You married? Girlfriend?"

I shook my head.

"I have a friend you should meet. She's real pretty, blonde, a lawyer, wicked sense of humor, just like you. Super sharp. Smarter than many of the old farts around here, to tell the truth."

"I should probably get settled in first, I imagine."

"I imagine that, too. But don't wait too long."

The first weeks were a blur of introductions and orientation seminars. The most important introduction was to my formal new faculty mentor. Because of the shortage of physics faculty, my assigned mentor was a chemistry professor, Uwe Meilleur. He was a little shorter than me, a bit more filled out, with a touch of gray at the temples of his receding hair. He was Black, but to my surprise, he had a strong German accent.

"Ja," he said, "you are probably wondering. My father was in the US Army, stationed near Heidelberg, and he met and married my mother, a German lady. When he finished his Army service, they stayed in Germany, and they're still there today. He's originally from near here. My Grandmere and my aunts and uncles and cousins and great aunts and second cousins live over in Lagrange

Parish next door. That's part of the reason I accepted a position here. I wanted
to be near family."

Uwe told me this at the faculty club, a rather shabby dining room with garish
orange carpet. Some universities have elegant faculty clubs with Michelin-Starred
chefs. Not LUSR. You went up to a counter and shouted your order to the
fry cook: hamburger, cheeseburger, chicken in gravy, chicken-fried steak, or
turkey-fried steak. You could also get gumbo, étouffée, po-boys, and the like.
"We don't have this 'chicken-fried steak' or 'turkey-fried steak' in Germany,"
Uwe confided in me, "and it confused me the first few times I ordered it."

"I've heard of chicken-fried steak," I said, "though I couldn't tell you what it
is. Maybe steak fried in chicken fat? But turkey-fried steak—that I've never heard
of."

"I have tasted them side by side for a comparison. The difference is subtle,
but I prefer the turkey-fried steak. I believe the gravy is the critical ingredient.
Perhaps it's made from turkey."

"Did you try asking the chef?"

Uwe glanced around. "Some of the people here, they have a strong accent. I
believe they think they're speaking English, but one could have a philosophical
debate on that point."

"So, why did you keep ordering it?"

"I do not give up on a puzzle easily." He sawed away at his turkey-fried steak.
"That makes for a good scientist, yes?"

I took a one-bedroom apartment at the corner of Trotter Boulevard and Jowl
Lane. Clearly, the town had taken its hog-rendering industry seriously.

One Saturday shortly before the start of classes, Uwe invited me to a barbecue
lunch at a cousin's place. "There will be lots of good food, much better than at
the faculty club."

When I hesitated, he added, "Almost every weekend, one cousin or another
holds a barbecue. Sometimes two of them hold a barbeque, and that's even
better, because they compete to see who gets the most people. I often bring
friends from the university."

"Sorry for being hesitant," I said. "I'm not very good with making small talk
with strangers."

Uwe gave a big smile. "My family always welcomes my friends. Remember, I
am their half-German cousin who talks strange. Compared to me, you will seem
completely normal."

"That'll be a first," I said.

When he picked me up from the corner of Trotter Boulevard and Jowl Lane, in the back was a slim Asian man with a receding hairline. Uwe waved me into the front seat. "This is my good friend Harold, Harold Tang from Visual Arts. He's a painter."

We shook hands over the seats. "Very nice to meet you," Harold said. He had a noticeable accent, but as I thought this, I realized that to me, most people in Louisiana had an accent, and I understood Uwe and Harold better than some of the rural folk I'd met. Probably to my students, I'd sound like some sort of Yankee, although I was hazy on exactly which states constituted Yankee-dom.

"Are you sure you don't want to sit up front?" I asked Harold.

"Oh, Harold doesn't mind," Uwe said. "This way, you can see the countryside better. Harold has seen it many times."

As Uwe drove off, I turned around in my seat to face Harold. Figuring I should continue to practice my small talk, I asked, "What kind of painting do you do? Is that the right kind of question, anyway?"

"Well, yes, the medium and the genre, and then the sub-genre and sub-sub-genre. I mostly work in oils on canvas, although I do some small paintings on wood. I trained with Wayne Thiebaud out in California."

"Thiebaud is a big thing," Uwe interjected, "though if you're not into modern American art, you might not know him."

"My work, my painting, it's partly photorealistic," Harold continued, "but with cultural commentary."

"I see."

"That does not really explain it," Uwe said. "He paints realistic scenes, like a dinner party, or an office, and most of the people, the white people in the painting, are painted in a photorealistic style. But then one of the people is a caricature, a cartoon Chinaman. I can get away with saying 'Chinaman' because I didn't grow up in America, and Harold tolerates it because I'm his good friend. You should go to his studio and see his paintings. It's not so easy to explain otherwise."

Uwe drove us across the lush green countryside, plowing through air thick with humidity. After a while, we pulled off the highway and onto a long gravel road that wound through the trees to a big house surrounded by verdant green. Out front, a plume of smoke rose from a big half-cylinder barbecue the size of a car, and tending to it was a plump man in a red apron, who waved his utensil at us in welcome.

Uwe's cousins and aunts and uncles and sundry other relatives, who had been sitting on the front porch, jumped up and swarmed the car, hugging Uwe and Harold both. The little ones, shy, hung back from me, but everyone else shook my hand as Uwe introduced me.

Uwe walked us up to the porch, where an old woman sat in a rocking chair with a quilt on her lap. Uwe kissed her, and she put her hands on his face, and then Harold kissed her, too. "Oh, Harold," she said, in a tremulous voice that was nonetheless thick with affection, "it's always so good to see you." She turned and looked at me. "He calls me *lao ma*—Chinese for 'grandma,' since his own isn't alive anymore."

"Grandmere, this is my friend John," Uwe said. "He's just started at the university."

"Uwe is showing me the ropes. And boy, is there a lot of rope!"

Grandmere lifted a hand, and I took it. She had surprising strength. "Always glad to meet a friend of my Uwe's. He was such a shy boy, I suppose from growing up with those Germans."

"I'm pretty shy myself," I said, suddenly noticing I was the only white person in attendance. Not far off, Harold was fist-bumping with Uwe's cousins.

"You want to make some friends, you should get Harold to take you to church. He takes me to church. Isn't that right, Harold? *Ni shi heng hao ren.* See, Harold's been teaching me some Chinese. I'm old, but my mind is still active. He's been such a good influence on my Uwe. I just love my Harold," Grandmere said, beaming.

The food was as delicious as promised: smoked tri-tip, sausages, mashed potatoes, hush puppies, collard greens, mustard greens with bacon, roasted beets, beet greens, green beans, black-eyed peas, piles of buttery, flaky biscuits, sweet potato pie... We ate until we were stuffed, then ate some more.

"Just roll me to the car and put me in the trunk," I groaned to Uwe. He laughed and leaned close to whisper, "I don't eat for two days after a visit!"

It took half an hour to say goodbye to everyone, and then we were driving back in the verdant, tree-filtered light of late afternoon. I was dozing in the front seat, probably snoring, when Uwe slowed the car and pulled over. I shook myself awake and looked over at him. He had both his hands on top of the steering wheel and was looking straight ahead. "Wha... What is it?" I mumbled with a sleep-numbed tongue.

From the back seat, Harold muttered something I didn't catch. Uwe jerked his head backwards as he switched off the engine. I turned around and saw the pulsing arterial light of a police car.

The engine ticked as it cooled. "Were you speeding?" I asked.

For the first time in our short acquaintance, Uwe cast me a withering look. He tapped the top of the steering wheel, both hands visible. The yellow dashes down the middle of the two-lane highway, faded and cracking, looked like an indecipherable version of Morse code. With the air conditioning off, the Louisiana heat and humidity seeped into the car, conjuring beads of sweat to trickle down my sides under my shirt.

"Sure taking a long time," I said.

"He's calling in our license plate," Harold said. "This your first time being pulled over by a cop? White folk get all the breaks."

At length, we heard the thump of the patrol car door, and a state trooper in khakis strolled over. He stopped and tapped my window, and I rolled it down. "Afternoon, Officer," I said.

The state trooper leaned in. He had a thick face and a thin mustache. "License and registration, son," he said past me.

"Ja, of course, Officer," Uwe said, reaching slowly for his wallet. He passed over his driver's license. "Here it iss."

"'Uh-wee,'" the trooper read off the license, mispronouncing it. "Not from around here, are we? Let me see you other fellows' IDs."

Before I could protest, Harold immediately proffered his driver's license. As I pulled out mine, Uwe said, "Ja, Officer, I am from Germany originally, but now I am teaching at dee oo-niversi-tee."

The trooper looked over all of us. "You all professor types?" he asked, and we nodded. "Got us a regular Yoo-nited Nations here, looks like," he said, chuckling at his own joke. Then he sobered and said, "Son, this ain't no German autobahn. You were fifteen miles an hour over the speed limit."

"My apologies, Officer."

"I'm going to write you up a ticket." Taking all our IDs and the car registration with him, he walked back to his patrol car.

Although there was no way the trooper could hear, I asked Uwe in a near whisper, "Am I crazy, or are you exaggerating your accent?"

For the first time during the stop, Uwe allowed himself a slight smile. "If he thinks me a foreign Black—not one of 'his' American Blacks—he will probably make some allowances."

"The German part helps, too," Harold put in from the back seat. "That cop, all the way walking back to his police car, he's thinking, *Is it possible to have an Aryan Black?*"

In truth, Harold used a different word than "'Black,'" and Uwe clucked his tongue. "You've picked up some bad habits from my cousin Frankie—and look, you've made John turn red with embarrassment." To me, he added, "He wouldn't dare say that around Grandmere."

"Damn straight," Harold said, gazing out the window. "That woman, she loves me."

The trooper came back and handed the ticket to Uwe, who took it wordlessly. "You drive safe now, son," he said. "Don't forget, we got some different customs around here." As he handed Harold his ID, then mine, he said pointedly, "And this isn't California, either, son."

"Ja," Uwe said.

"I hear you," I said.

As Uwe started the car and pulled back onto the two-lane highway, Harold laughed aloud. "'Got us a reg-yoo-lar Yoo-nite-ed Nay-shuns,'" he quoted, then leaned forward to put a hand on Uwe's shoulder, giving it a little squeeze. "You know I'm going to paint this."

"Ja, ja, I was thinking you would."

And he did. He got me to pose, both as reference for the trooper and for myself, though you could only see the back of my head. The trooper's face, jowly and glistening with greasy sweat, was only partly visible—but his badge, gleaming brass polished to shine like gold, as well as the dark handle of his service revolver, were clearly visible. The painting, very photorealistic, swam with tension, broken by the cartoonish scribble of the "Chinaman," painfully complete with coolie hat and buck teeth, representing Harold. While Uwe and I were turned towards the trooper, the backs of our heads to the viewer, Harold's toon figure grinned from the back seat, confronting the viewer. It ended up one of Harold's most famous paintings. You can see it at the Museum of Modern Art in New York: *We Got Us a Regular United Nations Here*, by Harold Haoran Tang.

One of the hallowed traditions of academia is the faculty meeting. I wish I could say it was a solemn ceremony, where professors dressed their sedentary bodies in ancient robes and adorned their graying heads with oak leaves and owl feathers, and we chanted in unison Maxwell's electromagnetic equations. But I swear on a stack of Feynman's lectures, it was just a meeting.

One of the surprises in the faculty was another new hire: Buford "Baka" Becker. "Great to see you again, John!" he said, pumping my hand with a slightly sweaty grip.

"I thought you were in Japan," I said.

Baka shrugged and wiped his glasses, which were fogging in the humidity. "My long-term contract at RIKEN was coming to an end, and, wellll, I got the sense I had worn out my welcome," he said. "So, I started looking around for positions back in the States. Not easy when you've been out of the country for fifteen years. But I got lucky: I landed here." Pointing at me, he turned to the other faculty drifting in and said, "This guy, he's done some sweet things in quantum tunneling."

Sally From Physics said, "All right, y'all, settle down, everyone."

One of the senior faculty members, Dr. Bobby Litsteen, raised a hand. He wore rimless glasses and had a salt-and-pepper beard, and he worked in soft materials. "When do we get a new chair for the department?" he asked in a somewhat reedy voice.

Sally looked around the room. "Well, that's a good question, Bobby. According to the university regulations, the faculty must elect a chair from among the full professors."

"We don't have any full professors left," Litsteen said. "They all got hauled off to jail."

"Can't an associate professor step in?" asked Dr. Barbara Muñoz, an expert in strange-quark hadrons.

Sally raised a finger. "Yes, an associate professor can be a chair—but only if the Dean of Inhumanities approves." A murmur rippled through the room; we were still missing a Dean of Inhumanities. "The best you can do until a new dean is hired," Sally continued, "is to form an ad hoc steering committee."

Litsteen raised his hand again. "Will that service count towards promotion to full professor?"

"You'd still have to be publishing more papers, Bobby," Sally told him. To the rest of us, she said, "I'll let you all discuss and vote on it. But if it were me, I'd think about Melody, and Sam," referencing Dr. Melody Bencik, experimental fluid dynamics, and Dr. Sam Soon, ultracold gases, both associate professors. "... and John." She glanced at me.

"Wait—what? Who?" I stammered. "Me? John, me? But I'm an assistant professor. I just arrived. I don't know how anything works around here."

"The assistant professors need a voice at the table," Sally said.

"And nothing around here works anyway," Sam added, "so you're perfect."

Classes started. I considered showing up the first day wearing my old red rubber nose and floppy shoes from my undergraduate days at a clown college, but I asked Uwe, and he advised against it. "Save it for Mardi Gras," he said. I had a hundred and twenty ambitious yet inattentive students in my "electricity and magnetism for resentful premeds" course (as it was surreptitiously called), and eleven grad students in mathematical methods. In the first course, I wheeled out a Van de Graaff generator and asked for volunteers. When they touched it, their hair stood on end. It took up a third of the class time, but it got the class laughing and chatting excitedly.

In the math methods course, I wrote on the board a forbidding-looking calculus integral and gave them twenty minutes to come up with strategies, none of which worked. Then in the last ten minutes, I used the method of steepest descents—the same method with which I had first impressed Ada—to get an approximate result. "If you evaluate this numerically," I announced, "you'll find it's good to within ten percent. Not bad for a quick-and-dirty approximation."

As the class streamed out, a young Black woman came up to me. "Hi, Professor, I'm Emmy Shore," she said shyly.

"Oh, yes, Sally mentioned you as a research assistant? You should come by my lab, and we can find something for you."

She nodded. "Professor, if you wanted to evaluate the integral numerically, what programming language would you use?"

"FORTRAN," I said. "It's an oldie, but a goodie."

"Maybe I'll pick it up, then," she said. "Thanks, Professor."

The late summer air was still thick as grease, and no matter what precautions I took, anytime I stepped outside, I was soon slick with sweat. I took to bringing two or three extra shirts into the office every day and changing frequently.

That first week of classes, the university held a welcome assembly in the football stadium, bribing students to attend with ice cream cones. The chancellor of the university, who had clung to power despite the depletion of the ranks of faculty, administrators, and coaches from the betting scandal, stood up, and with his voice amplified and echoing through the stadium, he admitted the university had gotten a black eye.

"Two black eyes, in fact," Chancellor Hebert said, "and a bloody nose."

I was far up in the stands with several of the other physics faculty members, and the chancellor looked like a tiny doll dressed in a suit. Despite the distance, I could see him mopping his forehead.

"But we're going to recover. We're the Butchers; we're not afraid of a little blood and guts." The Butchers was the name of the school sports team, the LUSR Butchers. The school mascot was Baron Butcher, portrayed by a student wearing a huge papier-mâché head with a maniacal grin and a thin black mustache and goatee, topped by a white chef's hat, and most importantly, waving an enormously oversized meat cleaver. Baron Butcher stood on stage next to the chancellor and occasionally thrust the cleaver into the air.

"I have a three-point plan to get this school back on track. I have consulted our university regents..." He gestured behind himself to four white men, one Black man, and one white woman. "... and we all agree."

"First, we're going to hire a new coach—the *best* coach, the best *clean* coach we can find. I'll double his salary over Coach Stabin's, even if I have to freeze faculty salaries for three years." Stabin was the disgraced former head football coach at the heart of the betting scandal.

"Next, to make sure this never, *ever* happens again, we're going to hire not one, not *two*, but *three* vice presidents for ethics and ethical behavior. In fact..." Here the chancellor took a long pause for effect. The crowd murmured, Baron Butcher put a finger to his papier-mâché lips, and a woolen silence settled over the stadium.

"Our goal, over the next five years, is to have the *most rigorously run* university in the nation. I promise you, we will have the *highest* ratio of assistant chancellors, vice presidents, deans, and assorted administrators per student, per faculty, of any educational institution anywhere. Not a single academic stone will go unturned or unmonitored by our massive management team.

"Once we have established our high moral principles and steely management, I will go to the state legislature, who slashed our budget after the recent failings of some of us, and I will say, 'We have *learned our lesson*, we have *proven* ourselves, and we deserve to have our budget restored, and maybe even increased a little, so that we can support our students, who, aside from the cheer squad and half the football team, had nothing to do with this recent unpleasantness.'"

Baron Butcher raised his cleaver in triumph.

One day in the faculty club, I started to sit down, but Uwe stopped me. "Not there. Over here." We sat two tables away.

I gestured with my head. "What's wrong with that table?"

"That's a Humanities table." Seeing my blank look, he continued, "That section is for faculty in the Humanities, over there are tables for Agriculture and Engineering, and here we are in the Inhumanities." He took a bite of turkey-fried steak and chewed for a moment. "When I first arrived here, someone had to explain it to me, too."

"But isn't Harold in Humanities? Hey, I just realized, you're often eating lunch with me and not with Harold."

"Well, Mondays, Wednesdays, and Fridays, he teaches at noon. Also, we decided not to be very obvious about our relationship on campus. It breaks no rules, but not everyone here is open-minded."

He dipped a French fry in some ketchup and waved it. "By the way, some lady is waving and trying to get your attention. No, over in Agriculture and Engineering."

I turned and saw a Black woman with a hand half raised. "You sure she's not waving at you?"

"Why, because she is Black and so am I? No, she is definitely looking at you. Let's see, I think I remember her name... Jones? No, wait... Johnston. No ... Johnson! She is young Professor Johnson!"

Though she was at a distance, and she had grown out her hair, recognition snapped into place: Junie Johnson, from my days with Phoenix. I stood up, then stopped and asked Uwe, "Am I allowed to encroach into the territory of Agriculture and Engineering?"

Uwe leaned back in his chair. "Only if you're holding a white flag, I believe. Or a white napkin, if that is more handy. I have never been bold enough to try."

With a shrug, I picked up my napkin, and waving it, I walked over to Junie.

"Hey, John," she said. "Fancy meeting you here. Welcome to Renderville. It's not LSU, but... Uh, what's with the napkin?"

I glanced back at Uwe. "I was told ... that to cross over here..."

She glared at Uwe, who smiled smugly back. "Never trust a German's sense of humor," she said.

My Academic Bestiary

M odern scientists focus on cause and effect. What causes the fairy folds of the northern lights, the rise of suicides in North American tweens, the melting of glaciers everywhere, the jet stream, hiccoughs, variant spellings of words, religious schisms, restless leg syndrome, magnetism, and finally, this narrow obsession with cause and effect?

During the Middle Ages, European scholars obsessed over categories. Some categorizations were practical. For example, on Fridays during Lent, Christians were supposed to eat only fish; hence, it was useful to know if whales or turtles are a kind of fish, and thus sanctioned, or some sort of aquatic cow or lizard to be avoided.

Medieval categorization was not a juvenile form of science, wishing to become biology or chemistry when it grew up. It had its own purposes, one of which was to instruct. Medieval scholars compiled bestiaries, books on animals real and imaginary. The point of bestiaries was to draw lessons for moral development. If I were to list subatomic hadrons and leptons and for each one give a short moralizing tale, I'd be tossed from a window of an ivory tower, or denied tenure. Yet rather than feel smugly superior to the medieval—look at them, ha ha, using ants and elephants as props in propaganda—I wish we ourselves were humbler. After all, some of the greatest intellectual triumphs of the twentieth century—relativity, quantum mechanics, chaos, incompleteness—are lessons in what we cannot know.

Scientists tend to be introverted, ranging from somewhat shy to very shy, with a few outlying extroverts. In the physics department at LUSR, Sally (not a scientist) was outgoing. She herself said she could talk the ear off an alligator, if it had an ear, and before lunch was over, the gator would have agreed to serve on three committees and four outreach events. Bobby Litsteen, who wore lifts to make him five-seven, was a compulsive glad-hander; he would have aspired to the higher pay of administration, if it hadn't required so much work.

Melody Bencik could be outgoing, or at least fake it, but didn't need to be the center of attention, unlike Litsteen. Sam Soon, born in Malaysia and raised in England, had received an accent that to American ears sounded like charm and wisdom, and fortunately, he had both. And Baka Becker was a compulsive talker. Whenever I passed by his lab, I overheard him talking to himself, narrating his adventures in science.

Of the newcomers besides me, Sanjay Nanda (neutron scattering off semiconductors) and Gabriela Lu (gravitational waves) were talkative; Lashawn Greene (exotic hadrons) was shy, but willing to go out for a beer; and Mischa Borozov (formal scattering theory) left his office only to grudgingly teach—after the first faculty meeting he never attended another one.

One faculty member I didn't get along with: Carson Whittaker, the department's string theorist, and for years, the department's sole Black professor. He himself was stringy, so thin that you wanted to buy him a sandwich. Upon meeting him, I made an offhanded joke about string theory, to which he took offense. I felt bad about it, until Melody told me that Whittaker, who'd been at LUSR for ten years, made no secret of the fact that he thought the place beneath him.

Uwe introduced me around to faculty in other science departments, such as Dick Cherrystone, the chair of Archeology and Anthropology, and his wife, Lina Mataros, from Geology. "We've made our peace with being here," Lina said, though the way she said it chilled my heart.

With Uwe and Harold, I went to a party thrown by Visual Arts, expecting either ethereal debates about the nature of art and perception, or a wild debauchery of dancing and drinking until the wee hours of the morning. To my disappointment, it was just middle-aged faculty discussing investment portfolios and vacation plans to Cancun or Canada.

And then there was Erstmann Codd.

The university chancellor put out a letter to all departments, announcing a presentation by Erstmann Codd ("former LUSR faculty and author of *The Science of Selfishness*") as a Big Event. Even if he hadn't, Baka Becker could not stop talking about it. He seemed to assume I was as big a fan of Codd as he was. Baka even materialized at my office half an hour before the event started, and with his eagerness like that of a puppy, I could not bring myself to say no.

Chancellor Hebert himself, in a suit and hideous green-and-brown tie (the school colors), introduced Codd. Baka leaned close to me, whispering something about Codd having greased the way for both Baka and me to get hired, but the crowd was so noisy that I did not catch all of it. Then Codd bounded onto the stage with the same energy and nearly the same clothes I'd seen in Sacramento: worn jeans and a tight green T-shirt. "Hello, Renderville! Hello, Butchers!" He paced back and forth, holding the mic as if it might flee, his bald head gleaming with perspiration. "You know, I'm glad your mascot is a butcher, because that's my life philosophy: hold a big knife, cut hard and fast, and never fear blood!"

"Never fear blood" was in fact the school sports motto, morbidly chanted at games. His reference earned some scattered applause.

"Never fear," he repeated, "because if you want to get ahead, if you want to win that game, you can't play it safe. Well, maybe you can if you're from a snooty school, like Harvard or Yale." People chuckled, though I noted he didn't mention Princeton, his own undergrad institution. "But if you're from Renderville in deepest Louisiana, you have to take chances. And when you take chances, you get cuts and bruises, the occasional broken bone or concussion, but you get back up, and you keep going! Just ask your coaches." He grinned.

"Now, life isn't always fair," Codd continued, pacing like a hungry panther. "It's a basic law of the universe. Just read my book, *The Thermodynamics of Poverty*, available in the lobby. In order to extract work, entropy has to increase. But entropy is a matter of statistics, and to beat the odds, you have to take chances. How do you think all those guys in Silicon Valley got rich? To beat the odds, they took chances."

I squirmed in my seat and leaned over to Baka. "He knows that's nonsense, right?" I said into his ear. "That most people who take chances *don't* beat the odds? He knows that, right?"

"Oh, sure. But with Codd, it's really more of a metaphor."

"A metaphor for what?" I asked, but Codd's amplified voice drowned me out.

"Now, let's face it, Renderville is a place where the odds are stacked high, and your university has recently faced some serious setbacks. Because Renderville has a special place in my heart, I talked to some friends in Silicon Valley, to get some elite coastal money here to support LUSR. I'm sorry to say, what I hear back is, *'Renderville? Never heard of it. Why should we take a chance on a place we've never even heard of?'*

"So, for you to succeed, it will require taking some mighty big chances." He paused, glancing to the side of the stage, where Chancellor Hebert was still standing. "The reason I am here tonight is that I—myself and Chancellor Hebert—are here to announce the founding of a new initiative: the Leap Before You Look Institute. The mission of this institute is to put forth bold new ideas, new thinking, to get the attention and investment of Wall Street and Silicon Valley. To start it, we are grateful for the generous support of one of our university regents, Regent Tode, owner of Tode's Reliable Motors.

"The Leap Before You Look Institute will question the unquestionable, think the unthinkable, take the chances that everyone else says are crazy." I glanced sideways at Baka, who glowed with excitement. "The institute will sponsor scholarships for thirty undergraduates—everything paid by the institute! There will also be twenty grad students given Leap Before You Look Scholarships.

"To kick off this institute, twelve university professors will be Leap Before You Look Fellows. We've already selected them; they didn't apply, they didn't even know. But they will lead this effort. Most of them are here tonight. I'd like to ask those in the audience to join me here on stage.

"So, come on down, Associate Professor Robert Osterman of civil engineering; Professor Sylvia Viviano of food science; Professor Beryl Knaught, English and literature; Associate Professor Hubert Biscuit, psychology; Professor Ekwunde Jones of religious studies..." I barely listened until I was shocked to hear him finish with "... and Assistant Professor John Chant of physics."

The people named were filtering down to the stage. I wanted to sneak away; I had never liked the spotlight. But Codd had spotted me in the audience and gestured for me to come forward.

Afterwards, as we streamed out, I was feeling a bit dazed, when someone fell in step with me. I turned and saw Junie.

"Hey, John," she said. "Congratulations, I guess."

"Thanks, I guess." We walked for a while, serenaded by the cicadas' love songs for the hideous. "Is it wrong to feel conflicted?"

"I'm not stepping into that."

"But he got someone to give him money for it, I suppose."

"Yeah, that Tode guy," Junie said. "You seen his billboards around town, right? 'Tode's Reliable Motors—Don't get towed, get Tode.'" I nodded. "Nothing wrong with local money, but Codd did approach a lot of tech companies and failed. I know for a fact that Codd approached Goosetech with a big pitch, but he got turned down cold."

"Goosetech? I think I've maybe heard of them."

"You've seen their logo? The goose with glasses? 'Honk if you love tech'? I got a job with them, medical accelerators, after I finished my PhD," Junie said. "But then decided I wanted to give academia a try. Bruce said there'd be a job for me if I wanted to come back."

"Bruce?"

"The founder and head guy. Gooseman, Bruce Gooseman."

I nearly missed a step as my heart squeezed. "Hey, I think I know..."

Junie stopped and faced me. Although it was dark, I made out a smile on her face. "You know, even though there are a lot of Johns out there, I wondered if you were the *same* John he talks about."

"Me?"

"Bruce, he wants to talk about the future, not the past. But then he brings up, well, this *John*—maybe you, maybe not you—who he says was the only person who befriended him when he was young. And saved his life. That's a direct quote."

Junie told me Bruce had invented a device to prevent nighttime snoring and sold it for a lot of money. Then he'd developed inexpensive devices to measure blood sugar, as well as sugar and fat content in food, and sold that start-up company, too. Now he had a whole company, Goosetech, which developed new ideas and spun them off.

"This is Big Bruce we're talking about, right? I mean, skyscraper big? Of course, I was a kid when I knew him, so maybe..."

"Oh, that's Bruce, all right. Huge. But a sweet guy, one of the nicest white guys I've met. Good to his employees. But he's no pushover. I heard he wouldn't even hear Codd's pitch."

We reached the parking lot, and Junie stopped by a car. "This is mine." She said it the way she said, *"Hey, John,"* almost as if she were singing. The melody in her voice filled me with a lightness I hadn't felt in a long time, and I started to wonder if I should ask her out.

Before I could say anything, as she dug into her purse for her keys, she said, "Say, my boyfriend and I are going to this zydeco festival this weekend... There's some festival or another nearly every weekend. Two things to do in Louisiana are eat and dance. Want to go with us? You won't be a third wheel, I promise."

I admit, I had hardly heard any of it after *"my boyfriend."* Those two words snuffed out the tiny flicker of hope in my heart.

"They give free dance lessons," she continued, "if you're worried about it. And nobody cares if you're any good or not. I mean, everyone admires the good dancers, but mostly folks are just having a good time. What do you say?"

"Sure," I said. "Sounds fun. Might as well start acting like the locals."

At that, Junie laughed. "Oh, John, I doubt you'll *ever* be like the locals. I like that about you." She touched my arm. "I'll call."

Meanwhile, as a newly hatched assistant professor, I was expected to hustle towards tenure via a great scavenger hunt of researching and writing papers. The university didn't take your papers and weigh them, but it wasn't far off.

My assistant, Emmy Shore, who had asked about FORTRAN, told me her father was an electrician, and from him she had learned how to wire anything. "Great," I said. Like most new science faculty, I'd been given a small sum of money to jumpstart my research. "I don't have enough start-up funds for a diamond anvil, but you can start building a photonic supertunneling apparatus." I did not have a clear plan in my head, but figured Emmy could try supertunneling through a wide variety of materials, just as I had in my graduate work.

"Lasers, cool!" she said.

When Junie came with her boyfriend to pick me up that Saturday, she took one look at me and shook her head. "You've got to dress cooler," she said. "Shorts and sandals, if you got them. You'll sweat to death in those jeans." She herself was dressed in a lavender tank top and matching shorts, with sandals.

I looked down at my clothes. "I thought it might be dusty."

"Yeah, dusty, but *hot*. Everyone else will dress the same. Put on sunscreen. And, oh, grab a hat. With a wide brim, not a baseball cap."

Her boyfriend was Harish Upadrashtra, a chiropodist in Lafayette, who had grown up in Orange County, California. "Which is why a lot of people here call me Chad," he said. "A lot of my friends think all guys in Orange County are named Chad."

"Your *white* friends," Junie corrected. She explained she was from Atlanta, and while Georgia was very different from Louisiana—"The South isn't a monolith"—it was still less of a shock for her than it had been for Harish.

A little after eleven in the morning, we pulled into a half-full dirt parking lot. From about a mile off, I could see tents and canopies, and already the looping strains of music floated through the air, as well as the thick scent of fried foods.

We strolled the freshly mown festival grounds. The crowd, still a bit thin before noon, was mixed, Black and white, all ages. Junie clearly enjoyed playing the tour guide. "Let's see, there's catfish po-boys, shrimp po-boys, hot links, boudin, deep-fried oysters, deep-fried frog legs, deep-fried gator... You can try gator, but it if you ask me, it tastes like greasy chicken. But pretty much anything deep fried. If you want crawfish, real Louisiana crawfish, you gotta wait 'til spring."

(Indeed, the following spring, I grew rather fond of spicy boiled crawfish. Uwe knew a gas station where the store sold boiled crawfish by the pound in garbage bags, and he'd bring back at least two or three pounds apiece. Uwe and Harold and I would spread out newspaper on the table and on the floor and open some cold Abita beers, then start in on the bright red mounds of crawfish. You had to twist off the tail, usually with a yellow smear of guts on the base, and with your thumbs, pinch and pull the meat out of the carapace.)

We headed to a canopied black-and-white-tiled dance floor, half filled with couples. Junie excused herself from Harish to partner up with me for lessons. A dance instructor, a man with a microphone and a boom box, led us through the basics: the two-step, the Cajun waltz, the zydeco swing. Later, Junie told me people who didn't know any better mixed up Cajun and zydeco. While she allowed that there were some similarities, at the most basic level, Cajun was the music of the poor, French-speaking white Acadians, while zydeco had originated in the Black community. Nowadays, many zydeco bands were mixed, but Cajun not so much.

"Looking good, John!" Harish said an hour later, though I felt ready to fall down. As a break, we bought some catfish po-boys and three Abitas, sharing a picnic table with three white girls from the university and an older Black couple.

We had just finished when music drifted from the stage next door. "Ooh, that's Little Red and the Zydeco Dukes!" Junie exclaimed, wiping her mouth with a paper napkin. She reached into the little black purse slung around her shoulder and refreshed her lipstick. "C'mon, *Chad*, let's see you shake your Orange County booty out there. John, you find yourself a partner; lots of folks come here just to dance."

She was right about the band, with Little Red singing and pumping away on his squeezebox accordion, accompanied by a lead guitar, a ponytailed white guy on bass guitar, a young fellow on drums, and Slim Something-or-other on harmonica, which I'd always thought of as a child's toy, only to be astounded by the way Slim made it wheeze and wail like a freight train of memory and regret bearing down upon us. While the lyrics were all about women who'd done Little Red wrong, or how Little Red did a woman wrong, I was struck by the joy in the crowd. Black and white, they clasped hands and waists and swung round and round.

Junie and Harish spun across the dance floor like a double star, faces shining with perspiration and happiness. Meanwhile, I only worked up the nerve to ask one woman to dance, a petite blonde who was probably ten or fifteen years older than I was. But I lost track of the beat more times than I could count, and I could see frustration in her face. After that, I sat on the side, listening to the next act, Sadie and the Swing Cats.

"You just need more confidence," Junie told me as we drove back.

"Yeah, the first ten times, I was sweating buckets," Harish said.

"Don't tell him that! John needs encouragement."

"John needs a lot more practice," I muttered.

"Yes, exactly," Junie said, smiling. "There's another festival next weekend. Shrimp and Petroleum, down Morgan City way."

Leap Before You Look Fellows were supposed to give lunchtime talks to our fellow fellows, as well as to the student scholars. The institute had been given space in Burlap Hall, which had once housed Ancient Languages. The first Leap Lecture, as it was called, was given by Lina Mataros, who discussed the unusual geology underlying our town. Along the way, she mentioned the high cadmium levels in the nearby Mouffetteenoyee Swamp. "That's why this parish is poorer than even the rest of Louisiana," she said. "Cadmium toxicity. There aren't any fish or gators to catch, and the trees are all stunted and half dead. The cadmium even leaches into fields near the swamp and kills crops."

"Isn't cadmium used in paints?" asked one of the other fellows, Professor Ramachandran, I think. "Cadmium yellow or red or something?"

I raised a hand. "It's also used in nuclear reactors, for control rods, because it absorbs neutrons like crazy." I can't help myself; I just blurt out facts. (Though I can keep secrets. After all, I never told anyone about you and that thing in Alaska NASA found.)

At this point, Sylvia Viviano, who'd been picked as director of the institute, spoke up. With a cloud of silver hair, she was one of the oldest faculty members on campus. "Yes," she said. "I believe that's why, when they shut down the nuclear reactor in the basement of Wunderkine Hall, they flooded it with swamp water."

"There's a nuclear reactor on campus?" asked a red-haired woman with a pretty if horsey face, wearing bright red lipstick.

"Nothing to worry about, Beryl," said Viviano. "It was sealed up in the eighties."

I raised a hand. "Do you mean decommissioned, as in they hauled away the fissile material? Or..."

"And you, are, dear...?" asked Viviano.

"Oh, John Chant. Physics."

"Well, it's under your department. Though I think the last person around at that time was Sonny Soleil, and he's gone now."

"So, wait, is there a nuclear reactor on campus, or not?" persisted the redhead.

I admit I rolled my eyes. "Nuclear power isn't as evil as a lot of people make it out to be."

"But ... we're possibly talking about a nuclear reactor no one is monitoring?" she said, her tone rising. "How is that a good idea?"

She had a point. "I'll ... I'll ask."

"Thanks. I'm Beryl Knaught, by the way. English and Literature." She pressed her fingers, replete with bright red nail polish, against her carotid. "Talking about nuclear reactors certainly got my heart rate up! So, Sylvia, who's the next speaker?"

Director Viviano smiled broadly. "Since he got people's hearts beating, let's have Professor Chant give the talk next week."

Back at Wunderkine Hall, I asked Sally From Physics if she knew anything about a nuclear reactor in the basement. At first she looked puzzled, but then her eyes widened. "I always wondered why that door was locked... I asked Sonny, you know, Dr. Soleil, several times about it, and he always said it went nowhere. He was a terrible liar, so I knew it wasn't true, but he never would say what it was down there."

So, we went into the basement, and then into a sub-basement, where decades of obsolete lab equipment was stored, slowly rusting away in the humidity. After pushing aside a cabinet filled with slide rules and old mechanical adding machines, we found a heavy steel door bound with a rusty chain and a heavy padlock.

We enlisted the help of Mick Guillory, the department's technician, who had a long, thin face and wore his graying hair back in a ponytail. Mick took a sledgehammer to the padlock. After a dozen whacks, he finally knocked it off.

With a crowbar, we pried open the door and shone a flashlight inside. Just a few feet down a steep, narrow flight of stairs, dark brown water lapped. The air held a weird, metallic stench.

"We have sump pumps keeping the basement dry down to this level. I could run a line down further, try to drain it," Mick said with a thick Cajun accent, but aside from *awn-yun* for "onion," I can't reproduce it in any way worth a spare muon.

I asked, "Aren't you worried about what might be in that water? What might go into the sewer system and then out to sea?"

Mick shrugged. "We're downstream from some of the world's largest petro-chemical plants. I doubt whatever's down here is nearly as nasty as what flows by on a daily basis."

I took some samples of the water and asked Uwe to analyze them. He told me it matched what I'd been told about the Mouffetteenoyee Swamp: high levels of cadmium. "Don't drink it," he said. "Don't even get it on your skin, if you can avoid it."

Emmy and I helped Mick drain the water, hoping to reveal the reactor room, or whatever was down there. The dark brown water was pungent, and Mick had a wet handkerchief tied around his face.

"Sorry about the stink," I told the two of them.

"Is that the cadmium?" Emmy asked, wrinkling her nose.

"No. Uwe—Professor Meilleur from chemistry—he told me the water is also saturated with gadolinium and other rare earth elements, and laced with phosphates and sulfates."

Emmy said, "It reminds me of the swamp, so it's nothing new. My dad, sometimes he has projects in the swamp. A couple of years ago, he took me along when he had to repair some power lines going out to this chimp haven."

"A what?"

"Let's see... I think it's called something like The Ape Angel Former Experimental Animal Rescue Haven. You know, for, like, monkeys that were experimented on. A place they can retire."

"In a swamp?"

"Well, the swamp is so poisoned that the land is almost free. Besides, though I'm sorry those poor monkeys were experimented on, whatever happened left them with a bad attitude. I remember, as we were bringing out a new power line through the swamp, just me and my dad in his dinghy, those monkeys were all along the top of the wall, screeching and screaming at us, making such an unearthly racket." She shuddered. "I never want to go near that place again."

"Don't worry," I said. "No chimp haven for me."

When it came my time to give my Leap Lecture, Director Viviano told me, "Erstmann has been going around saying that tunneling is a terrific metaphor for what he hopes for this institute: to break through barriers that should be impossible to surmount. So, everyone's looking forward to your talk. And you already have fans."

She gestured towards a door at the back of the room. Standing in the doorway was Baka Becker, who waved at me.

"I told him that technically, only fellows are allowed at the lecture," Viviano said, "but he was so insistent, I said he could listen from just outside. He had these big puppy-dog eyes, strange on a middle-aged man, but very effective."

That's how I ended up talking about quantum tunneling through energy barriers; how Heisenberg's uncertainty principle means that for short times, a particle can temporarily borrow enough energy to get through a barrier; and how this makes alpha decay and nuclear fusion possible.

"Sounds like embezzlement," said Beryl Knaught from the front row, and everyone laughed.

I smiled. "More like loose lending," I said. "The books always balance at the end of the day."

I spoke a bit more about my own experiments, trying to explain about coherent tunneling and how it may have facilitated the Big Bang, which faded into incoherent tunneling and the much gentler accelerated expansion of the universe we observe today.

From the back of the room, Baka waved a hand frantically. "What about time and space as barriers?" he called out.

I felt a little chill in my heart. Maybe my father had shared his speculations more than I realized. "For that, you need a quantum theory of space and time itself," I said. "Unfortunately, I don't see Carson Whittaker here." That was a mean dig on my part; Carson was wounded that he had not been selected as a Fellow of the institute and had thereafter sneered at it.

A plump sack of a man sitting directly behind Beryl raised a hand. "Hubert Biscuit, Psychology. I've heard it said that the observer affects the quantum wave function. Could it affect tunneling?"

I shook my head. "That old canard about an observer causing a wave function to collapse was abandoned long ago."

"But surely there are quantum effects in the brain. Don't those get entangled with other quantum wave functions?"

I paused. "I guess I don't know enough about neurophysiology to comment."

"Neural activity propagates back and forth in waves," Biscuit persisted. "Could something like Schrödinger's equation apply?"

I opened my mouth to dismiss it, but before the words came out, I had a vision of Rita, Freddy Pigeon's wired-together collection of rat brains in his sub-basement, thinking and predicting and advising. "Interesting suggestion," I said.

Harold Tang called me up. "Hey, John, it's me, Harold. I'm taking Uwe's Grandmere to church. Want to join us?"

"Is Uwe coming?"

"No, that bastard wriggled out of it. Says he has too much grading to do. To be honest, he wriggles out of going as much as he can. *Yes, Uwe, I'm talking about you!*" Harold shouted. "But Grandmere said I should phone you, and what Grandmere says, I do. So...?"

"Um ... okay."

Harold showed up driving the same car we'd taken out to Uwe's cousin's house, with Grandmere in the back and another gray-haired Black woman beside her. When I got into the front, Grandmere leaned forward. "So good to see you again, John. This here's my daughter, Lola, Uwe's aunt. This is John, Uwe's friend from work."

"He's been showing me the ropes around the university," I said.

"And boy, is there a lot of rope," Harold added.

The church wasn't large, holding maybe a hundred people, but it was packed, both in the pews and up front in the choir. I was one of the only white people; there were a couple of middle-aged blonde women, and one old, old white man bent over so far that he reminded me of my own grandma. But since I was accompanying Grandmere Meilleur, who was treated like a celebrity, people came up to shake my hand.

The choir sang a lot, at least five or six pieces—I lost count—and the congregation got in several hymns, too. The organ swelled and swept over us, just like the music at the zydeco festival, and the choir and congregation clapped and swayed. I tried to follow suit. The preacher thundered about the poor, how the most blessed thing we could do was to care for the penniless and the destitute. He declared that it didn't matter if they were drug addicts or prostitutes or otherwise unfortunate, because to take care of them was the same as caring for Jesus, and people shouted, "AMEN!" He preached that being rich didn't make us rich in God's eyes, and being famous didn't make us famous in God's eyes, and that the only thing that mattered was that we loved God and one another, AMEN! And the choir sang, and the congregation sang.

Afterward, there was coffee and sweet, moist cake, and though I had planned to keep my mouth shut—who was I to speak up here?—folks came up and asked where I came from, and how I liked Louisiana, and wasn't it different from what I was used to?

Later, after Harold dropped me off at my apartment, I cried, not sure if it was from sadness or happiness, and not even sure I wanted to go to church regularly. I didn't think I did—but I decided if this was life in Louisiana, I could make it my life.

Unfortunately, life in Louisiana was about to get more complicated.

The head of the university was Chancellor Willy Hebert. When the betting scandal hit LUSR, Hebert had been one of the few administrators to retain his job.

Fun fact: in Louisiana, the name Hebert can either be pronounced as the anglophone *HEE-burt*, or the francophone *ey-BEAR* (rhyming with *hey-BEAR*)—and Chancellor Hebert, wanting to be admired by all, used both. Sally claimed Hebert used *HEE-burt* in the spring semester and *ey-BEAR* in the fall, but I never paid enough attention to confirm this quirk.

The betting scandal crisis had provided Hebert an opportunity. Normally, it was impossible to fire tenured faculty, and nearly as difficult to shed fossilized deans. But with the university swept clean of thick-headed middle management and thinned of Cretaceous-era faculty, Chancellor Willy could remake the campus in *his* image, as he saw fit.

I had paperwork I couldn't make heads or tails of, so I looked for Sally. Before I could ask her about the forms, she said, "Are you going to the meeting, John?"

"Meeting? What meeting?"

She told me everyone in the College of Inhumanities had been invited to a special meeting with Chancellor Hebert, where the new dean would be announced.

"Was there a search?" I asked. "Aren't faculty usually part of a committee to screen and rank candidates for dean?"

Sally smiled. "It's so sweet that you think that." She swiveled herself out from behind her desk. "Let's go head on over. I think the rest are already there."

Faculty, staff, and students crowded into the main auditorium in Latourette Hall, the largest in the college. I spotted Uwe and waved to him, and he came over and sat by me. Despite the sweltering heat, he still wore his usual tie.

"I suppose this is exciting?" I said to him.

"Or terrifying," Uwe said firmly.

"Hey, guys," said Junie, plopping down in the other seat next to me. "How you doing, Uwe?"

"Why are you here?" I asked her. "I mean, I'm glad to see you, but you aren't in the College of Inhumanities."

"Well, the dean of Agriculture and Engineering is stepping down soon, and I hoped to get some insight into the kind of person the chancellor might pick for us."

Uwe leaned closer. "For myself, I'm not sure what to think about this," he said. "I don't even know if it's an internal or external candidate. It has been all super secret and hush-hush."

"Have y'all heard any rumors?" Junie asked.

"I didn't even know there was a search on," I admitted.

Junie crossed her arms. "I bet it's an external. If it were internal, someone around here would have blabbed."

Uwe said, "These days, it would be wiser not to bet at all." When his comment was met with stony silence, he added, "That was a joke. They say Germans have no sense of humor, but I think it's just too subtle for other people."

"No, it just wasn't funny," Junie said.

Just then, Chancellor Hebert walked onto the stage. The microphone squealed when he picked it up. When the knifing shriek had died down, Hebert said, "Better? Yes? Good. Thank you all for coming.

"I know it seems all I talk about is how we've had some rough times lately. In order to build back stronger than before, we need to restaff key positions. Few are more key than the dean of the College of Inhumanities. Engineering builds things, agriculture feeds our bodies, and humanities feed our souls. But inhumanities, with sciences and the like, is the fount of innovation—and of federally funded grant money.

"We need this college, *your* college, to color outside the box, to ignore the box altogether, and innovate as if there were no rules. Except of course the important federal laws governing research funds—no spending it on cocaine and hookers! And this innovation, this outside-the-box attitude, must come from the top, the dean himself.

"As it happens, I am announcing a new dean whose appointment will itself be an innovation, the signal that there *are* no boxes. The dean of inhumanities will be innovation incarnate: the first nonhuman dean."

Junie whispered, "What the eff is he talking about? He's making even *less* sense than usual."

The chancellor turned and gestured to someone in the wings. A small figure shambled onto the stage, wearing an ill-fitting black suit and a crumpled white shirt and tie, walking awkwardly upright in clumsy shoes. I felt as if an arsonist had lit a fire in the middle of my face. All around us, people gasped and muttered. Under his breath, Uwe said, *"Was ist das?"* while Junie blurted out, "Is that a *monkey?*"

"A chimpanzee," I corrected her. What I did not say aloud was that it was a chimpanzee I recognized. I felt an iron tightness in my chest, and for a moment, I wondered if I was having a heart attack.

"This ... *this* is a joke?" Uwe said. He turned to me and Junie. "Yes? A joke?"

Over the murmur of the crowd, which swelled like cicada song on a hot summer evening, Chancellor Hebert raised his voice, almost shouting like a circus barker, "I introduce to you the new head of the College of Inhumanities, Dean Pancake!"

"You were right," I told Uwe. "About the terrifying part."

Hidden Symmetries of Two Left Feet

M any people think of mathematics as arithmetic, accounting in a fancy suit and with a posh accent. But beyond arithmetic and accounting, even beyond calculus, math shines a light on many dark corners. Math shows that there is more than one kind of infinity, that some equations can be solved by a formula and others cannot, that any map needs at most four colors. Math can prove that unprovable truths exist. Abstract mathematics might seem as enticing as an empty water glass, but the power of math *is* the abstraction: boiling down ideas to reveal the bones hidden beneath fleshy, irrelevant details.

One area of abstract mathematics is group theory. This is not the theory of those cliques in middle school you never belonged to. Instead, it is the abstraction of dinner party seating arrangements, the organization of crystalline solids, the mysteries of parallel parking, and even dancing to a zydeco band in the swelter of a Louisiana summer.

You see, I wanted to be good at dancing. But it was no fun when I was so terrible at it. Then I thought that maybe I could import my competence in one area, mathematics, to another.

At night, I drew diagrams of the dance steps I had learned, assigned them abstract symbols—A, B, W, X, S, Z, and so on—and worked out mathematically how they combined. In the end, I fit everything onto a couple of pages of tables. This sounds crazy to anyone who's not an expert in group theory, which is to say pretty much everyone; but I found putting it into formal mathematics less panic-inducing than sweating on a dance floor surrounded by twenty other couples with years of two-stepping and foxtrotting experience. In the evenings in my apartment off Jowl Lane, I systematically practiced my tables: $A + B = S$; $S + W = V$; $V + Z = A$...

At the Morgan City Shrimp and Petroleum Festival, named for the two main industries of Morgan City (*not* a local recipe), I mustered the courage to dance with three different women. Up on stage, a ten-year-old accordion prodigy dressed all in white was leading a Cajun band, while my triumph was to not step on a single toe. When I exited the dance floor, mopping sweat from my brow, Harish gave me a grinning thumbs-up, and Junie said, "See, John? You're catching on!"

"Get any phone numbers?" Harish asked with a grin.

"One small dance step for a man, and so on," I said, still puffing.

The Cajun band had finished, and a gospel group broke into multi-voice harmony. Junie closed her eyes, as if inhaling the lush chords. "That brings me back... When I was a teenager, I sang every Sunday in the choir of my daddy's church. He's a preacher, see."

"So ... do you still go to church?"

She shook her head. "Not as such. That's a bit of a sore spot with my folks. But sometimes when I'm down or have had a long day, I put on some gospel to lift my spirits. Harish sure has to listen to enough of it."

"And I make her listen to bhangra and Bollywood," Harish said. Junie grabbed his hand, and they laughed together. I felt happy, albeit with a drop of bittersweet jealousy.

Sally met with Sam, Melody, and me as the ad hoc steering committee for Physics. "The new dean has sent out a directive to all departments: a top-to-bottom accounting of all time and money spent on research."

The three of us groaned.

"More paperwork. Just what we need," Melody grumbled, plopping her head into her hands.

"According to the dean, 'Paperwork is the life blood of academia,'" Sally reported. "And he says he wants to put resources where they'll be the most effective."

Sam asked Sally, "Can he—Dean Pancake—even read?"

Sally looked thoughtful. "I suppose. But he hired this new assistant, Mari, and mostly she reads to him, at least until he gets antsy."

I almost said, *"He can't spell worth a damn."* But I bit my tongue, reluctant to admit that I had a history with Pancake.

At the Leap Before You Look Institute in Burlap Hall, I found Hubert Biscuit, associate professor of psychology, eating half a thick, wet muffuletta, smelling of pickles and sharp mustard. Hubert cultivated the image of the Southern eccentric. Plump with thin, graying hair, he wore jeans and T-shirts emblazoned with obscure comic book heroes (Buzzardman, the Purple Puma, and The

Nothing). Over that, he wore a worn houndstooth blazer and clipped a tie to his T-shirt.

"Don't I usually see you at the faculty club for lunch?" I asked.

"Oh, hello, John," Hubert said around a mouthful of cold cuts, sliced cheese, and soft white bread. He put down his muffuletta and took off his glasses to wipe them on his T-shirt, which sported the blurred image of Lucy Legz, the world's fastest woman. "I'm avoiding my brother. We're having a spat."

"Your brother?"

"Yes, Humphrey, my twin. He's in English and Literature."

I said to Hubert, "Listen, I was thinking about quantum mechanics and the brain." In truth, I had been dwelling on the splattered bits of Rita, dying on the cold concrete of Pigeon's sub-basement floor. The only way to shake off those memories was to science them into silence.

"Splendid!" cried Hubert. He took a big bite of his muffuletta.

"But I don't really know much about the brain."

"My own specialty is states of consciousness," said Hubert, "and I can tell you, we know both a lot and very little about the brain." He finished his muffuletta, licked mustard from his fingers, and wiped them on his pants. "Let's go back to my office."

Outside, as we strolled beneath the magnolia trees, Hubert said, "When you talked about 'coherent tunneling,' all those particles in the same wave state, I thought, what if we got the brain waves of a group of people all in sync, all in the same state? What would happen then?"

We walked up sandstone steps and into Egas Moniz Hall, a long, slender building housing the psychology department. As we approached Hubert's office, we saw a student waiting: a young woman with well-coiffed hair, heavy lipstick and eyeshadow, cutoff shorts, and a rather tight halter top, hugging a bookbag against her chest.

"Professor Biscuit? I've come for my make-up quiz." She looked down as she spoke.

"Oh, dear, Katie, I lost track of time. Can you come back tomorrow? That's a good girl."

She nodded and slipped down the hallway.

"She's from my Altered States of Consciousness class," he told me. "Popular course. Most students pass, but I take care not to make it too easy, or else I'd never have pretty girls visit me in my office.

"By the way," he said, as he unlocked his door and flicked on the light, "they probably didn't say this in faculty orientation, but you know how some schools have prohibitions against faculty dating students? That's not the case here at Renderville." Hubert plopped himself behind a large desk. "Though I often find myself disappointed with the young women here," he continued. "They seem so fresh and full of potential, but then their immaturity pops up like dandelions: pretty, but easily blown away by the wind." He sighed. "Sorry... My almost-ex-wife is a former student. Another reason I was hiding out at the institute... She's hunting me down with final paperwork to sign, and I am finding it difficult to let go. I suppose I must."

"Your ex, uh, wife was your student?"

"Yes." His body quaked a little. "My first ex-wife was also a former student. Maybe you shouldn't date students, no matter how tempting."

"I'll keep that in mind," I said. "Back to the brain... What do you think will happen if they, uh, get in sync?"

Hubert slid down in his leather chair and folded his fingers in front of him. "Let me confess, I have a side interest in the paranormal. Don't make a face! I don't believe in ghosts, or go to séances, but I do believe strange, unexplained things happen from time to time. You say quantum mechanics is all statistics, and while you also say the observer doesn't affect quantum mechanics, what if—hear me out here—what if on occasion, our minds could, say, bend the statistics? The way a casino might load the dice or weight the roulette wheel. Just enough to make a better guess at thoughts, the future, distant events."

I opened my mouth to object, but then I realized: shifting probabilities were how the probability pump worked—how Hile had won the Nobel Prize; how Ada had miraculously saved her father's life.

"What if," Hubert Biscuit continued, "many minds were all following the same waveform? Coherently, as you say? Could that increase the chances of something happening?"

"Something's always happening" was my inadequate response.

Baka Becker knocked on the door of my lab. "C'mere, John, I want to show you something."

I got up from my bench, where I had been soldering electronics, and followed him down the hall. Although like me, he had only been here a few months, already his lab was so stuffed that it made my father's garage look neat and tidy. "RIKEN let me take my equipment," he said when he noticed me staring. "Actually, they told me to get rid of it, or they would dock my final paycheck to cover junking it."

Baka wiped the gleaming top of his head with a cloth, took off his glasses, and squatted until his eyes were level with a workbench. He gestured for me to do the same. There were two glass cylinders, each a centimeter in diameter, surrounded by huge magnets, fairy-frosted cryostats, and other exotic equipment I could barely guess at.

"What's it do?" I asked.

He pointed out a grain of sand in the left-hand cylinder, then threw a switch. I felt the air crackle with electrical potential, and a bass buzz rose in pitch and intensity into an eardrum-piercing whine. The grain of sand jiggled a little, then was still.

Baka sighed and stood up. The whine faded to silence. "I was hoping to teleport it. After the APS conference, after your talk, I rooted around in the literature on quantum tunneling. In some very obscure Albanian journals, I found allusions to theories treating space like an energy barrier—one that could be tunneled through. The original papers were never published; I can't even find the name of the author. That's why I asked my question at your Leap Lecture. For a while, I've been trying to make this work."

"But no luck?" My heart was beating a little faster, but I was not going to admit that my father was the author of this crazy idea.

Baka bent back down, tapping at the cylinder holding the grain of sand. "Not yet," he admitted. "I was hoping to get it to work, so I could show it to the dean. You know that Dean Pancake is now demanding that we all give presentations and demonstrations of our research projects? Rumor has it he wants to eject people from their labs if he's not impressed." When he said this, I felt a small glacier form in my gut. "Apparently, he heckled the chair of Biology, and threw poo at the chair of Archaeology and Anthropology, didn't let him get a word in." He stood up and sighed again. "I already know I don't have enough power to pull it off. But someone told me there's a nuclear reactor in the bowels of this building ... and that you're rehabilitating it?"

I had in fact slowly mucked out the control room, wearing a hooded hazmat suit while I scraped up gadolinium-laced ooze and scrubbed and painted corroded metal. As far as I could tell, the actual core was still intact and sealed, with a few kilos of fissile material left. Much of it had decayed away in the intervening decades, but I estimated that enough remained to produce tens of kilowatts.

We were well into fall now, so the heat had dissipated when the three waltz-a-teers—Junie, Harish, and I—went to the Gator-n-Oyster Festival over in L'Hôpital Parish.

"I'd skip the oysters," Junie advised as she locked her car and we walked from the parking lot. "I had some my first year here, and I got sick. But if you all want some, go ahead."

For a while, I watched Harish twirl Junie like a gyroscope, as I silently categorized each step from the side. Junie gestured for me to join in, but my shyness kept me rooted. Then Junie broke away from Harish and disappeared into the crowd.

A few minutes later, a tall woman of medium complexion with a cloud of tightly curled brown hair approached. "My friend Junie, she said you're a good dancer, but shy?"

As we danced, I saw in my mind's eye the entries in my math tables flash before me. $V + T = B$. $A + B = S$. $S + W = V$...

"You thinking about something?"

"Huh? Oh, just concentrating on dancing. I'm still, uh, learning."

"Well, you're not bad, not at all." Junie's friend had leaned in close to speak in my ear over the music, and I could feel moist warmth radiating off her body as she brushed against me.

When the band—The Cajun Crusaders—finished, I asked if she wanted to get something to eat. She said she was meeting someone, but thanked me for the dance.

I met up with Harish and Junie. "You looked like you were having fun," Junie said.

"Yeah, but I never got her name."

"Actually, she's got a boyfriend, I think. But it was fun to dance, right?"

To get my mind off the sting of yet another universe closing off to me, I explained about using group theory to help with my dancing. Harish threw me an incredulous look, while Junie laughed. "That sounds *so* John to me."

"I wasn't sure if I should admit it."

"It's a bit different," Junie said, "but it's not like you're confessing to a murder or being secretly married or anything. You *haven't* murdered anyone, have you?"

After we finished our jambalaya and fried okra, I heard the voices of a gospel choir. "You want to go listen?" I asked, adding, "I find I'm sometimes surprised how much I like gospel and church music."

"You asked me about going to church, but I never asked back," Junie said as we walked toward the pavilion. "If you go to church, I mean. I assumed you don't, just because, well, a lot of scientists don't go to church. But then again, some do." She paused, then said, "I made complicated what I meant to be a simple question, though I know it can be delicate for some folk: You go to church? You a believer?"

"Not as such," I said, "though I'm finding, if I get invited, I often go." I told her about Uwe's Grandmere and going with her and Harold to church. I did not bring up Ada.

We reached the outskirts of the crowd. We listened to the DeWayne Family Singers wax lyrical about how Jesus loved us all, and when the next group, Zydeco Zyncopation, came on, Junie and Harish danced some more. I asked a woman to dance, but she said, "Sorry, got a blister."

As we drove back, Harish turned around and said, "You're awfully quiet; you doing some math in your head?" And I could only say, "Something like that."

Soon, my turn to present my research to the dean came. I brought the apparatus that I'd had Emmy build and talked about supertunneling. In fact, I had wanted to bring Emmy, thinking to showcase a promising grad student, but that was shot down. "The dean of inhumanities is reluctant to waste research on students," his assistant, a severely dressed young Asian woman, told me. "Students are only here for a few years, then they leave, and we lose those skills and knowledge."

"That's the whole point of a university," I said. "To teach students skills and knowledge they can take away and apply elsewhere. You know, for the good of society."

"But the dean is concerned with the good of the college," she told me, and when I opened my mouth to argue, she added, "and it's his opinion that counts."

So, by myself, I wheeled the apparatus on a cart into the dean's spacious office, which was nearly as large as my entire lab, full of dark, polished furniture. The air thick was with humidity—I felt like I was in a giant coffeepot—as I gave my prepared speech. Dean Pancake sat in an enormous chair, his back to me the whole time, tossing a baseball into the air over and over. When I finished and asked if he had any questions, he just kept tossing the ball into the air, a perfect parabolic motion. For a while, I wondered if he would throw it at me. When nothing happened, I just left.

I hadn't thought any more about Hubert Biscuit's idea, but he showed up at my office with a sheaf of papers in his hand. "I've got my IRB proposal ready," he said. When I looked blank, he told me any experiments on animals or humans had to be approved by the Institutional Review Board.

I wanted to say physicists seldom experimented on animals or humans, but instead I asked, "Approval of what experiments?"

He showed me the documents. The proposed experiment was "remote send-ing." A person or group of people would attempt to send a randomly chosen message to someone across campus. Comparisons would be done between single senders and receivers, versus multiple senders and receivers, and the latter with and without with synchronized brain waves. "People have tried multiple senders before, like Charles Tart at UC Davis," Biscuit said, "but no one has tried to synchronize brain waves before." He pointed at the experimental protocols. "Notice the control groups. Control groups are very important, as you physicists also know."

I flipped through the pages. "How do you synchronize the brain waves?"

"*We* will synchronize the brain waves with a modified EEG device." He pointed to a certain paragraph. "That's where you come in. I need you to build EEG electrodes that both detect and send electrical signals." He saw the look on my face. "A very gentle signal," he added. "Surely that's a cakewalk for you."

I thought that compared to other things, building complicated electronics was by far the easier thing.

"How long will it take to get approved?" I asked, hoping it would be several months, leaving me free to focus on other things.

"Hard to say, but the dean is on the IRB, and he loves it. When I presented it to him, you know, as part of his review of research programs, he gave me a one-monkey standing ovation."

"Hmph," I said. "Not the ringing endorsement I'd be looking for."

I felt bad about being a third wheel at festivals with Junie and Harish, even though it blunted the blade of my loneliness. I was going to bow out of the next festival, tell Junie I should go on my own. But as the weekend approached, we had three days of heavy rain, as if the Mississippi had moved a hundred miles west and was pouring directly into Mouffettenoyee Parish.

"It will be just a field of mud," Junie told me over the phone. "We'd all sink up to our hips. Why don't you come over for dinner this weekend? Harish and I are having a few friends over."

I arrived to find that "a few friends" was Junie's travel agent, Charla, a petite white woman with mousy-brown hair. I glanced at Harish, who was trying hard to keep a grin off his face, which only confirmed my suspicion. Harish asked, "Want some wine? Or would you prefer beer?"

"Just a sip of wine."

"I know you're not a big drinker, and that's okay," Junie said as Harish carefully measured out the dark liquid. "Charla here isn't a drinker, either."

"What do you drink?" I asked.

She looked as trapped and miserable as I felt. "Dr. Pepper, mostly," she said in a small voice.

"Charla's shy like you, John," Junie said. "Maybe even more so."

"But if you're a travel agent, you have to talk to people all the time, right?" I asked.

"That's different," Charla said. "It's my job."

"And you have to lecture to all those students," Harish pointed out.

"It's like Charla said. I guess introversion is contextual."

Dinner was smoked pork in a thick red-eye gravy, though not in the massive portions served at Uwe's cousin's house, and on the side was some wild rice and a spinach salad with a tart dressing. Dessert was sweet potato pie. "I bought this at the store. I'm not much of a baker," Junie confessed.

As we sat in the living room afterwards, drinking Community Coffee, Junie said, "John here's been going to festivals with us and learning how to dance. He's gotten pretty good."

"Hey, maybe you two could go sometime," Harish said. I wondered if they had rehearsed these lines.

If so, Junie hadn't done her research. "I'm too much of a klutz to dance," Charla said, looking down. "I have two left feet."

I made a point of looking at her feet. "Looks like left and right to me," I said, trying to make a joke. She smiled feebly.

"I'm sure if John could learn, so could you," Harish said. "What was it you said you used to improve your dancing, John?"

I quickly lied, "Practice," but at the same time, Harish said, "Oh, yeah: math."

"Math?" said Charla, eyes widening as if someone had put her fingers in a vise. "I'm no good at math. Not like a professor, like you."

"So, what do you do for fun?" I asked to change the subject.

"Oh! I like to crochet." She paused, and her eyes had a faraway look, as if she were daydreaming about crocheting. Then her attention was back in the room. "What about you? What do you do for fun? Besides dancing."

I paused, realizing dancing was the most normal thing I did. I was wracking my brain for something else passably normal, when Harish leaned forward and said, "John here's rebuilding a nuclear reactor."

Maybe if Harish had said I had a side gig as a serial killer, Charla's face might have looked more horrified. I quickly said, "It's a research reactor from decades ago. I'm just trying to make sure it's safe."

"You get it working yet?" Harish asked, unaware of Junie glaring at him.

"Um, yeah, I actually pulled out a control rod today and got about a kilowatt of power, and I'm preparing for a regulatory inspection... But that's not really that interesting. What kind of things do you crochet, Charla?" I asked.

"Pot holders," she said, not quite looking at me. She bit her lips while considering for a moment. "Mostly pot holders."

After that, the evening limped along to its conclusion. Charla said she was tired, and I shook her hand good night.

When she was gone, Harish said, "Junie can give you her phone number. I'm sure you can find some things in common."

Junie rolled her eyes. "My man here spends his days looking at feet, so he's no good at reading faces. I'm sorry it didn't work out, John." She gave me a hug, I shook Harish's hand, and then I said good night.

The reactor was finally running. Soon I had it producing twelve kilowatts, and I thought I might get it up to fifty. An inspector from the nuclear regulatory agency stopped by, but it was a surprisingly brief visit—or perhaps not. As he left, the inspector mentioned knowing one of the regents. In the meantime, I ran power cables up the basement stairs and into Baka's lab. From the joyous look on his face, you'd have thought he'd gotten a twelve-speed bike for Christmas, or maybe a flying pony.

Hubert Biscuit came by my lab and waved some sketches at me and Emmy Shore. "I was given a design to do exactly what we need. It turns out the dean has a connection."

My stomach twisted like a trapeze artist when he mentioned the dean. "What is it written in, crayon? Monkey poop? Besides," I said, pointing at Emmy's supertunneling apparatus and her whiteboard listing dozens of materials, "we kinda got our hands full already."

Meanwhile, Emmy was leafing through the blueprints. "Actually, these plans are very clear," she said. "Nothing tricky about them."

"Terrific!" said Hubert. "A good project for an undergraduate. Professor Chant here can show you how."

I said, "Miss Shore is a graduate student, and very skilled with building electrical equipment—even better than me."

"I don't know about that, Professor," Emmy protested, though she looked pleased.

"Well, then, I'll go recruit some volunteers, and you can get to work, young lady," said Hubert, turning to the door.

"When she has time!" I called after him.

Emmy asked me, "What are these for again?"

I made a face and explained, then said, "If they're from Dean Pancake, there's something wrong. Check them again. Please. I'm going to check on the reactor."

We had put a new padlock on the door leading down to the reactor room. The reactor itself was humming. I'd rigged up a recording power meter and saw spikes of up to fifteen kilowatts being drawn.

The only person hooked up to the reactor was Baka, so I went and knocked on his lab door. "John!" he said, looking over his glasses, which were fogged from the humidity. "Just the person I wanted to see! Let me show you something *amazing*." He darted back to his bench.

"How is teleporting sand going?" I asked. "Putting that reactor power to good use?"

He grinned with a hand extended towards his apparatus. "Sand, I can't teleport. But I can..." And he pointed.

I leaned in close and squinted at the leftmost cylinder. Inside, I saw a fly, buzzing in dizzy circles.

"Here we go," Baka said solemnly. The click of a switch, the hum of a transformer, a silver flash of light, and then the fly was in the right-hand cylinder. It lay on its side for moment, but then it twitched and began to buzz and bang against the glass.

I felt slightly dizzy myself. "Wow," I said. "That *is* amazing. What else have you teleported?"

"So far, I can only teleport flies. Dead flies, living flies... Nothing else works."

"Still, even to teleport a fly... Say, do you have IRB approval?"

He adjusted his glasses and looked at me. "What's an IRB?"

At the end of September, Dean Pancake called a meeting of the department chairs in the College of Inhumanities. Since physics didn't have a chair, the ad hoc steering committee had to choose a representative. When I admitted I knew Pancake, Melody and Sam deputized me.

We gathered in the dean's conference room. Pancake, dressed in a suit and tie, sat at the head of a long, polished dark wood table. He had a bottle of syrup at hand, which from time to time he poured into a shot glass and drank. Standing next to him, hands behind her back, was his assistant, dressed in a stark black-and-white outfit.

Around the table were name cards for the chairs and representatives of the departments, indicating where we should sit. I was seated at the end, farthest from Pancake.

"Hello. My name is Mari Hsu, and I am Dean Pancake's assistant. He has given me detailed instructions on what to say."

Pancake nodded and chuffed.

"The dean has reviewed the departments in the College of Inhumanities and put them into three separate ranks." She pointed. The table was divided into four parts, separated by three lines of masking tape. "The highest is the alpha rank, the next is beta, and the last is zeta. Over all of you, of course, is the dean, the super-alpha."

"How were these rankings created?" someone asked.

Mari ignored the question. "The alpha rank has the most privileges. They will have first claim on equipment and lab space, and reduced teaching loads, and the dean has negotiated a discounted menu rate for them at the faculty club."

"The beta rank will have second choice of equipment and lab space. Following the chancellor's goal of Renderville being the most well-administered university in the country, if not the world, the dean is hiring three sub-deans. To pay the salaries of the new sub-deans, most of the secretarial staff in the college has been let go. Beta faculty will take up secretarial duties for faculty in the alpha rank."

A murmur went up around the table, like a low buzzing of bees.

"Last and least is the zeta rank. If there is any lab space left over, zeta faculty can apply to use it. They will have additional teaching duties starting next semester, however, and they will pay a surplus at the faculty club. To further save on costs, janitorial staff have been let go, and zeta faculty will assume their duties, emptying trash, mopping floors, and so on."

With dismay, I looked at the yellow tape marking the physics department, and myself, in zeta.

The table burst into shouting. Dean Pancake chuffed and poured himself a shot of syrup. "He can't do this!" said Dick Cherrystone, chair of Archaeology and Anthropology, seated next to me in the zeta zone. His face was as red as a baboon's butt.

Mari said, "The university lawyers have carefully examined your contracts, and they said we can."

Dean Pancake hooted and slapped the table, as if it were the funniest thing he had ever heard, though of course the joke was on all of us.

Swing Low, Sweet Chariot of the Gods

The next week, all the janitors for the College of Inhumanities were gone. Slipped into each of our mail cubbyholes were our assignments. I had trash and mopping duty for the first floor of physics and the second floor of biology, and would empty wastebaskets for psychology on Wednesdays.

To avoid being seen, on Wednesday I arrived at the university at 6:51 a.m. Soon I was in Egas Moniz Hall, wheeling a large garbage can, keys jingling at my waist. The psychology offices were all dark except one: Hubert Biscuit's. I almost skipped it, but I could not risk it: I didn't have tenure. I knocked, waited two beats, then opened the door.

Hubert Biscuit, sitting behind his desk, was saying, "... just the jani— John! My God, John, they assigned you to psychology? What luck!"

I felt my face grow hot. I had planned to duck in, grab the wastebasket, empty it, and be gone, less than fifteen seconds.

Another person sat off to one side. I blinked.

"John, this is my twin, Humphrey. Associate professor, English and Literature. Hump, this is John Chant from Physics. You know, *zeta rank*," he stage-whispered.

Humphrey Biscuit's face and physique mirrored Hubert's, although they dressed differently: Humphrey wore a lavender button-down shirt, in contrast to Hubert's superhero T-shirt (the Purple Puma), khaki slacks to Hubert's fraying jeans, and black suspenders and no tie, unlike Hubert's clip-on. Both held glasses containing ice and brown liquid. From the sharp smell, it was not iced tea they were drinking at seven in the morning.

"Oh, yes," Humphrey said. He swiveled on his chair. "You told me about this. I wish we could get one for my department."

"I'm sure you could," I said. "It's called a janitor."

"Ah, he retorts!" Humphrey cried. He swung all the way around in his chair, a complete circle. "Tell me, is this your regular day and time? Beryl would love this," he said to Hubert.

"Your imaginary Beryl would," Hubert said with an amused drawl, "but the real one won't give a rat's ass." To me, Hubert said, "Hump has a crush on

Beryl Knaught. You might know her from the institute. He has a thing for unobtainable women."

"Not unobtainable," Humphrey said. "Just out of my league. How about you, John? You're not a lump like us two. Get much yet?"

I ducked my head. "I'll leave you gentlemen to it."

"Oh, pish, ignore Hump, he's drunk. We both are. Well, buzzed, anyway. Been out on the town. My ex finally tracked me down, made me sign the papers. Divorce finalized."

"Divorce number *two*," Humphrey noted.

"Hump is younger than me by ten minutes," Hubert said, "and ever since, he has felt inadequate, taking any chance to swipe at me."

"Well, sorry about the divorce ... er, divorces," I said.

"Don't feel bad for Hubert," Humphrey said, swiveling furiously back and forth on his chair, as if drilling into the floor. "He's already got number three lined up."

Hubert grinned. I goggled at him. "You don't mean that girl, Katie?"

"What—who? Oh, the one you met. God, no! She's a freshman. Please. I've made mistakes in the past, but I've learned my lesson." He gulped from his glass. "Only juniors and seniors from now on."

I started to back out of the office, but Hubert put up a hand. "How is your student coming with the EEG caps?" He was taken aback when I said she hadn't gotten around to them. "Why on earth not?"

"School, her research with me, and having a life."

Hubert blew a raspberry. "Having a life is overrated," he said. "Listen, I got a note saying we got expedited approval from the IRB. Apparently, the dean made a push for us. I heard he's favoring experiments on humans over animal experimentation. Lucky, huh?"

Later, I found Emmy Shore sitting at her bench in my lab, staring at the wall. "Anything wrong?" I asked. Normally, she sat down and immediately got to work.

She shook herself, as if freeing herself from the cobwebs of a daydream. "Sorry, Professor." Then she confessed she had heard some disturbing rumors, that the Dean of Inhumanities was looking to shut down some labs, and to rent out those spaces to start-up companies or local private K-12 schools. "I also heard he doesn't like physics." Her voice faltered a little. "Do you think he might target us?"

It would be a very Pancake thing to do, but not wanting to worry her with speculation, I told her truthfully, "I don't know anything. I understand your concern. All we can do now is to keep working. If we produce results, there's less reason to take away the lab."

She relaxed when I told her this. "I built a couple of those EEG caps Professor Biscuit wanted," she said, gesturing to a pair of heavily wired headsets on the bench.

"I hope that will satisfy him," I said.

"Well, he's a lot less scary than the dean," she said, and smiled when I laughed.

Noticing we both were discombobulated by the swirling rumors, I changed the subject and asked why she had chosen LUSR for grad school. She shrugged. "I'm comfortable here. I live at home, save money."

She told me her brothers—Elmont, Edwin, and Eamon—all went to LUSR, had been on the football team, despite offers from LSU in Baton Rouge and other universities. In high school, her brothers had each been in the model rocket club, and Bobby Litsteen had been the club advisor.

"Litsteen? As in, Professor Litsteen from physics, our department?" I asked, incredulous. He struck me as grasping and self-centered.

She nodded. "He helped them, spent a lot of time with them on the rockets, taught them how to be safe, even gave them tips on applying to college." She stretched like a cat, then picked up a soldering iron. "Well, I guess I'd better get back to it."

For a few minutes, I watched her work in silence. As little wisps rose from the soldering iron, I thought that I had misread Litsteen. I wondered who or what else I was misreading, too.

Junie called a couple of days later. "I hear your dean is really shaking up the place."

"He sure is shaking something. I'm just not sure what."

"Listen, the real reason I'm calling is to apologize for that evening with my friend Charla. I'm sorry it was such a disaster."

"It's okay. Charla seems like a nice person. I don't think we have much in common, though."

"Uh-huh, I know. It's just, you always look like you expect that an asteroid is about to crash into the Earth. Harish and me, we hoped you might hit it off with her."

"I appreciate you looking out for me," I said. "It's strange. I mean, in a way, this is my dream job, my destiny. Yet I feel split, like I'm in a quantum superposition, half ecstatic to be a physics professor, half in despair, because... Well, you said it."

"Don't take this the wrong way, but it's partly 'cause of remarks like that that you aren't getting many dates."

Then she said very seriously, "There's something else I wanted to ask you. I remember you said when you're invited out dancing, or to church, you usually go. So, we were thinking to invite you."

"Dancing? Or to church? I thought you didn't go."

"Not to regular church, not to a Christian church, though I don't have a problem with those, what with my daddy and all. This is a different kind of church. I don't talk about it much, 'cause it's different, but you seem more open-minded than most."

I wasn't sure what I was supposed to say to that. Junie finally said very gently, "It's the Church of the Flying Saucer."

With effort, I turned my snort of laughter into an aborted sneeze. "'Scuse me! I got a tickle up my nose." I put down the phone and blew my nose into a tissue before picking it up again. "I haven't heard of that church before."

"Well, we do keep a low profile, on account that people confuse it with crazy space cults, where people kill themselves and such. This church isn't one of those. Also, it's over in Lafayette. That's where I met Harish: in church. Anyway, you remember back when I told you about *Iron Genius*, how I've always been interested in such things?"

"Oh. Yes. Um... So, how does your family feel about this ... interest? Or do they know?"

"They think I'm crazy. Daddy tells me all the time how he's praying for me. It's kind of hard when your own family doesn't see you as you."

"Oh, *that* I get," I said.

The trees were turning red and orange in late October when I brought over to Hubert Biscuit's lab two EEG caps Emmy had built. The design, which looked like an inverted metal colander bristling with wires, didn't require electrodes to be glued to the scalp.

Hubert had recruited a couple of undergraduates from his Altered States of Consciousness class to test the caps. I couldn't help but notice they were both pretty, petite young women who favored heavy lipstick. I also noted that Hubert's three grad students, Lana, Lorri, and Leesa, were stamped from the same mold as the undergrads, only a few years older.

Lana, who had done a brief course on EEG at a hospital in Baton Rouge, placed the bulky caps on first one undergrad, then the other. "It tickles," said the first.

"Those are the electrodes," I said. "You might feel a slight tingling. It's perfectly harmless."

"It makes you look like a robot gal from the future, Bethany," the second undergrad said to her.

"Same for you, Brittany," said Bethany. She giggled. "We should go out like this for Halloween. Say, Professor, can we borrow these?"

Hubert smiled and patted Bethany on the hand. "Sorry, my dears, they are valuable equipment."

Lorri connected cables to the caps, and Leesa switched on the analog-to-digital converter. On the EEG recorder screen, we watched the signals swing up and down to shaky and independent rhythms. Hubert nodded with gravitas at Lorri, who pressed a button.

"Ooh, I feel that!" said Brittany.

"It feels kinda nice, actually," said Bethany.

Soon their brain waves were moving up and down in sync. "Looks like we're on our way to making scientific history!" exclaimed Hubert.

"Sure looks like it," I said. Privately, I wondered what kind of history it would be.

After we finished, as I was heading out of the building, an office door opened, and a portly man with a Lincoln beard thrust a wastebasket at me. "You missed this," he grunted.

It took me a second to respond. "Uh, sorry..."

He shook the wastebasket. "You can take it now, *zeta*."

I raised a hand and kept walking. "I'll come for it in the morning."

From behind me, I heard, "I'm reporting this to the dean!"

I marched to Wunderkine Hall, went into the main office, and stopped before Sally's desk, my pulse jackhammering in my temples. Sally had escaped the administrative purge because her part-time work in the dean's office kept it from falling into utter chaos. "Say, Sally, that lawyer friend of yours—"

"Yes?"

"Do you think you could ask her to look at my contract? Can the dean really make us take out the garbage and stuff? I know the university lawyers looked at it, but..."

"But you suspect the university lawyers might be just a bunch of good ol' boys in bow ties who were fraternity brothers with Chancellor Hebert? Sorry, my friend doesn't do employment law." Sally paused for a minute, as if I might be inspired to ask other questions about her friend, but I was in such a dark mood that I just wanted to cheer myself up as best I could with integral calculus.

The next Sunday, Junie picked me up and drove us down the four-lane highway to Lafayette. When I kept looking nervously over my shoulder, she asked me why. I told her about the state trooper pulling over Uwe, me, and Harold. She wrinkled her nose. "John, how many times did you get pulled over in Seattle? Zero? Thought so. In Seattle, I got pulled over *six times* for 'driving while Black.' *Six.* You have no idea."

"Isn't it worse here?"

Junie glanced at me sideways. "At least here, they don't pretend."

We drove on in silence most of the rest of the way, arriving fifteen minutes before the service started. Harish, who lived in Lafayette, met us at the door.

The inside had been remodeled to look like a church from the seventies, all wood paneling, though the pulpit resembled, without irony, a small flying saucer. The congregation consisted of about forty people. They did not have a formal minister, no prayers or a liturgy. Instead, they took turns each Sunday giving a talk.

This week, two people spoke. The first was a man in his early thirties, vaguely Hispanic, with a prominent ring in his ear. He recited ancient Sumerian legends about gods, or possibly alien astronauts, bringing knowledge to humanity. "Scientists—and I know there are a few of you here—exhort us to appreciate the wonder of the universe, and to see ourselves as a small part of a bigger picture. That's the same story we're telling here: humility about ourselves. Most people assume humans picked ourselves up by our bootstraps, but it's not true."

The second speaker addressed the topic, "Was Confucius from Outer Space?"

"It's part of a series," Junie whispered in my ear.

The speaker, a thin white man with snowy hair, summarized Confucius's life and teachings, placing them in the context of other ancient prophets. Mohammed: definitely not an alien. The Buddha: definitely an alien. Jesus could go either way, though the miracles, if taken seriously, would put him in the alien camp. As Junie and Harish listened raptly, I found my thoughts wandering. I never did learn if Confucius was an alien or not.

At the coffee hour afterwards, Junie introduced me to people, and they asked me about being a physicist. One fellow said he had worked out some ideas about the star drive aliens used, and could he talk to me about it sometime? I said it wasn't my area of expertise.

Harish steered a couple of young women towards me, one white and blonde, the other Asian with a purple streak in her black hair. The blonde, who was tall and wore heels, making her tower over even me, asked, "Did you see the show about the alien autopsy?"

"I missed that one," I said. Then, unable to resist, I added, "But I did catch one where Hollywood special effects artists showed how someone could fake an alien autopsy."

She made a sour face, as if biting into a lemon. "Oh, that's just part of the cover-up!" she exclaimed.

Afterwards, we went out to lunch in Lafayette. Harish asked me if I wanted to invite either of those young women. I declined.

The restaurant's specialty was fried shrimp, smothered in a heavy white sauce with smaller shrimp. With it, we drank sweet tea. "What do you think?" Harish asked.

"Tasty, but if I ate like this all the time, I'd put on fifty pounds."

"No, silly," Junie said. "He means our church."

I was quiet for a while, probably for too long. "The people seemed really nice."

"Some of the folk, maybe they don't believe so much in UFOs, per se," Junie said defensively, "but they like the message. And the message is, if our ancestors came from light-years away and helped seed us, it makes all our squabbles seem petty and small."

"You think we have alien ancestors?" I blurted out.

"Well, I don't *know* that," she said, an edge of irritation in her voice, "but think about it. The Bible says how God led the Israelites in a pillar of cloud by day, and a pillar of fire by night. Doesn't that sound just like a rocket? And how on the mountain of God, there was the sound of many mighty trumpets: doesn't that sound like a rocket?"

I agreed it did. "But do you think UFOs are still actively visiting Earth, and the government is covering it up?"

Junie and Harish exchanged glances. "Well," Junie said, "since the US government has been gaslighting Black folks since forever, I would have no trouble believing they're lying about this. But just because they *would* lie doesn't mean there *is* something to lie about."

Taking her hand, Harish said, "This is one of the few things we disagree about. Junie is more about the ancient astronauts, but is dubious of whether UFOs are here today, while I'm certain they're here and visiting, and the government is definitely covering it up." He kissed her fingers tenderly. "We joke about being a 'mixed' couple."

"I don't think the government is competent enough to keep such a big secret," Junie said, smirking at Harish. "Besides, how did we get here? How did we all of a sudden leave the trees and make fire and stone tools? Someone must've taught us. Someone gave us our big brains."

Harish rolled his eyes. "But what about the DNA evidence, hon? We're ninety-eight percent chimpanzee."

When I shuddered, Junie put a hand on Harish's arm. "John's a bit sensitive to the topic of chimps, dear."

Everyone in the College of Inhumanities, or at least all the zeta departments in the college, was on edge, waiting for the dean's threat to close unproductive or unloved labs. (You know from personal experience how it feels to have your lab unfairly shut down.) We might have said we were waiting for the other shoe to drop, only Dean Pancake seldom wore shoes.

Instead, the dean came to the Leap Before You Look Institute and looked on as his assistant, Mari, cleared her throat. "Dean Pancake has a new initiative, very much in the spirit of the institute, which he believes can bring additional financial resources to the college." She paused dramatically, then explained: Pancake wanted to partner with local tribal casinos, to host and place bets on middle school and high school science fairs.

There were a few coughs, and someone laughed nervously. Mari Hsu looked straight at Dick Cherrystone, chair of Archaeology and Anthropology. "The dean believes the institute has unique connections to move this exciting possibility forward."

"You've gotta be shitting me," Cherrystone said, and I probably don't have to explain the hostile tone in his voice. "Yes, I've become good friends with Chairman Bullrunning of the Wet Creek band. But that's because I've shown him respect, helped to repatriate indigenous remains and artifacts."

"This is a chance for a zeta department to show its worth," Mari said, her voice polished steel. Behind her, Pancake chuffed and slapped a hand on his head.

"Bill would laugh at me if I brought him such a proposal. Betting on *children*? He would never speak to me again."

"Once a zeta, forever a zeta," Mari said, in a tone that would make an iceberg reach for a jacket.

Pancake hooted and spun on his chair.

Two days later Baka dragged me into his lab. "I can send flies all the way across the lab, four meters," he said. "I can send a lot of flies, all at once." He pointed to a large glass-enclosed chamber, buzzing with tiny winged bodies.

"Butterflies, bees, ants...?"

"No, they all explode. I can only teleport members of the order Diptera. But..." He gestured me towards another, smaller chamber. Inside was a huge cockroach with a dark amber carapace—they grew large in Louisiana, popping up at inopportune moments in my kitchen—scrabbling horribly at the glass. Baka theatrically pushed a large red button, and with a flash of light, the cockroach disappeared.

"Seems like a complicated way to kill a cockroach," I said. "I mean, you can step on them, and they still manage to run away, but even so..."

"Wait, wait," he said. He glanced at his watch, then pushed the button again. Another flash of light, and the cockroach reappeared.

Baka stood up. "Right now, I can send cockroaches—but not just cockroaches; anything—thirty seconds into the future. At first, it was just five seconds, so I think I can get it even longer."

"Okay, that is amazing," I said. "Can you send them into the past?"

He shook his head. "I worked it out. The amount of power needed to go even a few minutes into the past would be greater than the entire output of the sun." He tapped on the glass. "Next I'm trying mice."

"Don't forget the IRB," I said.

For Thanksgiving, my sister invited me home, but I declined. "Travel is terrible that week, and I have a bunch of projects to do," I told her.

"Ah, so what do you have on the ol' Bunsen burner?"

In fact, I'd been assigned to clean and wax the hallway floors in Egas Moniz Hall over Thanksgiving break. To Jane, I said, "Oh, you know how it is... It looks promising, until it doesn't."

"I get it. You don't want to jinx it."

"Exactly," I lied.

Lucky for me, Uwe invited me to join him and Harold for Thanksgiving at the family homestead. Grandmere greeted me like a prodigal son. After kissing my cheek, she said, "Why haven't you joined me and Harold for church lately? We've missed you."

"I keep inviting him," Harold put in.

"Work's been so exhausting that I catch up on sleep on Sundays," I said. It was even partly true.

The Thanksgiving spread was even more expansive than when I had visited before—three turkeys, two of them fried and one smoked, plus ham, slow-smoked brisket, whole mountains of mashed potatoes with oceans of red-eye gravy, stacks of corn dripping with butter, piles of greens cooked with bacon and a splash of vinegar... Afterwards, two of Uwe's aunts led everyone in singing some gospel tunes. I mouthed along silently, as I had a terrible singing voice. Then we had dessert.

On the drive back, I fell asleep and dreamed I was sinking into a vast pumpkin pie, unable to get a grip on the whipped cream. When a vast hand came out of the sky, I thought someone, maybe God, was rescuing me. Then I saw thick black hair on the back of the hand, and far away yet still enormous, Pancake's grimacing face.

I didn't think my dream was any sort of premonition, but the week after Thanksgiving, the dean announced that the college had a new slogan. Wrapping our buildings and halls were banners proclaiming, *The student is our customer, and the customer is always right.*

After one of my less successful lectures on Gauss's law, which left the pre-med students confused, I went back to my office, dejected, only to find Hubert waiting for me.

"Hey, John. Listen, for our experiment, I got a bunch of volunteers from the football team. It won't even cost us anything. They'll do it for class credit."

I frowned as I unlocked my door. "But they won't learn anything."

"Ah, but *we* will learn from *them*." He followed me in and plopped down in a chair. "We need those caps built. I've been meeting with the dean regularly, and I tell you, he is keen on this experiment. I convinced him to agree to reduce your teaching load next semester, back down to two courses, if we can get this moving forward."

I frowned. "Well, Emmy's made a lot of progress with her supertunneling trials—"

"Splendid!" He stood up. "Gotta go. Lana will be waiting patiently outside my office, so we can discuss experimental protocols. She's remarkably bright, for such a pretty girl."

I had a sour feeling in my stomach. "Wait... Why is Dean Pancake so interested?"

Hubert shrugged. "Maybe he wants credit. It doesn't matter. If you play ball with the dean, you can get a reduced teaching load."

His words lit an incandescent fury within me, or maybe it was heartburn from the barely digestible sandwich I'd made for myself. "The last time I played ball with Pancake," I said, barely restraining myself, "I got a concussion, and then exiled."

I was still a novice professor. For my first set of final exams, I tried to construct questions to test how deeply students understood the material. Wisely, I showed my drafts to Melody Bencik. She read them over and handed them back with a sigh.

"Don't be clever on a final," she said. "It'll be wasted and will bring only confusion, disappointment, and heartbreak. Make your finals straightforward, boring variations on problems they've encountered before. At this point, they're exhausted."

I followed her advice. I had imagined that my students would look back and marvel at the new insights and mental dexterity they had gained. Instead, the exams revealed the material through my students' eyes: haphazard piles of random facts, accompanied by equations as incomprehensible and context-free (in their understanding) as a magical incantation. The grad students did a little better, and I was pleased that Emmy was the top scorer in my math methods class, though even she made a few errors.

"Don't worry about the EEG caps," Emmy told me. "I have free time over the holiday break. I talked to Mr. Mick, and he'll help out some."

I was ready for a break. My first semester of teaching had been more stressful and far weirder than I expected, leaving me wrung out like an old dishrag. Jane suggested we rendezvous at my father's house for Christmas. While the family home held a maelstrom of emotions for me, I knew it would be good to see Jane.

The day before I was to leave, I checked the reactor. The data recorder showed a lot of power being drawn. I went up to Baka Becker's lab. "How's the teleportation going?" I asked. "Can you send anything other than flies?"

"Oh, hi, John," he said cheerily. "Still only flies, though I can send several hundred at a time. And I can send mice sixteen minutes into the future. Do you think I should try a dog next?"

"Please don't," I said.

"I have something new," he said. "Let me show you." He waved me over to a workbench, where huge coils hummed and radiated heat.

I glanced around his lab. It was more crowded than before, which was saying a lot. While previously it had been mostly beat-up junk, salvaged from his RIKEN days, the additional equipment looked new and top-of-the-line. In particular, I noticed a high-end neon-krypton laser from Newport that I knew cost over a hundred grand.

"Your start-up funds cover all this?" I admit I felt jealous.

"Mmm? No, I, um, I'm—"

"I noticed you're drawing a lot of power from the reactor," I said.

"Yeah, thanks so much for that! I wouldn't have gotten nearly so far without it. Now listen to this." Baka turned a dial, and static poured out of a small loudspeaker. After a couple of minutes, he cocked his head and said, "There! Did you catch that?"

"Catch what?"

"It's a radio transmission from another universe. You know, like in the many-worlds hypothesis."

I closed my eyes and listened again. In the midst of the static, there could have been some words, maybe a woman's voice, tense, clipped. But I could have been imagining it.

I opened my eyes. "Are they speaking English?"

Baka glared at me. "Yes! It doesn't seem that different from our universe. For this one..." He checked a dial. "Hmm, yes, with this one, the main difference, as far as I can tell, is that Jimmy Carter served two terms as president. In another one, there are references to some terrorist attack that traumatized the nation."

"Can you talk to them?"

Baka looked crestfallen. "I've been trying, but no response so far."

"Keep at it. And if you get through, wish them a merry Christmas."

Back home—whatever *that* meant—my father said, "Good to see you," while not quite looking at me. He was distracted by the vortex of Jane's kids as they ran in and out of every room, chased by the au pair. Jane herself had padlocked our father's garage laboratory to keep her children away from the dangerous electrical equipment.

Despite that, Christmas morning, my father gave each of his grandchildren, even the five-year-old, soldering irons. "It turns out they don't sell chemistry sets for children anymore," he said to me and Jane.

"For good reason!" Jane said. "John almost burned the house down, remember?"

"That's wasn't me." I pointed to our father. "That was *him*. He mixed up acids and bases or something."

"It wasn't acids and bases, it was something else," my father said. "Besides, we learn from our mistakes."

"In which case, we must all be geniuses," I said.

Jane watched her two oldest kids fence with soldering irons as if they were lightsabers. "God, this brings back memories... Not the good kind."

At three o'clock on Christmas Day, we ate dry turkey with mushy green beans and a thin gravy. "Still, it's home-cooked, right?" Jane asked. She leaned towards me. "Dad mostly eats microwave meals these days; look in the freezer. Billy-boy, do *not* draw on the walls with a green crayon!" she shouted. "No, not with a purple one either!"

"You seem subdued, John," my father said. "I remember that my first year of teaching was a shock."

"You don't know the half of it," I said, declining seconds of soggy stovetop stuffing. "I might as well tell you who I ran into."

Jane blurted out, "That girl Becky you liked?" When I frowned, she added, "You never know."

"Pancake," I said to my father. "Your chimpanzee, Pancake. But get this: now he's my boss. The dean of the College of Inhumanities. And he's still out to get me. Some things never change."

"College of *what?*" my father asked.

Later that evening, after Jane's kids had gone to bed and the au pair went outside to smoke a cigarette ("the only time she allows herself to have one," Jane told me), Jane and I put on coats and drifted into the backyard. When we were kids, we could see brilliant stars on a dark night, but with the new houses built behind us, the sky was the gray of a turned-off TV screen.

"Should I stop by her grave?" I asked.

In the distance, a dog barked.

"We did on the way in," Jane finally said. "Wanted to introduce her to the kids. She wasn't talkative. By my estimate, she's about ninety-nine percent—"

"Dead," I put in. "Ninety-nine percent dead."

"We didn't stay long. The kids were antsy and didn't understand what it meant."

"Remember when we buried her out here?" I asked.

"I also remember when you dug for fossils and broke the sewer line. And wasn't there some little girl you got a crush on?"

"She moved away the next day. I've always wondered about her. As for the sewer, I thought it was the bone of a huge dinosaur."

She turned her face up the sky, hunting in vain for the glint of a star. "Do you think it was all real? That we remember it right?"

"I don't know. A lot of things don't feel real. Today, it felt like we were actors pretending to be us: me, you, dad." I kicked at clod of earth. "But it had to have been real. The pain and grief I remember, the loneliness... That was real."

"Yeah. I'm sorry I wasn't a better big sister." Her breath made white clouds in the night air. "And I bet Pancake is being a real dick, isn't he?"

When we reached the back door, Jane paused. "You know, when you asked if you should stop by her grave, my first thought wasn't mom. I thought you meant Ada."

I don't know if Ada was ever really mine, but my sister was perceptive as always. After Christmas, I did not go straight back to Louisiana, but instead detoured to Montana. I had located Ada's grave.

Snow blanketed the vast Montana landscape. I drove in silence; if the radio played a song about love and loss, or even one I had listened to with Ada, I might crash the car or spontaneously combust in a supernova wiping out all life on Earth. Yet driving cross-country, I also found peace and calm. Like a sleeping colossus, the scale and the beauty of the land dwarfed both me and my griefs. Here, my life and losses that seemed so huge to me were only tiny pieces of infinity.

At the cemetery, I parked at the bottom of a slight slope. The snow crunched beneath my steps. I scanned the gravestones until I found hers, crowned with white. Hers didn't say much, and anyway, how could a slab of granite express the bright, brilliant, beautiful spark of light that she had been?

For a long while, I tried to imagine myself in her presence. I took from my wallet the picture of Ada and me in our Halloween costumes. After brushing off the snow, I put the photo on top of her gravestone and held it in place with a couple of small rocks.

"I can't go on comparing everyone to you," I told her. "I can't keep imagining what you would say about everything. I don't want to let you go, but I have to. Even though no one will ever measure up to you."

I was wrong, but at the time, I didn't know it.

The Dissent of Man

When I returned to Louisiana shortly before New Year's, I learned I had missed a riot—a riot for which I was blamed.

Students in my Electricity and Magnetism class had been unhappy with their grades. "I needed an A-plus in that course," one student told a reporter from the *Renderville Revealer*, "if I'm going to get into a top medical school. But Professor Chant dismissed my needs; he said he doesn't even *give* A-pluses!" Then the student quoted Dean Pancake's slogan: "'The student is our customer, and the customer is always right.' So, that means my answers are always right, right?" he concluded with stunning logic.

According to the article, a crowd of twenty or so students had stood outside Wunderkine Hall and chanted, *"Our hopes and dreams won't fade! Give us a better grade!"* for half an hour, and set a small pile of physics textbooks on fire. They tried to overturn one of the cars in the faculty parking lot, but none of them had mastered the principles of leverage, and they gave up. As I read the article, I wondered if similar things had happened in Baka's alternate universes.

Uwe called to invite me to a New Year's Eve celebration with his family. I told him he was very kind, but that I wanted to be alone.

"Hold on," Uwe said. "Harold wants to say something."

"Hello? John?" Harold said, getting on the line. "You gotta come."

"I'm not just feeling it."

"Grandmere will be disappointed."

"Well, I'm disappointed in myself, all the time."

When the phone rang again, I thought it might be Uwe, given his German persistence. Instead, I heard Mari Hsu's voice. "The dean is very unhappy with you. You caused a riot. Those students are our customers."

"So, give them a refund," I snapped.

There was a long pause. "That's a good idea. I'll run it by the dean." She paused again. "Of course, it would have to come out of *your* salary."

When the first day of the new semester came, I planned to start my Nuclear Physics course by recounting some of my personal adventures with accelerators and reactors, suitably edited. *"We learn from our mistakes,"* I would say, *"and boy, have I learned a lot."* In the movie theater of my mind, the class laughed heartily.

But before I could charm a single student, I was startled to find, standing outside the glass doors to Wunderkine Hall, a fat, balding orangutan, dressed in military green. The orangutan held up a hand and made a gesture. "I work here," I said. But it would not let me through, only pointing at a patch on the shoulder of its jacket. The patch read PRIME-APE, the letters circling what I first thought was a squadron of UFOs leaking fluid, only to later realize they were pancakes soaked in syrup.

One of the glass doors pushed open, and I spotted Sally. "He needs your school ID," she said softly.

The orangutan put my ID into its mouth and sucked for a while, as if it could taste my veracity, before returning it, slick with saliva.

Inside, Sally had waited for me. It was the first time I had ever seen her look flustered. "What the hell?" I said.

Sally continued to speak in a low voice, though I doubted the orangutan outside could hear her. "The dean used the riot, though nothing really happened, as an excuse to increase security. He recruited from that Ape Angel Former Experimental Animal Rescue Haven. Chancellor Hebert questioned that decision, but the dean accused him of 'speciesism,' so the chancellor backed down. I guess he's nervous about another scandal so soon."

The Prime-Apes quickly became a disheartening presence on campus. They were empowered to stop anyone, student, staff, or faculty, and demand an ID. They searched through backpacks, frequently confiscating food as well as the occasional textbook they deemed to "slander the first apes." Humans were categorized as "second apes," or latecomers. The Prime-Apes patrolled the halls, entered classrooms and labs, and disrupted experiments.

"And I had just succeeded in sending a fly to another universe!" Baka complained to me.

"What if you accidentally transmit a disease that universe has no immunity against?" I asked.

Baka slapped his forehead. "Ooh, I didn't think about that!"

On a rainy Saturday, we gathered the football team volunteers into a small auditorium in Wunderkine Hall. Emmy Shore had them sign release forms.

Across campus in Egas Moniz Hall, a similar group of young men from the basketball team were getting organized by Hubert's students Lana, Lorri, and Leesa.

The EEG caps were laid out in a shiny row up front, bristling with electronics, looking like a squadron of flying saucers. One by one, Emmy and Lorri began to place the caps on the heads of the volunteers. When they began cracking loud jokes and jostling around, Emmy shushed them firmly. She was always soft-spoken with me, but with these young men, her voice took on a hardness I hadn't heard before.

While they worked, Hubert told me about control runs he and his students had done: mass remote sending experiments without EEG caps. "Consistent with random chance, as I expected," he said.

"What are your error bars on that? The standard deviation?"

"Ah, yes, you physicists and your 'good statistics' and 'reproducible data.'" Hubert smiled blandly. "Erstmann thinks that as a psychologist, I must suffer from 'physics envy'—as if that were an official diagnosis from the DSM. I've long suspected that it's really the obverse: that physicists, mathematicians, astronomers, and chemists suffer from *psychology* envy. Because we psychologists deal with the fundamental issue: what is it like to be human?"

He was smirking at me when the doors to the auditorium flew open, and a dozen or more Prime-Apes trooped in wearing military-green jackets, led by Dean Pancake in his ill-fitting suit and tie. He knuckled over to me and handed me a piece of paper. Someone else must have typed it out for him; it contained no spelling mistakes.

"He's commandeering the EEG caps," I told Hubert.

The Prime-Apes snatched the EEG caps out of Emmy's hands and off the heads of the volunteers. One young man protested, "Hey, man, that's mine!" But the chimpanzee grasping the EEG cap bared its teeth at him.

Hubert said to Dean Pancake, "But sir, but ... you approved this experiment!"

I showed Hubert the letter. "It says, 'PRIME-APES GO FIRST.' Whatever that means."

The chimps, orangutans, a couple of gibbons, and a lone gorilla placed the EEG caps on their own heads. Pancake marched up and down, inspecting his Prime-Apes and their inverted-colander headwear. He chuffed heartily, then led his troops out the door.

"So, what's it like to be human *now*?" I asked Hubert.

I wondered what Pancake wanted the caps for. The Prime-Apes had left behind the connecting cables. Instead, the they wandered around campus, demanding IDs, interrupting lectures, and pilfering sandwiches, while wearing the EEG caps like fashionable hats, if you could call an inverted colander on your head "fashionable."

But a week later, I noticed some EEG caps sprouting antennae. Someone had been modifying them. This was confirmed when Junie phoned me to complain. "That monkey of yours marched into my office, can you believe the nerve? Wanted me to add radio to those caps. I slammed my door in his face. I'm in Agriculture and Engineering; he has nothing over me."

I soon learned Dean Pancake had intimidated Baka Becker into modifying the EEG caps. "He got up real close and bared those teeth at me," Baka told me while he was soldering wires on an EEG cap. "He wrote on that chalkboard of his that he could bite off my face and get away with it. He couldn't really ... could he?"

"I think there's a limit to what even a dean can do," I said.

Baka leaned closer. "And just when I'm getting close to a breakthrough... I discovered that when I teleport flies, whatever is inside their bodies, in their little fly stomachs, also gets teleported. I've been inserting microdots into flies to teleport a message, maybe even to another universe."

"Who'd want to dissect a fly just to get a message?" I picked up one of the modified EEG caps and poked at the electronics. "Pretty elegant modification. Yours?"

Baka shook his head. "Thanks, but no, not mine. Dean Pancake brought me the blueprints. He said he has a source, a mole inside a committee, something to do with quarks..."

At first, with his Southern accent, by *"kwahks,"* I thought he was talking about ducks. Then understanding tumbled into place, and my heart clanged like a fire alarm. "C-QUARK?" I asked.

He nodded. "Yeah, that's it. What does it mean?"

"Trouble," I said. "That's what it means."

Most of the College of Inhumanities, the lecture halls, laboratories, and of-fices, were housed in the northeast corner of the campus. Wearing their fly-ing-saucer-like EEG caps, the Prime-Apes enthusiastically marched in sync along the boundary, which they had demarcated with a line of thick yellow paint. I heard rumors that Chancellor Hebert had insisted that Dean Pancake keep the Prime-Apes within that boundary. Still other rumors had Hebert thinking to expand it university-wide. Uwe told me he'd overheard the campus ROTC commander wonder aloud if he could get those caps for his cadets.

Hubert Biscuit was dismayed that his plans for synchronized remote sending had been disrupted. "Is that any way to treat an alpha department?" he asked me as he sat in my office, his sneaker-clad feet hoisted up onto my desk.

"As a zeta, I wouldn't know," I said, shifting a pile of ungraded homework away from his shoes. As I did so, a pair of gibbons, who had for all practical purposes taken up residence in my office, grabbed several of the sheets and began chasing each other, leaping from file cabinet to bookshelf and swinging from the overhead light fixture.

"You should get that student of yours, Annie—"

"Emmy."

"—to make more EEG sets. In secret, maybe? Then we can continue the experiment."

I shook my head. "The Prime-Apes are everywhere. Don't they show up at your lectures, hooting at random? I heard that over in biology, whenever someone mentions evolution, they start screeching and jumping around and frightening students. The chair of biology went to Dean Pancake, but he dismissed it as 'FReeDoM oF eXPReSSIoN.'"

I suspected she spent a lot of time at home analyzing her supertunneling data, as an excuse to get away from the Prime-Apes. I couldn't blame her. As Burlap Hall was outside the boundaries of the college, I often sat at a desk at the Leap Before You Look Institute to get any work done, away from the gibbons.

That's where I was in early February when I ran into Codd. He showed up a few days each month. He still wore jeans and a green T-shirt, but in deference to the cold, also wore a purple hoodie.

"You look awful. You teaching this afternoon? Let me take you to lunch."

He took me to Little Larry's Bar-B-Q and Crawfish Emporium, a campus favorite. As we waited for our fried oysters and a shrimp po-boy, Codd said, "Hubert Biscuit tells me your experiment got sidetracked."

"Not my experiment. His. But everything is sidetracked these days." I made an *ook-ook* sound and hunched over in an imitation of an ape.

Codd laughed and coughed into a fist. "I suppose it's my fault. I had commented to the chancellor that a lot of management could be accomplished by a grumpy monkey with a sharp stick. I didn't think he would take it literally."

After Codd gobbled down three fried oysters with remoulade, he wiped his mouth and told me he was off to South Africa for a big conference. Mostly, though, he'd be working on his next book. *Against Love*, he told me, was the working title. Either that, or, *The Tyranny of Love*.

"I guess you won't be missing Valentine's Day next week, then," I said, and he chuckled.

Jane sent me a newspaper clipping, an obituary for my old fifth grade teacher, Mrs. Jarczynski. She had been caught embezzling schoolroom funds, and although she avoided criminal charges, she'd been fired and reduced to selling luggage at the mall. The obituary said she had died after a brief unspecified illness. Reading it, I thought about everything that had happened in fifth grade—making friends with Big Bruce, the omelet breakfast, and the gigantified Mexican beaded lizard, Ernie. None of that was in her obituary. I had mixed feelings about Mrs. Jarczynski, but this bland obscurity—she didn't deserve it. No one did, and yet billions of people lived and died the same obscure way. The world suddenly felt not large, but small and petty.

I received the clipping in the mail the day before Valentine's Day. The next morning, I taught my class, grabbed my sandwich from my office (fortunately the gibbons were somewhere else), and headed to the institute. Passing by the faculty club, I saw the entrance decked out in big red heart-shaped balloons, and I felt glad I was skipping it. I walked on, telling myself I didn't care about Valentine's Day.

The institute was quiet and nearly empty, save for Beryl Knaught. She sat on a swivel chair, staring into space. Her face held a touch of sadness, as if she had just learned of the death of a distant cousin.

"Hi, Beryl," I said. "You're not usually here."

She smiled wanly at me. "No, but on Valentine's Day, I actively stay away from the department. Humphrey Biscuit pants like a dog in heat, and..." She shuddered.

"Is that why you look like you're mourning Valentine's Day?"

Beryl looked down and laughed, as she was dressed all in black, complete with deep, dark red lipstick. "Ah. This was my only clean outfit this morning." She turned to me. "And you? You got big plans?" I shook my head. "So, here we are, both all alone."

"Yeah, well, you want to grab some lunch, maybe off campus?" I asked, keeping my tired sandwich behind my back.

"Why, John, are you asking me out on a date on Valentine's Day?"

I shrugged. "If you want it to be."

"That's not very romantic."

I sat down, facing away from her. I told her one of my old grade school teachers had died.

"Oh, I'm sorry. Was she, or he, a favorite of yours?"

"We, uh, kind of butted heads, but... Well, um, a lot happened in my life that year. And she was part of that."

Beryl stood up, touching my arm. "C'mon," she said gently. "Why don't we go get lunch?"

"You got a favorite place?"

"My house is just a few blocks from campus. Tonight, I was going to make fettucine and a salad for myself, but I've got enough for two. And there's already a bottle of pinot grigio chilling in the fridge." Before I could protest, she put a hand on mine. "I think we both could use an afternoon off. Let's try to cheer each other up."

I know it's cliché, but afterwards, I cried, just a little. Lying next to me, Beryl stroked my arm. "I bet you've got a lot going on in that four-chambered heart of yours, don't you?" she said softly.

I sniffled. "Did you say 'four-chambered' because I'm in the sciences?"

Beryl laughed and kissed my bare shoulder. "You really *are* so much smarter than the average bear. I'll make a note not to expect to slip anything by you."

"I'm sorry," I said, wiping at my eyes. "But you're right, there's a lot going on right now."

Beryl whispered, "If it helps, you could just imagine how jealous Humphrey Biscuit would be if he knew about this."

"Wait... You're not ... using this to get at him, right?"

"Oh, God, no!" She gave a gasping laugh. "I can easily deflate Humphrey on my own."

"He seems sad and lonely."

Beryl propped herself up on an elbow. "He left a note in my departmental mailbox yesterday. Do you know what it said? 'I believe our friendship can survive a purely physical interlude.'" She made a gagging sound.

"That *is* creepy," I said. "And though I shouldn't gossip—you know about Hubert, right? How he—"

"Please! Humphrey is icky, but Hubert's a predator. Don't spoil the mood by discussing him." She snuggled closer. "Thank you."

"For not discussing Hubert Biscuit?"

"For this afternoon. I was a bit down and needed some cheering up myself. So, thank you."

Louisiana has festivals year-round, but the most famous, of course, is Mardi Gras and its run-up.

"So, you coming with?" Junie Johnson asked me, meaning heading to New Orleans for Endymion, the Saturday before Mardi Gras.

I shook my head. "What, jam myself in with half a million drunks along Canal Street? I don't have a moment to breathe, what with additional teaching and my janitorial duties."

Junie sighed. "That damned monkey..." she said, her tone softening.

"It really irritates him when you call him a monkey."

"Yeah, that's why I do it," Junie said. "You know, there's a local parade on Sunday. The Krewe of Porque. Won't be as packed as New Orleans; you can park on campus and walk. Grab some beads, drink some hurricanes. Forget your troubles for a while, John."

I was not going to go, but come Sunday, I found myself unable to focus. So, I walked to Ham Street, which was all of four blocks long, and stood at the back of the crowd, watching the floats go by—all six of them, plus the high school marching band. Five of the floats were pig-themed, with the krewe members giddily tossing cheap beads to the grasping crowds, but the last one depicted the head of a giant ape, with the king and queen of Porque standing in its open mouth. The ape looked just like Pancake. I raised my hand, and the queen turned and tossed me a thick set of beads and a large plastic medallion depicting an ape riding a pig. I put the beads and medallion around my neck and walked home, feeling slightly lighter for a few moments.

One day, I received a phone call summoning me to Dean Pancake's office. At first, I thought it was because I had worn my old red rubber nose and floppy shoes in lectures during Mardi Gras week. Then I wondered if someone had spotted me at the Krewe of Porque, cheering madly at the chimp-themed float. Surely attending a parade with a thousand other people could not be grounds for dismissal, I told myself.

I walked across McClendon Quadrangle, where at least two dozen Prime-Apes, sporting their metal EEG caps, were rapidly swinging from magnolia to dogwood to magnolia again, causing the branches to shake and the few remaining brown leaves to fall to the dying lawn.

In Haricot Hall, in the office of the Dean of Humanities, Mari ushered me into Pancake's office. He proffered a shot glass of a sticky brown fluid, but I declined. He shrugged and quickly wrote on his slate, then turned it around. "*I NeeD YouR ReACToR.*"

"For what?"

"*ClAssIFIeD.*"

"No."

"*NoT A RequesT. oRDeR.*"

"Still no."

Pancake eyed me. I expected him to bare his teeth, to throw things around the office, but he just poured himself another shot glass of syrup and downed it, then pressed a button on his desk.

As I left Dean Pancake's office, Mari handed me a piece of paper.

"What's this?" I asked.

"You have been relieved of your oversight of the campus reactor."

I stood there, trying to read the words, but my heart was pounding, and I could feel the hot sweat sliding down from my armpits. The letters on the page swirled, and for a moment, I wondered if Pancake himself had typed it out.

"Who's going to maintain it, then?" I asked, my mouth dry.

"The dean is assigning the task to Bobo." When I looked confused, she softened her voice and said, "I think that's the orangutan."

"And does Bobo the orangutan know anything about fissile isotopes or chain reactions, or how to use control rods to tamp the neutron flux?"

Her voice regained its brittleness. "Bobo knows how to take orders from the dean."

I handed her back the slightly crumped letter. "Stock up on iodine pills," I told her. "One of the components of radioactive fallout is radio-bromine, which gets taken up in the thyroid and resides there for a long while. Saturating yourself with iodine helps prevent that." Then I walked out.

Back in my office, it took half an hour before I stopped shaking with anger enough to call the chancellor's office. Unfortunately, I was told that the request to talk to the chancellor had to go through my dean's office.

"But it's the dean who's the problem," I said, trying to keep from shouting.

"I'm sorry, sir, I'm just following protocol. There's no need to get testy with me."

I guess I had shouted after all. "Sorry, sorry," I said.

"Perhaps you should get your chair to talk to your dean."

I rubbed at my eyes. "Ah, we don't have a chair, and the dean has made excuses for not appointing one."

"According to campus rules, you don't need the dean to appoint a chair. Any department can elect a chair from among the full professors."

"Well, see, we lost all our full professors in that betting scandal…"

There was a long pause. "What department are you from again?"

A few days later, thick black power lines had been run out of the sub-basement of Physics and into McClendon Quadrangle. The lines were patrolled by a pair of chimps, plus a gorilla who held up a red STOP sign whenever any human strayed too close.

I went down into the sub-basement of Wunderkine Hall, and indeed, the orangutan, Bobo, sat stubbornly outside the door leading down to the reactor. When I approached, it held out its hand. Reluctantly, I handed over my ID. Bobo put it in its mouth, sucked thoughtfully for a minute, and then carefully handed it back. Then it shook its head and spread its arms wide to block my passage.

I went over to Chemistry to look for Uwe, but couldn't find him. He wasn't at the faculty club, either. In desperation, I walked up the sandstone steps to Egas Moniz Hall, nearly choking as I swallowed my pride, and knocked on Hubert Biscuit's door.

There was no answer, but I heard low sounds inside.

"Hubert? Are you in there?" I banged on the door. "Hello?"

Finally, I heard Hubert clear his throat. "Come back later."

"It's an emergency." I fished out the janitorial master key for Psychology and unlocked the door.

By this time, the young brunette with him was mostly dressed and buttoning up her blouse, although she'd gotten the buttons misaligned. Hubert was still struggling to step into his pants. "She's not my student!" he shouted. "It's consensual! *Consensual!* She's not my student!"

"Not your student *now*, you mean," the young woman said.

"Maybe you should go," I told her.

The young woman ducked her head and dashed out of the office.

Hubert sank down into his chair, his pants still tangled around his ankles. "I've been working on that one for a long time," he said wistfully.

"I need your help," I told him. I explained about the reactor. "You can go to your chair. Maybe she can go around the dean, get to the chancellor."

Hubert considered this as he pulled up his pants. "Hmm... That will take too long. There will be memos to write, and some committee will have to approve it. No, I know a faster way to get to the chancellor," he said, leaning back in his chair and zipping himself up.

The key to Hubert's plan: Beryl Knaught, who was best friends with the chancellor's wife.

"John!" said Beryl when I knocked on her office door in Absinthe Hall. "Are you here to seduce me again?"

I could feel my face flush hot. "You said it was a one-time thing."

"You shouldn't believe me when I say such things. But I'm guessing from your face that you're here for something else."

"I do have a favor to ask."

She raised an eyebrow. "It'll cost you."

I had yet to hear back from either the chancellor or Beryl. I was walking from the faculty parking lot to Wunderkine Hall when I spotted a crowd in McClendon Quadrangle. The thick black power lines from the reactor now terminated in a boxy control panel sitting in the middle of the brown lawn. From the control panel, a web of brightly colored cables ran to silver saucer EEG caps on the heads of apes perched in the trees of the quadrangle—twenty or thirty of them, mostly chimpanzees, but also several gibbons, a couple of gorillas, and a lone baboon. The branches rustled under their weight, but otherwise they were strangely silent, staring at the humans who were staring at them.

I noticed Baka Becker off to one side, looking as nervous as a sheep at a wolf convention. He kept rubbing his hand over his bald pate. I started to edge through the crowd, but with everyone jostling for a view of the monkey show, my progress was slow.

I was about halfway to Baka when out of the corner of my eye, I spotted the ugliest imaginable green-and-brown tie: Chancellor Hebert, at the edge of the quad, speaking to the people around him and occasionally raising himself up on his tiptoes. Changing direction, I elbowed past a gaggle of undergraduates to reach the chancellor. I was about to introduce myself, but when he saw me, he said, "Ah, Professor Chant. Beryl said you were trying to contact me. Can you explain what's going on?"

I was momentarily stunned that he had any idea who I was, and I wondered if he spent his evenings memorizing the photos and names of faculty. "I'm not sure," and then remembering I was in Louisiana, I added, "sir." I went on, "But I'm concerned, because whatever it is, it's drawing power from the nuclear reactor."

He furrowed his brow. "Aren't you in charge of the campus reactor?"

"Pancake... *Dean* Pancake relieved me. He put an orangutan named Bobo in charge of the reactor, and Bobo won't let me near it." I turned and crooked my head into the crowd. "I don't know what's going on, but I think Professor Becker there may know more."

Chancellor Hebert turned and crooked a finger at Baka. Baka spent all his time in his lab, and he was pale, even for a white person; but at Hebert's gesture, he went paler still. Mopping his bald head with a handkerchief, he waded through the restless crowd.

As Baka nudged past faculty and students towards the chancellor and me, Dean Pancake emerged from Haricot Hall and waddled down the steps to the quadrangle. The crowd parted for Pancake, who positively strutted to the control panel. All around, conversation buzzed like a massive beehive.

Baka reached us, sweating profusely. He took off his glasses and wiped them on his shirt. Hebert asked, firmly yet not unkindly, "Do *you* know what's going on here, son?"

Baka looked furtively at Pancake, who had reached the control panel. "I had no choice; he forced me. I had to help the dean..."

"To do what?"

Baka swallowed. "He, the dean, Dean Pancake, I mean, he says this will give them ... will make them..." He looked like he was about to faint, or vomit, or maybe both.

"It's okay, son," Hebert said. "Just tell me what you know."

The crowd had fallen silent. I turned and saw Pancake with both arms held high in the air. He paused to share his grin with all the watching humans, then dropped his right arm to slap a big red button.

The air tensed with palpable electric potential. The apes in the trees, their caps connected to power cables, stiffened; their mouths all opened to emit an eerie crooning sound. The hairs on the back of my neck stood up as I heard it.

Over the crooning of the apes, Baka said, his voice squeaking, "He's trying to boost their brainpower. Make them superintelligent, ascend to a higher level. According to the plans he got from C-QUARK..."

"Oh, God," I groaned. "Don't believe *anything* from C-QUARK."

Hebert narrowed his eyes and turned to me. "Shut down that reactor."

I swiveled to run into Wunderkine Hall, but it was too late. The crooning increased in volume and pitch, shading from eerie to a sound like sheet metal being torn, and then to outright screaming. The apes trembled, shaking so hard that dead leaves rained from the trees, and I saw smoke rise from the body of a gibbon, then a chimp, then a gorilla, and another chimp. The humans began to shout and scream too as the apes convulsed, and their fur caught fire with blue flames. I tore my gaze away to look to Pancake. He had a shocked look on his face, his eyes wide with horror, like the rest of us. Finally, sparks shot out of the control panel, and one by one, the apes tumbled out of the trees onto the ground, dead.

A woolen silence settled on the quad. With the reek of burnt fur and flesh heavy in the air, I felt queasy. Next to me, Hebert groaned, "I don't need this..."

Pancake whirled around, facing the crowd of humans. In an instant, his look of horror and grief switched to snarling defiance. He screamed wordlessly at us, leapt atop the control panel, and bounced up into the nearest tree.

"Somebody get him!"

"*You* get him!"

"Call the sheriff!"

Pancake swung from tree to tree, and as he circled the quad, reaching down to swat at any human who came too close, he dropped his jacket and pulled off his tie. He tore off his white shirt, which fluttered to the ground like the ghost of one of the dead apes, and let his ill-fitting trousers slip off. He swung up and onto the low roof of the nearest building, then paused to scream at us once more, unleashing all his simian rage and frustration. Then he scampered over the crest of the roof and was gone.

Postmodern Love

The ancient Greeks, or at least Aristotle, believed the universe was eternal. It's not a bad assumption. After all, Copernicus argued we are not the center of the universe. Perhaps neither are we at the center of history.

This humility led to Einstein's biggest blunder. When working out the motion of the cosmos, he found that the universe either expanded or collapsed in upon itself. This seemed patently ridiculous, so he added a special term: the cosmological constant, which acted as a brake, pinning the universe to an unchanging eternity. A few years later, Edwin Hubble, using techniques painstakingly developed by Henrietta Leavitt, found that the universe was in fact expanding outwards like shrapnel from a bomb. Einstein was flummoxed.

The problem with the Big Bang theory is that it suggests something came from nothing, violating all other principles of physics. A variation is the "ekpyrotic" universe, from the Greek for "out of fire": the universe expands, eventually stalls out, collapses back upon itself, and is then reborn like a phoenix in one of an infinite number of Big Bangs. But while there is tons of evidence for the Big Bang, we have no additional evidence for ekpyrotic cycles. The ekpyrotic universe is thus merely a hunch.

Nonetheless, the idea of a cyclical universe—found in cultures around the world—is appealing, if only because it captures our own lives, our cycles of expansion, collapse, and rebirth in fire, fury, loss, and pain.

Beryl did demand a favor for a favor. Spring semester, she taught Rhetoric from Ancient Greece to Postmodernism, and she wanted me and Humphrey Biscuit to have a discussion in front of her class.

"Hope you're not disappointed that's my 'favor,'" she said.

"You can call it in as anything you want," I said. "But .... you want us to just ... talk ... about things?"

"Rhetorical standards and styles differ in the humanities and the sciences," Beryl said. "Sometimes radically. It'll be a golden-ticket opportunity for my students, like experimental demonstrations in science classes. I'm asking them to write a short paper on their observations. Do you mind if we record it on video?"

A week later, Humphrey Biscuit and I were sitting on stools in front of two dozen students in a room in Absinthe Hall. Beryl introduced us and sat down.

"So, Professor Biscuit, what shall we talk about?" I asked. "The price of milk? Our favorite works of art? How the baseball team is doing? Though I'm not a big baseball fan."

"Neither am I," Humphrey said. "My specialty is the analysis of rhetoric from a Marxist framework."

"Then it may be a short conversation," I said, "as physicists, and scientists in general, try to avoid relying upon rhetoric. It's so easy to fool yourself with words. And nature knows no politics."

"Ah, not according to *all* scientists. Erstmann Codd has written books applying a theory of thermodynamics to economics."

I started to say I had dipped a toe into the ocean of economic data and could not find evidence to support Codd's claims, but before I could, Humphrey went on to interpret thermodynamics in Marxist terms: useless and lazy heat, the bourgeoisie, and tidy and noble work, the proletariat. When I protested, he swiveled and brought up the phlogiston theory, which posited heat as a physical fluid.

I said, "Experiments disproved phlogiston by the end of the eighteenth century. No one ascribes to it anymore."

"So, thermodynamics as a one-party political rule? See, there *is* politics in science," he said, triumph in his voice.

I looked to Beryl, but she just shrugged. "Are you saying facts aren't important?" I asked.

"I'm saying that argument based on 'facts'..." Humphrey added air quotes. "... is just rhetoric by another means. The sciences are so invested in this mode of rhetoric, they can't see how culturally trapped they are by it."

I put my head in my hands. "If that were true," I said, feeling a headache coming on, "if it's all culture, then there would be no surprises. Becquerel wouldn't have discovered radioactivity. Roentgen, x-rays. Rutherford, the nucleus. Fleming, penicillin."

"New ideas come about in culture all the time," Humphrey countered. "The Enlightenment. My own tool, Marxism. Feminism," he said, gesturing to Beryl, "which of course is merely a subset of Marxism."

"We could debate that, Humphrey," Beryl called out, "and we have."

"Is Newton's law cultural?" I asked. "The radioactive decay law? Gravity? The expansion of the universe? All of these are cultural artifacts?"

"I'm sure one could make such an argument. I haven't tried." Humphrey leaned forward, his eyes shining, clearly thinking he had me on the ropes. He glanced at Beryl, and I could almost see him imagining a later scene of seduction. I shuddered.

Perhaps Beryl saw it, too, for she stood up. "Well, this is all *very* interesting, but we're out of time. May I ask you, gentlemen, perhaps we could take this up again, say, in three weeks' time?"

Emmy Shore showed me her compiled supertunneling data. She could consistently produce the phenomenon, through a wide range of materials, but even when using the same kind of substance, the rates varied greatly.

"It must be minute variations and imperfections," I said. "I had hoped that it was like superconductivity, which has zero resistance because the pairs of electrons ignore impurities."

"So, why didn't that happen here, Professor?"

I shrugged. "Just because two things are called 'super' doesn't mean they'll behave the same, I guess."

As we were about to comb through the data again, Erstmann Codd walked through my open office door. "John!" he said, barely nodding at Emmy. "I heard you finally rid yourself of that monkey."

"Actually, he did it all by himself." No one had seen Pancake since the incident. The whole campus had been traumatized, and it had taken two days to cart away all the bodies of the electrocuted apes. The only survivor of the unintended massacre had been Bobo the orangutan, saved by his assignment of guard duty over the reactor. "The good news is, Uwe Meilleur and Dick Cherrystone are interim acting co-deans. The alpha, beta, and zeta ranks have been abolished, the janitors and secretaries have all been rehired, and I don't have to mop floors or empty trash for Psychology anymore."

Codd crossed his arms and nodded. "So, back to that synchronized remote sending experiment with Hubert?"

I shook my head. "After what happened to the Prime-Apes, who would possibly volunteer? Besides, Emmy has a ton of supertunneling data."

Emmy showed Codd her results. Codd said, "Let's talk to Baka; he always has lots of ideas."

I noted he didn't say Baka had lots of *good* ideas, but I didn't object. Emmy had to go to her stat mech class, so Codd and I trooped downstairs to Baka's lab. I said, "He's been scarce lately. I'm sure he feels bad about his role in Pancake's fiasco. But I know he's been working in his lab; I've seen the power draw from the reactor."

We stopped at the door marked B. BECKER EXPT LAB. Codd banged a couple of times, then rattled the doorknob. When there was no answer, Codd asked me for the key, then unlocked the door. I followed as he stepped through.

"Oh, boy," I heard Baka say, reminding me of my father. "Guys, listen—"

But we weren't listening. Even Codd, who always affected a bemused nonchalance, was stunned, his mouth open.

Crammed into a glass chamber, surrounded by coils and frost-encrusted cryogenics, was our former dean, Pancake. The chimp threw us a look of panic and fury.

"What are you doing?" Codd asked.

Baka stuttered, "He asked... He demanded... He threatened—"

I stepped closer to the chamber. Pancake bared his teeth at me, face pressed against the glass, his breath fogging it. "What's that covering him?" I asked. His dark fur glistened as if oiled. At first, I thought it was Vaseline, perhaps to help squeeze him into the cramped chamber—but then I noticed bits of tiny legs and wings smeared over his face and hands and body. "Are those...?"

"Mashed-up flies," Baka said, misery dripping from his voice. "My entire supply. I had thousands of them, and I had to... He demanded I send him to another universe."

Before either Codd or I could speak, Baka wiped his nose and flipped a switch. The sudden increase in electric potential made my hair stand on end, and I heard the familiar whine of transformers. Pancake closed his eyes and began to make a long sound—"ooooo-*ooooo*-OOOO-*OOOO*..."

The chimp opened his eyes once more, looking straight at me, before there was a flash of light and a high-pitched scream—I don't know if it was him or the machinery—and then he was gone.

"Wait, what were you doing again?" Codd asked.

I left as Baka began to explain to Codd his experiments in teleportation and time displacement and communicating with other universes. Back in my office, I wasn't sure if I should throw up or dance a jig. Perhaps this was what people meant by "getting a monkey off your back." Perhaps it was endorphins. Perhaps that neurochemical intoxication is why I phoned Beryl in her office.

"Hi, John. What's up?"

"I just saw off... Well, I feel the freest I have in months. Want to go out to dinner?" I could feel the flutter of my pulse in my neck.

"That's so sweet of you. But let me be clear; I don't want you to have the wrong expectations."

"No expectations," I lied. "But you're fun to talk to."

"And you're one of the few here who can challenge me intellectually. I suppose that's a sad statement about my colleagues... I'll do it, as long as you know we're not going to jump into bed at the end of the evening."

She suggested we go to Lafayette. "It's a bit of a drive, but the restaurants in Renderville are mostly pork-themed. I know a great Italian place in Lafayette."

When I picked her up, she was wearing a deep pelagic-blue sheath dress with a matching handbag, and dangling earrings like miniature wind chimes, a faint tinkling wafting through the air whenever she moved her head. I said the dress was a beautiful color, and she thanked me.

"So, your field is feminist analysis, right?" I asked.

"Of literature and rhetoric in general, yes."

"Okay, and I ask this out of curiosity..."

"Uh-oh, it's never good when someone says that."

"... but does anyone, not me, but anyone else ever comment on the contrast with your, uh, um..."

"Slinky dresses?"

"I think I was going to say something like 'stereotypical feminine clothing choices.' I just hadn't rehearsed it enough times in my head."

"That's better than saying I dress like a slut, which I have been told, by the way. Well, there are seven different kinds of feminism, at least, and none demand that a woman dress like a lumberjack. They just assert that if a woman *wants* to dress like a lumberjack, she should be able to, without castigation. And this is how *I* like to dress—without castigation."

As I drove us to Lafayette, we talked about the downfall of Pancake. Uwe Meilleur and Dick Cherrystone had been appointed interim co-deans. Thankfully, they had immediately rescinded Pancake's motto, *The student is our customer, and the customer is always right.*

"Besides simian archenemies," Beryl asked, "do you feel you've adjusted to life here in Renderville?"

"It's been so crazy, I've hardly had time to think. Except when I lie awake at night."

"What keeps you awake at night?"

After a pause, I said, "I wonder what friends I'll make here. I mean, Uwe and Harold have been really kind to me, very generous with their time. So has Junie, Junie Johnson in electrical engineering, and her boyfriend. But this is a small town, and I've never been good at fitting in. So, I wonder, how was it for you? Making friends, finding people to date?"

"It was hard at first, because yeah, it is a small town. Eventually, I figured it out ... mostly." She was silhouetted in ghostly green by the dashboard light. "Life is complicated."

I was far from figuring it out. Part of me ached to tell her about Ada, to ask, *"Is it like that for everyone? That void?"* But I didn't know how.

The restaurant was atmospheric, by which I mean it was dark. "I can barely see you," I said after we were seated. "And part of the point was to see you."

"Is that a subtle way of complimenting me?" She squinted at the menu.

"I was trying for subtle and non-creepy, yes."

She put down the menu. "You succeeded. What are you having? I'll have the mushroom ravioli, I think."

When the waiter brought us a grassy chardonnay, we clinked glasses. "May your papers all be swiftly accepted," Beryl said. "So, do you know how many papers you need for tenure?"

"I don't know—as many as I can write. What about you?"

"In English and Literature, it's a book. You need a book to land a position, another to get tenure, and another to get promoted to full professor. Luckily, writing comes easy to me. People like Humphrey Biscuit, he's very voluble, but he finds it torturous to write."

We talked a long while, then drove the midnight highway back to Renderville. When I pulled into her driveway, Beryl said, "I really enjoyed talking with you, John." She looked down at her handbag. "I appreciate that you didn't argue with me about not jumping in bed at the end of the evening..."

"I didn't want to be a jerk."

"I'm glad you're not." She moved a hand over mine. "But ... it wouldn't be so bad if you argued with me a little..."

Three weeks after the first debate, I again crossed rhetorical swords with Humphrey Biscuit for Beryl's class. "Though I'm beginning to regret this," Beryl told me. "Humphrey is interpreting this as, well, a wider invitation from me to him. And he just won't let up."

I wondered if this was meant as a subtle message to me. After our date, I had asked Beryl out twice more. Both times, Beryl said she wished she could, but she was plowed under with commitments.

When I arrived at Beryl's classroom, however, it was overflowing. Beryl approached me and said, "Apparently Humphrey has been advertising this, as if it's some sort of boxing match. I hope you don't mind."

Humphrey Biscuit strolled in, wearing a white straw hat banded with the school colors. Surveying the overfilled seats and the spectators lining the walls, he gave a doughy smile. He made a show of shaking hands. I'm not one to give much of a handshake, but with him, it was like shaking a recently dead trout.

Humphrey Biscuit wasn't as stupid as I make him out to be. He quoted Linus
Pauling, then other people I'd never heard of. I protested that quotes did not
make an argument. He said he both agreed and disagreed. He said a pile of words,
then another pile of words, and soon my head began to throb. After what felt
like three hours (but couldn't have been more than forty-five minutes), Beryl
stood and said time was up.

Erstmann Codd blew into town. He was advertising a new book, *The Tyranny
of Romance*, and even signed copies at the bookstore. Afterwards, he shut
himself in with Baka Becker in Baka's lab.

The book—he gave me a free copy—made the same argument that Ada had:
looked at coldly, love was a chemical response, an evolutionary strategy, an
illusion foisted on us by our genes, like some sort of secret conspiracy. Unlike
Ada, however, he took this as a serious flaw. *We should decry the gauzy notion
of love as foolishness,* he wrote. Only then could we be truly unshackled from
self-deception.

Codd proposed that families be contractual and paid for by society, as re-
production kept civilization chugging along. He wasn't against sex; in fact, he
argued, his analysis was sex-positive. We should seek out pleasure in sex, food,
and comfort. We just shouldn't imbue them with mythical qualities they didn't
possess. In the same way that the Christian Eucharist was merely cheap wine and
stale bread, he wrote, not the blood and flesh of a man who lived two thousand
years ago, we shouldn't attribute our sex drive or the bond between parent and
child to anything more than an intoxicating orchestra of hormones.

He even addressed marriage. Codd wrote, *A contractual relationship between
two people—or more, I don't see why not—who work together effectively can
be a positive thing. The problem is when it gets elevated from a practicality to
magical thinking.*

I leafed quickly through the book, then starting writing out my next day's
lecture notes. It had grown dark outside when Codd knocked on my office door.
"Got a moment?" he asked, and without waiting for an answer, sat down across
from me. He noticed his book on my desk. "How do you like it so far?"

"Oh... Interesting, I guess."

He laughed. "'Interesting' is code for 'I didn't like it.'"

"Well," I said, then paused.

Codd picked up on my hesitation. "It probably sounds frightening, doesn't
it, to say there is no such thing as love. It's a hard truth to face."

"Well," I said again, and then... You have to understand, I was reluctant to make myself vulnerable, to anyone, in particular to Codd, but I was holding so much inside of myself, it was like all the alternate universes Baka had contacted were crammed into my chest, and I went around every day feeling like I was about to burst. So, I said in a tight voice, "It's just that Renderville is a pretty lonely town."

"Yeah, I understand." I expected Codd to repeat his arguments from the book. Instead, he said, "Say, John, you're in charge of the campus nuclear reactor, is that right?"

I licked my lips before answering. "I don't know if it's 'in charge' so much as 'no one else was willing to take care of it.' I think I do a better job than an orangutan, at least."

"Great, great. Listen, in a few weeks, I'm hoping to do a demonstration. Something game-changing. It will really light a fire under this place, set the whole university on a path somewhere. But I'm going to need that reactor power."

I rubbed at my eyes. If Ada's God existed, He or She surely was testing me. "You realize, after Pancake, that's a pretty big ask."

Codd laughed. "I know, right? Downright arrogant of me. But listen, I'm not a *chimpanzee*, yeah?"

We're all kind of chimpanzees, I thought, but I only said, "I'll have to run it by the chancellor first."

"You do that." He reached over and patted his book. "I'm really looking forward to what you have to say when you're finished."

At a faculty meeting, Sam Soon brought up Codd's demonstration. Codd asked to use the main physics auditorium, room 137. Sam looked at me. "And using power from the reactor, I gather?"

"That's what he wants. Chancellor Hebert gave his okay." This time when I'd called the chancellor's office, I was put straight through. What surprised me was when Hebert agreed. He said while he understood my hesitation, Codd was a completely different animal, and again, I thought to myself, *We're all kind of chimpanzees*. Then the chancellor added that Codd had the financial backing of a major supporter of the university, as if capitalism eliminated any chance of electrocution or radioactive fallout or zombie apocalypse.

In the faculty meeting, I simply said, "Everyone wants power. I don't know what it's for, though." I turned to Baka Becker. "Do *you* know what he's doing? You're friends with him."

Baka took off his glasses and shook his head, his bushy beard rustling against his chest. "Erstmann likes to spring things on people, see their surprise." For the first time, I thought I detected a note of resentment. "Though he sure has taken an interest in my experiments. To be honest, he never seemed to care before."

Carson Whittaker, who seldom spoke during faculty meetings, cleared his throat. "We shouldn't participate in this farce. It's going to be a circus," he said, and glanced at me; everyone vaguely knew that part of my history. "A circus whose sole purpose is to promote Erstmann Codd. Even if no one gets electrocuted, we won't come out of this looking good, I'm telling you."

Two weeks later, flyers appeared on campus, announcing a *stunning demonstration that will embody the bold new direction of the Leap Before You Look Institute,* featuring a big black-and-white picture of Codd with his arms crossed. At the bottom, it said, *Sponsored by Tode's Reliable Motors.*

I found one on a table at the faculty club when I sat down with a bowl of gumbo. I was reading it when Beryl came and stood next to me, holding a plate of salad. "Mind if I join you, John?"

I gestured at a chair. I thought, *If God plays dice with the universe, maybe I should gamble, too.* I said, "I was wondering, do you want to go to New Orleans sometime? You know, have some dinner at a famous restaurant, go listen to some jazz, dance the night away?"

"Sounds fun, but I'm trying to finish my book... Maybe next weekend?"

Not wanting to push, I changed the topic by sliding Codd's flyer over to her. "Think you'll go?"

"No, no. I really need to finish my last chapter. But I hear this is getting a lot of buzz."

I finished my gumbo. An awkward silence had settled over us, so I wished Beryl a nice day and left, wondering if she would keep her promise for the trip to New Orleans.

I reached the exit at the same time as Carson Whittaker. We both set off in the direction of Wunderkine Hall. As we fell into step, I handed him the flyer. He adjusted his glasses and read it as we walked. I said, "Yeah, yeah: a circus. I know some people think of me as a clown, but when I lived in the circus, the clowns were the kindest people."

"John," Carson said, with a strange, plaintive note to his voice. "I know we don't get along. But you shouldn't get involved."

"I don't see that I have much choice. The chancellor approved—"

"Not that." He stopped, took off his glasses, and closed his eyes. "I saw you with Beryl Knaught. You should know: Beryl is married. A long-distance relationship—but still, married."

It was as if he had slammed a hammer against my temple. My body stood still, but my mind staggered, trying to calculate sixty things at once: about Beryl, everything we had talked about, and Carson. Why would he make up such an accusation?

"It's none of my business," Carson said, "but ... you need to know."

Midterms and running a nuclear reactor kept me busy. But at night, I lay awake, tossing and turning over Beryl. The uncertainty alone gnawed at me, an unsolved problem. I would sleep better, I told myself, if only I knew for certain whether or not Carson's accusations were true.

Beryl phoned me at my office a week later. "You're not home," she said. "I tried calling there."

"Some of us work," I said. "Some of us don't have tenure."

"It's eight o'clock at night! Anyway, I'm sorry, I've been distracted. Does that offer to go to New Orleans still stand? Maybe we should stay overnight, get a hotel, so we don't have a long drive back at three a.m."

I wanted to ask her, right then, about her husband, real or imaginary, but that could be a long conversation. Instead, I decided to ask her to join me on the drive to New Orleans. But on the highway, Beryl asked if I'd be willing to have one more final debate with Humphrey Biscuit. She admitted that Humphrey thought he had crushed me in the previous round, though she thought the opposite. I asked, more sarcastically than I needed to, if that was a *fact*, or merely rhetoric. Beryl calmly replied that rhetoric and worldviews could hobble us in more ways than we realized. She pointed out Einstein's introduction of the cosmological constant and Newton's fudged calculation of the speed of sound. I shot back with Jacques Derrida's non sequitur about the speed of light, c, and Sandra Harding's tarring-by-association of Newton with Bacon. Beryl said those arguments should not be taken as stand-alone statements, but understood in a larger context. And then we arrived in New Orleans.

I was going to bring it up over dinner, but we got to talking about the books she'd written after her promotion to full professor, and I asked if that made her a superprofessor. She said she liked that and would introduce a resolution to the faculty senate next time they met. Afterward, we went out dancing, and I felt her warmth through her dress. Beryl told me how impressed she was with my dancing skills as we arrived at our hotel. It was only when she turned and asked me to unzip her dress, and I had my hand on the zipper, that I finally asked, "Beryl ... are you married?"

She stepped away and sat on the bed. "Someone told you."

"You've said you're a private person, but don't you think this is relevant?"

She swallowed. "He's not around very much. Hardly at all. He lives in another city."

"Are you separated? Getting a divorce?"

She shook her head. "It's far from ideal, but neither of us want to break it off. We agreed to an open relationship."

"Okay... So, does he know about me?"

She sighed. "We found it best if we don't share about our lovers."

"Okay," I said. "Does the plural apply to both of you?"

Beryl crossed her legs. "There's no need to get jealous. My husband gets jealous, despite himself, despite everything. That's why we agreed to not talk about our lovers."

I sat down next to her. "The trick of physics," I said, "is to isolate a system, pretend the rest of the universe doesn't exist, and work only on that tiny speck of existence." I spoke tensely, trying to keep my voice from breaking, keep my tears from flowing. "Do you still love him?"

"I don't know. What is love, anyway? What does the word *love* really mean?"

I found it hard to breathe. "Didn't you promise, when you got married, 'to love and to cherish,' all that?"

"Those are just words, John." She put a hand on my leg. "I kept it from you because I thought it might hurt you. Well, that backfired. But this is the way things are. If you can't accept that, I understand. In the meantime..." She turned her back to me again. "... unzip me, and then I'm getting into this bed. Then you can decide whatever it is you want to do. I know what *I* want to do."

It's difficult to be resolute in the darkness when you lie mere inches away from the humid warmth of someone else's body, aware of the weight of solitude in a nearly empty universe, and she reaches out and touches your bare skin, and you wonder, *Will anyone else ever touch me again*? Because of that, I tried to have compassion for myself, for being foolish, for making excuses—even compassion for her.

A few weeks before the end of the semester, on a beautiful spring day with a blue sky that painted a shimmering picture of forever, Erstmann Codd threw open the doors of Auditorium 137 in Wunderkine Hall. Two days prior, a large truck had backed up to the loading dock, and several burly Black men staggered as they carried in large pieces of equipment wrapped in canvas tarps. Baka Becker and I stood by, watching. "Can we help?" Baka asked Codd.

Codd grinned. "That would ruin the surprise."

I thought to myself that we'd had enough surprises for one year.

At four o'clock in the afternoon, a crowd of several hundred streamed into the auditorium. At the front of the crowd was Chancellor Willy Hebert, wearing a charcoal suit with his horrid green-and-brown school tie, along with his teen daughter, Rachel, who wore a purple T-shirt and distressed jeans.

Uwe was there, frowning. He simply said, "Dick and I flipped a coin. I lost."

"And you dragged me here," said Harold, who was standing next to Uwe. To me, he said, "I've been working on this massive painting; you should come see it when it's finished. I'm calling it either *How the West Was Really Won*, or *Fool's Gold Mountain*. You can see turn-of-the-century San Francisco broken and on fire while up in the mountains—"

Uwe pushed him into a seat before he could finish.

Carson Whittaker was not there, but the rest of the physics department was present, even the reclusive Mischa Borozov. I slid into a seat between Baka Becker, who looked unusually pensive, and Uwe and Harold.

Codd hopped up on the stage in front of the closed, heavy curtains in the school colors. As people settled into the seats, he tapped the mic, then welcomed everyone.

"All physicists know that the great conundrum of quantum mechanics is its statistical nature. Does God—if there were a God, which there isn't—play dice with the universe? Are we living in a gigantic, fourteen-billion-year-old casino?"

Codd began to pace. "One way out was suggested by Hugh Everett: that every quantum event spawns new universes in proportion to their probabilities. This creates a new problem: can we find evidence of those other universes?

"Recently, my good friend, Professor Buford Becker of the Department of Physics here at Renderville, inspired by the discovery of quantum supertunneling by my other good friend, Professor John Chant, who I see is also in the audience, was able to receive radio transmissions from those other universes. He even made preliminary forays into sending ... well, material to those other universes.

"Yes, I hear you murmuring in disbelief. I don't blame you. Science is built on evidence. *I will give you evidence.* Standing on the shoulders of those giants, I have been able to push this discovery and the technology further. Before I demonstrate, I want to acknowledge the generous financial support of University Regent Tode." He gestured towards the back of the room. I saw a stout figure in shadow, but could not make out the face.

Codd glanced down at his massive stainless-steel watch, then smiled at his audience. His face shone, as if some secret nuclear reaction had ignited within him. Then the curtains drew back, revealing a large apparatus. The exterior was crudely welded, as if constructed in a hurry, but it looked much like the round, empty casing of a huge, human-sized clock, surrounded by copper coils and frost-encased cryogenics. With a theatrical gesture, he threw a switch. As transformers hummed and capacitors charged, Codd said in his booming Yahweh voice, "Not only have I successfully contacted other universes, I can bring people here from them. Including some familiar faces."

The audience sat in stunned silence, not that you could tell with all the noise on stage. The air inside the empty clock casing shimmered, and with a flash of bluish light, a figure appeared. He was tall and broad-shouldered, bald and clean-shaven, wearing a tight-fitting yellow T-shirt.

"Sorry if it seems self-indulgent, but it seemed easiest to invite over an alternate version of myself!" crowed Codd.

This time, the surprised shouts of the audience were audible even over the noise of the apparatus, for indeed, aside from the lack of beard and the different color of shirt, the mirror image of Erstmann Codd stepped forward and raised a hand to greet the crowd. The first Codd, our Codd, handed his alternate version the microphone.

"Hello, Renderville!" the other Codd said, using the same out-of-the-burning-bush intonation as our version. "So very glad to get confirmation of the Everett hypothesis. I want you to know, in my universe, I was also working on trans-universe teleportation. Alas, in my world, I do not know a Professor Becker, and so I was stymied—until my alternate self from *your* universe showed up."

The murmuring had grown so loud that our Codd had to raise a hand. "That's not all!" he bellowed. Another flash of bluish light, and another figure stepped forward, shorter, rounded, balding on top, but with a fringe of gray hair. He wore denim coveralls and a white T-shirt and looked slightly abashed.

Codd grinned. "Welcome, sir!" he said and handed him the mic.

"Um, hello." He blinked at the audience. "My name is Will Hebert. I'm told that in this universe, I'm an important man, but back home, I'm just a plumber." He reddened slightly as he said this. In the front row, Rachel Hebert gave a long, braying laugh and elbowed her father.

Next was a thirty-something Black woman, Gemma Wells, a best-selling author in her universe, but a secretary for the Department of Pomology in ours, Codd informed us.

Beside me, Baka pursed his lips and muttered, "How is he doing this without flies? How? *How?*"

Another bluish flash of light, and out stepped a young man: late twenties, dark brown hair, slightly stoop-shouldered, wearing a striped long-sleeved shirt and jeans. I didn't catch on until Baka elbowed me in the side and said, "It's *you!*"

"Hi, I'm Johnny Chant," said the young man, taking the mic. "I have to say, it's a bit strange to be here."

Erstmann Codd saved the most spectacular for last: an alternate-universe version of Elvis Presley, old, but still very much alive, causing consternation in the crowd.

Codd invited all of us up on stage. For a moment, I stayed in my seat, stunned as if I'd been hit on the head with a mallet. Baka pushed at my shoulder, so I stood up, slowly; I wasn't sure if my legs would work. But they did, and with Baka trailing, I went up.

Naturally, most people crowded around the alternate Elvis, who said, "Now, hold on, everyone. I understand from Mr. Erstmann here that your Elvis Presley—but most folks call *me* Aaron—was pretty famous. In my universe, I'm just a retired truck driver who sings from time to time in bars and at weddings."

While alternate Elvis answered questions and signed autographs, on the edge of the stage, I faced my own alternate. It was like looking in the mirror, if the mirror had a life of its own. "Oh, hello," said the other me. "Mr. Codd said you'd be here. I don't know if we should shake or what."

"Yeah," I said. "Strangers, and yet not."

"You're a professor here?" the other me asked. "My father was a professor."

"So is mine."

"Is he still alive? Mine died when I was five. Then my mom fell apart, and she died in a car crash when I was nine."

My guts twisted. "I'm ... I'm so sorry."

"It's okay. Family friends adopted me and my sister. We turned out okay."

My brain was spinning to process all this. "I'm glad to hear that. Here, our father, *my* father is still alive. My mother, um ... not so much." After a brief awkward pause, I asked, "So, what do you do?"

"Oh, I drive a taxi. It's not as important as being a professor or anything, but it pays the bills."

Baka was leaning in close to the other me, squinting as he inspected him.

"Ignore him," I told other-me. "He's looking for bits of flies."

Other-me laughed. "You sure have some strange customs in this universe."

Out of the corner of my eye, I spotted Rachel and Chancellor Willy Hebert with plumber Will Hebert. Chancellor Hebert had his arms folded, but Rachel was joking and laughing with plumber Hebert, turning every so often to poke her father in the arm or in the gut.

Other-me was asking something, but I missed it. He repeated, "Are you married?"

"Me? Oh, no. You?"

"Oh, yes, to this nice girl I met in high school. Enid. We have two girls: Shasta, who's five, and Sierra, who's just eighteen months." He fished pictures out of his wallet. Enid was plain, but had a big, warm smile, and the girls, both with brown curls, were cute.

"Thanks," I said, handing him back the photos, although inside I felt a frigid hollowness. "I'm still all alone."

"Well, my Enid says she's lucky to have me, and I'm sure someone here will be lucky to have you."

I nodded. If I had opened my mouth to say anything, I would have burst into tears.

Codd pushed to the front of the stage and picked up the microphone. "Folks, I know you all are enjoying this, but since we don't know the effects of staying too long in an alternate universe, I'm sending everyone back now, for their own safety."

One by one, in the same order they had arrived, the alternates stepped into the big circular casing and disappeared in flashes of bluish light. Alternate Elvis bowed as people cheered him, but right before that, alternate Johnny looked over at me and gave a thumbs-up.

Soon, Codd herded everyone out of the auditorium. He promised he was writing up everything in a paper, but said that in the meantime, his patent attorney had advised him to keep his equipment and methods under wraps.

Uwe said as we walked out, "I have a meeting—too many meetings—but are you okay? That must have been strange for you."

I simply nodded.

Uwe looked at Harold, who was fiddling with his tie. I'd noticed Harold did that when he was envisioning a painting.

"You want to paint this, don't you?"

"I don't know how, but I'm going to have to," Harold said. "Don't worry, John, I won't ask you to relive it. It will be more of a self-portrait..." He was gesturing to Uwe as they walked out.

Outside on the steps, Baka said, "I still can't figure out how he did it. Can you, John?"

"Hmm? No, I can't." I was dazed, my head dizzy with alternate universes. Would I have been better off as a happy taxi driver with a loving family than as a lonely, too-smart-for-his-own-good bachelor physicist?

"Are you jealous of Codd? You have this strange look on your face."

"Jealous? No. That's not what I'm feeling right now."

"Oh," he said. "Maybe I'm just projecting. Because I'm definitely jealous. How did he do it without flies?"

I was divided, half wanting to be alone to wallow in the loneliness of *this* universe, and half wanting the warm presence of another human, even obsessive Baka Becker. I said, "I don't even know how you did it *with* flies. Are you sure it worked? Did you really send Pancake to another universe?"

"I sure hope so," he mumbled.

"Why did you help Pancake, anyway? Did he have something on you?"

Baka looked at me sideways, then closed his eyes and sighed. "Yeah," he said. I thought he was going to confess to some weird pornography habit, or to exaggerating his CV, but instead he said, "I had funding under the table. And I wasn't paying overhead," he added in a low, conspiratorial voice.

I gave a harsh laugh. All universities take a cut of grant money, anywhere between a third and a half, ostensibly to cover the cost of maintaining buildings, provide secretaries and bookkeepers, and so on. "You were avoiding the taxman! Who was funding you, anyway?"

Baka reddened slightly. "Codd arranged it. That regent of the university—Tode, you know, Tode's Reliable Motors." He looked down at his grubby, worn sneakers, as if they could console him. "I feel like I sold my soul," he said, then slunk off.

My thoughts of other universes and other lives had receded like a distant galaxy, but my body still felt numb. To occupy myself, I went to do a routine check on the nuclear reactor.

Only it was not routine. A data recorder kept track of the power draw, and I saw, in addition to spikes at the beginning and end of Codd's demonstration, that there was a spike, a big one, half an hour *before* the alternates had stepped out of the apparatus.

After closing up the reactor room, I climbed the stairs back to the first floor. The auditorium was locked, but I still had pass keys from my stint as a janitor.

The lights were dimmed in the hall, save for the stage. I climbed on the stage and circled around the apparatus. I was surprised to hear the hum of transformers, and a dial showed that the capacitors were fully charged.

"That's dangerous equipment!" Codd called from off stage. He stepped into the light. "Oh, it's you, John. I'm sorry, but I'm going to have to ask you to leave."

"It's okay, I'm not going to steal your modification of Baka's experiments. You know, it's driving him crazy, how you got it to work without flies."

"Sometimes a different point of view solves the problem." Codd gestured towards the back of the auditorium with a brawny arm. "But seriously, I'm going to be packing this up, and I'd rather not be distracted by someone looking over my shoulder."

"I can help with the power lines. I provided you the power, after all."

"And I appreciate it. But I work best alone."

I turned and looked into the darkened auditorium. "It gave me a lot of think about, talking to the alternate me."

He stepped closer, looming over me. "I bet. Don't you have homework to grade or something? A hot date, maybe?"

I shrugged. "No hot date. Beryl's busy."

Codd's face turned to stone—the kind about to fall and crush you. He shoved me with both hands, hard. "What did you say? *What did you say about Beryl?*"

I stumbled backwards. Then I braced myself, in case he came at me again, but before either of us could move, the apparatus hummed and flashed, and out of it stepped the other Codd.

"What did you think, bro?" the other Codd asked. Then he noticed me and winced.

The real Erstmann Codd, our Codd, also glanced at me. A moment before, he'd had murderous intent on his face, but that had blown away, leaving behind a sheen of panic.

The apparatus flashed again, and the other Will Hebert stepped out. He saw me and said, "Are we still doing this, or...?"

Then the alternate Gemma Wells materialized. Our Codd grabbed the other Codd, said sotto voce, "Not a word," and dragged him towards the back of the auditorium.

As the door slammed behind them, the other me appeared. "Where are they going?" alternate Johnny Chant asked. He turned to me. "Am I still going to get paid?"

The other me's real name was Luther Jones. He was indeed a taxi driver, married to his high school sweetheart, with two girls. The rest of it had all been an act.

Codd had not materialized him, or any of them, from alternate universes. He had simply improved Baka's time displacement device, to the point of sending people thirty minutes into the future.

As Luther understood it, the alternate Codd was actually Codd's real-life twin brother. Codd had hired a private detective to find look-alikes for various people on campus. Luther had overheard Codd say that Hebert and I were "generic-looking," so it wasn't too hard to find doppelgangers.

The alternate Elvis was, in fact, a real-life Elvis impersonator. He handed me his card. "I came all the way down here; might as well do some business. I do weddings, birthdays, baby showers, bar and bat mitzvahs, I'm not choosy. I even did a divorce announcement party once."

My head was spinning so much, it was only when I thought I ought to tell the real Chancellor Hebert that I thought of his wife, Elaine, and then I thought of her best friend, Beryl, and how Codd had acted when I mentioned Beryl, that I finally put it all together, and I almost threw up.

I was still buzzing with anger, fear, and embarrassment when I called Hebert that evening. He sighed and said tightly, "Thanks, John. I should let you go. I have a lot of phone calls to make."

I didn't sleep much that night. In the morning, I arrived at campus at 7:00 a.m., the same time as a small convoy of vehicles in military camouflage pulled up. I spotted Chancellor Hebert walking swiftly towards Wunderkine Hall, followed by Uwe Meilleur and Dick Cherrystone. Hebert raised a hand to greet a military officer in khakis, probably a colonel, though it could have been a rear admiral or a sideways general, for all I knew. Together they quickstepped to Auditorium 137. It was locked, but I presented myself and my key.

When I flipped on the lights, the stage was empty, save for a dark-haired woman in a beetle-blue pantsuit, examining the back of the stage. Chancellor Hebert charged forward, with me and the colonel close behind. "Where did it all go?" he demanded.

The woman turned around. "Where did all what go?" asked Shahra, or Sharon, or whatever she was calling herself that day. The agent of C-QUARK gave us an innocent smile. "Oh, hi, John. Good to see you."

Shortly after finals, Chancellor Hebert called a meeting of the Leap Before You Look Institute. All of us Leap scholars were there, except Beryl Knaught. She had taken a sudden leave of absence, right after Codd disappeared.

The chancellor said, "I have good news and bad news. Although I am by nature reluctant to leap to conclusions, before or after looking, it seems Erstmann Codd absconded with the institute's funds." He held up his hands to quell the murmuring. "But there's good news! We've secured new funding. Let me introduce to you the sponsor of the new Goosetech Institute, the CEO of Goosetech Industries, Bruce Gooseman!"

Out stepped Bruce, larger than life, wearing a vast Goosetech T-shirt complete with a goose and *Honk if you love tech!* Next to him, looking almost diminutive, was Junie Johnson.

"Goosetech is developing a new medical device," Bruce said to the gathered audience. "It's similar to magnetic resonance imaging, but instead of requiring huge magnets, it uses supertunneling photons to directly and harmlessly image tissue anywhere in the body." He smiled. "John, would you be a volunteer for a demonstration? Since you first discovered supertunneling photons."

I came forward, and he hugged me in his huge arms. "It's so great to see you," he said. "Junie didn't tell me you were here until a month ago."

"I was keeping it a surprise," Junie said.

Bruce and Junie had me stand between two laser cavities mounted on motor-driven tracks, like two gun barrels simultaneously aimed at me. Raising his voice again, Bruce said, "John here noticed that supertunneling is sensitive to the material between the laser cavities. Goosetech has been boosting that sensitivity, and we hope to soon make it competitive with CAT scans and MRI."

The laser cavities rode upwards, level with my skull. On a color monitor, I could see the folds of my brain tissue, as easily as if someone had peeled away the skin and skull. "This is John's enormous brain," Bruce intoned. "There is none bigger!"

"Only my ego," I said, and people laughed.

The laser cavities moved downward in tandem. "There's John's larynx, and his thyroid... There's his esophagus... And there is John's heart." I could see it in full color, nothing like a Valentine's heart, but more like a reddish squash. As he talked, it squeezed faster and faster, probably because I felt exposed in front of everyone.

Bruce had stopped talking. Looking up, I saw him swipe at his nose, saw a glint of tears in his placid, cow-like eyes. He sniffed, then, his voice breaking, he said, "No one has a bigger heart than John."

The gathered crowd of Leap scholars applauded.

"Jeez, should I be worried?" I said, and they laughed, even Bruce, who hugged me once more.

Back at my office, I found a largish white man wearing plaid wool slacks held up by dull red suspenders. He wore one of the ugliest and least convincing wigs I have ever seen, and beneath his face, thick rolls of flesh hid any sign of a neck.

"Can I help you?" I said as I unlocked my door.

The man stiffly rotated his whole body to face me. "Yes, you can," he said. He had a strange, breathy accent. "Do you know who I am?"

I tilted my head. "I've only seen you from a distance. You're Tode, the university regent."

He rocked his whole upper body back and forth, which I took as an awkward nod.

"You slipped money to Baka Becker," I added. "And funded Codd's institute."

Tode closed his eyes and hissed, a kind of sigh. "Your Codd embezzled my money. After making big promises, he talked me into putting most of my considerable funds into an account for his projects. And he took it all. I have little left. He stole it." He opened his eyes, which had a startling amount of yellow in them. "He had promised... But no matter; I should have expected promises to be lies."

"Promises from Codd?" I asked. "Or do you mean, promises from a human?" I sat down in my chair behind my desk.

His mouth opened and closed several times without making a sound. Then he said, "So, you also know *what* I am."

"Not know. I guessed."

"I can show you." He grabbed the rolls of flesh and started to pull up.

"No! Don't bother." I sighed. "I'm not in a mood for this."

"Not in the *mood*? We have been waiting a *very* long time."

"Why not wait a few hundred years more? Maybe we'll have licked asteroid defense."

"There are so few of us left, and all past reproductive age. When we fled underground after the calamity, we thought you would develop civilization much faster. Frankly, we could not believe how lazy mammals turned out to be. So much for warm-bloodedness."

"For an ancient civilization, you sure are petty. You know, I dreamed that you, or your ancestors, cursed my life." From a drawer, I took out a half-written proposal and began to mark it up.

"Ah. That was *you*. You humiliated a prince, caused a million-year dynasty to fall. Our vengeance was, by comparison, very small."

Still scribbling in red pen, I said, "In my life, it was huge."

"Not as huge as the loss when the last of us die. The songs and poetry of my people would shame your Shake-spear, your Li Bai, your John Lennon." He put a thick hand on my desk. "We have millions of years of discoveries. You can claim them, be renowned among mammal kind." He paused. "I need the probability pump."

I did not bother to look at him. "I'd rather make my own small discoveries, or none at all, than take credit for yours."

"I beg you. If you give us the probability pump, we can build a time window, warn our ancestors to flee Earth for another world."

"I don't have the probability pump. It was fully discharged, anyway." Now I glanced up. "Besides, I read this science fiction novel that says colonization of other planets will probably fail."

My visitor's mouth opened and closed several times. Then he stood. "You have condemned us."

"Could be. I once built a cannon of mercy, tried it on myself. If you'd come sooner, I might have had a drop of empathy left for you." I crossed out a few words. "You can ask Baka Becker to smear flies all over you and send you to another universe. It might work."

When I looked up, my office door was ajar, my visitor gone. I opened the lowest drawer of my desk. Beneath a pile of ratty T-shirts was the inert husk of the probability pump. Sometimes I tapped it, like a talisman. More often, I just stared at it, thinking of ancient hopes and painful losses.

I brushed it with my fingertips and felt a faint *zap!*—the barest static discharge. My hand twitched away; then I reached to touch it again. Nothing. It had been drained, after all, leaving only a hunk of metal and rare isotopes. Must have been my overactive imagination, once more.

I had just gotten off the phone with Uwe—he invited me that weekend for a barbecue at a cousin's place, adding that I had to come see Harold's new painting, *Self-Portrait in a Mirror Universe*—when Sally knocked on my office door.

"Got any plans for the summer?" she asked.

"At some point, I'll go out to Los Alamos, see how Emmy Shore's summer internship is going. Meanwhile, I'll write my proposal to fund more lasers for supertunneling. That will keep me busy."

"Well, seeing as you'll be mostly around, how about meeting my friend for lunch? The lawyer?"

I suppressed a sigh. "I'm sure she's very nice and all, but I don't think I'm up for it."

I hunched over the Physical Review paper I was reading, but Sally didn't leave. "Lunch, John. She's free today for lunch. One o'clock."

"I don't know what to say to a lawyer. Can I plead the Fifth?"

Sally punched me playfully on the arm. "She's smart. *Really* smart. Didn't I tell you? You'll find something to talk about. She's also good-looking. I know you'd care about smart first, but the other doesn't hurt. If it goes badly, I'll pay for your lunch."

"I'm not going to sue you or anything. Maybe your friend..."

"She's not that kind of lawyer. Not a *mean* lawyer, as she likes to say. She does patents, inventions, and such. Does most of the university's IP." She just stood in my office, doing a very good impression of an Immovable Object. As I'm no good at approximating an Unstoppable Force, I had no choice but to agree.

At one o'clock, I walked into Little Larry's Bar-B-Q and Crawfish Emporium, where I wandered around, looking for a blonde lawyer. I was about to give up, when I saw your hand waving to catch my attention.

"John? You're looking a bit lost."

"Yeah," I said, standing by your table. "And you..."

"Well," you said, "*I'm* not lost. I've been sitting here for fifteen minutes. You kept walking right past." When I just stared at you, you said, "You can sit; I didn't put thumb tacks on the seat or anything."

I eased myself into the chair. I needed to sit, because when you said, *"I'm not lost,"* my heart shattered, like one of the glass jars in Freddy Pigeon's sub-basement; I felt like I'd suddenly appeared in an alternate universe. I said with forced lightness, "I was more worried about torts, or writs, or thumbscrews, whatever lawyers do."

"I'm not that kind of lawyer." You rolled your eyes.

"Sally From... Your friend Sally told me that. Patents? Inventions?"

"Yeah. I used to be a scientist, but I got tired of chasing grants."

"Really?"

"I was originally funded by NASA, studying how plants grow in zero g. And then they asked me to... Well, it got a bit crazy." You sighed and looked down at the plastic menu. "I hardly tell anyone; no one would understand my weird adventure."

"I might," I said.

You looked dubious, so I told you about how when I was young, I wanted to be a paleontologist, and dug for dinosaurs bones in the yard until I broke the sewer line, and it backed up the toilets.

You laughed. "Isn't it funny how childhood remembrances shape our lives? I have this memory of when I was little: I met a boy searching for pirate treasure."

"Treasure?"

"Yes, I'd run off—I was about six—because my family was moving, and I didn't want to go. I found this boy looking for buried treasure, and a nice lady gave me lunch, and then my mom fetched me home. He'd dug a big hole, I'd almost forgotten that part, and now, I remember something about a sewer, just like with you, and a backhoe, and—"

"You sure he wasn't digging for dinosaur bones?"

"I've always remembered it as pirate treasure. But I was an early reader and was into this Pippi Longstocking knockoff, a girl pirate who..." You leaned forward. "Where did you grow up?"

I told you. Your eyes widened—I noticed then that they were green—and I felt a slight electric tingle, a tiny shock, like the one I had imagined when I touched the probability pump. Maybe I hadn't imagined it.

You spoke in a subdued tone. "My mom said I couldn't stop talking about that boy for the longest time, wondering if he'd ever found his treasure. She called him my first crush." A wry smile spread across your face. "But you say it was dinosaur bones? I suppose it could have been dinosaurs. They *are* both terrifying and safely long dead."

"Or maybe it was pirate treasure. I suppose I've been looking for some sort of treasure all my life." I took a deep breath. "At any rate, it was only the beginning."

As the waiter came to take our order, you asked me, "So, how does it end?"

That, love, you already know.

Acknowledgements

The story on the page is seldom as beautiful and as compelling as the epic narrative in my brain. Readers help me see what I actually wrote, not what I dreamed. I am grateful to the first readers of an early draft who encouraged me to continue: Zak Jarvis and Sharon Mock, Lise Breakey, Rob Pritchard, and Karen Fowler. Later—much later—Preye Iwowari, Starr Baumann, and Shadae Mallory provided valuable comments on a complete beta draft. After revisions, I received additional helpful responses from Jerrold Stubblefield, Dawn Lyons, and Steve Rodgers. Steve has gone much earlier and further than I in the rugged terrain of self-publishing and provided much guidance and support.

I was lucky to find an editor in Olivia Batker Pritzker. She understood what I was trying to say, and her feedback made the story more truly itself. Olive Reekie designed the wonderful cover art, encapsulating the book's whimsical darkness. Robin Fuller meticulously copy-edited the final manuscript. Any remaining infelicities I own, though Mark Caprio caught a few that slipped through.

Even before I started this novel, I had many wise and generous teachers: my high school English teacher Jim Speakman; later Joanna Russ and Peter S. Beagle, Tim Powers and Algis Budrys; the poets Becky Larkin, Shannon Marquez Maguire, and Sue Owens; and most of all Kim Stanley Robinson, whose insights have profoundly influenced my views on writing and science fiction.

Although I lived and worked in some of the places depicted, this book and the characters within are fictional. (So is much of the science, deliberately so.) But, you, Donna, and your love are the most real things in my life, the only story that truly matters

About the author

As a child, C. W. Johnson lived in a world of his own, much to the exasperation of his family. He trained in theoretical physics, mathematics, computers, science fiction, poetry, and many other impractical topics. Today he is a professor of physics at a university best left anonymous. He has published more than a dozen short stories in professional science fiction magazines such as Analog, Asimov's, and others, as well as more than two dozen poems. This novel is largely an extension of his many obsessions.